SCRIPT OF THE HEART

A CELTA HEARTMATE NOVEL

ROBIN D. OWENS

FOLLOW YOUR HEART

COPYRIGHT

❀ Created with Vellum

DEDICATION

To my Mom and brothers, Tom and Pat, who continue to demonstrate what family really is.

ACKNOWLEDGMENTS

For research help with Heart Journey and this spin-off story, I'm thanking my facebook friends: Terrie Adams, Betty Glsgow Hanawa, Polly Nichols Cassady, Kathleen Therese. For the copy edits, the wonderful Rose Beetem of Final Eyes.

Cast of Characters

Giniana Filix: FirstLevel Healer, on-site staff Healer for First-Family GrandLord T'Spindle, daughter of feckless actors.

Thrisca Filix: the FamCat Giniana inherited from her father, who got her from his father.

Melis Filix: Thrisca's FamKitten.

Klay Saint (St.) Johnswort (Johns): MasterLevel Actor with the lead in the play *Firewalker*. He is the last of an old merchant family, and was raised by his grandmother on his father's side (FatherDam), and his mother in near poverty. Secondary character in *Heart Journey*.

The Actors & Theater Folk:

Amberose: Genius playwright whose plays can make actors' careers, she is reclusive and difficult.

Cerasus (Raz) Cherry: MasterLevel actor, friendly rival to Johns. Hero of *Heart Journey*. Secondary character in *Heart Fate* and *Heart Change*.

Mas Filix: Giniana's father, famous MasterLevel actor who left Druida City to pursue his career on the continent of Chinju.

Ovata Forsythia: MasterLevel actor, she is the Theatrical Guild representative and President of the Thespian Club.

Lily Fescue: Leading lady in the mystery Raz Cherry is starring in. Lily was the only person to get the original script.

Ellis Gardenia: Character actor, becoming a counselor.

Austro Gentian: Amberose's second agent.

Chatt Geyer: Johns's agent

Trillia Juniper: An actor from an acting Family, she's been in the business all of her life, another rising star, working in Gael City.

T'Spindle: FirstFamily GrandLord who owns the theater, The Evening Primrose, and the estate where the opening party takes place. A man with his finger in many pies, employer to Giniana Filix.

Blakely Wattle, Amberose's original agent.

Other Characters:

GreatLady Danith Mallow D'Ash: HeartMate of T'Ash, Danith is an Animal Healer and the person who usually matches intelligent animal companions (Fams) with people. (*HeartMate*).

GreatLord Rand T'Ash: Jeweler/blacksmith, (*HeartMate*).

GraceLord Majus T'Daisy: Journalist, newspaper publisher, new father, employer of Giniana Filix for night shifts.

Morifa Daisy: Socialite, ex-lover of Raz Cherry, sister to T'Daisy.

Helena D'Elecampane (Del): She is a master cartographer and has charted the western part of two continents. Del is often on the road and in the field, HeartMate to Raz Cherry. (*Heart Journey*).

Shunuk Elecampane: FamFox to Del (*Heart Journey*).

Marti Samphire: Boy neighbor of St. Johnswort, botanical talent.

Dufleur D'Thyme-D'Willow: FirstFamily GreatLady, her Flair is manipulating time, and she provides Time Healing procedures quarterly (*Heart Dance*).

Palli Willow: Assistant to D'Willow.

TIMELINE NOTE

Script of the Heart is out of chronological order in the Celta HeartMate series. This story takes place during the events of *Heart Journey*, book 9 in the series.

CHAPTER 1

GRANDLORD T'SPINDLE'S ESTATE, Druida City, 407 Years After Colonization, Late Summer, Night

Klay Saint Johnswort—Johns—surveyed the large ballroom of white marble and chandeliers dripping with cut crystal. A place of work, not pleasure. Every actor there scrabbling for influence. Everyone self-aware and competing each minute of the gathering. Including himself.

T'Spindle, Johns's host and the owner of the Primrose Theater, stood listening to a beaming and fast-talking agent—something shady about that guy.

Raz Cherry, Johns's friendly rival, walked up and said, "Good thing brooding looks good on you."

Johns grunted, tipped his glass of springreen wine in salute. "Congratulations on the one hundred twentieth performance of your play."

Raz appeared humbled. "Thank you." He cleared his throat, pitched his voice low. "Have you heard the rumors that *Firewalker* might be closing down?"

"Yeah." Johns had. The play that he starred in. He kept his expression impassive, made sure the twinge of envy that Raz's play seemed to be continuing indefinitely didn't show either. On the other hand, if Raz remained tied up, he wouldn't be competing with Johns if his run ended in a couple of weeks.

Johns drank some springreen wine from a delicate flute. Not really part of his image as a tough alpha hero, but he probably wouldn't be able to buy this vintage for another half decade, even if his career took off.

Right now Johns would fight with all he had to keep his career from falling into even the briefest hiatus. He needed continuous work to climb to the top.

Suppressing all emotion from his visage, Johns said, "I also heard the rumor there's a new play by Amberose circulating the producers. First time in a decade. Big deal." It could be. And his big break.

Raz paused in his own drinking. "Yes, Amberose's agent spoke with me. I saw you giving the slimy guy your best rockface imitation." Raz grimaced. "I pushed him a little too hard for information about the play, and I'm sorry I did that because he dried up." Another slight pause—for emphasis as opposed to indecision, Johns thought. "The leading lady in my show got a script. I saw pages of it yesterday."

A thrill zipped through Johns, he lowered his eyelids even more. "Not just rumor, then. Real deal."

"I believe so. We had thefts at the Primrose Theater yesterday. I think some of the script pages were stolen."

Johns grunted again. "Don't see an eccentric playwright like Amberose being happy about having some of her work stolen. Far as I know, she always wants to keep a script under wraps until the production is funded and the actors cast. With miscellaneous pages floating around in the public, I think she'll try and yank the script back from her agent. Get the story back under her control." The brief hope of landing a job in that play anytime soon faded. It would take too long to get up and running.

Raz's eyes, bluer than John's own gray-shaded blue, met his. "*Try* is the word. *Try* to get the script back." Raz angled slightly, and Johns shifted to follow his gaze to see the agent who'd approached them.

After another sip of excellent wine, Johns shook his head. "She didn't pick a good representative. He won't obey any orders to gather all the copies and send 'em back to Amberose. He's more interested in his commission to get the play financed than what she wants. Bet the deal will go underground." Slowing the production even more.

Raz shrugged. "Probably."

Of course the delay in the staging wouldn't matter to Raz. He had a solid current job.

Johns caught himself clenching his jaw and loosened it.

"Well, I'll be off," Raz waved a hand. "Leave the audience wanting more." He placed his wineglass on a nearby table, scanned the room and gathered attention. Then he gave a bow of courteous leave-taking, received applause, and left through an open door to the terrace at the side of the house.

Johns eyed the man. He moved well, striding with more of a glide whereas Johns preferred a prowl ... Raz was an actor with a smoother manner and build than Johns himself, but Johns thought he had an edge on the alpha-type.

He wondered what kind of hero Amberose had written.

Glancing at the people engaged in conversations—theatrical wheeling and dealing in a loud, stifling, and overly perfumed room—he decided to take a break. Get some air before more networking. He moved toward the terrace.

Shouts! Glider alarms! Sounds of fighting.

Johns shot onto the terrace. Heard Raz's vehicle's alarm pronounce, "My virtue is threatened." Saw Raz struggling with a large man. Another thief sat in the glider, lit by the inner light, searching the vehicle.

"Hey!" Johns yelled in a voice that would reach the ballroom, alert others. He dropped the three meters from terrace to parking field, rushed toward Raz.

Raz fought better than Johns had anticipated, but bled from a graze on his temple.

"Get him and hold him," the bigger man panted at the smaller one in the glider. "Play actor too damn much trouble. Who'da thought?"

A growl erupted from Johns. "Have a problem with actors?" He grabbed the big guy from the back and threw him aside. The man turned and grappled with him. Johns trained in fighting, had moves. Adrenaline kicked in, surging through him. He hit the man on the jaw, saw his head snap back. The guy swept a leg aimed at Johns's crotch. He dodged.

Then the guy angled back to Raz.

"I'm getting out of here!" cried the smaller man in a higher voice.

Tearing from Johns's grip and leaving some of his shirt in Johns's hands, the big guy attacked Raz. They exchanged blows. Johns lunged toward the struggle and landed a hit on the guy just as the smaller man popped from the car and flung himself on them.

They all went down, Raz's elbow jerked into Johns's solar plexus and his breath whoofed out of him, leaving no air.

"Gotcha!" The smaller man grabbed the larger and they teleported away.

Thankfully, Raz rolled off Johns. Through slightly bleary eyes, Johns could see Raz rub his cheek. It swelled, nearly blocking his eye. Raz groaned.

Snatching short breaths of air, Johns let them out along with frustration that his prey escaped. "Sorry, too late." As he spoke, something seemed to rip loose. Fligger. He'd broken a rib in the fight. He grunted out a pained breath.

"You did fine," Raz told him.

"Gotta take care of your friends," Johns mumbled, though he didn't know that anyone heard him.

Footsteps and voices came closer. Several other glider alarms that had been shrieking fell silent.

The first person to tower over them was Cratag Maytree T'Marigold, even taller and broader than Johns. Unlike Johns and the hero he currently played, this guy was the real thing, a fighter and a bodyguard.

Extending a hand to each of them, Cratag hauled them to their feet, then said, "Want to quiet that glider alarm?" His hand rested on his blazer hilt as he scanned the trees.

"Alarm stop, Cherry," Raz said.

Johns stared. The man had named his vehicle. Johns shook his head, then pressed his hand against his ribs, endured the sickening wash of pain. Looking at Cratag, he growled, "The thieves got away. Teleported."

"I'll check the grounds anyway." Cratag jerked a nod, strode into the small parking area for the rare gliders.

The curious party-goers hanging back drew up to crowd around Johns and Raz.

A quiet woman's sob came. "Oh, my poor glider. My poor baby, I didn't shield you and look what happened, your jeweled timer, stolen!"

"This is a bad thing," T'Spindle, their host, said from the bottom of the terrace stairs. People cleared the way for him. "Healer needed here!" he shouted, making both Johns and Raz wince.

"Arriving from my cottage to the ballroom teleportation pad transnow!" boomed a woman's voice, amplified by the intelligent Residence itself. The Spindles must have a staff Healer.

"This is a very bad thing," GrandLord T'Spindle repeated. His gaze went flinty, reminding Johns that the rotund man belonged to the FirstFamilies. A lord accustomed to playing dangerous politics. Johns's anger eased at the thought that the vandals had made a very powerful enemy.

T'Spindle displayed an easygoing but stubborn personality. He wouldn't rest until the men who'd dared to invade his property and distress his guests were caught and punished. No doubt he'd also make sure the city guards assigned to this case were equally stubborn about solving the crimes.

Lord and Lady knew the GrandLord had a whole lot more power and influence than Johns. He could leave the villain catching to the noble and guards.

Yes, those intruders would regret this night.

Cratag returned. "Hoodlums are definitely gone, but vandalized several gliders. We'll need a list of the thefts and damage." He gestured to Raz's *Cherry*. "This one's the worst."

"I have contacted the city guards," T'Spindle said. "They are sending a liaison to speak with those affected." He bit off each word.

At that moment a lithe and graceful young woman in Healer green and holding a medical bag ran toward them. She stopped before the GrandLord. "GrandLady D'Spindle said not to teleport down here since the danger of accident would be great. Your lady stated no one was injured enough to be 'ported to a HealingHall and told me that I could handle all wounds."

"Thank you, Giniana," said T'Spindle. He snapped his fingers and all the lights in the Residence flashed on. So did minor lightspells circling the terrace like suns. Some shone over the side grassyard designated as a parking area for those who had gliders. Three short rows.

Hands on hips, Cratag studied Johns with narrowed eyes, snorted. "You did well enough in the fight, I guess."

Pivoting to Raz he stated, "Looks to me like you need more than stage fighting instruction. You can come to me."

"I don't think—" Raz began, then stopped to wipe away blood from his lip that split when he spoke.

"I'll give you a discount since you know a good friend of mine," Cratag ended.

While Johns felt glad he'd passed as acceptable by such a warrior as Cratag, a worm of continuing envy wound through him. Once again, Raz had received a good offer from a nobleman. Johns would have snapped up that one up himself.

Tilting his head, Cratag speared Johns with a look. "You can take me up on that, too."

Johns wondered what had given his wish away. Not his expression, so some part of his manner or body language that the observant fighter had picked up on. He could learn more than just better fighting techniques from the man. He inclined his head. "Thank you, I appreciate the offer."

"Well, then," the Healer stated and huffed a breath, as if the discussion of fighting disgusted her. "Let's move this discussion, *and* my Healing, into the Residence."

T'Spindle raised his hand and the ensemble that had played background and dance music blasted out a cheerful tune. Cratag T'Marigold led the return to the ballroom. People smiled and their chatter rose about the exciting incident. Johns figured this had been a good break for them and now they wanted to drink more of the Spindles' good liquor, eat more of the good food, and dance.

GrandLady D'Spindle arrived and took the arm of the older woman who'd had her glider broken into, and T'Spindle escorted the other two noble victims away with him. Of course, for their convenience, the guards would talk with them first. Johns and Raz, as actors, essentially employees, would be left for last.

Raz grunted in pain, and Johns glanced at him, saw the

Healer's hand on his cheek. Her thumb traced his split lip, her Flair, psi magic power, mending his mouth as Johns watched. "Deeply bruised cheekbone, bad bruise on the temple ..." She pressed on Raz's side and he yelped. Turning to Johns her hands reached to where he cradled his ribs. As much as he liked her looks and would enjoy her hands on him, he raised a palm. "I've got one broken rib and maybe another cracked one."

"I hear you." Her beautiful features scrunched as she frowned, her full lips thinning. "What happened?"

"Two guys got through security and trashed some of the gliders." Johns gestured to the vehicles, aware of how the light and shadow fell on his hand with the motion. He rather hoped the Healer preferred broad, strong hands to Raz's elegant fingers, and that thought had him wondering why he cared.

Johns really liked the looks of this Healer. Not too short, a slender figure, understated curves, not overblown. She moved well and with supple poise.

Shaking his head, he said, "That was a real pretty glider, Raz."

The Healer said, "Come along, I'd prefer to see you both inside. We'll walk so I don't spend our Flair teleporting." Removing her hand from Raz's face she went ahead of them.

Raz stumbled and Johns steadied him with an arm around his shoulders, gritting his teeth at the shooting pain of his own ribs. "I'll help him along."

"That hurts," Raz muttered. "Everything hurts."

Glancing over her shoulder, the Healer smiled approval at Johns. "That's kind of you."

"Let's get you going, friend." Johns provided balance as

Raz wove a little. He also limped. The guy might have broken toes. He wore once-elegant dancing shoes. Johns wore heavier, polished boots.

Raz lifted his right hand and sucked on his knuckles. "Fligger."

Now that his friend mentioned it, Johns's own hands felt scraped from hard contact with muscle and bone.

Raz tripped again. Johns shortened his stride and slowed his steps.

"Thanks, Johns," Raz said, sounding like he meant it.

"'Welcome. Sorry about you and your glider."

"You've always envied my glider," Raz said. He came from a noble Family well-known for their transportation and shipping company. "Tell you what—" They took the steps up to the terrace slowly. "Why don't I ask my father to get another sportcoupe at cost, sell it to you for the same price? As a thank you."

Johns grinned. "In blue?"

"Metallic blue-gray, the color you wear most often," Raz agreed.

Johns did tend to use that tint in his wardrobe, same color as his eyes. "Done," he said. He'd raid his savings to buy the glider, a good investment. He'd go with a solid model with classic lines that would age well.

They walked to the last door on the terrace and entered the Residence into a corridor covered in a thick maroon carpet, the walls tinted a pale peach.

Johns had never been in the living quarters of a First-Family Residence, an intelligent house. The itchiness between his shoulder blades that had ruffled his nerves all evening intensified. His personal Flair, good for acting, also included a preternatural awareness of his surroundings and people. The Residence watched him—probably kept an eye on all the guests, an entity aware of each life-form inside its walls.

The doors along the hallway showed individual carvings on each, impressing him. Raz kept rubbing and flexing his fingers, not reacting to the luxury.

Johns glanced down, wondering whether his boots had picked up twigs and dirt from the parking field. Or his clothes. Yeah. And they flaked off as he walked the pretty corridor.

He had the gloomy feeling that he had a few rips in his second best go-to-party-and-network clothes that would take some gilt to repair.

A door opened down the hall and they angled through it to a sitting room furnished in a masculine fashion where blood and grime wouldn't show—much.

The Healer—Giniana of unknown Family—motioned to a couch where Johns deposited Raz and gingerly sat down himself, giving the woman plenty of room to work.

"Residence, more lightspells, please," she requested. Two tiny sun-like balls coalesced and circled the room, brightening it.

Johns couldn't take his eyes off her. Beautiful features, lovely body. The light struck her hair showing a deep, true brown all the way, no hint of red or touch of blond or black. Johns was used to streaky hair in his profession, actors and actresses modifying their looks for their jobs ... or for their vanity.

She wore no enhancements, either external herbal cosmetics or illusion spells that Johns could always spot. Also extremely unusual amongst his friends and acquaintances. Every little difference endeared her to him, and fascinated him.

As she bent over Raz, using her Flair to finish Healing his cheek, then placed her hands on his shoulders and let her psi power flow through him to mend his other hurts, her scent drifted to Johns. The fragrance distracted him from watching a true professional work, something he considered part of his ongoing training. She smelled of peaches and spring blossoms and ... a spice he couldn't quite place but drew him in. A dark fragrance that hinted at hidden depths at odds with her open, practical manner.

In a few minutes, she stepped back and her eyes widened. They appeared a few shades darker than the light amber he'd noticed before.

Raz groaned and stretched languidly, his joints popping. Everything from his cheek to his hands had been Healed. Johns narrowed his eyes to see if he seemed interested in Giniana more than any man would be in such a situation.

No. Raz had been attracted to another woman he'd met earlier—one that Johns had made a point of dancing with just to irritate Raz. She'd made Johns laugh, too, at her trenchant observations of the arty crowd in the ballroom.

Now Raz had risen to his feet, taken the Healer's hand and bowed over it. "My greatest thanks, FirstLevel Healer."

"I'm just doing my job."

He continued to hold her hand, smiling charmingly, and to Johns's annoyance, she softened. "You're quite welcome, MasterLevel Actor Cherry."

So she knew the rankings of theater people, most outsiders didn't. Interesting, though she did work for T'Spindle, perhaps she picked it up from the household. Still, a simple glance around the room showed that the GrandLord and GrandLady, like all FirstFamily nobles, had other pastimes. Fingers in many pies.

Healer Giniana withdrew her hand from Raz and turned to Johns. "Let me take a look at those ribs of yours."

He smiled. "Sure."

"And your hands."

His hands, his body, his voice were the main tools of his trade. He held out his fingers, some of them swollen, most of them scraped.

"Lady and Lord, Johns, they look worse than mine," Raz said.

"I got in a few good blows." He smiled. "And unlike on stage I didn't have to pretend to hit, or hold back."

"Yeah, yeah," Raz said. "Thanks again for the help." He grimaced. "They'd have taken me out, otherwise," he added in a tone that conveyed he didn't believe that. The Healer snapped a glance at him, then back at Johns, who let the ends of his lips curve up.

"Anything I can do." Johns angled his torso, with only a hint of mockery.

The Healer made a disapproving noise. "Always acting."

CHAPTER 2

"NOT ALWAYS," Raz protested. "My gratitude to you and Johns is real."

But Giniana had wrapped her fingers around Johns's own and her touch sent hot licks of desire coursing through him. Good thing he hadn't worn the skintight trous that some of his colleagues favored. Even Raz's trous were more form fitting than his own.

Soothing heat radiated from her hands and Johns quashed a moan at the pain relief. He hurt more than he'd realized. The continuing warmth prickled along his nerves leaving a great feeling behind, not only Healed and pumped full of health, but extremely aware of the woman— the soft capability of her hands, the smoothness of her skin, her touch, her energy.

He swallowed at his unusual reaction to the woman's attractiveness, kept his gaze on where their hands joined. After far too little time, she said, "Let me mend your ribs."

Smiling slowly, he offered, "Want me to take off my shirt and jacket?"

"That's not necessary."

This time she pulled up a stool before him, then placed

her hands on his chest—checking the health of his heart, no doubt—and removing the newly-blooming bruises with a whisk of her fingers. Glancing down, he saw his rumpled and torn shirt, thought he'd ripped out the shoulders of his jacket. Not dressed to impress anymore, and the loss would cost him, too.

Then her hands lay right above his ribs. She pressed and he sucked in a sharp breath at the pain that dizzied his head. An instant later he *felt* the bone move and align and meld together, whole once more. Her fingers stroked—and, yeah, he liked that a whole lot—and the other two cracked ribs Healed.

After that, as she checked out his other bones and muscles, he simply enjoyed the feel of her hands on him.

"There, I'm done," she said and he thought—he hoped— he heard a breathless note in her voice. Maybe the attraction was mutual. "You should be fine, but should I notify your Families? Your parents?"

"My parents are dead," Johns said too quickly, forgetting to put any spin on the bald statement.

"I'll take care of contacting my Family," Raz said at the same time.

Her mouth relaxed, compassion radiated from her.

"Thank you very much for your Healing." Johns gave her a crooked smile. "Since I'm no longer a patient of yours I'd like to see you later.... Why don't we go out for—"

With a definitive snap she closed her Healing bag, one of those shaped oddly after ancient Earthan ones. Her lip curled. "I am completely uninterested in socializing with actors." She rose and walked gracefully away, hips swaying, to a chair near the fireplace.

The rebuff hurt, then anger spurted above the sting and his determination solidified to prove her wrong about enjoying one particular actor's company.

Raz hooted with laughter, swallowed it when T'Spindle entered the room.

The lord nodded to them, then said, "I've spoken with the guardsman and we agree, Raz, that this incident must tie in with the burglaries of your apartment and my theater. We should discuss this." He turned to Johns and said, "And I thank you, MasterLevel Actor Saint Johnswort, for your intervention on behalf of my employee."

A dismissal. Johns stood and smiled, saying sincerely, "Friendship's important." The Healer shot him a wary look like she thought he lied.

The lord gave a stiff nod. "Yes. I will remember you, Saint Johnswort."

Johns bowed with the exact degree of depth due to a FirstFamily Lord. "Thank *you*, sir." He glanced around, smiled deprecatingly. "I'm the odd man out of your theatrical family here. So I'll take my leave." He said individual good-byes and strode away in a man-of-action manner.

Once outside in the hallway, he blew out a held breath, rolled his shoulders and shook out his arms, let the cheer inside him stretch his smile to a grin.

T'Spindle didn't own only one theater, and had, of course, contacts with all the other high-status lords and ladies who funded the arts. Johns's luck was looking up. Maybe he'd land a job soon after *Firewalker* closed.

The door opened behind him and Giniana the Healer exited. Her face showed tightened muscles and narrowed eyes. "T'Spindle would like you to escort me to my cottage here on the estate," she told Johns stiffly, "just in case the assailants are lurking in the woods between this Residence and my home. He doesn't wish me to teleport there." Her lips pressed together before she continued, "I hardly think I'll have any trouble, but T'Spindle insisted."

Johns's pulse picked up pace at being alone with her to

talk, but he bowed to her, no flourishes. "My pleasure to be of service."

She jerked a nod, murmured a Word and her Healing bag vanished, no doubt translocated to her home. But that left both her hands free. Johns wished he knew her better so he could hold one of those hands.

They walked—Johns kept the pace to a stroll—down the corridor to the cross hallway that led to the terrace door.

"As if I couldn't just teleport away if someone comes at me," she grumbled.

"I've done that," he said, aware of the buzz on his skin at her presence, her scent, the luxurious surroundings they moved through.

"What?"

"I've been grappling with a villain and teleported away." He hadn't grown up in the best part of Druida City. "It doesn't always help."

"Really?" She sounded curious. If he had to reveal himself, tell stories of his youth, he'd do it to keep her interested in him, set up for a date. Get her to his theater, maybe. At least prove to her that whatever ideas and stereotypes of actors she believed in were wrong with regard to him.

"Yes." He backed up the story a bit. "Happened when I was a teen and hadn't gotten my growth spurt." He stopped at the door to the terrace. "This way?"

"Yes, we can reach the path to my cottage from here."

He opened the door to the now very dim terrace and took her elbow to help her down the stairs. Sparing some Flair, he sent a small lightspell bobbing in front of them.

"So what happened?" Giniana asked.

Stopping a grunt as punctuation, he replied, "I miscalculated and we both landed in my FatherDam's, my father's mother's, back vegetable garden. The screech of that woman." He shuddered. "I mashed some of her ripe tomatoes. Enough to wipe them out for a few weeks." And go without that tasty fruit in his limited diet.

"Oh."

Johns got the idea that whatever background she'd come from, it didn't include growing vegetables for dinner or his own genteel poverty. His family *had* been prominent once. They had a street named after them.

"But that wasn't the worst," he said, infusing his tone with a grim note.

"No?"

"No."

§⦿

They'd reached the bottom of the steps. She glanced up at him. Oh, yes, he had her with his story. It wasn't one he told often so he didn't have it down pat. As an actor, *not* a story-teller, he could ramble or flub a personal story, so the fact that this one kept his audience involved pleased him.

With a gesture indicating the way, Giniana moved diagonally onto a white graveled path. It wound through the grassyard surrounding the house into a large, dense stand of trees. Her cottage might be in a far corner of the Spindles' estate. Their decision to house her there, or hers?

"What was the worst?" she prompted, her eyes wide with concern, her full lips parted.

"The bigger bully who'd jumped me on the way home from grovestudy barely missed having his head as a part of the corner of our house."

She gasped. "That would have killed him, being teleported into an inanimate object."

"Oh, yes. If he hadn't had his noggin angled close to mine ...." Johns shook his own head, gave her a triumphant smile. "Lady and Lord, he turned white. Began trembling. Almost wet his pants. Then my FatherDam began beating the both of us with a rolled up newssheet and he crawled away."

She choked on a laugh.

So he gave her the punchline. "Never had any trouble with him or his friends after that. They didn't know I could teleport, you see. I hadn't done it very often, and never from grovestudy to home." He shrugged. "Later that summer I grew and put on some weight."

He thought he saw her give his build a quick, admiring glance.

"Bullies picking on smaller children." She sighed.

"Yes, and I wanted to be an actor even then, and during grovestudy we worked on apprenticeship applications. Mine was to the Masks Theater. They had a scholarship—" But her body had stiffened and her steps picked up pace.

He'd lost her by reminding her he was an actor.

Dammit.

Was she worth so much work?

He didn't know.

Maybe not.

But then she tripped over a tree root and he caught her, pulled her close to him, against his chest. Again her scent rose to his nostrils, along with a faint sheen of her sweat that triggered a deep need in him.

She looked up at him with wide eyes, and the lightspell that had out-distanced them zoomed back and he could distinguish the amber color of her irises.

Her body seemed to fit against his. Minimal but very soft curves of breasts and slight belly.

Keeping his voice low and intimate, he said, "I do want to thank you. More than just words. Have you seen the play I'm in? *Firewalker*?"

"You're *starring* in *Firewalker*," she corrected.

He shrugged off the compliment as he'd trained himself to

do, so he didn't seem conceited. He'd give the play his best for the remainder of the run, but already considered that role in the past. He'd start looking for another job tomorrow.

Her lips curved as glanced at him from under her lashes. "No, I haven't seen *Firewalker*." Inhaling, and he deeply appreciated the rise of her breasts closer to him, she placed her hands on his chest and again he felt her natural energy, the Flair she used for Healing in the warmth of her fingers. The atmosphere suddenly heated...and soothed...and the wave of her personal energy seemed to seep into his blood, lap through him like ocean surf.

"Though, of course," she said, "I've heard the play is fabulous" Her tone remained only courteous.

"I can get you a pass for the play," Johns murmured. Something he could obtain easily and without cost.

"Really?"

"Yeah."

"Then I'd be glad to go."

"And who should I say the pass is for?"

"Giniana Filix."

A well-known acting Family surname, and facts about her Family tumbled into Johns's mind. He kept the warm smile on his face, thought he even controlled his gaze as he recalled that both her parents had been actors. Her mother, the mistress of a rich lord and supported by him, had died a few years before. Giniana's father had abandoned his wife and child decades ago for a career on a continent across the ocean, Chinju.

Now he understood her air of wariness.

But still she challenged him.

Next, how to get her.

Johns trod lightly with Giniana through the untamed brush at the edge of T'Spindle's estate. The stone path had become a dirt trail.

A prickle along his spine indicated someone watched them. They'd come within sight of her lit cottage at the end of the track. Did one of the intruders wait for her there?

His pulse surged faster. He stopped her with a touch of his hand on her elbow, then turned in a circle, *search-sensing* the area until he discovered the individual.

The one who lay on a branch, then dropped its paws and waggled them.

A Fam. Great. He disliked and distrusted Fams, naturally intelligent animals, particularly cats.

Another dreadful memory of grovestudy rose. With one arrogant contraction of his butt and a spray, his FatherDam's, father's mother's, FamCat had ruined his entire wardrobe.

Nothing, no cleanser, no cheap spell, no stupid ideas of his FatherDam had eradicated the odor. He still remembered the reaction of his grovestudy group. And the ugly charity clothes he'd had to accept from the local temple just so he wouldn't stink. Then he had to hide that garb from his FatherDam to spare her feelings. Change back and forth morning and evening, until he finally grew out of the odorous clothes.

Too much damn trouble, cats.

The cat's head lowered, muzzle and whiskers shining silver with age. Purring filled the space. *Greetyou, FamWoman. Greetyou, man.* Even its mental voice held a creak and crackle of age, accompanying the rough purr.

"Greetyou, Thrisca," said Giniana, her voice lilting with love.

The cat leapt from the tree in a move Johns recognized as showy to impress. He didn't think the thing often sat in trees ... so .... "Anyone come near here, Thrisca?" he asked gruffly.

I heard much commotion, heard running and teleporting pops, but no one came near here. All is well.

"Thank you, Thrisca," Giniana said.

For a moment, the big feline stood in the twinmoons light, beige fur patterned with black stripes on its head and shoulders, the rest of its body spotted. Looked like an old-earth-type cat.

I am a large Earthan Cat, a serval, and female, hissed the thing in his mind. It slunk close to Giniana, accepted a quick pet on its head and turned to Johns.

He braced himself.

Sure enough, the large thing, about fifty-eight centimeters high, rubbed against him, trying to throw him off-balance and leaving a load of hair on his trous.

Yep, maybe he'd better rethink his association with Giniana.

꽃

Thrisca coughed. Giniana reached out with glowing fingers towards the cat. Words sounded in Johns's mind from the FamCat. *Do not fuss.*

Her hand dropped. Angling toward Johns, she said stiffly, as if she returned to Healer mode and slotted him in the low category of actor, "Thank you for walking me home."

Obviously, she would not invite him into her cottage.

He moved on impulse and desire. He took her hand and inclined his torso, kissing the back in a formal farewell. And, yeah, attraction zinged between them. He liked the vibration that sizzled through them both, the tremor of her fingers under his lips. Reluctantly, he let her hand go and straightened, gave her a real smile.

"I'll leave tickets for *Firewalker* for you."

"Thank you," she replied in a stiffly proper voice.

When she tugged at her hand, he said, "One moment, let me scan the area." He pulled on his Flair, sensed only the night, throbbing with possibilities between himself and Giniana. No other humans around.

"Nobody's lurking in your home, or around it," he said, still keeping her fingers trapped in his hand.

I could have told you that, Thrisca stated, then sniffed richly.

Johns ignored the beast.

Giniana's face went from tightly expressionless to relaxed. "Do you teleport home?" A lightness entered her tone.

Her question wasn't quite flattery on her part. She complimented him in believing he had the Flair, psi magic strength, and the will, to teleport home—outside the area of these large estates called Noble Country. 'Port from this estate of T'Spindle's back to inner Druida City, where she probably thought he lived. He didn't.

"Not tonight," he replied. "It's a beautiful night and autumn will come soon enough." He gave her another of his patented crooked smiles. "And I don't often get to Noble Country. I can walk out to the main avenue with public carrier routes and take a carrier home."

She glanced down at his feet, noted his sturdy boots, then nodded and gestured the way they came. "Go back down the path until it becomes gravel again. Turn right and it will take you to the front gate." Her manner had loosened up.

He wouldn't have to walk far, T'Spindle's estate was the closest to the rest of the city.

"Thank you. I'll see you to your door."

I can do that, MAN. Thrisca flicked the black tip of her ringed tail.

He didn't stop himself from stealing a kiss from Giniana, and her soft and tender lips thrilled him. Her breath went in with a quick inhalation, her mouth trembled under his, heating.

The cat snorted.

Giniana chuckled and stepped away. "Thanks again, MasterLevel Saint Johnswort."

"Johns," he corrected. "My friends ... I go by Johns."

Her head tilted. "What's your given name?"

"Klay."

Her brows raised. "That's a good name. Very tough hero-ish."

He shrugged. "I play those roles, but not only those type of parts. Please, call me Johns."

"Yes, Johns. Good night."

Thrisca butted her head against Giniana's thigh. *Let's go.*

"Yes, you need your food."

Not hungry for special food.

"It's to tempt your appetite." Giniana seemed to have forgotten him, but Johns figured she felt the thin bond spinning between them. He'd wait and see.

Woman and cat walked away, and the tense set of her shoulders showed him that she carried a heavy burden. But with grace. Everything about her spoke of compassion and grace under pressure.

Despite the cat, she appeared lonely ... vulnerable.

At the tiny stoop of the cottage, she dropped the dwelling's spellshield with a murmured word and gesture and opened the door. Thrisca, of course, sashayed in first. Giniana turned and raised a hand to Johns. Mental words reached him. *Merry meet.*

He liked the touch of her telepathy ... warm and intimate, whether she intended that or not.

Projecting the ritual reply, he said, *And merry part.*

"*And merry meet again,*" they replied in unison, with him adding a slight reverberation to his tone with telepathy.

He spoke aloud, "Yes, we *will* meet again."

The door closed behind her and the spellshield turned blue in protection.

Johns let air sigh from his lungs. No, he wouldn't be staying away from Giniana Filix who appeared to dislike actors as much as he did Fam animals.

CHAPTER 3

GINIANA'S SMILE lingered as she stepped into the small mainspace room of her cottage. No bigger than four meters square, she'd tinted the walls a rich cream color over an undertone of gold. The antique patterned blue-on-blue draperies over the large windows added to the atmosphere of quiet elegance.

Thrisca lay, panting a little too hard, on her dark blue velvet twoseat. The leap to and from the tree would have taken a lot of energy for her. She said, *Man smells interesting and good.*

Giniana flinched. Klay St. Johnswort, *Johns*, had smelled good, working sweat and... "You just say that because he smells like...."

Family. All My Families, Your Sires and before, and Your Dam.

"All actors, yes." Johns's kiss on her hand yet tingled. "I wonder how much posturing and lying went on at the party tonight? Plenty, I'm sure. Actors spend their lives dissimulating." Giniana marched into the kitchen area, a larger space that betrayed the age of the cottage. True meal preparation could happen here ... if she ever had the time.

Instead she relied on a few no-time cabinets, already

stocked with food, drink, and full meals. A no-time would keep the temperature the same as when the meal went in it. These old and sturdy no-times would be good for another century.

She yanked the food storage door open, pulled out the slightly cool mixture of furrabeast and a few greens that she purchased from the animal Healer. Just at the temperature that Thrisca preferred.

"Come eat your food," Giniana said. More of an order than Thrisca usually obeyed, but Giniana's good mood had evaporated with the irritation that the most interesting man she'd met lately ... all right, since she'd dated far too long ago ... practiced the profession of acting, of pretense.

You snapped at me, Thrisca said, sauntering in. She gave the food a sniff, then stepped away, then sniffed again and put her head down to the expensive meal.

I am old, Thrisca said mentally as she lapped. *Perhaps I am ready for My next adventure on the Wheel of Stars.*

As always, Giniana's stomach clutched—no, her whole being. Thrisca referred to death and rising to the Wheel of Stars and cycling to be reborn.

"I am a Healer. I fight death." Deep and steady breath in, release. "You could add another decade or more to your life without that lung disease and cough that weakens your whole system."

One of Thrisca's ears rotated in Giniana's direction. *I am still old. All of my litter mates are long dead.*

That would have shocked Giniana more if she hadn't heard the smugness in her Fam's tone.

Steady breath, steady words. "We have spoken about this before. If you wish me to let you die, I will. If you wish me to take you to the animal Healers so one of them can move you on to the Wheel of Stars ___"

Tail thrashing, but no yellow eyes staring at Giniana,

Thrisca daintily ate the last few bites. When her mental voice came, it sounded both energetic and casually studied, *I am interested in this new Time Healing Procedure that will cure my cough.*

Giniana's shoulders slumped. She and Thrisca had this conversation weekly. Live or die. The indecision wore on Giniana.

She straightened her spine. She loved Thrisca and had since Giniana had been a baby. The one member of the Family who'd loved her and had never abandoned her.

Once every quarter of the year, D'Willow conducted her time experiments, and Giniana hadn't had the fee last quarter. She worked and scraped and saved so Thrisca could attend the next session, which was coming up in less than two weeks. At the rate the lung-congesting disease progressed, Giniana didn't think Thrisca would last another few months.

To keep those thoughts at bay, Giniana busied herself restocking her Healing bag with herbs she'd used on the actors, made the case tidy and ready for the next emergency.

A few minutes later she left Thrisca snoozing on the two seat. As Giniana took the public carrier to her next job—a six septhour stint at new GraceLord Daisy's to nanny his infant at night—she totted up the gilt she made at her multiple jobs and gritted her teeth. Maybe she'd have enough to pay for the treatment.

But not if she took a night off for a play.

On the whole, Johns's spirits remained high. When he'd reached home, there'd been no formal notification that *Firewalker* would close in his message cache. He'd deal with that problem when it appeared.

In the dim twinmoonslight silvering the windows of his

bedroom, he stripped and carefully put aside his clothes. He'd take them to the Thespian Club and leave them with a wardrobe person who'd mend them in exchange for tickets to *Firewalker*.

Then he headed for the waterfall in the heir's suite of the old St. Johnswort mansion. His property included a large shabby house that held only him. Last of his line. Not uncommon on Celta.

His body felt fine, no bruising or even muscle stiffness, Healer Giniana Filix had done a damn good job.

He grinned, completely naturally. Yeah, everything considered, the night had gone well. He'd networked with producers and agents and rich patrons and other actors. He'd helped a friend in a good fight, had an offer from Cratag T'Marigold to be taught better fighting moves that would enhance his alpha male actor persona.

And Raz Cherry would be tapping his Family for a glider for Johns! Like springreen wine, it would have been years before Johns could afford a personal glider if Raz didn't gift him one at cost. A vehicle all his own! Oh, yeah, and he could take care of it so it lasted until he reached the pinnacle of his career and he could buy another.

His unthinking and altruistic actions sure had brought benefits, and the attention of T'Spindle, a producer, to him. Maybe Johns could finesse the next few weeks and not have a hiatus in his career.

Most of all, he'd met a fascinating woman. Too bad he was contrary enough to be attracted to the Healer who *dis*liked actors.

When he finally rested in bed, it was the golden amber eyes of the Healer, Giniana, that lingered in his mind's eye as he fell asleep.

Bells tolling woke him. The sound he used as his agent's ring-tone, pealing from the old-fashioned scrybowl in the sitting room of his bedroom suite. By the time he struggled awake and blinked in that direction, the ringing stopped.

His before-sleep optimism morphed into morning gloomi-ness matching the gray heat of the summer day. The sun had risen and his timer showed about an hour before WorkBell.

He sat up, rubbing his face. No matinee today, only an evening show. He'd've liked to have slept in. Every instinct he had, supplemented by the gossip at the party, indicated that the play he starred in would be closing and he'd be out of a job.

No doubt that's why his agent scried him, and used the house scrybowl instead of Johns's personal and mobile scry pebble. The man needed to give Johns formal notice his job was ending, but didn't really want to talk to him right now.

His agent probably already put Johns's name up as avail-able at the Theatrical Guild. Everyone at the social club, the Thespian Club, would know, too. Time to cut back on eating breakfast there, an expense he didn't need.

Definitely time to consider his future seriously. He mentally reviewed the state of his finances. Enough set by for a few months without a job. After that, he'd have to find work, even if not acting.

Slipping out of the bed, he pulled on a nice trous suit and scried his agent back. Making sure his voice held complete self-confidence, he said, "Greetyou, Chatt."

A plump man with sandy hair, Chatt Geyer smiled with false cheer. "Greetyou, Johns. Just got the word *Firewalker's* last show will be at the end of the month."

Johns couldn't help himself, he snarled.

"Be calm," soothed Chatt, a man who usually pushed enthusiasm at him, since, of course, Johns was the dark and brooding sort. "Everybody knows *Firewalker* is closing and you'll be available. I notified the Theatrical Guild."

"Any nibbles?" Johns forced out smooth, not choked, words.

"Ah, not right now. But it's only been *minutes*."

Johns grunted.

"Gael City has a couple of productions hiring—"

"No. I want to stay here, where I can make an outstanding career."

"That was true once, but Gael City's an up and coming—"

"Here in Druida City, Chatt," Johns said, moving to the window and looking out at the weeds carpeting the back of his "estate." Very run down, had been since before he'd been born. He'd put muscle and effort into it as a boy under the rule of his FatherDam, but let much go after she passed on to the Wheel of Stars. He'd rather not pay rent on anything else.

Especially if he'd have to use saved gilt to live on.

A squeal came from Chatt's end of the scry. "Gotta go. Keep cool, Johns. This interval won't harm your career." Another beaming smile Johns didn't believe.

Chatt signed off on Johns's second grunt.

He'd only managed to get down to the kitchen room that held one ancient no-time and grab some stocked hot black caff in a stained pottery mug before his perscry, personal scry pebble, in his pocket clanged. Pulling it out, he studied a flashy golden BW logo he didn't recognize.

After a sip of caff, he thumbed the perscry on, accepting the call.

"Geetyou, MasterLevel Actor Saint Johnswort." Blakely Wattle, the sleazy agent who'd talked to Johns the night before about a new play by Amberose, showed too-white teeth in a too-large smile dominating his round and pasty face, accented by a dark mole by his mouth. Johns couldn't figure out why anyone would keep a flaw like that.

Johns had almost forgotten about the new script by Amberose. His heart thumped a hard beat in his chest. He could hold out for a play that might zoom him to stardom, sure. He'd listen more to what the guy had to say.

He kept impassive. "Yeah?"

"Marvelous to see you last night." The man's voice grated but held an occasional squeak at the same time. Johns listened, wondering if a tone like that could ever come in use ... not soon, not while he continued to play rough and ready heroes, but maybe if he ever got a character acting part ....

"Wonderful party at T'Spindle's. So many luminaries, great networking ..."

Natter. Natter. Natter.

"You're not *listening* to me!" Yeah, that phrase went damn high pitched. Shifty and nervous.

"I am," Johns replied, adding a soupçon of boredom to prod the guy into actually saying something of worth.

"Like I said last night, I represent the great, great play-wright Amberose. Her first play in a decade."

"Yeah, so you said." Neither Johns nor his friends liked the man's reputation. With her near-legendary status, Amberose should have been able to do a whole lot better than this guy. Johns frowned. "You're really representing Amberose?"

Puffing out his chest, Wattle held up a card, flicked it and Amberose's logo became a banner, with confirmation of the man's status as her agent.

"Huh," Johns said. He wondered if anyone had asked how Wattle had landed such a top-of-the-pyramid client ... at least any one of Johns's actor friends. Most, like Raz Cherry, would have danced around the subject trying to persuade the man instead of being blunt. Johns shrugged, may as well ask. "How'd she come to you?"

Wattle stiffened, scowled. "She's living on ... an estate in the south ... and I'm ... relatively ... local."

The playwright thought she could control Wattle better than a bigger agent with a name. Amberose had the name and probably thought that was enough.

The man's eyes shifted. "And she had some requirements."

Johns had heard rumors that the playwright wanted more creative control that producers preferred to keep to themselves. He stared at Wattle, who remained mum.

Nervous twitch of the man's mouth, the mole rising and falling as Wattle's smile disappeared. "There's a good part for you. One tailored to you," the agent enthused, rushing words onto a topic Johns liked better to hear.

"Nice to know." Johns regulated his breath so it sounded as if he suppressed a sigh. Keep cool, don't reveal he wanted this so much he could taste sweet success on his tongue. Chill.

"I can show the script to you." That came out oily. An oily offer.

"Heard one of the copies of the script was stolen a coupla days ago from Lily Fescue's dressing room at the Primrose Theater," Johns kept his voice casual. "I'm sure Amberose wouldn't be happy—"

A squeak. "Lies! All lies. I have a script. A full script. Amberose has complete faith in me." But the shiftiness of his eyes, the waving of his hands, his flinching manner betrayed his lie.

Johns raised a disbelieving brow, sipped his tepid caff.

"We can meet. Let's meet! I promise you, Amberose is interested in you. Wrote the part for you! And I know *Fire-walker* is closing. I'm your best bet for future work."

One beat of silence. Two. "Oh? Haven't heard that any real producer, like T'Spindle, is interested in Amberose's play."

"Just playing hard to get. Listen!"

"Don't think so—"

"I promise you the job."

"Yeah?"

"Just for a small percentage of your first week's salary, I'll make sure you get the job!" A completely unethical proposal.

Johns snapped, "A casting director negotiates with my agent. Not you, never you negotiating with me."

Wattle winked and the cheek with the mole jerked. "A little side deal between the two of us."

"No." Johns's whole mouth turned sour. "You got nothin'. Even if the job came through, I wouldn't pay you." He cut the scry, anger surging and mixing with longing. The notion of a play by Amberose, a part specifically written for him, hit him hard at this particular time. Especially since he could tick off the names of at least five actors whose careers had been made by being in an Amberose play.

Yeah, he wanted that part bad. He paced the kitchen.

But he couldn't let Wattle play games like this.

And, hell, the man could be lying through his teeth about the part and stringing Johns along. From what he recalled about the gossip last night, one of the copies of the script was stolen. He didn't see the touchy Amberose giving the agent very many. In fact, Johns figured the woman would have spellbound whatever copies she let out of her grasp so they couldn't be replicated.

Nope, discount the whole damn conversation that left his mouth tasting bitter.

Concentrate on reality. As he washed his cup, he contemplated what food he had in the no-time and figured it, too, could last him about three months. Wouldn't have to buy any groceries, have meals prepared or struggle with food preparation himself. But his FatherDam, an indifferent cook, had made most of the meals.

Better if he had a job, of course, and didn't have to draw down his stock.

But he *wouldn't* let even the hint of desperation slither through him. Move on to a more cheerful thought!

An Amberose play. He *would* like to see the part. May as well try that angle, first. Wattle should have understood from their conversation that Johns wouldn't be paying him any gilt for anything. Calling now would give the guy the upper hand, so Johns would wait and hope the man would call back.

As an exercise, Johns extended his senses, trying to catch the vestige of any connection he might have with the guy and discovered a faint thread. Scowling in concentration, Johns traced the link to the becoming-familiar direction of T'Spindle's estate. Interesting, but Johns figured the man had no chance to sell the play to the producer. Not a guy as shaky in his ethics as Wattle. He wouldn't be at the Spindles for long.

But he sure had reminded Johns of one of his priorities of the day—arrange for tickets for Giniana Filix to his play, *Firewalker*.

He considered going to the Spindles and dropping off the pass there for Giniana. Johns might even be able to convince the guards to let him leave the tickets at the Healer's cottage … but then he'd definitely have to face the FamCat as well as Giniana. And he sensed last night that he'd already pushed the woman as far as he could into being with him. More pressure now could very well be counterproductive. Much as he yearned to see her again, it would be a mis-step. He'd leave her alone, for the moment.

The lady sure stirred something in him that hadn't been touched before. Johns should be wary of that, but his curiosity about his own emotions had been piqued.

Yeah, better to wait and get her in the playhouse, on his territory. *Show* her what he could do. Entice her.

CHAPTER 4

DAWN LIGHTENED the sky and Giniana handed over the baby girl to a fresh and beaming mother. The babe didn't really need Giniana's care, the slight case of croup had passed two weeks ago, but the Daisys kept her on and Giniana felt deeply grateful.

On the way to the public carrier plinth where she'd catch transport to Noble Country and the Spindles, her personal scry pebble vibrated with a quick written message from D'Willow's assistant: *The number of individuals scheduled for the next Time Healing Procedure has dropped from seven to six, thus the shared fee has increased for each of the remaining clients.*

Giniana stopped in her tracks. The summer morning suddenly became hot as slick dread coated her body. She'd be short of the payment.

She understood the costs, mostly to Dufleur D'Willow in health and Flair, energy and strength as the lady moved beings through time to Heal them. Also, the expenses involved in preparing the area where the process would take place. But, *Lady and Lord*, Giniana currently worked to the end of her own strength in coming up with the fee to Heal Thrisca.

Most people, particularly Healers, considered the new treatment of using time to cure maladies as highly experimental. D'Willow had initiated the procedure no more than two and a half years before. Only in the last year had she offered such a proceeding once a quarter.

Though Giniana hadn't watched the experiment, she'd seen the results. D'Willow, whose Flair included bending *time*, explained the operation as moving her clients a few minutes back in time, then forward to a minute after the start of the experiment. Some of the illnesses in the patients couldn't transition with the people and simply vanished. Or dried up and disappeared...or...who knew? Only D'Willow herself might know more and she didn't reveal anything else.

But one of Giniana's patients had had a cyclical disease that couldn't be totally Healed and with every recurrence, became worse. A young mother and beloved HeartMate, her spouse had begged her to try the treatment. She'd been completely cured.

Even the most important Healers on Celta couldn't argue with such results.

Since the Animal Healers couldn't help Thrisca any further, Giniana had scheduled Thrisca to take part in the Time Healing Procedure ... as soon as Giniana could raise enough gilt.

Wetting her dry lips, she scried D'Willow's personal assistant who handled her business. Giniana pasted on a smile, wishing for once that she'd inherited some acting talent from her parents. She felt like she projected desperation instead of cool inquiry.

"D'Willow's," the woman snapped. Giniana decided she wasn't the first to reply regarding the announcement of an increase in cost. Though Giniana's scry pebble could frame a face, the woman didn't bother to look up from her writestick and papyrus.

"Greetyou, Palli," Giniana said mildly. She'd interacted with D'Willow's assistant over the last three and a half months she researched the procedure. "I received your scry note that someone has dropped out of the experiment in a week and a half."

"That's what I wrote. Why are you scrying me?" Palli still didn't meet Giniana's eyes.

"I was afraid someone took a turn for the worse," Giniana said. "That a health problem might have come up, particularly with a person I referred to you and D'Willow." As far as Giniana knew, two people had already been through—and cured by—the experiment due to information Giniana gave them. Two more were booked in the same session as Thrisca.

"You would know better than me about health issues." Palli grunted her words. "The client who dropped out informed me that traditional Healing methods helped her and she didn't want to put herself through the fear of being experimented on with time."

"Oh."

The assistant gave Giniana the name of a person she knew only casually. Not one of the individuals she'd referred.

"Thank you," she said politely, and drew in a breath. "I would like to speak with D'Willow—"

Now Palli jerked her head up. "No!" She scowled. "You know we don't do payments because some people are terminal and we *don't* get paid. No, you can't speak with D'Willow."

"All right," Giniana soothed. "Thank you for your assistance."

"Later," Palli replied, head back down and writestick scritching across papyrus.

Deep inside, Giniana's nerves trembled and she stopped them from showing, then watched the public carrier pass her. She *wouldn't* give up. Rolling her shoulders to release tension, she called T'Willow Residence. Dufleur D'Willow held her own inherited title of D'Thyme, but had married a First-Family GreatLord.

"T'Willow's," answered the cheerful housekeeper, obviously a Family member.

"I would like to speak with D'Willow's secretary about making an appointment with her, please," Giniana said.

A calendarsphere pinged into existence. "I can do that for you, dear. You're a Healer?"

"Yes. FirstLevel Healer Giniana Filix."

"Very good. The best appointment would be tomorrow at Mid-Afternoon Bell." The housekeeper met her eyes, glanced away, coughed. "Is this about the upcoming Time Healing Procedure?"

Despite herself, Giniana stiffened. "Yes."

With a sigh, the housekeeper shook her head. "Palli *does* need to be tough, but, perhaps her manner is a little too grating."

Giniana didn't comment.

"We'll see you then, dear," said the housekeeper and signed off.

Maybe Giniana would be able to finesse this, perhaps finance this. After all, *she* was young and well-employed and healthy. Her FamCat was the patient.

Worse came to worst, she'd use the very last of her savings, perhaps even ask for an advance on her salary from T'Spindle. She cringed at that.

Her mother, the failed actress, had lived off her lovers.

Her mother's existence, and Giniana's as a child, depended on lovers. Mostly patrons of her acting career, and their favors. The career that never quite got off the ground because Verna Winterbloom Filix didn't work to make it so. She took an easier path.

She borrowed gilt she couldn't repay, had no intention of

repaying, lost all the friends they'd had … except for her rich lovers.

Like all actors, like Giniana's father, her mother made promises she never kept, to Family, friends and to Giniana.

And Giniana's feelings about her mother had always been mixed—love and despair.

Giniana suspected the reason she'd been hired by the Citronella Family as soon as she'd finished her training was because her mother had been the GraceLord's lover at the time. A humiliating situation that she hadn't learned about until months on the job. Because she'd been estranged from her mother.

Giniana had been proud to send gilt to her mother's cache earned on her first job, thinking that *she* would be able to support them both, then learned of her mother's lover who'd indulged Verna by giving her daughter a job.

But Giniana had proven her worth, and when the Spindles had offered her a better position, she'd taken it.

She liked the easy-going Spindles, perhaps the least intense of the FirstFamilies, and she admired and respected them.

The only drawback was the actors she had to deal with.

Giniana trudged from the public carrier stop in Noble Country nearest to T'Spindle Residence. Unlike the rest of the city, here in Noble Country such plinths indicating public transport were few and far between. Most people here would teleport or use antique Family gliders or modern sports models.

She sighed as Tinne and Lahsin Holly zoomed past her, ensconced in a new luxurious twoseat glider. And Giniana said a spell to relieve the ache in her feet. Even the small

Flair needed for her Healer bag to follow her with anti-grav depleted her energy.

Working too hard, for too long. Her thoughts circled to Thrisca again, a FamCat who had been in her family since her father's childhood.

In the back of Giniana's mind she'd been aware of her cat rising from an ever lengthening sleep, stretching, thinning the Fam door in the cottage from wall to air and padding into grassyard—without eating.

Not only had Giniana's parents *not* taken care of her, they hadn't paid any attention to the Familiar companion, Thrisca, her father had inherited from his father. Her parents hadn't loved the cat, either. But Thrisca had always been there for Giniana.

She'd find the gilt to pay for the time Healing.

Greetyou, FamWoman, Thrisca's mental voice held a note of animation at odds with her usual boredom.

Greetyou, FamCat, Giniana replied. She tilted her head as she pinpointed Thrisca's location beyond the yard of the cottage and close to the ivied door in the outside wall for the first time in a month, attention fixed on—something. Though the cat's attitude seemed calm, Giniana's heart thumped hard and she picked up pace. Significantly younger than her FamCat, Giniana hadn't reached the serenity of her Fam.

What's wrong? she asked. A spurt of adrenaline boosted her energy and she hurried along the path outside the estate wall to the door near her cottage, a trail her feet had defined from grass to hard dirt in the last few weeks.

We have an intruder. A dry mental cackle. *He is not in good shape.*

What have you done? demanded Giniana.

I did not eviscerate him, Thrisca continued in a light tone.

Lady and Lord. Giniana snatched her bag back into her hands and sped up. Though she knew the grounds very well, it would be faster to run than for Thrisca to send her detailed images for Giniana to teleport—hoping to miss any bushes and trees that could kill her if she landed with a branch inside her.

She reached the small human-sized door, heard muttering from the other side. "Gotta be here somewhere, found one flappin' in brush, gotta be more."

That didn't make sense right now, so she said the spell-words T'Spindle coded to her, and pushed through the iron portal. Just inside, leaning against the stone wall, she found a thin and twiggy man with a round sweating face, a mole near his mouth stood out dark against his pallor. Limp fingers held a crumpled and dirt stained papyrus page.

One glance told her he'd contracted the flill sickness, one of the viri moving through the Druida populace this season. Debilitating but not fatal.

Narrowing her eyes, she examined him. He'd have felt minor symptoms of nausea and sleepiness. And if he'd *gone* to sleep instead of pushing on, he'd have been fine. Now the sickness had moved into a more active mode.

She'd noticed him last night at the party, hadn't she? Milling around with some of the others below the terrace? An actor? No, he couldn't pass for even a character actor, build all wrong, plain features, definite mole. It would be an uphill battle for this one to get parts.

"Lady and Lord," she gasped.

Tremors racking his body, the man opened watery green eyes. "Healer," he gasped.

"I'll teleport you to AllClass Healing Hall," she assured. It would strain her resources, but she should have just enough energy to take them both.

"No, please! Just let me rest here a little bit."

"You need a HealingHall or your own place. I can call a HealingHall glider."

"Please," he coughed, then grimaced, spoke slowly as if completely forming his words. "I just pitched a play to T'Spindle. He rejected the project and dismissed me. Don't tell him that I'm here." He gulped. "I have my pride."

And that request hit Giniana directly. One of her flaws, too, pride. She didn't ask for help. Never. Not when she recalled her mother prettily begging for some bauble or another from an indulgent lover she slept with.

"Can't you just let me rest?" he mumbled, sliding down the wall.

Giniana leapt to help him, *felt* his fever, checked on his vitals. He'd moved into the second stage of the sickness. "Who do you have at home?" she demanded.

His eyelids raised showing glassy orbs. "I'm single," he leered.

"You shouldn't be alone—"

He might be interesting company, Thrisca stated. She slunk through the bushes, put her muzzle close to the man's and swiped his face with her tongue.

Giniana didn't admonish her. Like many diseases, this particular sickness didn't affect animals.

Has interesting taste, Thrisca said.

The fallen man sucked in air. "Good kitty, nice Fam." His face contorted, probably thinking that he smiled at Giniana, but she saw the perspiration beaded on his forehead, smelled more. "Lemme stay. Lemme rest." His eyes closed.

"This is a FirstFamily Lord's estate. I could lose my job if I harbored you." She opened her bag and placed a cool pad on his chest.

He raised limp fingers. "No trouble. Man of peace. Wouldn't never harm the Spindles, anyone here. My Vow of

Honor on that." Then he put his hand on the pad and sighed.

I like him, Thrisca said. Giniana sensed her amusement at someone not as intelligent as her, someone to toy with.

"Listen to the cat," he murmured.

"This is wrong."

"Just need to rest a coupla days, then I'll get out of your life, I promise." He coughed.

Here she'd been arguing with someone in need of Healing! Giniana knelt beside him, did a more intense exam. He'd need nursing for the next few days, some potions and medicines.

Thrisca sat and licked a paw. *I know this sickness. He is weak now, will be weak for days.* She snapped her paw down next to his hand on the ground holding the papyrus, barely missing his fingers. *He can't outrun Me. He can't beat Me in anything!*

"No." Giniana sighed the word out. The Healers had learned long ago that it was easiest on everyone not to pour energy into Healing this particular virus. Such Healing demanded Flair reserves Giniana didn't have, and would wring the strength from the patient, too. Best if he'd simply gone to bed when he realized he'd picked up the bug, but of course he hadn't done that. Few people did.

The warmth of the sun, the quiet around them, seemed emphasized by a cheerful hum of bees tending the flowers, full of vitality when she, like this man, felt exhausted.

She sat back on her heels. The man had fallen into an uneasy sleep. She *could* teleport him to AllClass HealingHall, strain their always limited resources. But, as a threat, he didn't appear great. And he wouldn't be going anywhere soon, particularly without her help. He'd be lucky to get out of bed to move to a toilet and relieve himself.

She studied Thrisca. The Fam felt livelier than usual, her ears rotated with curiosity. Perhaps giving Thrisca a duty would help. That had never been true in the past, because Thrisca embodied cat disdain, but the situation had changed since spring and the Fam's unHealable malady.

Meeting her cat's yellow eyes, Giniana sent telepathically, *You must guard the Spindles against this man.*

Thrisca snorted, extended her claws on her left forepaw and groomed them. *As if Residence wouldn't stop man, or house guards arrest him.*

Giniana replied mentally, *Right now I don't know whether the Residence or the guards know this man is still on the estate.*

A studied stare over her shoulder and no response from Thrisca.

Speaking aloud, Giniana said, "All right, I'll call the Spindle guards and have him taken to AllClass HealingHall."

After a huffing snort, Thrisca said, *I will watch him. All the time.* She opened her mouth, tongue curling in the extra smell-taste sense cats had, sniffed, then lifted the top of her muzzle to show fangs in a predator's grin. *He is hiding a secret. Perhaps more than one,* Thrisca finished with perky glee, sinking her claws into the papyrus and leaving little holes. *I like to find out secrets.*

Yes, this guy would be a play toy for Thrisca. Ah, well, it would do no harm to nurse the man until he recovered enough to stand up a few septhours on his own, since Thrisca would keep him under her scrutiny.

Giniana believed the cat would, because if Thrisca didn't, Giniana would teleport the guy out of the estate and into the HealingHall as soon as she recovered her energy, and Thrisca knew that.

Against her best judgment, but under the supervision of her purring FamCat, Giniana settled the man in a small lean-to attached to the back of her cottage. Since she'd fitted it up as an emergency sickroom that her trainers always stated every Healer should have, the tiny space *did* contain a toilet cubicle with sink and extremely basic waterfall, a no-time for food and drink, and a bed.

I will keep track of him, Thrisca assured Giniana.

She had no doubt of that, but since the whole thing seemed to liven up her Fam, Giniana let it go. She'd inform the Residence, at least, of the situation next time she was there. Right now, fatigue pressed upon her.

Once inside her own cottage—and alone for the first time in days, a luxury she'd appreciate for as long as it lasted—she saw an alert of bright yellow air swirling above her old-fashioned scrybowl—indicating a message in her cache. Her personal scry pebble in her trous pocket emitted no sound, so the person calling her only knew her scry image here at the Spindles.

She crossed to the kitchen counter and touched the rim of the bowl. Immediately star-shaped yellow St. Johnswort blossoms fluttered down, revealing the hard-planed virile face of the man. She could have sworn her heart skipped a beat or two.

CHAPTER 5

IN HIS SCRY MESSAGE, Klay St. Johnswort didn't look like an actor, not incredibly handsome and carrying smooth charm ... like Raz Cherry whom she'd treated.

No, this determined man emanated sheer male magnetism. That had attracted her from the start. Realizing she'd swallowed at the sight of his crooked smile and intent eyes and stared at the image for long seconds instead of listening to his message, she finally touched the bowl again. "Play."

"Greetyou FirstLevel Healer," nice that he acknowledged the mastery of her craft at the same level of his own. That he started with respect. "Giniana Filix," his deep voice seemed to caress her first name and that caused unexpected tingles to shiver through her, too, mesmerizing her.

"I've left a pass for you to view *Firewalker* at any time from this evening to the final performance at the end of the month." A corner of his mouth lifted wryly. "I'm sorry I can't offer you tickets after that. As you may have heard, the play is closing at that time." He shrugged, accepting the vagaries of his career.

The uncertainty and risk of such a profession would have driven Giniana mad. She shuddered. Perhaps she would have given up and given in and found others to support her, like her mother had done.

No. Giniana would always fight. Healers did. They fought for their patients, they battled disease and sterility and all the other ills that plagued the descendants of the Earthan colonists and kept the Celtan population too low.

Healers knew that humans still held only a slippery grasp on complete survival on the planet.

She tuned back into the message as Johns's voice stroked her again when he said her name. "Giniana, I'll be glad if you would come backstage after the show, and...." His eyelids lowered until his gaze glittered with sensuality, "I'd be delighted to treat you to dinner and any other entertainment after the play."

A breath whooshed from her, and before she could consciously stop them, her fingers initiated the replay spell.

After the third repetition, the dazzle diminished and she decided to watch the whole thing once more to study his manner. She'd grown up with actors, her parents and their friends. They'd rarely been "off," always performing.

But she didn't think St. Johnswort, Johns, did. She blinked at the thought. Oh, she'd seen him studying Raz Cherry, and T'Spindle, and some of the society people milling around the terrace before she'd Healed Raz and Johns himself. Observing people with those keen actor eyes, but he hadn't done much playacting then. Perhaps the adrenaline running through him had edged his manner even more, eroded his actor training to reveal the man.

Raz Cherry, hurt worse than Johns, had kept that easy charm, that surface actor skin during the time she'd spent with them and T'Spindle. As far as she could recall, Johns hadn't.

Nor did it seem like he acted in this simple scry.

He'd been himself and allowed her to *see* himself.

Also a sign of respect.

On the scry he blinked and his expression turned bland, his gaze opaque. "I will leave *two* passes for you, should you care to bring a gallant or a friend."

He'd let her bring a lover, even though they both knew he wanted to act on the allure between them. He wanted to be her gallant, squire her around … take her to bed. And, yes, every time she thought of that her pulse jumped. She was a medical professional, she knew heart thumping when she felt it.

That final offer, which cost him since he made it while behind a mask, also spoke of respect.

This time when he signed off, she let the scrybowl stay dark.

The whole message spoke of interest, and respect. She wasn't used to respect in acting circles. She always thought they used and manipulated people as much as they could, and believed others weak for allowing that. When thinking of those parties of her parents', her ears rang with the sharp insincerity of laughter, of derision her parents and their actor friends held for others.

And her parents had used her mother's Healing Family for as long as they could, until they totally wrecked that relationship for themselves and Giniana herself. Not that her parents had cared.

Giniana cared about people, and from the small interaction she'd had with Johns, he did, too.

Perhaps.

Perhaps she should give him a chance.

But not now. She had other priorities now. She had to work herself thin to afford Thrisca's treatment. She and Johns would both see if he'd still be interested in her or would have moved on, after the time treatment to Heal Thrisca.

An emptiness left by flattened hope filled her, and she

ignored it as she mentally checked one last time on Thrisca lying in the sun near the lean-to. Then Giniana went to bed and embraced sleep.

🕯️

Johns finished dressing in a good, professional tunic and trous. Classic cut and fashion, like his glider would be, if Raz Cherry came through on his offer to sell one to Johns at cost. Johns sure didn't plan on reminding his friend and sometime rival of that, let alone nagging the man.

Just as well if Raz forgot the issue, Johns shouldn't be spending gilt on a large expense at this point anyway. And the pang of regret that he might lose the vehicle sunk him into more gloom.

Didn't help that his sitting room scrybowl had pinged that Giniana Filix had picked up his message in her cache, and his own offer of the monthly pass, but she didn't scry him back. Tried not to let that fact prick his pride, ego, or any deeper self.

Time to hit the Theatrical Guild to show his confidence to his peers, confirm his freedom from employment at the end of the month, and make sure his name was on the hiring lists for certain. He trusted his agent, Chatt, but best to be proactive.

He wouldn't let the once-again-clouding-over morning smudge his spirits any further.

His scry pebble clanged the standard ring and he grabbed it from his pocket, answered it. Then saw Lily Fescue's face staring out at him—the lovely blond actor who played the leading lady role opposite Raz Cherry in their very successful show. Johns recalled that Raz had told him the night before that *she* had gotten the elusive script from the playwright genius, Amberose.

Interesting.

She simpered at him. She thought the heavy-lidded gaze and slight curve of lips looked sexy. He didn't, and he did that expression better, too.

"Greetyou, Lily." He stayed courteous. No use irritating anyone who might help him in the slightest, especially a notoriously touchy person like Lily who believed he liked her. He thought her a good actress, at the moment. As far as he was concerned, she didn't hone her skills enough, didn't train with others, but depended on her natural talent and passion which wasn't enough to see her through to a strong career.

Wasn't enough to sustain anyone's acting career.

"Johns?" she asked, pouting.

"Here."

A mock sympathetic expression dropped onto her face. "I understand if you've gone into brood mode, since *Firewalker* is closing." She paused delicately, then said, "I saw you at the party last night to celebrate the run of my play."

All right, that irritated him. "Yeah." He'd danced with her, hadn't he? Yeah, done that duty. Checkmark.

Lily looked around and lowered her voice to a whisper. "And I saw you talking with BW." A small cough. "I've tried and tried scrying BW this morning." Her lips pursed, showing irritated vertical lines that would age her faster if she didn't watch out.

"Who?" he asked.

"BW, Blakely Wattle, the playwright Amberose's representative."

"Oh, yeah." Lily called the guy BW. Didn't take Johns's sharpening senses to understand Lily had a closer connection with the man than anyone else he'd talked to recently.

"Last night, BW said that he'd scry you more about the script, has he?" Lily pressed.

"Yeah, but I didn't like his attitude."

Lily rolled her eyes. "Oh, Johns."

"Tried to shake me down for gilt. I should pay him to get a part in that play, as well as pay my agent. Told me a string of lies."

Now she widened her eyes. "But, Johns, Amberose wrote the main hero part for you!"

His heart gave a huge thump, but he kept his expression bland, sighed inwardly that he had to act for this woman, this colleague, but he didn't trust her. "Yeah? He told you so?"

"Yes, but more. I had the script. I *read* the script. The main part, the heroine's, was obviously meant for me, but the description of the hero matched *you*." Her face scanned what she could see of him, his head and torso, lingered on his shoulders and chest. "Big guy with a honed build, rugged good looks, dark hair, gray-blue eyes, tough alpha manner, that's you."

"If you say so."

"I do. Just like the secondary lead was for Raz Cherry."

"Is that so?"

"Yes, there's a part for Raz, too." But she flicked that aside with a finger motion.

"Yeah?' Johns scowled, played a little dumb for more clarification. "What kind of role?"

"Two couples," she explained briefly. "But *our* characters and our relationship is the primary one."

He'd be working opposite her. Just great. He managed to dredge up a slight curve of lips as if pleased.

Lilly continued, "I recognized who Amberose meant to play my character, and yours, and Raz's. I don't know who she might have intended for Raz's love interest." Another flick of the hand. "But that doesn't really matter."

She didn't recognize the secondary female lead because she didn't pay attention to other women in her profession unless they directly competed with her. Another flaw in her own character, ignoring her female peers.

Clearing her throat, Lily glanced aside, then back at him, nervous for some reason. "BW didn't mention giving you the script, did he? What of the pages, do you have them?"

Why she seemed secretive, Johns didn't know. He stood alone in his family home—and Lily knew he lived in single solitude—and she appeared to be by herself in her upscale townhouse. But Lily had to be dramatic. He really regretted that brief fling with her years ago, a mistake.

Johns said, "Of course he didn't give me pages." He let her see a small frown. "Raz Cherry told me *you* had the script." And everyone knew the theater where she and Raz worked had been burgled. Johns had gotten the idea that most, if not all, of Amberose's newest play had been stolen from Lily's dressing room.

Lily put her face far too close to her scry pebble and said, "BW told me when he loaned me the play that it was the only copy Amberose allowed him to have!"

Ah, so the agent *had* lied that morning. And Lily had lost the script, typical of her indifference to anything but the absolute now. A couple of her pores showed the dampness of sweat.

Johns grunted.

"Don't you do that to me!" Lily snapped, aimed a too-sharp-pointed fingernail at him. "Answer me in words, dammit, Johns!"

"Tough luck the script's gone."

"Johns!"

Well, what had she wanted him to say? "T'Spindle is involved in going after the thieves, now. He'll get action. Pretty sure that when Amberose hears that Wattle lost the script she'll yank her representation from him, maybe he won't tell the woman that you had her play when it disappeared."

Lily's hands fisted. "I want that role, dammit."

Johns didn't see her getting it now, fine by him.

She stalked back and forth, diminishing and enlarging in her scrybowl. "I hoped BW had more than one copy," she muttered. "Too bad he's the only one who has the play."

"You mean the only one who did," Johns said sardonically. "Sure sounds like the thieves that hit your theater and T'Spindle's last night got it."

"They *can't* believe it's worth much!" Lily protested.

Johns shrugged. "Who knows? Amberose has a huge name and rep in theatrical circles. One copy of a new play by her when she hasn't written one in a decade might command a lot of gilt." He contemplated it. "A lot. Depends on the thieves, and what they know, doesn't it? Whether they were only after jewelry and money."

Lily puffed out a breath. "I wrote down what I could best remember, my part." She glittered a smile at him. "And inter-actions with you."

Lady and Lord help him, seemed all his interactions with Lily, on and off the stage, would be acting. He raised a brow in bored interest. He didn't want her to know how he'd pounce on such a role. She'd use him if she could. "Yeah, you wrote down lines?" Then he rolled an offhand shoulder. She wouldn't have gotten the language right, for sure, the rhythm. Maybe for her part, a bit of his ... but it might be interesting to get a glimpse and a gist.

A few breaths from heaving overblown breasts that caught his eye as a guy, but he didn't admire, then she'd found her sultry tone again. "I'll definitely show what I've got to you."

That yanked his gaze up to her face, her sharp eyes and pouty lips.

"Your memories of the script? Not sure it's worth it. Gone now, and when Amberose hears about the theft, gone for a good long time. Won't help me since the production won't be up and running soon." He stated the worst case scenario.

"Meet me for breakfast at the Thespian Club." Her tone went from breathy to brisk. She glanced at her jeweled wrist timer. "I know it's slightly early for most of us *working* actors, but you're up and I'm up."

And he'd already had three scries and made one. How did regular people handle mornings?

"Can't meet you," he said.

"Why?" Lily whined.

"Because I'm due to teach at Moores House for Lady-Blessed Children," he fibbed. That standing appointment was early afternoon, tomorrow. "I have the teaching, then rehearsal and the show." He wanted to go to the Theatrical' Guild. He'd have to watch the timing, because Lily would hear when he'd shown up and he wouldn't be caught in a lie. So he'd wait a septhour or so. She would believe that he'd only give a few minutes to the children, do a drop-by.

Lily's already dissatisfied mouth turned down. "Are you still doing that gig the Thespian Club sponsored last new year for publicity?" She flicked fingers. "No one's reporting on it *now*. It's old news."

He let his tough guy persona come to the front, said coolly enough, "I like working with the children."

"They're ... slow."

"They're great. They welcome every moment. I find it fulfilling when I teach and some become better seated in their bodies."

She made a moue. "You're lucky they remember you from one session to the next. They didn't me."

Oh, yes, the children had remembered Lily. Just not in a good way.

"They remember me. They love me."

"How pitiful that you need such adoration," she sneered.

He heaved a breath. "Later, Lily."

"Wait, I want to talk to you about Amberose's play, maybe finding it."

Shaking his head, he said, "Not worth it to me."

"Please, Johns!" Tears filled her eyes. "If not today, then breakfast tomorrow? Please, the role is really something. It will make me—you—make us all!" She paused. "If we can salvage this fiasco."

He figured she wanted him to do all the work. But the only way to see if he should contemplate the role would be to look at whatever portion of the script Lily had. He suspected he wouldn't get her notes until he actually met with her and she'd handed them to him.

"All right," he agreed. "Tomorrow, MidMorning Bell, Thespian Club."

"*Thank you!*" she trilled. Then her lips curved and her eyes sparkled. "I saw Raz with that new woman last night. His attention to her really steamed Morifa Daisy...."

And Lily had moved on to boring gossip, Lord and Lady help Johns. He pasted an *intent* expression on his face, slipped his hand in his trous pocket where he kept his perscry, below Lily's line of vision. With a touch, he had it ringing and stating, "Incoming scry for Saint Johnswort."

"Gotta go," he said, raised his fingers for a sign-off gesture.

"Tomorrow morning, then," she caroled in a cheerful tone with a wiggle of fingers, though her gaze held dark sharpness as if she doubted his honesty. She smiled with an unamused smile. "I'll treat." Her lilting voice mocked.

His expression solidified into the stone of offended pride, then he made himself relax. Returned her mocking look with a smoldering one of his own. "Fine with me. I always enjoy when a woman picks up the tab." A lie, but who cared?

She hissed, and flounced, and cut the scry.

Johns sighed. He hated playing games, didn't do that as often as most of his colleagues. And he disliked Lily Fescue, didn't know if breakfast with her would be worthwhile or not, even for more information about the elusive Amberose script. He should put that out of his mind, he had better things to think of.

On impulse he scried Blakely Wattle, to touch base with the agent. No answer.

Too bad he *hadn't* received a scry from a much more honest and fascinating woman than Lily Fescue.

When would Giniana Filix call? Would she?

He hoped for that more than any prospective role. Odd, but true. Just the thought of her stirred him more deeply than anything else in a long time, a pervasive feeling of aching need.

CHAPTER 6

THAT NIGHT, Giniana had no sooner gotten to the Daisys than she'd been met at the door by the new GraceLady who wore a diaphanous gown and a sly smile. "We've decided to stay in tonight. And play. Play with the baby, too. We won't be needing you, but we'll still pay for the evening and your time and trouble since you came all the way here." She pushed gilt coins and bills into Giniana's hands, then shut the door in her face.

Giniana stood open mouthed, breathing sparkling evening summer air as her evening widened with freedom. Dizzying. And her heart, as well as her body, knew what she wanted to do. She didn't want to go home and check on her patient— whom she'd just looked in on and refilled his bedside water pitcher—didn't want to listen to Thrisca.

Slowly she walked, experiencing all the night had to offer, the lingering scent released by the summer flowers during the day, the insects whirring cheerfully in the bushes, the feel of the ground under her lighter step.

She smiled with the release of care, the living in the moment of *now* instead of worrying about later.

Then an urgent call from Intake at AllClass HealingHall shrilled through her pebble. *Scrying all contract or consulting Healers. Please 'port to AllClass HealingHall Intake to treat emergency victims of a boating accident.*

More gilt to pay for Thrisca's time procedure. Giniana's options vanished and her shoulders slumped a moment as the previously lifted burden thunked back down upon her.

She flicked a word reply with her thumb. *I'll be right there.*

And she used the lovely mood and surrounding energy of the evening darkening into night as energy to teleport to the HealingHall.

Not only Giniana, as an independent Healer, showed up at AllClass HealingHall. Two others had, too, and some journeymen and journeywomen Healers, interns, had been at the center. Lark Holly briskly organized them into teams, with Giniana leading one full team, and teaching the journeypeople as they Healed.

A septhour later, one of the HealingHall gliders took her home, dazed and nearly spent, but with more coin in her pocket than she'd anticipated.

A peevish Thrisca, who'd wanted to sleep outside in a huge bed of catnip that Giniana forbade, refused to listen to reason. *There is no life without some fun, and sleeping in catnip is marrvvelllous—GO AWAY! I watch man from here.* A cat snort. *He didn't come out door at all today.*

Giniana stared at her Fam. *Did you eat?*

Thrisca rolled over and showed catnip in her mouth. *I ate.*

Food? she persisted.

I munched some food. Another roll and the cat's back showed Giniana a long, flexible and irritated spine. *You weren't supposed to be here tonight. Go. Away.*

Giniana should stay, watch over her Fam and human patient. But if she hurried, she could make the play, *Firewalker*, and instead watch Johns perform his craft.

Johns knew Giniana Filix sat in the audience. Even if his general situational senses hadn't given him that information, the tiny bond between them had. He wanted to analyze that bond—from her Healing him, spending a little time together and layered with mutual attraction? But his cue came up in five seconds. Big breath, check his balance, inside and out. Four, three, two, one. He surged onto stage, leading with his fist to take a punk down....

His Fire Mage character battled flames burning a First-Family Residence, and as he jumped away from a falling beam, he *felt* the spurt of fear of Giniana Filix.

Their bond expanded.

Good. Distracted only for an instant or two during an action scene that his body continued, rolling, leaping to his feet, snatching the heroine from mid-air. Perfect timing.

Heroine pushed him away as another burning beam hit, gave him a quick sideways look not in the play, he rolled out spellwords, raising and lowering his arms, putting out the blaze like a real Fire Mage would do

And he *acted*, less involved in his character than normally, but the excitement of having a lovely woman he liked and respected in the house gave him a boost. Rather a split attention, moving well, saying his words with the passion and inflection they needed, but also hooked into Giniana Filix's reactions. Despite her family background, the play affected her. Particularly since it featured several strong women characters. His link with Giniana gave him an edgy interaction with his female co-star and romantic lead, which she, also an excellent actress, picked up on and gave back to him in an equally intense performance.

The story swept Giniana into it. At the end, the firewalker and the heroine battled villains who'd set a fire, the couple broke free just in time for the firewalker to extinguish the blaze, then ran through a building collapsing behind them. Once outside, the hero declared his love, the heroine hers and they flung themselves together in a kiss that looked as hot as the flames that had graced the stage.

Seeing the fascinating guy who seemed interested in locking mouths, crushing bodies together with another woman jolted Giniana from the story. As the curtain fell and applause roared, she thought once more how her parents had had affairs with their co-stars, especially her father.

Actors, pretending feelings they didn't have.

Like love for their daughter.

Making promises they never kept, like to each other and their child and their Fam.

Yes, she clapped with those all around her who'd enjoyed the story, suspended their disbelief that such exciting events rolled on right before their eyes, experienced the emotions the actors had pulled out of them through their craft and some Flair.

Those who'd manipulated their emotions.

But the audience calling for another bow from the cast had made the choice to come and have their emotions tugged, hadn't they? To be entertained, swept out of the now and the problems of their lives, to an urgent and dangerous *then* of a story.

Still, she wondered how much Johns felt for his co-star when he kissed the woman—until Giniana's pocket perscry vibrated. The note stated that one of the patients she'd helped earlier at AllClass HealingHall needed the next layer of Healing.

Giniana bit her lip. She didn't want to leave. She wanted to go backstage and talk to Johns, even if surrounding fans burbled huge admiration at him. The first time she'd wanted to linger in a theater for decades.

She teleported to do *her* job, her duty.

At the end of the play, the audience yelled and stood and the cast received more curtain calls than ever. Johns briefly regretted the closing of the show, obviously he and the cast hadn't explored all the nuances of the characters, but so life went.

Giniana didn't come backstage to the green room or to his dressing room. He'd even used the ebullient Flair from a good performance to fund a whirlwind spell so he could change faster and see her. But she'd left. From the faint anxiety of her bond, he understood she hurried to a job. He hadn't thought the Spindles would be that strict, or that injury-prone.

He circulated in the green room, interacting with the audience, also considered part of his job, though the lack of Giniana's presence smudged his enjoyment of the praise from people packed in the green room. The compliments along with the glass of inexpensive wine he sipped, fumed through his head with possibilities that the production would continue.

Simple denial of bad circumstances.

Better to think that he'd find a new part, *soon*.

Instead of enjoying speaking with the captivating Giniana, a noble and wealthy patron of the arts, Morifa Daisy, stepped in front of Johns just as he had calculated it was time he could leave. Morifa touched his arm and gushed at him and he knew he'd better give her attention or she'd spread vicious gossip. Like she had about Raz and *their* meeting last night.

Suppressing a sigh, Johns went back to his other job,

promoting himself, being Klay St. Johnswort, larger-than-life actor.

When, at last, her female butt sashayed out of the room, *without* getting him to commit to any kind of a date, he looked around to see only the rest of the cast. A couple of the guys appeared envious, everyone else, amused.

"Time to wrap it up, folks," the stage manager said. She glanced at her wrist timer. "Theater hours have been cut. Don't come in more than a half septhour before a rehearsal or performance, and we're past time on when this place should close, now."

Someone muttered about the producer being cheap. Another person said the reason the play had been canceled was because the guy wanted to launch a new production featuring his lover rather than keep *Firewalker* going, though the play continued to make money. Johns didn't know about that, but his mood definitely deflated at the reminder that he'd be living on savings in two and a half weeks.

Yeah, his face fell into a brooding expression.

The weak-guy-secondary-character who died in the last scene, Ellis Gardenia, a good if aging actor, buffeted Johns on the shoulder. "Cheer up. And *do* something to *keep* your spirits cheerful."

Johns narrowed his eyes at the man. "You're continuing to take those lessons in counseling."

Ellis rocked back and forth on his heels, thumbs tucked into his belt, gave Johns a wide, *cheerful* grin. "Yep, I'll have professional SecondLevel Counselor status by the end of the month. Got a few referral clients from my teacher already." He rolled his shoulders, glanced around. "I'll miss acting, but the counseling business is so much steadier." He winked at Johns, "And still deals with characters."

That pulled a chuckle from Johns. "Best of luck."

Meeting his eyes, Ellis put his hand on Johns shoulder and he felt sheer optimism flow from his fellow actor to him.

"Truly, Johns. Don't be negative about this. You're an extremely good actor and should be proud of your past work, and confident that your career will be strong."

Johns wanted to be a great actor. A phenomenal actor.

Ellis flashed a smile. "I know you and a group of colleagues meet for breakfast every morning at the Thespian Club, and while you exchange news and gossip, you also do a daily divination, yes?" Ellis' thin, plucked brows rose with the question. No doubt he'd let his eyebrows revert back to their natural heavier state once he became a counselor.

"Yes, we all pull a daily divination card," Johns confirmed.

"And what did you draw the last time?" Ellis persisted.

Johns relaxed, let the slight bounce of confidence within him rise to curve his lips. "The Oak King."

With a nod, Ellis said, "A brilliant career ahead of you."

"I hope so," Johns said. He was determined to make it so.

"And I'll remind you that helping others helps yourself. I know you volunteer at Moores House for Lady-Blessed Children. That's common knowledge in the counseling and Mind Healing circles." Ellis squeezed Johns shoulder. "Keep on doing that."

The thought of the kids *did* buoy Johns. Or at least remind him that he should be thankful for what he'd received. Time to do a gratitude ritual.

Giniana knew she should go home. Johns didn't need her enthusing at him. If she knew actors, he'd be plenty puffed up already after the green room. He—and the rest of the cast —had done an extraordinary job tonight.

Return home ... to a dying Thrisca and the sick patient. At the thought, she checked on both of them, the man had lapsed into Healing sleep, though Giniana should change his linens within the next couple of septhours. She preferred to do that personally instead of initiating the cleansing spells set in the sheets as well as in her tiny infirmary.

Instead of heading home, as soon as she finished the next course of Healing, Giniana took a public carrier to the theater district. There she strolled in the large rectangular space of marble benches and fountains of the main plaza.

She'd forgotten just how lovely this area was, how energizing and soothing at once, depending on which a person needed. Studying the fountains, the echoes of sounds and the reflections of light, she admired what the designers and architects had constructed. Surely they'd worked with Healers.

And Giniana waited for Johns to leave his theater, hardly scolding herself.

Johns walked out of the theater. Like most of the staff, he skirted the building from the back door to the front. He'd find good transportation by public carrier from the district to the rest of the city, and home, along the streets of the large central plaza.

The sight of Giniana Filix sitting on a bench watching for him struck him like a palpable force. A hot blow spreading satisfaction from his chest out. He began to arrange his face in a superficial smile, then his instincts rose and he stopped. When she looked up at him, she'd see his raw and natural grin.

He strode forward quickly, and her gaze switched from

the fountain to him, and her brows went up as her eyes widened. Good. He hoped she *felt* his pleasure at seeing her, perhaps felt the lifting of his spirits, too. As he got within a meter of her, he held out his hand. Yeah, he wanted to touch her. Let that need buzz down their bond, too.

"Greetyou, Giniana Filix." He kept his hand out and she placed hers within it and he tugged to request her to stand. "You came." Then he gave her a truth. "I'm glad you did, and I felt you in the audience." He didn't say he'd missed her when she hadn't come backstage.

Glancing around, he asked, "Did you come alone?"

"Yes." She flushed slightly and smiled. "You did very well." Her words sounded breathy, and he hoped that indicated she felt the desire swirling between them, but ...

"I'm not the man in the play," he said. "I'm not that courageous, and not as intensely conflicted." He paused, found an easy smile for her. "I have my own strengths and issues."

Her head tilted and her mouth dropped from the previous curve. She looked away and removed her fingers from his own. "I know that."

She moved slightly away and began walking to the busiest street with the most public carrier routes. He took a step to her and caught her hand. This time she didn't pull it from his clasp, nor did she make any nasty comments about actors.

He revealed a little more about himself, in words and along their bond. "I miss your touch." He linked fingers with her...and followed where she led.

Now that he was paying more attention to her instead of his own emotions reacting to her, he felt her weariness, and sent her some residual energy from the boost of the play.

She caught her breath and tilted her head, for an instant her hand stiffened in his. "Thank you."

He glanced at her, noticed lines of strain beside her eyes,

darker smudges under them. She hadn't put on any physical facial enhancements or masked the signs of weariness with a spell. Totally unlike any other woman of his acquaintance. A corner of his mouth lifted in appreciation of the charm of an honest woman.

She stumbled and he steadied her, and she unbalanced again on the next step. He caught her arm, pulled her close to steady her. "What's wrong?" he asked, saw her wince, and went with his own bluntness. "Are you tired?"

She shrugged, stepped back from him but didn't pull her arm away and he loosened his grip on her biceps, moving his fingers to above her elbow. "I sensed that you went to Heal. Is someone at the Spindles hurt?"

"No," she responded. "In fact, they are a very healthy bunch. Healing you and Raz Cherry last night was the first after-hours emergency I've had at the estate in months."

"Oh."

Before he could follow up on his comment, she continued, "Since I want to keep in practice with all types of Healing, I'm also on call with two HealingHalls—AllClass and Primary."

"Ah." Like most folk he knew, Johns used the Celtan Councils' subsidized AllClass HealingHall that charged him a minimal amount.

By this time they'd reached the public carrier plinth for the vehicle heading into Noble Country. "You *are* tired from working."

"Boating accident this evening. I have several patients who will need continuing care."

Must have been bad to have tired her so. "I'll see you home," he stated.

"That's what a gallant would do," she murmured.

Keep real, she didn't like actors, but, damn, he kept

exposing himself tonight, and that sure left him vulnerable to her hurting him. Hell, he was supposed to be a tough guy, right? He could handle it. "I'd be—" he stopped. If he said, "honored" it sounded more flowery and actor-like. Be real. "I'd like being your gallant."

Her glance slid in his direction, and, yes, he could feel the pumping and pulsing of his blood.

"That's moving fast," she said in a quiet voice.

He didn't reply, and she lifted her hand up to touch his fingers where they curved around her arm.

"You gonna let me accompany you home?" he asked gruffly.

She sighed, then the public carrier pulled up and they both got on, showing their passes to the driver. They sat on a twoseat bench and when she leaned against him, he felt the true exhaustion of her energy. The fact she had so little shocked him. So he did what any friend, friendly acquaintance, gallant, would. As soon as she dropped into a doze next to him, he sifted energy to her from himself. He'd gained plenty from the success of the play that night, the gift sent with applause as well as ambient stuff that just floated through the theater after the play ended.

As the carrier proceeded through the darkness, Johns enjoyed simply being with Giniana. Throughout the day, he'd thought of her often, and never would have expected to be happy simply sitting next to her while she slept. But contentment filled him. She'd come to the play, had watched him, told him she appreciated him as an actor. And she hadn't brought a gallant. Didn't have a steady lover in her life. She wasn't the kind of person to take favors from one guy while seeing or sexing with another.

He also received the impression from her that she stuck strictly to heterosexual relationships, as he did.

He woke her at the first stop in Noble Country, the one closest to T'Spindle's estate. She she seemed groggier than he'd expected since he'd slipped her energy to support her own. But perhaps their energies clashed instead of merging well. A depressing thought.

CHAPTER 7

By the time they went through the wall door and along the path toward her cottage, Johns noted that Giniana moved with her usual grace.

He stopped below the stoop of her small house, placed his hands on her waist and swung her up to the small permacrete square. Now she looked him in the eyes.

Lifting his hand, he trailed his fingers down her cheek, touched the corner of her straight mouth and smiled at her, waited until her own lips curved before leaning in, close, until their breaths sighed together. A brush of his lips against hers. Then slightly more pressure, testing their softness, how their mouths matched.

She withdrew. "Don't kiss me like you did the woman onstage."

He felt a corner of his mouth lift. "That wasn't me. That was Icos Phytolac, Fire Mage, the firewalker."

Her brows dipped and she put her hands on his shoulders. He liked the spurt of warmth that filtered through his body at her touch. "I've never really understood such a concept."

He raised his brows in contrast to her frown. "No?"

"You are who you are. You spend time refining yourself until you know who you are, then strive to be the best you can."

"That's a philosophy," he murmured, and while she frowned, he bent and took her mouth. Softer lips than they looked. Quite fabulous taste, light and peachy and with that deeper note. Before he could define it, desire punched through him. He wrapped his arm around her, curved a hand on her butt, tested the firm muscles....

No, not any actress or play kiss, not any other woman in his life felt like this in his arms. Only primal need drove him and he kissed her, sweeping his tongue over her lips, then gliding between them, demanding she open for him so he could draw her taste into himself, soak it up. Remember it forever.

Yes, the light outer scent taste of Ostara, of spring itself coated her lips, peach blossom but something darker, earthier, in the depths of her mouth. He probed inside and all the moist smoothness, finally identified the taste, saffron. An herb associated with actors.

A very expensive herb that he didn't taste often in food, but now he knew he adored. His sex hardened and rose and he needed to surge inside her, experience all her textures, everywhere of her with everywhere of him. He stepped up, lifting her, keeping her against him. One pace and they pressed against the plastered wall of the cottage. Good enough.

But he had to break the kiss to breathe and opened his eyes that had closed to the sight of her own wide eyes, the flush against pale skin in her cheeks. Her swollen mouth seemed more bruised by his kiss than plush with passion.

Dammit! He was not an uncontrolled stup, a man with no finesse, no matter how he looked and the manner he donned.

Breathing heavily, he stepped back and lowered her to the

porch. He would not take her physically, move fast and hard like he wanted to. "We should wait—"

She hissed, then scowled up at him. "You—*actors*—are all show, all pretense, you change your aspects and feelings and *values* in an instant, pivoting from love to hate in a breath." Harsh emotion broke from her in cracked words on her jagged breath.

Gently, he set his hands on her shoulders, enveloped them. "No," he whispered. "No." He dipped low with his knees so he could try and meet her downcast gaze. He would not tilt her head up to force her to look at him.

Tears filmed her eyes, her mouth drooped.

Lord and Lady, he'd—they'd—screwed up a simple kiss. No, it hadn't been simple, not for either of them and that's why this was so important. "I could swear I was—*am*—an honest man," he said roughly, lifting a palm out to her. She could take it or slap it away.

"But that doesn't mean you'd believe me. I can only prove it with my actions. But, believe me, that kiss I gave you I could never manage on stage because it wasn't acting."

She sniffed and took out a softleaf from her sleeve, not shrugging away his fingers, and he released his hand on her shoulder, slowly straightened. After wiping her eyes, her gaze followed him up.

"There's been an attraction between us—at least for you and significant on my end—since we met. I want to act on that." Since his throat had tightened, he went ahead and cleared it, not a defensive action he'd usually do. "I *really* wanted to, uh, move to the next level of intimacy when I had my hands on you."

"Best you ended the kiss then." She cleansed her softleaf with a Word, folded it and tucked it back in her long sleeve pocket. "I like to go slowly with relationships."

Too bad. He wanted to race to her bed with her. But she hadn't pushed him off the stoop.

He quirked a smile despite the fact she'd hurt him, this time touched her chin with a finger and she met his gaze as he'd wished.

"You kissed me just like your character kissed your leading lady," she stated.

"No. Earlier, during the play, that was a stage kiss of two lovers who are *fictional characters* performed by excellent actors. *This* is a real theatrical kiss."

With wide, dramatic gestures, he swooped upon her, one arm behind her shoulders, the other at her waist, and in this position he truly felt how feminine, how lovely her body was formed. He dipped her, chuckled at her hands grasping his shoulders, her wide eyes, her slightly opened mouth. He pressed his lips to hers, did not take advantage of her parted lips to touch his tongue to hers. All the same her floral underlayed by saffron flavor filled his mouth with her sighed breath.

No tongues in this kiss, he sent her the amused thought telepathically, *unless both want it.* And he yearned for a longer and deeper sampling of her flavors. Keep his head, keep the kiss light. *This was the first dramatic kiss I learned, we all learned as apprentice actors.*

Yes, she stiffened in his arms, and he sensed that she'd seen her parents kiss like this—each other and other actors—and now doubted the honesty between them even more.

Distract her! *We practice on everyone. I've even kissed Raz Cherry like this!* He let a bubble of amusement rise through him, impinge upon her. *The man really DID taste like cherry.* Then Johns swept his tongue over her lips, did not dip inside again as he yearned to, though she still hadn't closed her mouth. With every moment of closeness, his sex hardened until his body craved being inside her wet heat.

He would not lose control.

Never, and absolutely not with this tender woman.

His physical voice would crack if he said words aloud, but he endeavored to keep the mental ones smooth. *I have ever and only been attracted to women.* He let his tone whisper, become more feeling than words. *Strong, honest women like you.*

A gurgle escaped her, she was definitely thinking more than feeling, and in this moment, that was fine. They'd both stepped back from quick sexual intimacy. She tapped his arm and he raised her, and doing so said a spell he hadn't used since his adolescence to erase lust.

Passion gone, he felt the connection to her more, liked the warmth, the mutual respect.

Standing, she gasped and laughed, waved a hand. "A real theatrical kiss, all right." Her gaze shadowed as if with memories, but she looked directly into his eyes. "Thank you for the kiss and the explanation."

He angled his chin. "You're always welcome. And a kiss is always available for you."

"Yes?"

"Yeah."

She swept a look over him and he got the idea she'd scanned with Healer's eyes and actually noticed the diminishment of his erection. Healer, she'd be able to read his body very easily. Something he hadn't realized before. She'd absolutely know when he mimed passion, or reached the edge of his control, or banished lust as he just had.

With a slow smile, she traced her fingertips along his cheek, the line of his jaw. He sank into his balance so his inner trembling from the hum of her touch didn't show.

"Kiss me, Johns," she whispered and stood as if seeing what kind of kiss he'd give her ... the one she thought she remembered from his character in the play, the fierce one he'd laid on her in the beginning, or the fake theatrical one he'd demonstrated.

So this time, he made the kiss a tender, gentle press of his lips on hers. When her mouth opened, he didn't delve, but slid his tongue in barely behind her teeth, and when her tongue touched his, he retreated after catching only a rare taste of her. He let his lips graze the delicacy of her jaw, enjoyed the softness of her skin, glide down to the pulse of her neck and feel the throb of her life against his mouth.

She relaxed in his arms, giving herself up to him, and he held her like he'd never let her fall.

Very nice kiss, actor, the cool cat voice seeped into his head like winter chill, kicking his mind back to thinking. Hell.

My FamWoman likes YOUR taste, too, Thrisca sounded slyly amused.

He liked hearing that.

And your body readies to mate. I am inside on Giniana's bed. You wish me to go outside and sleep on the bird bath and give you some privacy?

A couple of quick kisses on her mouth, another to taste her throat pulse, then below her ear, as kept his arm behind her waist. And he drew away.

Once more he cherished the sight of a dazed Giniana, her lips parted sipping breaths, eyes dilated so he'd be blurred to her vision, beautiful breasts rising and falling rapidly. Oh-yeah.

He panted himself, all too aware of his semi-erection that had revved to full and hard with passion until that damn cat had interrupted a fantastic kiss.

On a rough breath, he said, "Yeah, we'll take it as slow as you like. I'll leave now. Can I see you tomorrow?"

Shaking her head, but putting out a hand to touch him on his chest—checking his heartbeat? the link between them for honesty?—she said, "You confuse me."

All right, he used his best slow smile, hoping for the effect it usually had. "Good."

She blinked.

"When can I see you tomorrow?"

"Ah—"

Before he could press the question, her scry pebble rolled out a snappy tune from her sleeve pocket. Her hand fisted on his chest, her face paled.

"Sorry, work," Giniana said to Johns as she grabbed her pebble from her pocket, flicked it on.

Johns recognized Lark Holly's voice and image against the background of AllClass HealingHall. The woman appeared distracted. "Can you finish up a two septhour shift for Myrrh? She's taken sick with the flill sickness going around." Then Lark narrowed her eyes. "Are *you* all right?"

Giniana straightened her spine, Johns saw her dredge up energy from her core, as she glowed a serene smile at the Healer. "I'm fine. I'll be glad to take the shift. I must check on Thrisca and I'll be there shortly."

A frowning Lark studied her in the scry. "Very well, and since you've already put in so many septhours here, you'll be paid overtime." The Healer signed off.

I am fine. Go, Thrisca projected loud enough for Johns to hear the FamCat.

Opening her bag, Giniana drew out an orange tablet, tapped the energy surge spell and murmured the word to activate the pill, and swallowed it down.

Dammit. He thought she'd gotten some sizzling energy from their kiss, and he'd given her some on the ride here, but she thought she still needed more? "How often do you do that?" he demanded roughly.

Her lips twitched up in a smile. "Not very often."

He stopped himself from commenting further. She'd know more than he about the downside of taking the vitalizer.

"What's going on?" he asked, trying to keep his tone easy, requesting facts.

She gazed at him.

He put his hands in his pockets, but didn't move. Not going anywhere until she answered him. He figured he'd opened up enough to her that she should reciprocate.

A quick smile formed on her lips, then her mouth straightened. "The short explanation is that Danith D'Ash, the Animal Healer, can't Heal Thrisca and she is ... fading."

I am fine, Thrisca added, but Johns sensed she coughed.

"So *we've* decided to try one of D'Willow's time procedures to cure her cough and the underlying disease and give her many more years. I need to work harder in the short term to afford the new treatment."

He blinked, trying to comprehend the statement along with all the intense emotions ladening her words.

"Can you go inside and make sure Thrisca eats?" she asked, then leaned over and kissed his cheek. The zip of desire surged through him again, continuing to muddle his mind. "I need to get to work," she ended.

He grasped her fingers before she could slip away. "You need to take care of yourself as well as Thrisca."

Giniana's brows dipped. "It's only for the short term."

More echoes of raw emotions that he didn't have time to process, especially since his body reacted to the sight of her in a patch of twinmoonslight, appearing more like a fantasy woman who stopped his breath than a real, flesh and blood female.

Wait, the real flesh and blood woman affected his own flesh and blood, made thought drain out of his head. He opened his mouth, grunted—not what he wanted this time—saw her tilt her head attentively.

"You take care of yourself," he managed to repeat and scowled at her to emphasize his instruction.

Her lips curved only slightly, the shadows around her eyes seemed to gather with haunted thoughts. "I'll be home in under three septhours." She tugged at her fingers.

He lifted them to his lips. "I want to see you tomorrow, I'll scry you late in the morning."

"Sure." Dismissive tone. When she pulled at her hand again, he let her go. He would never constrain her against her will.

He heard her inhale a deep breath, as if counting down for a teleportation.

"I'll check on Thrisca," Johns found himself offering.

I don't need checking on, Thrisca objected.

A brilliant smile from Giniana melded the ethereal fantasy woman with the real human sexy one, then she vanished.

He turned and considered the cottage. Well designed and built a couple of centuries ago, he believed, though he thought the Spindles had hired a construction mage, had no Family member with such Flair fabricate it. Johns would have felt that, the resonance of a Spindle builder, since he *did* have such Flair. What he considered his secondary Flair. He liked raising small buildings, had several tree houses and play-houses on his land that he'd constructed at various times in his life.

Move his feet and carry out his promise. Johns stepped up to the door. He hadn't seen Giniana unlock it, but he tried the latch and it opened, yet he felt some wards still up as if she shielded a private place or two. Fair enough.

A small area, the whole front of her cottage, mainspace, kitchen, hallway to the bedroom could fit in his home's Residence Den. Cozy, tidy, and smelling like Giniana, he felt comfortable immediately.

Until Thrisca appeared at the end of the short hall moving from the bedroom toward the kitchen. Johns felt her low growl more than heard it, discovered resignedly that he had a link with this Fam, too.

She sauntered to him, and now that he studied her in good light, she appeared even older, thinner than a cat should be, and damned arrogant.

She lifted the top of her muzzle, showing long fangs. *I do not need 'checking on.'* She glanced toward the back of the house. *I do not want you here. Go away.*

Raising his hands, he said, "You look fine to me. Just say you'll eat some food and I'll go." Naturally, he trusted no cat's word, but he didn't care about the thing, either.

She showed long, yellowed fangs. *I will eat.*

"I'm sure Giniana knows exactly how much of your food is in the no-time and will see whether you eat or not," he pointed out.

You call her by her given name.

"She gave me leave."

A rough sigh that caught on a cough. *You are an actor and smell like My old Family, but you are not.*

From what Johns had heard, her old Family, at least Giniana's actor parents, weren't that nice so he took no offense. "You said you'd eat. I believe you." He gave her a false smile. "Leaving now."

Good! Then she coughed so hard she hunkered down. Her eyes closed … with him, a stranger in her house.

The spasm went on too long. Johns inched forward to just outside paw-strike distance. When she paused between hacks, he asked, "What can I do for you?"

CHAPTER 8

NOTHING. Go away, Thrisca demanded mentally.

"Not until I believe you won't croak right here and now. I can't have that. It would spoil the relationship I'm building with Giniana."

Thrisca hissed between coughs. *GO AWAY!*

Johns took a pace back. "Nope, changed my mind. Finish coughing, eat a coupla bites of food, and I'll be gone."

Her eyes slitted open, showing a virulent green. Johns reached out to the nearby no-time, but didn't want to look away from the now-rising and stalking cat to open the appliance and get her food.

When she reached him, she angled her butt toward him and switched her tail aside.

"Don't you piss on me," he rumbled a threat.

She glanced back. *Or you will do what? You will NOT hurt me. You are a big alpha-type male and will not tell My FamWoman.*

"No," he replied calmly.

Even if you did, My FamWoman thinks all actors lie all the time. She will not believe you.

That confirming insight into the Healer's personality didn't sound good, but he'd think on it later. "I won't have to tell Giniana. I'll just step out of my clothes and leave them, teleport home." He smiled down at the cat, with teeth. "Then she'll have to clean them *and* return them to me. We'll have more privacy at my home than here." He glanced around.

Thrisca grumbled in her throat.

Johns cocked his head. "A good sound. I'll think on that sound for the future."

Lash, lash of the tail. *Actors,* she sneered, as if now reversing her attitude.

Cats. "That's right," Johns said. "Giniana Filix comes from a long line of actors."

She is a Healer, a Winterbloom, Thrisca said, then coughed again.

Johns looked at the no-time and checked the meals. A whole section belonged to special food for Thrisca. He glanced at her. "There are five flavors of meat and greens here, you got a preference?"

One wet hawk of *stuff* that hit the floor, then disappeared. She sat up straight and licked her paw. And he knew an actor's gesture when he saw one.

He waited.

Her eyelids half-lowered. *Is there fish with clucker egg and greens?*

Sounded terrible to Johns. He glanced at the menu. "Yeah, you want that?"

She lifted her nose in a superior manner. *In the brown bowl.* With a flick of a forepaw, she indicated one of three on the counter. She wanted him to wait on her. Eh, may as well. Keep the FamCat happy, make Giniana appreciative. He opened his mouth to quiz the cat more about Giniana and the Filix family, then shut it again. This cat would squeal on him.

He took out the lukewarm meal, the same temperature as

it went into the appliance, and dumped it from a white crockery plate to the brown bowl, put that down for Thrisca.

The cat sniffed and sniffed again at her meal, stuck out her tongue to taste it, stared at Johns.

He raised his hands. "All yours."

You won't pounce on Me?

Yeah, she expected him to do to her what she'd been planning to do to him. He practiced his own sniff. Sounded a little dry, but good enough. "I am not a cat, Thrisca." Still, he stepped around her in the old fashioned kitchen. One counter contained a sink like his place, and he washed and dried the dish and left it on the counter, then three paces and he'd returned to the hallway to watch her.

Boring. "How do you really feel?" He smiled another insincere smile but the cat seemed to buy it.

I cough, and I COULD go to the Wheel of Stars, if I wished. But I do not wish to leave FamWoman alone. She did not take her father leaving well.

Johns grunted in response as he thought of the right thing to say, wondered if the cat tested him.

"Rough," he commented.

Her father, Mas Filix, said he would send gilt for Me and Verna and Giniana and We should come to him in Chinju. He did not.

"Rough," Johns repeated.

Or he sent the gilt once and Verna spent it and did not take US to Chinju.

Uh-oh, family secrets and drama and how really fast Johns sank deep into Giniana's family mess. She wouldn't like him knowing this stuff.

I am not going to the Wheel of Stars. I am more interested in going back and forth through time and having My lungs and My cough cured that way. The FamCat glanced up at him, eyes gleaming, mouth dropped a little in amusement.

Of course she would be. Lord and Lady, most people

would be. With one whisk of a red tongue she cleaned her bowl, belched, then stretched long and lean and he saw her ribs.

I am an old Cat and I will be older still. I may become the Oldest Cat Who Ever Lived.

Some goal, but at what cost to Giniana? Traveling through time sounded damn expensive to Johns.

Thrisca sat and stared at him. *You may wash and dry My bowl, now.*

He stared back.

Then her head tilted and one of her ears rotated toward the back of the cottage. *Then you may go.*

"Move from the kitchen and get out of my way, then." He wasn't going to step over her or near her so she could snag his trous.

She rose slowly to her feet, sauntered into the mainspace.

Not wanting to leave even the smallest chore for Giniana to do, he put the bowl and no-time cooking dish in the cleanser and started the appliance running on an anti-bacterial setting.

Are you finally DONE? snipped Thrisca.

"Yeah." He walked to the front door, found her sitting right in front of it. *Tell the lights to lower to twenty per cent,* she ordered.

He gave the verbal command and she stropped his boots and trous and left hair and something wet ... he hoped that was old-cat drool ... before she trotted back into the bedroom, radiating satisfaction.

The next morning, Giniana rose a half-septhour before Workbell. She'd taken herself into trance-sleep the night before to recharge her energy naturally. She only had to work her very hardest for a while, until she accumulated enough gilt for Thrisca's time Healing procedure.

Just work hard for an eightday and a half. That reminded her, she had the appointment with D'Willow this afternoon during her break from the annual Spindle staff physical examinations.

As usual, they'd been scheduled to begin at this time of year, the nearest full twinmoons to T'Spindle's nameday, and, as usual, the FirstFamily GrandLord himself would be the first to be checked out.

Very poor timing for Giniana this year.

As soon as she went to T'Spindle Residence's Healing suite, she double-checked the order of her supplies, cleansed the rooms again. Before the FirstFamily GrandLord arrived, she contacted the Residence telepathically. *I have a patient in my infirmary …*

The Residence replied immediately, using a more austere tone than its standard cheerful lilt. *I noted the man, the agent Blakely Wattle, did not sign out with any of the guards. But I also understood he sickened with some illness and went in your direction. I extrapolated that you found him and cared for him.*

I did. As I said, he is staying in the sickroom attached to my cottage. He succumbed to a case of flill. I trust you sanitized the areas he passed through.

Naturally, FirstLevel Healer Filix. All my in-dwelling staff are hale. You will see that I take excellent care of them as you proceed through their annual examinations.

I know you are a dedicated Family member, Giniana stated only the truth.

The walls literally glowed around her.

She continued mind-to-mind with the Residence, *I anticipate my patient will be well enough to send him to an empty home within three days.*

An empty home! the Residence sounded completely

shocked. It hadn't been empty or without Family for centuries. The thought would be nearly inconceivable.

Yes, he lives alone. He probably has rooms somewhere.

We can watch over him when sick, then. It is the decent thing to do, the Residence replied stoutly.

So I believe. You take care of us all very well, Residence.

Thank you, Healer. A tiny window creak. *I think the puny man poses no threat, so I will not tell T'Spindle unless he asks specifically about that one. My lord is deep in important business negotiations with T'Hawthorn. T'Spindle is also considering running for the office of Captain of All the Councils.*

The most important position on Celta. Giniana hesitated, but she was being paid for her own professional opinion on the physical, mental and emotional health of her employer. *I think that may be a mistake for T'Spindle, and might toughen him in ways we would not care for.*

I agree! the Residence trilled by stirring a windchime hung outside the window. *We are not considered the highest or smartest or richest of the FirstFamilies—*

But the Spindles are valued for their generosity and common sense. She paused, thought of her basic education in the FirstFamilies and their characteristics. *For their… sweetness.*

YES! We do NOT want to lose that, ever—

But any further conversation between her and the Residence stopped as T'Spindle walked through the door. Still, she felt better that the Residence confirmed it knew of her "guest" in the Healer's Cottage infirmary.

Though T'Spindle seemed more restless and impatient than usual, Giniana refused to rush through his examination, and he finally settled down. She pronounced him extremely healthy, but as he placed his fingers on the door lever to leave, she reminded him that before he ran for political office he must have a deep session with D'Sea, *the* mental and emotional Healer of Celta. She must certify him sane and healthy and able to fulfill the solemn Vows of Honor toward the people and the planet a Captain of AllCouncils promised.

He sent her a narrowed-eyed, considering look, nodded brusquely and left without another word.

Giniana sighed.

You did well, the Residence stated. Neither T'Spindle nor she had asked the Residence to keep the Healing Suite private and not to observe.

Thank you, she responded mentally.

But you are low in energy. I will send you some.

Not necess— but huge Flair gushed into her from the massive reservoirs of the Residence. She choked, windmilled, and stumbled to her chair in the examination room, fell into it. When she could breathe normally again, she said, *Thank you, Residence.*

You are always welcome. I am also rescheduling the staff physicals. I told you last year that you organized too many appointments a day. Three this morning, only, the Residence decreed. *Since you scanned T'Spindle himself. Break, then two this afternoon.*

An "I told you so" from the Residence. She smiled. Nothing it liked better. Last year her workload had been fine, this year not so much. *All right, Residence,* she agreed meekly. She should be able to pick up extra work from the Healing-Halls, and easily fit in the meeting with D'Willow. The Daisys hadn't canceled her nightshift with the baby. She could handle that, too.

When Giniana finished with her duties at T'Spindle Residence—the two other Family staff checkups and a quick caff break with the GrandLord and Lady—she walked back to her cottage. Her steps slowed as she let the ambiance of nature surround her, breathed in the sweet smell of summer leaves in the sun, let the dappled light paint pretty pictures of bright and shadowed flowers.

Enjoy the moment. Too many times lately she'd let

moments of her life slip by without notice, focused too much on the future instead of the now.

And, she realized that in the back of her mind, along her bond with her FamCat, Thrisca seemed more her old mischievous self, also contented.

The cat must have caught the slight health check, and sent pure satisfaction down their bond. *The man has been most amusing,* Thrisca said. *He talks to himself.*

So did Giniana, or, rather, she talked to Thrisca often, but knew the cat ignored her. If Giniana had been alone, she'd have talked to herself. Not a bad thing, in her opinion. She wondered if the actor St. Johnswort talked to himself, somehow, she didn't think so. She felt her mouth turning down. If he was like her father—other actors—he might try on different personalities, posture in front of a mirror.

But something in Thrisca's dismissive tone clued her in that the cat had much more to say.

Yes, Thrisca? Giniana prompted.

Man has secrets. Didn't tell you everything.

That often happened with Healers, patients didn't tell them everything, and especially not all at once. Giniana grimaced out a sigh. She reached the shed, opened the door and discovered he'd suffered a relapse of the illness. He must be more susceptible than she'd thought. And he *was* talking to himself. Also thrashing around in a fever, which Thrisca hadn't bothered to tell Giniana...

He mumbled, "Gotta find the pages. Gotta. Best chance for good gilt. *Need* the whole thing. Maybe they don't know what they stole, how valuable. Must find pages..."

She checked his progress, found that though he'd hit a setback, he still followed the regular parameters of flill sufferers. Then she cleansed the cottage, the man, the linens, as she had when she'd gotten off shift in the early morning, and did what palliative Healing she could.

Thrisca watched all, lying in the sunshine on the outside step to the sickroom. *I sniffed at the papyrus he had in his hand.* The cat pointed with her nose to the side table where Giniana had placed the crumpled sheet, not even smoothing it out. Not her business.

Page smells like this man, like sweat of scared men and rough men—

"Johns?" the question spurted from Giniana's lips.

Of course not. Brute man.

Well, Giniana didn't know of any brutish male actor, past or present.

Odors of this man, scared men, rough men, brute man, too-sweet perfume. A definite sniff. *Most interesting smell is like Our estate, some grass, some pine, some mousie droppings.*

"Oh," Giniana said.

I looked around Our cottage and near the place where the gliders were parked during the party and the terrace.

Thrisca had ranged farther from the cottage lately than she had in a year. All to the good, stretching and movement and activity, mental as well as physical. That kept a person healthy.

Giniana lay down on a lounge, half in shade, half sunny, and let herself doze and her mind relax. Thought she might be soaking in more strength and Flair from the estate. How lucky she was!

For some reason, she let Klay St. Johnswort dance through her thoughts.

🐾

Johns awoke and stretched long and luxuriously, allowed a grin to curve his lips. Things were looking up. He felt great, physically, and not inclined to slip into a brood because the run of his play might end in a couple of weeks.

All because Giniana Filix came to his play, admired his work ... responded to his kiss. Oh, yeah. He hopped out of bed and into the waterfall, scrubbed, groomed.

He grinned until his calendarsphere reminded him of a breakfast date with Lily Fescue.

What had she wanted to talk to him about? Ah, the script by the playwright Amberose with a role for him! He'd forgotten that fabulous bit of information and the idea lifted his spirits.

He glanced at his scrybowl cache and the one on his perscry. That agent of Amberose's, Blakely Wattle, hadn't called him. Huh. Johns had sure figured the man would. Johns tried reaching for the guy along the tiny bond they'd developed but it had fizzled away.

Dressing like an actor who'd received seven curtain calls the night before—successful, confident—he prepared to leave his home. As professional as he'd been when he dropped by the Theatrical Guild the day before. He'd acted well, then, pretending to be unconcerned when he saw no upcoming casting calls posted, heard no rumors of a new show. Of course his own agent would have contacted Johns if the man got wind of a prospective part. The guy might even get industry or production rumors before Johns...but always best to put in an appearance at the guild and let people know in person you were available. And he'd liked talking with others in his profession.

Lily Fescue preferred good costuming by her escorts, and Johns must admit that her current leading man, Raz Cherry, outdid Johns regularly on that issue.

Johns belonged to a group of MasterLevel actors who routinely breakfasted at the Thespian Club, men and women he admired, who worked at their craft, who shared stories and techniques and a common outlook. There were six of them, three men and three women, none of them romantically involved with each other. Those who currently weren't working ate early—and he'd be in that crowd next month, if he continued the habit, which he doubted—and those in a show met later.

Eating at this particular time with Lily Fescue, who thought the whole get-together beneath her, would have him missing both sets of his friends. Just as well. He didn't mind being seen with Lily, but felt sensitive enough about his brand-new relationship with Giniana Filix that he didn't want a lot of gossip floating around. He'd keep the meeting as business-like as possible.

CHAPTER 9

JOHNS MET Lily Fescue at the Thespian Club. He was a little late and waved to friends and admirers as the maître d' led him to a table in the center of the room that Lily reserved.

She arrived later still and made an entrance, though she didn't appear to like the smattering of applause. Maybe she expected a roar of acclaim.

Trying his patience, she picked through the menu, ordered expensive items with a flourish of rolling tones, and he said to the waiter, "My usual, please."

After the man took their orders, she wiggled her butt on the chair cushion and began to look around. "Oh, there's Guy Balsam, he's showing his age, isn't he? He'll be taking older character parts, soon. And Morifa Daisy, who invited her? She's saying *terrible* things about Raz, since he dumped her at that party the other night. Oooh! The Marigolds are here!" Lily sat straight and waved her softleaf at the nobles as they walked through the dining room toward the door.

Johns saw the big bodyguard, T'Marigold, angle his body away as if protecting his lady. Johns snorted, turned that into a cough, and lifted his cup of caff to swallow. As soon as he let liquid slide down his throat, he said, "You wanted to talk about Amberose's play?" Lily was the only one who'd actually read it that he knew.

She glanced around and lowered her voice. "Though Amberose's agent said not to, I made a copy."

"Great! Can I see it?"

Pouting, she responded, "The copy didn't last more than a half septhour, and I hadn't thought to write things down." She coughed discreetly behind her softleaf. "And the original papyrus tinted slightly gray and the print lightened and I didn't think it would be good to try and copy it again."

Johns brows rose. "That's some good security on the script."

"I know! And I was told it was the only copy, and I was the first to see it because Amberose wanted me in the part particularly." Lily preened.

"And you lost it."

"It was stolen! Along with other minor items during that burglary we had at the theater. I lost the most." Her pout returned.

"You said the new play had roles for you and me, and Raz and another actress—"

"Yes, but the papyrus wasn't in Raz's dressing room, but mine, and someone stole it all the same."

"Tell me about the story."

Her eyes lit. "It has a *fabulous* part for me, except slightly less lines and stage time than the male lead." She flashed Johns a false and scintillating smile. "But we can have a little agreement about that, adding more to my part, if I tell you everything I know about it, right? You can request a better part for me from Amberose, right?"

Why did everyone think they could play him for a fool? "Like hell." He pushed back from the table and stood.

"Oh, you!" Lily huffed. Johns watched her from half-lidded

eyes. The thing about Lily, she wanted to show off, be the one in the know. And she always figured that if she couldn't get what she wished one way, she'd be able to manipulate you into giving her what she wanted some other way in the future.

So, as he thought, she broke as he took a pace away.

I will let you read the notes I made of the script, she sent him mentally on a private channel.

Johns let his lips curl in a sardonic smile. Lily might get some of the passages right for her role, but he wouldn't bet on anyone else's. Still, it might be enough to give him an idea of how good his part might be...whether he should hold out for a production of it, if that appeared to be likely. Another unknown, who might produce it and how quickly they would cast.

Sitting back down, he jutted his chin. "Let's see those notes."

With a frown, she replied telepathically, *I haven't finished them yet. I will send them to your scry cache.*

Waste of time meeting her this morning then. Except for a better breakfast than he'd pull out of the no-time at home, and Lily would be paying. Johns stifled *more* thoughts of the lack of gilt coming up and pursued the nice idea of starring in an Amberose play that would send his career soaring ...

The waiter delivered their food. Lily applied herself to the meal with gusto.

Good breakfast.

"You *did* manage to get the general plot of the story down, didn't you?" he asked, between bites.

"Yes, of course." She peeked at him from under her lashes. "It's a wonderful story. *Fabulous* characters and parts."

Johns grunted, "Too bad it's gone."

"We could look for the script," she said. "If the thieves

don't know what they have, they might have just dumped it on someone or sold it to someone for minor gilt ..."

"Who'd want it?" But Johns would.

"I would," Lily said.

"Yeah. Raz would like it, too." And other actresses who might like the secondary female role. But, face it, not many actors had a lot of gilt to spend on an iffy stolen script.

Lily sipped her caff, gave him a sideways glance, "You could scry Amberose and ask for another copy of the script."

"You're the one who knows Amberose's agent well," Johns shot back.

Lily's lips thinned. "He's not returning my scries. In fact, I've asked around and no one's seen him lately."

"Huh." As she opened her mouth again, Johns said, "Or *you* could contact Amberose. She sent the script to you, first."

"I think Blakely arranged that for me, and I don't want to bother her."

"Don't want to tell her the script has been stolen if she doesn't know? Admit someone took it from your dressing room?" he pressed.

"Johns!" she sniffled, picked up her softleaf from her lap to dab at her eyes, and a small piece of porcine strip fell from the thick folds.

And was caught in the open mouth of a male fox that zoomed toward them.

Lily screeched, "Go away, go *away, you filthy animal!*"

The gray fox sat on his haunches, lifted his muzzle, replied loudly enough that whoever in the chamber had a minor amount of Flair could hear him, *I am NOT dirty. I am a very clean FoxFam.*

Must be the mottled pattern of his fur that made him look dirty, then. Johns glanced around, most people smiled at the scene. He didn't care for animals, or for this FoxFam, but didn't react so poorly to them as Lily.

She jumped up, knocking down her chair, and Johns caught it before it hit the floor and tipped it back up in place, pushed back his own chair and stood.

Meanwhile, Lily, now the focus of the room as she liked, pointed at the fox and shrieked, "An animal should not be here with *human* food." Then she did worse, she threw herself on Johns's chest, yelling, "Get him out!"

"I don't—" Johns began.

This is my third day here! Wonderful with peoples and smells and tastes! I am welcome here— insisted the FamFox at the same time, rising to his paws and arrogantly coming over to sniff at Lily and Johns.

"Save me!" Lily slumped in a fake faint against Johns.

Growling under his breath, Johns did the right thing and picked her up, carried her across the large dining room to the nods and smiles of his peers, opened the door with Flair, and set her outside on the threshold.

He turned back, and received a modicum of applause. That didn't stop his scowl at the sight of the FoxFam on their table, eating *their* food, the meal Johns had barely touched. The furrabeast steak and eggs his mouth yet watered for.

And Lily had stuck him with the bill. Ungracious to tell the grinning manager, in front of everyone, to put the meal on her account. Swallowing saliva bittering in his mouth, Johns pulled a couple of large gilt coins and tossed them with Flair to land on the table, turned on his heel and made a good exit.

Gazes on him burned, sending the heat of irritation and embarrassment between his shoulder blades.

No use for it, after this scene, he'd have to come here again, and soon, to make the place comfortable for him and to prove to everyone that this little drama hadn't bothered him, even though it had.

A Fam ruined his breakfast, cost him time and good gilt.

These were his people, his clan, he would not let himself be separated from them, even by one of them herself.

A thought struck him. Giniana's parents would have brought her here, but he'd have bet his own old estate that she hadn't returned in years.

He stopped in the entryway and trod back to the threshold of the dining room. Fully formal with linens and long rows of flatware, it was a teaching situation and practice set as much as anything else. Babble rose cheerfully, people already over Lily's scene, and the fox mooched around at the tables.

Giniana would like this place, wouldn't she? Maybe there wouldn't be very many terrible memories of her parents here. Johns had started his career as a pre-teen, and had come with groups to the social club since. He never recalled seeing her mother.

People would welcome Giniana. Not simply because she was her parents' daughter, but because she was a Healer.

Turning aside, he went to the Thespian Club's small office. At the open door, he looked in to see Ovata Forsythia and knocked on the jamb.

The woman stood, tall and statuesque. "Can I help you?" she asked, and her expression folded into bland curiosity.

Since she not only held the Presidency of the Thespian Club, but also the office of a Theatrical Guild Representative for actors, Johns realized she expected him to whine or something about *Firewalker* closing. As if he would voice dissatisfaction anywhere except in his own mind.

He gave her his rough-and-ready smile. "Yes, just checking on a membership here in the Thespian Club. Giniana Filix? Did her parents sign her up for a lifetime membership?"

Ovata's smile hit him with charm and sincerity and a splash of feminine charisma. "Ah. She works for the Spindles.

I'd heard that you helped Raz Cherry in a fight at T'Spindle Residence, good job."

"Thanks." He dipped his head at the compliment, deciding to be absolutely honest with this woman, a MasterLevel actor of great repute. She'd see through any false manner.

Her glance went up and down him in simple scrutiny. "I know the Spindles employ Giniana Filix as their staff Healer, you were injured?"

Johns jerked a shoulder. "Nothing to speak of, Raz was, too. Giniana Healed us up quick and fine."

"I understand." Ovata waved and a holographic data globe sprang into existence. She stared at it, frowned, considered Johns again as if she parsed all his emotions, his feelings for Giniana from his stance, his manner, his expression. Maybe Ovata's particular Flair included some sort of empathy.

A tiny catch of her breath. "Yes, her parents paid a first installment on a lifetime membership, but, ah, neither her father or mother kept up the minimum payments."

Johns grunted.

Without looking at him, Ovata snapped her fingers, grinned in satisfaction as she dismissed the data sphere and glanced at him. "I completed FirstLevel Healer Giniana Filix's lifetime membership with Thespian Club general funds."

"She will never be an actress."

Ovata's visage became austere. "The Filixes have been actors for five generations." She winked at Johns. "We'll see if any of her children might want to follow that career."

The notion of Giniana having children, then Ovata's implication that Giniana might have *his* children, a woman with whom he'd only had *one* date, shocked Johns. Unpleasantly. He had so much to do for his own career.

"And it's always good to have members of other professions in the Club, and Healers are always welcome with us."

"Uh-huh. Well, good talking with you. Thanks for the

membership, I'll let her know, maybe will be able to talk her into coming here."

Ovata inclined her head. "Give her my best regards. Merry meet."

"And merry part," he responded.

"And merry meet again."

Johns left the building. He'd turned the corner and reached the alley when he heard it.

Meeeewwwwwww, a mental cry.

"Mewwwww."

No. He would *not* investigate. No.

Is anyone there? Pleease? came a tiny voice in his mind, as if a mist of sound had condensed around his head and sunk into his brain.

No. Someone else would come along soon.

Me. Hurt.

Hell.

Hurt. Help! Heellpp! Whimpering.

No. He couldn't ignore that.

Huffing a breath, he strode down the alley, past the back of the squat and solid corner store, and stopped next to the narrow passageway between two other buildings, more like a crack than a space a person could actually walk through.

"All right, cat, where are you?"

A savior! Here! Here! HERE! came the telepathic cry, then a physical screech.

Narrowing his eyes to see better in the always-dim alley, he caught a motion from under a plank leaning against the brick wall—large furrily-feathered ears twitching. Large for a kitten.

Yep, small, young cat. No use for it, he had to help the thing.

There he is! A WONDERFUL, BIG MAN! Hooray!

Johns squatted and a wave of cat piss odor wafted out as the thing wriggled. Oh. No.

He had no spell to coat his hands from touching nasty things. Giniana might. Maybe such a thing as a keep-skin-sterile spell. Sucking in a breath, a mistake, he reached in and tugged gently. Nothing happened except a teeny tongue spread drool on his thumb.

Me STUCK.

"I got that." He set the kitten down, reached around and found long, matted fur, couldn't even get his fingers through the strands. Carefully he found the point where one of the hair clumps tangled with splintered wood and rough brick. Kitten might have bled on that, too, making it worse.

Nope, absolutely couldn't leave a creature, even a cat, in this much distress. Feeling around, his fingers touched something squishy and stench of rotting dead thing rose.

Me found dead mousie to eat! Me got stuck!

The cat sounded thrilled, which meant it hadn't been eating well, either.

Johns withdrew his arm from the depth of the crack. With his other hand, he took a softleaf out of his pocket and initiated a cleanse spell as he wiped filthy fingers.

He flipped out a pocket knife, snicked it open. He figured he should explain to minimize any more bad cat experiences so streamed steady, calm words. He also took the precaution of blanketing the area with as much soothing emotion as he could. "I'm going to use both my hands to free you. I'll hold you in one hand and free you with my other."

Good! Me FREE soon!

"Sure." Slowly, he reached in again, slid his left hand along gritty, slimy ground, touched a warm and damp fur covered body, cradled the too-light beastie in his hand. It even fit, not overflowing at all. Felt bony.

He scraped the knuckles of his right hand along brick,

leading with his knife, thrust through a mass of soft density, stopped. This he could do.

A few gruff spellwords later, he'd freed the kitten, translocated his knife back home to the high intensity cleanser.

When he brought the little animal into the dim light, he could only see more dirt and grime. No telling what color the creature actually was.

But its stench was amazing.

THANKYOU, THANKYOU, THANKYOU!

It looked completely gross. Johns couldn't imagine how he'd start cleaning up the thing. And among the stink of it rose the odor of fresh blood.

"You hurt, kitten?"

Put Me down and Me will go Me way. Me said 'Thankyou' three times, that's enough. Me is Cat. Me can take care of Meself!

Johns grunted. He'd like to believe that, just put it down and let it go on its way, but he thought the kitten lied. He did have to get rid of it soon before he bonded with a Fam. Unlike most folk, he didn't want a Fam now. Didn't trust them. Hell, one of them screwed him out of breakfast this morning.

Couldn't let the creature go, though, too small. Couldn't have a life on his conscience. "Okay, you're a cat and can fend for yourself, but what's the most hurt?"

It held up a tiny paw covered in blood and looking a little mangled.

Lord and Lady dammit! No use for it, he'd have to take the Fam to be Healed by FirstFamily GreatLady Danith D'Ash, the main Animal Healer. And he'd have to pay for that.

Then, the idea sparked. Person who liked cats. Woman who Healed. She should be able to help such a small being, right?

A woman with whom he desired to spend more time.

He *could* take the tiny creature to D'Ash, give the cat to her for her Fam adoption rooms. Someone might like it.

Or he could take it to Giniana Filix.

He stared down at the kitten and a slight chill slid down his spine. *not* due to its state, but another cold thought. Both Giniana and Thrisca believed the time procedure would cure the old FamCat. But what if it didn't? Giniana would be crushed.

She should have the kitten. Absolutely. Yes.

CHAPTER 10

So Johns smiled down at the little being, his acting skills would outmatch this kitten anytime and always. "You know," he said in his softest, silkiest tones. "I think you should have a companion."

The thing gasped, ears rotating. *Me? You get Me a pet?*

It would be the other way around. Giniana would adopt another FamCat. This one Giniana's own since kittenhood, maybe less bossy to a FamWoman than Thrisca.

Giniana. Since their evening together last night, their sense-suffusing kisses and the emotions that tore between them, their bond had instinctively become stronger. He checked their link, yes, it expanded and formed emotional hooks caught deeply into him. And, as he experienced the connection between himself and Giniana, he realized that he now linked with the FamCat Thrisca, too.

Not something he wanted. But Giniana loved the cat and Johns was fascinated by the woman. He'd also spent too much time with the damn FamCat, enough to weave that strand.

But, at this moment, having that extra tie would help.

He stared dubiously down at the kitten who, despite its

request, had fallen asleep in his hand. Not prepossessing at all. But looking desperately in need of help. Worse came to worst, maybe Giniana could tell him how to help the mite himself.

To discover her location, he sent energy and *awareness* down the bond growing between Giniana and himself.

He sensed that Giniana relaxed outside her cottage, appreciating nature, lightly tranced, her mind in restful awareness and not busy with Healing or getting ready to leave for any job.

So he flicked an easy thought down their bond, called softly, *Giniana?*

Her mind lit with attention and he caught a wisp of delight, which increased his own pleasure, as well as his ego. She liked him.

May I come? I have a small problem I need your help with. In sleep, the kitten in his hand wrapped around his thumb and tried out tiny fangs that barely dented his skin. A very small problem.

Now?

Yes, transnow. I can 'port to T'Spindle's front gatehouse. No one could teleport into a FirstFamily estate, of course.

It's that important? Her mind clicked into thinking mode.

Yes, important enough for me to teleport. He didn't have a lot of energy to spend on teleportation, but he believed the situation to be serious. One teleportation this morning should be fine. He still had a show tonight that demanded his best, and he hoped he could convince Giniana to come tonight to the play, too. Or maybe meet him tomorrow for breakfast, at the Thespian Club even.

Best way to woo a woman into a relationship was to see her every day.

The kitten awoke, stirred and stretched. It rolled and Johns closed his fingers to stop it from falling from his hand.

From his home, he translocated a very old towel he'd planned on throwing into the deconstructor. He wrapped the cloth around the matted little being.

It mewed, opened eyes up at him, and one of those appeared cloudy, Lord and Lady dammit! Then it snuggled into the towel and fell asleep as if sheer relief had finally caught up with it. Yeah, the fabric would smell and have stuff on it now. Best he threw it away. Without the FamKitten, of course.

Come ahead, Giniana sent telepathically. She paused. *And come on to my cottage. I'll tell the guards to admit you.*

My great thanks, Johns replied, squelching exultation from tinging his mental tone.

Giniana did another check on her sleeping patient in her infirmary, once again set privacy wards around the shed, and readied a carafe of spring water and bowl of fruit if Johns cared to spend a few minutes talking with her.

You did not ask the actor why he comes. Thrisca disapproved since suspenseful curiosity plagued her.

We'll find out soon enough, Giniana replied, aware of a flash of contrariness. Let her FamCat be riled, the feeling would be good for her, keep her blood moving. Now Thrisca showed more vivacity, Giniana wanted her to continue. She'd been eating better the last few meals, too.

Sooner than Giniana anticipated, she sensed Johns prowling down the path to her cottage. When he came into sight, he carried a small rolled bundle in one hand.

What is that? Thrisca demanded, peeking around the corner of the cottage. Perhaps she'd planned on shooting out to surprise Johns, but he'd certainly caught her interest. *What? What?*

I don't know, Giniana replied telepathically to her Fam as she rose from the chair beside the front stoop. She smiled at him, and though his lips curved, his brows remained down and his gaze serious.

He stopped close to her, gently unfolded the top of a threadbare towel.

Giniana stared in horror at the sleeping kitten. Scowling up at Johns, she demanded, "You didn't clean her up?"

His expression dropped into stolidity. "I don't know how without hurting it ... her."

On an intake of breath, Giniana took the towel and limp kitten. Thinner than Thrisca, not at all well. Hard to see any injuries, though Giniana smelled both new and dried blood.

Thrisca dashed from the side of the house where she'd lurked. *Let Me see! Let Me SEE the little One.* The older FamCat's nose wrinkled and she snorted, then opened her mouth in the extra cat smell-taste sense. *INTERESTING. More interesting than the ma—*

Quiet! Giniana warned Thrisca mentally, then stated aloud to Johns, "I daren't help her. I don't know enough. She's in too poor a state for me to try human Healing on her."

"Oh," Johns said. He swallowed, one of his big fingers came out and stroked the kitten's head. "It—she has a bad paw and eye."

Fear welled up in Giniana. "We need to get her to D'Ash's."

Johns's mouth bowed down. "Do we need to teleport, or will a glider or walking do?"

"I can commandeer a Spindle business glider. The Ashes are in Noble Country, after all, but the estates are too big to walk in a timely manner." Even as she spoke, she drew her scrypebble from her sleeve pocket and requested a glider at the front gate for a trip to D'Ash's. Since she'd gone there often with Thrisca, before GreatLady D'Ash told them that she could no longer Heal the FamCat, no one at T'Spindle's questioned Giniana.

I will come, too. You have not let Me See the Kitten, or really smell Her, or—

Again Giniana interrupted her FamCat and stared down her. "You can't come. *You* must continue that particular duty you promised."

Thrisca growled loudly enough that Johns stared down at her. *I don't want to,* the cat whined. *I want to go to D'Ash's again. I want to sniff and lick the little Person the actor brought. I want—*

Replying tersely mind-to-mind, Giniana insisted, *You promised. Do not break your word. I can stay with you and send Johns to D'Ash's by himself.*

With a deep rumble in her throat, Thrisca turned, and, tail whipping, stalked back around the house to the shed. *Stup man is sleeping. Won't wake up when You are gone. I could have had treat of going to D'Ash's with You.* A pause. *Make sure You bring back the Kitten. Should not go with Johns. He does not like Cats.*

Giniana demanded, *Did you do something to him last night?*

Thrisca didn't answer.

Giniana's perscry sounded the Spindle's song and she turned to Johns. "I'm sorry for speaking privately to my FamCat."

A smile hovered on his lips. "I'd imagine that's natural when one has a Familiar animal companion, especially a FamCat, no apologies needed."

Reluctantly, she put the still unconscious kitten into his large hand that nearly enveloped her, then Giniana linked arms with him. "A Spindle glider awaits at the gate."

"Sure." He turned toward the gate and walked with a smooth and gliding step, holding the kitten against his chest. She kept pace but didn't, couldn't, move like he did. Now that she thought on it, she usually kept her steps brisk and efficient.

Best to get bad news over with quickly. "Thrisca insists I bring the kitten back here."

"Sure," he agreed.

"You don't like cats?"

"Cats don't like me," he replied. "Maybe not foxes, either." She glanced up to find him watching her, still negotiating the path perfectly.

He continued, "I've had incidents with FamCats and a FamFox." His smile turned wry, but she felt irritation pulse through him and to her by their bond.

The man didn't like animals. How could that be? She opened her mouth to say something, and unbalanced on a tree root, began to fall. Johns drew her up, easily and steadily, with his free hand, and her gaze fell to the kitten snuggled in his large and completely stable grasp. He'd brought the kitten to her, and now they were on their way to the Animal Healer. He'd agreed to that and she had no doubt he intended to pay the bill … and he hadn't even brought that subject up, even though he knew he'd be unemployed soon.

"I'll pay for the kitten's Healing," she blurted.

His expression went haughty but his inflection didn't hold any chill. "My responsibility."

Giniana flinched beside him. Maybe he'd been too harsh. Hell. He paused and she stopped, too. He didn't have much time with her to himself, here and now. He'd be blunt. "You seem better this morning."

Her head lowered and she flushed. "I have the annual physical examinations of the staff—the Spindle Family—the next couple of weeks, up at the Residence. The Residence itself gave me some Flair and energy, and I began with GrandLord T'Spindle himself. Simply being in his presence in his Residence, on his estate, generates ambient Flair that I can use in addition to my own."

"Uh-huh. Good." Johns began walking again, wanted to link fingers with her. Instead he must mind a kitten.

They came in sight of artistically curved greeniron gates that would accommodate a wide Family glider. Not much time to say everything he had to. "Don't you get any time for yourself, for Giniana Filix?"

Her head lifted and her cheeks flushed more, this from the irritation he sensed in their bond. "Time enough," she replied shortly.

They paused near the glider as the guards nodded and the gates opened. Still flushed, she shot back a question. "Did you bring the kitten to me because you planned on using her to see me?"

"Yes. No. Not entirely. She needs Healing and I thought you could do it." His mouth compressed as he tried to think of a smooth way to say the next concept that had worried at his mind. "You ... have an old and ailing FamCat ... who will be going through ... a strange, uh, medical procedure." Without thought his hand lifted and his fingers flexed in a helpless gesture he didn't often allow himself. "The kitten needs a home. I thought you might want her, care for her better than D'Ash and her adoption rooms with a lot of other Fams."

Giniana turned her head to him and met his gaze, her color fading, her amber eyes wide. "Oh. I understand," she said softly, then shrugged. "You think Thrisca might die during the time Healing process."

"I don't know." And he was a blunt guy, but hadn't said such stark words. "I don't know anything about the time thing. Barely even heard about it." And hadn't paid any attention when he had since it never occurred to him that any such weird thing as time experimentation would impinge on his life. Added gruffly, "And I wouldn't've said it that way."

Nodding, Giniana said, "I understand. Death isn't as prevalent in your life as mine."

One of the guards gestured and Johns lifted the door of the passenger side of the glider, carefully held out the kitten to Giniana.

His care with the mite softened her, as had the anxiety he'd felt at broaching the death of Thrisca that Giniana had felt through her link with him. And he'd actually admitted to using the kitten to see Giniana, though she believed his explanation. She believed him, that he didn't act around her, didn't lie. That could be dangerous to her well-being ... but now they had a kitten whose well-being hung in the balance.

Johns sat next to Giniana, who stroked the kitten on her lap. She seemed more ... lively. Giniana, not the kitten. He wanted to think of Giniana, keep his gaze on her, because he felt a huge stone of dread weigh in his chest as he stared at the small lump of fur. His responsibility. He'd said that and he meant it. And obviously the injuries of the catling were worse than he'd hoped.

Yes, nicer to contemplate Giniana. He realized that since he'd known her, her energy had been depleted, even the very first night when T'Spindle called on her to Heal him and Raz Cherry. She'd helped them so quickly, so easily as a FirstLevel Healer, Johns had thought nothing of it.

But her strong Flair had masked her weariness.

He thrummed his fingers on the steering bar. It seemed as if she ruined her current health due to worry for her Fam and overwork. And that made him recall those nightmare months when he and his FatherDam took whatever jobs they could get to provide his mother with ultimate comforts as she faded with an untreatable sickness and died.

A member of his Family. Like Giniana considered Thrisca. In fact, sounded like Giniana thought Thrisca her *only* Family. How sad.

So nothing else was wrong with Giniana. No physical illness, her colleagues would have discovered that and taken care of that at once, if Giniana hadn't Healed herself.

She hummed, her hand on the kitten. Not quite a Healing tune, or rather a very minor one everyone knew for cuts and scrapes. More like simple soothing and caring and … love. How could she love a being so soon?

Happened, he guessed. For a passing instant, he wondered if Giniana was worth all this time and effort—a relationship with her would demand much of him. Including him getting to know, and somehow winning over, that old FamCat.

But a woman had never affected Johns like this. He'd never had such a deep and intense relationship, linked so closely with a female, and they'd only kissed!

Yes, he intended to keep the fascinating Giniana Filix in his life as long as possible to peel and reveal each layer of her. Even though the woman had problems, would be complicated, and had that miserable FamCat, too.

No, he couldn't walk away.

He'd have to learn to cope with Thrisca. Find some common ground, though he couldn't imagine what.

"What's your schedule?" The question came out more brusquely than he'd anticipated, but what the hell. She should *feel* how much she attracted him through their bond. Too much to walk away.

She looked at him sideways. "You really want to know?"

"I asked, so, yeah."

Her breasts rose and fell in two deep breaths, then she said, "Annual physical examinations of the T'Spindle staff, most of whom are, as usual, Spindles themselves, in the morning and the afternoon."

"Any breaks?"

"Of course, more than generous breaks." Her mouth

thinned. "Long enough I can usually pick up some additional work at the emergency intake of the HealingHalls."

"Ah."

"And in the evenings and at night, I'm over at a private client's watching their new baby while they sleep."

"All night long?"

"Yes, from RetireBell to dawn."

"Ah."

"What about you? What are your performance days?"

Good that she was interested enough to ask. Glancing at her, he smiled. "I've got matinees and evening performances on the days of Qwert and Midweekend," he paused.

"Yes?"

"And some volunteer work at Moores House for Lady-Blessed Children after noon today, and every week."

"You do?"

"Yes."

"That's wonderful!"

He'd have basked in her approval if he hadn't been annoyed that she sounded so surprised. "My regular schedule's full, but I have plenty of time for a relationship."

Not looking at him, she said, "I'll only be working hard, taking as many shifts as I can at other HealingHalls, staying with my clients at night until I make enough gilt to pay for Thrisca's procedure."

He hesitated at offering her gilt. In the last couple of days, he'd heard that her mother had lived off others' generosity, so such a notion would be a sore point with Giniana. In her position, he'd be offended if a new friend offered financial help, even a loan. They weren't close enough yet for her to feel comfortable being obligated to him. While he thought about feelings and stuff, she asked, "Will you wait for me? Until I have more time to spend with you?"

He took her hand, found her fingers tense. "Naturally, I'll

wait. But I'm not giving up now, either. If you can't be with me—and I think we could arrange a meal or two, at least, you must eat—I'll scry you for a moment or two, every day." He smiled his famous crooked smile, not for show, but because he felt wry emotion. "I find I'm unable to say no to you, to even think of not seeing you every day," he added lightly, exposing himself as he'd never done to a woman, "You have all the power in this relationship."

She looked at him, then away again. "Now," she said, choked. "When I'm new to you."

She needed more from him, and though he didn't want to give it, what he'd just said was true, he'd fulfill all her needs if she'd allow that. And how had he gotten in so deep so quickly, with only shared kisses? Not the hunter instinct, not her apparent unavailability. Lord and Lady, going by the bond between them, and all outer problems aside, she just *fit* him.

CHAPTER 11

"I'M MORE than interested in you, and it's more than the shiny new desire for an affair with a fascinating woman. You should feel, already, the bond spinning between us. More than I'd allow with a woman I only anticipated having a few weeks of hot sex with," he replied brutally. "I want more than that with you, so, yeah, I repeat that I'll contact you every day. I won't be waiting for you because I'll *be* with you." He sucked in a breath, told her something he didn't recall saying to any other woman. "I'm here for you. You can lean on me."

Giniana turned her head and stared at him until he began to feel uncomfortable, but didn't show that, of course.

"What about you?" she asked softly. "And your career? What will happen after your play *Firewalker* closes? How will you cope?"

All right. He could hide behind a mask, but sensed that wouldn't work with her. He had to open up, *be* himself, Klay Saint Johnswort, and not a hint of any other character. She'd sense any falsity, any fibbing, any shading of the truth, through the tie weaving strongly between them. *She'd* walk away from him.

So he let out a sigh. "I've already contacted my agent, and

gone down to the Theatrical Guild to let them know officially that I'll be free at the end of the month, and ready for a job, of course."

"Of course." She sounded stifled. Paused a couple of breaths, then said, "You want good work."

"Yeah, I do. I want really good work, a fabulous part in a long-running show." Amberose's play flashed across his mind. "But I'll settle for steady work. Acting, first, of course, but something else if I can't get a job there. Construction, maybe. Even Flaired builders need strong laborers sometime, and my secondary Flair is for construction."

She gasped, turned in her seat to look at him, and blinked as if in startled surprise. "Really?"

"Sure." He rolled his shoulders. "Gilt is gilt, and I'll need income in a couple of months."

"How will you live until then?"

Another shrug. "Got no rent, do got savings." He grimaced. "And I have some stocked no-times. Not the greatest food, neither my mother nor my grandmother, my FatherDam, were great cooks, but I'll get by."

"What of your father and your father's father, your FatherSire?"

"Both long gone. Barely remember my father, he died so early in my life, and FatherSire before I was born. My mother and FatherDam raised me."

"Oh. All three of you lived alone on the Saint Johnswort estate?"

He snorted. "Not much of an estate, a house and some land on the outskirts of town." Reluctantly, he admitted, "And both are shabbier than I like and need some rehab."

"How lovely that you have a respectable name and good estate, land of your own that can't be taken from you. Unless you mortgage it, of course."

The very idea sent shock flashing through him. He choked.

Giniana blinked at him. "I see you didn't even think of that. But you could get gilt from the house and land."

"No." He would never short the future for immediate gilt. He could work, now, had prospects and a rising career, everyone said so. Who knew what the future would hold?

And his FatherDam and his mother had had the house and land when they'd needed it. He might need that, too, later in his life.

Now Giniana stared straight ahead out the windshield, her smile strained and bordering on false. "We had a house and a little land when I was a child. From my father's parents and older generations." She waved a hand. "I barely remember it because my parents mortgaged it, then did not keep up the payments."

Dreadful.

Her parents had more to answer for than he'd thought. He would *never* mortgage his home if he had a child. Even if he had to give up his acting career—a deep and scary thought—he'd ensure his child lived well. Pretty much why he'd steered clear of relationships and supported no dependents.

But he meant to keep time and company with Giniana Filix, who matched him in this, he knew, being solid and responsible. Too responsible for Thrisca, to his mind.

As they entered the T'Ash estate through the Visitor's Gate and gliderway that went straight to the Animal Healer's section of the Residence, Johns yanked the topic back to Giniana and off of him and his prospects.

"Back to your schedule. You have a night job and morning exams at T'Spindle Residence," he repeated. "You did those last night and today?"

"Yes." Giniana continued to pet the kitten, looked ahead.

Not much to see since they drove straight down a tunnel of hedgerows and trees.

"Did you eat a good breakfast this morning?" he persisted.

Her gaze, her whole body, shifted away from him. "Oh. No," she mumbled.

"I'm sure I've heard Healers say that breakfast is the most important meal of the day."

She turned to him with flashing eyes. "Did *you* eat a good breakfast?"

"I sure ordered one, at the Thespian Club. You remember that place? Very good food for starving actors at reasonable prices? Unfortunately, as sometimes happens at the Thespian Club, drama interrupted my meal ..." Now that he thought on it, and not his empty belly, it seemed almost humorous. "Actually a FoxFam ate my steak and eggs."

She stared at him, mouth open.

"Why don't *we* try it again, tomorrow? We can both have good breakfasts to start the morning right, and early. We can meet after you finish your night job. You can come to the Thespian Club and I'll treat you to a full breakfast. Then you can head home for some sleep on a full stomach." He thought that was okay, healing and energy wise, wasn't it? "You can sleep before you go in to work at the Residence? When is that?"

"T'Spindle Residence schedules my time, and I start half-past MidMorning bell." She shrugged. "Healers, especially those who work in the HealingHalls, become accustomed to working after a few septhours of sleep. And I'm good at dropping into a renewing sleep."

"Hm-mm." He raised his brows at her.

She sighed. "I tried to keep a regular sleeping schedule instead of altering it. But I've moved into efficient trance sleep, now."

"Thought so."

"It's only for a short while," she repeated under her breath as if a mantra. Meeting his eyes, she said, "You know how living on little sleep and efficient sleep can be."

He inclined his head. "Like during auditions and rehearsals and the first performances of a new play. But you need to eat, too. We can meet a little after dawn at the Thespian Club." He'd be going short of sleep, too, and was sure he didn't have such a good technique manage his sleep patterns as she did, but so it went. "If we meet for breakfast, will that give you enough time to sleep? I want to see you every day if possible, and I'll endeavor to make that happen."

"I … ah." She exhaled, looked away, then back to meet his eyes, replied firmly, "Yes, I'd like that. I'd like to continue to see you."

"Good. Maybe you can use the pass for the play now and again—"

But she shook her head, so he changed direction, "Or come by before the show or afterwards, perhaps the afternoon matinees, if your schedule allows."

"Maybe …" She eyed him, frowned, "… though I imagine the green room will be crowded since the play's closing soon and people will want to talk more about the play to the cast."

He shrugged, bit off some words. "Maybe. Come if you like. I don't do regrets, like having the play closing too soon. That's looking back and negative. I prefer to look forward."

And since they'd arrived at the small glider parking area outside the Animal Healer's, he stopped any more thought and scrubbed bitterness from his emotions.

She waited for him to circle and open the glider door, treating the kitten she held gently.

"How's she doing?" he asked.

"She's alive."

"Good. We should be able to keep her that way."

"I hope so."

A few minutes later Johns stood with Giniana in a basic examination room, smaller than he'd expected. Pale sage-colored walls soothed and matched the tile floor. The Animal Healer, GreatLady Danith D'Ash, stood behind a low counter with a thick bedsponge atop it, obviously sized for her to work at comfortably.

"Ooooh, poor kitten. Poor little girl," D'Ash cooed.

She confirmed the beastie was female, not that Johns doubted Giniana, who'd known at a glance.

D'Ash stroked the small cat and her fur smoothed, short-ened over most of her body as the mats fell away, leaving an awful smell that neither the Animal Healer nor Giniana seemed to notice.

"Now—" D'Ash began.

"Bad eye, first," Johns insisted, suppressing a shudder at the thought of relearning his acting techniques if he had vision in only one eye.

"Oh, of course." The Lady turned the kitten around. It had awakened when they'd brought it in, then its eyes had closed as soon as D'Ash touched it. Now it rumbled a purr larger than itself that filled the room. Excellent projection.

Thumbs stroking the eye slits, D'Ash cleaned the gunk, stared down. "Oooh! Infection." A pause. "I can fix this." But she sounded as if it would take a lot out of her.

"I'll pay for it," Johns said. "I'm paying for everything." Lord and Lady, would it cost as much as the glider Raz promised? It could. He found that his body went stiff at the thought, the danger of poverty.

Giniana glanced his way, head tilted. He relaxed each muscle, but didn't bother with a fake smile, she wouldn't like that.

"We'll work something out," D'Ash said absently, drawing in a large breath.

But Giniana went behind the counter, set her hand on D'Ash's forearm. "Use some of my energy."

"FirstLevel Healer—" D'Ash began.

"I worked with T'Spindle this morning, he gave me some energy."

Yeah, that was a fib on Giniana's part. Giniana wouldn't tell her boss—any of her bosses—of her problems. They'd have to guess at her struggles and confront her. He reached over and caught her free hand. "Take my strength, too. I don't go to work until late this evening." He linked fingers with Giniana, summoned his energy. It bubbled through him, holding strength and pleasure at being with the woman, touching her, sharing an experience.

"Thank you," D'Ash said, "Usually I'm fine for strength and Flair, but right before you walked in, I'd finished a four septhour labor of a dog, delivering six puppies." She grinned. "I saved them all! A first in the annals of Celta, I think."

"Wonderful!" Giniana enthused.

Johns didn't even know dogs could have six pups at once. He wondered about cats, if they'd been equally fertile on Earth. Not many descendants of the Earthan colonists, animal or man, produced large families.

"Yes, wonderful," D'Ash said, then focused on the kitten, murmuring a short poem-spell. Johns felt the siphoning of his Flair, tried to ensure the Animal Healer tapped from him before Giniana. Then Giniana pushed his draining stream aside, with a powerful rush. *I told you, the Residence helped me.*

Not what you said to D'Ash.

In my case, it's much the same thing, T'Spindle emitted Flair during his physical testing, the Residence picked it up and cycled it, and sent some to me.

That complete cycle hadn't occurred to Johns.

FirstFamily GreatLady D'Ash paused a moment, scrutinizing the kitten who lay breathing heavily. "Best if we rest a bit before proceeding further." She disentangled her fingers from Giniana, who moved back to the same side of the bedsponge as Johns.

The Animal Healer looked at him. "You're in *Firewalker*, aren't you?"

"Yeah."

"I heard it's closing."

"At the end of the month, yeah." Simple fact, no emotion.

She smiled. "Then I think we can do a trade. My Heart-Mate is a blacksmith and works with fire, and we're sure our son is a Fire Mage. Could you get tickets for my husband and me?"

"For sure." Johns smiled down at the small woman. "It's kid friendly—"

"There are some very exciting parts, with, ah, raging and threatening fire," Giniana added.

D'Ash said, "Nuin is a toddler. We won't take him." She chuckled. "We've already had some exciting times." Then her expression turned thoughtful. "Though perhaps it would be better if only I went, and took a friend."

Recollection struck Johns that all the former Ashes except the current Lord perished in a fire, along with the Residence. T'Ash had built this smooth armorcrete home less than two decades ago.

"I'll leave passes for you at Will Call," Johns stated. "For the rest of the month for as many times as you'd care to see the show. You can treat as many friends as you like." And, whew, that relieved his mind as to payment. He'd previously hadn't used any passes at all, until Giniana, and now, Danith D'Ash.

The GreatLady dipped her head. "Thank you."

Me, Me, Me! whined the kitten, twitching a little.

"Yes, let's get back to Healing you," D'Ash murmured, her stance relaxed as if not expecting further difficulties.

Johns sent energy toward Giniana, who also added her Flair to D'Ash, who continued to feather her fingers over the kitten's eyes. They cycled strength like that for a good three minutes before D'Ash raised her thumbs and the kitten opened bright green eyes.

Another verse of the spellchant, then D'Ash cheerfully announced, "Done with your eyes!"

Eeek! Me feels so GOOD! The kitten opened wide eyes, a brilliant green, slithered around in D'Ash's hand until she could stare at Johns and Giniana. *Lady is pretty. Man is not.*

Johns cracked laughter along with Giniana and D'Ash, mostly from relief.

Me can SEE, the young cat shrilled. *Me can SEE good!* She wiggled away from D'Ash and hopped all along the bedsponge, her head turning this way and that.

Both the women sniffled. Johns swallowed.

After her own few sniffs, the kitten inspected herself. *My furs is GONE.* Her high-pitched squeal seemed to pierce Johns's eardrum, left it ringing. Great.

"You're absolutely fine," D'Ash soothed. "You have a few long tufts left. Your fur, *you*, are clean."

"Probably for the first time ever," Johns said, rubbing his ears.

Ouch! squealed the kitten mentally.

"Oh, your poor paw!" Giniana said.

"Now sit still while I deal with your paw," D'Ash commanded.

The kitten stopped and lifted her deformed paw. Johns winced. Looked bad, all right, as if most of the teeny digits had been broken and not Healed well.

The little cat gave them all wide eyes and pitiful expression. Very effective.

Johns tensed.

Setting her hand under kitten's paw, D'Ash said, "This isn't so bad."

Looked terrible to Johns. He flinched.

The Animal Healer sent him a reassuring smile. "Feral Fam animal companions who were born and lived on the streets come to me now, for me to place them in my Fam adoption rooms. I've mended broken and infected and smashed and splintered bones—"

Johns coughed to break up the litany.

"This will be much easier," D'Ash stated. She domed her fingers over the small limb.

"Wait," Giniana said.

D'Ash looked at her and Giniana stepped close again. "This is how we do it for humans," Giniana said, and taking Danith's hand in her own, placing two of the GreatLady's fingers exactly atop the paw.

D'Ash frowned. "I didn't learn that. I didn't know that." She raised her gaze to Giniana. "I studied with the Heathers."

Giniana blinked. "The Heathers taught you this method for digit and bone—"

"No, that wasn't part of my original training, but my secondary training with the Panaxes ..." D'Ash's lips flattened. "Though the GuildHall paid the Panaxes for my education, their ... attitude ... towards me, a commoner raised to GrandHouse status, was ... poor. Until I wed with T'Ash, of course."

Giniana had stiffened as if in deep offense. "The Panaxes do have a stiff manner, though I had not heard this before. You should request the GuildHall try to get their payment back. Obviously the GuildHall was shorted."

D'Ash shrugged. "Seven years ago. I'm sure the GuildHall would believe such an action isn't worth the effort."

Johns shared a look with Giniana. Neither of them stood in a place where they could take that perspective.

"Paw is Healed," D'Ash stated with satisfaction.

A terrible, pulsing siren went off and Danith D'Ash vanished, then she screamed, *FirstLevel Healer, to me, now!*

CHAPTER 12

JOHNS FELT Giniana fling the door open, saw her rush through it. He followed, and his brain processed that he heard screaming.

He ran behind her, stopped when he saw a bloody tangle of large animal and human. Both showed wide red swatches of blood on their hides.

Ears throbbing, he went to the teleportation box and turned off the siren, left the light showing the pad remained in use.

"My horse, my horse ... help my ... hor—" Abrupt silence from the woman Giniana had run to.

Adrenaline surged through the Healer, heat and Flair flashed and poured out of her into the human who seemed to be holding onto life by a frail thread. Johns stepped back, gave the women room to work.

A lot of blood and gore, D'Ash tending the heaving barrel of a horse, and was that wrinkled thing a bit of protruding intestine? Johns yanked his gaze toward Giniana whose equally bloody hands pushed against the pale skin of the unconscious woman.

Long seconds passed into even longer minutes and Johns could only watch, helpless, as Healing sucked energy from the healthy to the critical.

Both Giniana and D'Ash panted, their eyes glazed.

"Residence!" Johns called.

"Yes, MasterLevel Actor Saint Johnswort?" it replied in a light female voice.

He snapped, "Your Lady and the FirstLevel Healer Giniana Filix are saving lives and need energy! Can you send strength or Flair to them?"

"Yes!" A smell like a fully flowering summer meadow dropped on them, permeating the room. Both Healers choked, then drew even breaths and applied themselves to their patients. The air around all four sparkled.

"Better," gasped Giniana. She levitated her patient, inhaled the shiny motes, and moved her hands above the woman, chanting what Johns recognized as the final chorus to a deep Healing spell.

The rider opened her eyes, gazed around with full comprehension, set a hand on her side that had been crumpled bones under deep red stained clothing. "Zow." She stood, staggered a step and Giniana steadied her.

"Zow," the woman repeated. "Excellent Healing. Didn't expect that here. Oh, my mare!" She swung toward where GreatLady D'Ash continued to mutter Healing spells over the animal.

"Oh!" She fell forward and Johns stepped up, caught her and yanked her out of the way.

"Wait," he commanded, but she struggled in his grasp. He didn't let her go to interfere, said, "No. You want your horse to survive, you let the Healer you brought her to do her job."

She snuffled and moved away from him to lean against a wall. "You're right."

The Residence spoke. "I have a great store of energy, D'Ash, do you need more?"

When D'Ash didn't answer another puff of scent wafted from the walls, Johns felt his soles warm as the floor radiated Flair that spiraled up into him. From the reaction of D'Ash and the horse, they received much larger doses.

D'Ash let out a small groan, uncurled herself from the awkward position over the mare, smoothed the animal's sides that flaked away blood but showed whole and unscarred.

With a whinny, the mare rose to her feet.

"Oh. Oh. Oh." The horsewoman burst into tears, hurried to her mare and flung her arms around the animal.

FirstFamily GreatLord T'Ash shot through the office suite door, ran to his HeartMate and whisked her up into his arms. "I felt the change of energy in the Residence, smelled the use of spells."

He glanced around, saw woman and horse standing Healed. "Greetyou, GraceMistrys Sallow. How can I help?"

She wiped an arm across her brow. Johns finally noticed she wore what must be special horse training clothes. He observed them, figured them to be tailored, fashionable and expensive. "Noth—nothing." Her voice came out creaky, and once again she studied her horse. "Unbelievable. Truly, D'Ash, you are an extraordinary Healer." The Sallow woman bowed. "You will be well compensated for saving my mare. Not only do I love her, but she produces excellent get. I will let my elders decide on a good price for your Healing."

D'Ash quoted a figure.

The woman shook her head. "No. I know that the Residence funneled stores of energy and Flair to you, so that must also be taken into account."

T'Ash rumbled in his chest. Johns kept an eye on the legendary and formidable man, studying every gesture, his whole manner for future use in Johns's acting career.

Waving to Giniana, the Sallow woman continued, "This lady, whom I don't know—"

"FirstLevel Healer Giniana Filix, on the staff of the Spindles," D'Ash replied, apparently comfortable being held by her husband. Johns narrowed his eyes, might be a standard habit of theirs. Interesting.

A nod from Sallow. "As for my own injuries. I will consult the cost of those emergency services at Primary HealingHall and forward the amount to T'Spindle to put in your account."

Giniana dipped a curtsy. "Thank you. But T'Ash Residence also gave me energizing Flair—"

T'Ash's growl finally emerged as words. "No matter. You owe us nothing. You helped when my wife called you. That's enough." He still held his wife tightly.

GraceMistrys Sallow bowed to all of them, thanks gushing from her, then teleported away with her mare. Johns didn't know whether the mare held enough Flair to help with the teleportation or not, but both woman and horse looked in prime fettle.

"Payment for D'Ash's services received from the Sallows, along with a note from the GraceLord himself for saving a beloved daughter and mare," the Residence stated.

"Good," T'Ash said.

A squeak came and the kitten pranced through the open door from the examination room to the main office area. *Me sleeps and You all left Me! Did You forget about Me? How could You?*

"No, I don't want that one here," T'Ash said. "Absolutely not."

"No," Johns agreed. "She won't be staying."

"Good."

Me look around, announced the kitten, lowered her nose to the sturdy rug and trotted along a scent trail.

"Let's get this cleaned up. Residence?" asked T'Ash.

"I can do a full cleaning spell on the Animal Healer

offices," the house replied eagerly, and wind breezed through the whole place.

"I don't like those—" D'Ash began, too late.

Johns watched all the stains in the teleportation area vanish. The spell even cleaned up the sweat on Johns's skin as it whooshed by him. He strode to the newly cleansed large animal teleportation pad and flicked the switch showing its availability, then joined Giniana.

Smoothing her tunic down with both hands, and vanishing the blood and bodily stains at the same time, Giniana looked at him with large eyes and murmured, "You helped incredibly."

He replied, "I wouldn't have even thought of speaking to the Residence, of requesting such a thing from the entity, but you told me about it earlier."

She sighed and rocked a bit. Stepping up, he held her, let her lean on him. Wished she'd do so more than physically.

D'Ash coughed slightly.

"Yes?" Johns asked.

"I want to thank FirstLevel Healer Filix, too," the Great-Lady said.

"You're quite welcome," Giniana answered.

"And I also want to request that you come and teach me proper techniques for Healing humans that I might be able to apply for Fams and other animals. Obviously the Panaxes gave me substandard techniques they thought would be appropriate for animals and not primary ones used for humans." D'Ash smiled. "I'll charge them for the remedial education, at current prices. I can also document how they thought specific injuries should be treated and how you Heal humans."

Giniana stepped away from Johns and curtsied to D'Ash. "Thank you."

"I'll work out a list of what I think needs to be done and

we can decide on the price and the time schedule." D'Ash frowned. "I am now in the position of not knowing which of my procedures are good and which are bad."

Time to go home, the kitten pronounced. *Back to the cottage and Thrisca.*

Johns stared at her, had the elderly FamCat contacted the kitten? Maybe.

"Later," said T'Ash, and as Johns and Giniana walked toward the door, he addressed his wife, "Beloved, I don't want you calling on the Residence for stored Flair energy unless it's a major emergency."

"This was a major emergency. I was depleted from the dog and the puppies—"

T'Ash grunted.

"—And Healing the kitten and the horse *and* rider teleported in with major injuries, dying."

"All right." Finally, the man put his HeartMate on her feet, looked around. "Residence, I didn't know you could supply us with strength and energy and Flair."

Johns should have hauled Giniana out of there, but his curiosity caused his steps to lag. The kitten, distracted again, coursed through the large room checking out the desk and teleportation pads and nosing the cracks under shut doors ...

T'Ash Residence answered, "We were lost, long ago, when my first shell burned and you ran away as a child. You might not have known all I can do, what we can do together, and I forgot."

Giniana's steps slowed. She obviously listened, too.

"It's good we can remember things together," T'Ash said.

"Yes, we can do things together. Because you are generous with your Flair and perform rituals sending power into me and funding all my spells, I had Flair to return to you. But I did not recall such a gifting of power by myself. It was the actor who told me what to do, who reminded me what I could do for my Family."

T'Ash and D'Ash swung toward Johns, yet a full meter from the door. He felt their gazes, and the Residence's scrutiny, as if he stood under a spotlight.

"Ah, Saint Johnswort," T'Ash said. "An old name, an old heritage. Your house is becoming a Residence?"

The question jolted Johns, blanked his mind. "I—"

"Of course you shouldn't tell me, for security and privacy reasons," T'Ash stated. "Know that I am indebted to you. I owe you a favor."

Johns made a half-bow. "I appreciate that." He wouldn't be so stupid as to turn the man down, nor would he ever remind T'Ash.

But the FirstFamily GreatLord snapped his fingers, then held out a silver Ash Family token to Johns. "You saved my HeartMate from over-extending herself trying to Heal the horse. You saved the FirstLevel Healer from doing the same with GentleLady Sallow, so Sallow lived, too. You reminded my Residence of its power, made me and my wife aware of its capabilities. For all this you deserve a silver token."

Johns took the coin. He didn't quite remember what all a silver token meant, what aid, or even gilt he might get from T'Ash should he cash it in. It made him wonder what other tokens the Saint Johnswort family, he, might have. Maybe better than gilt in the bank. He'd research all that, later.

Since he didn't want to betray his ignorance, he pocketed the coin and returned the man's bow with his best.

Taking Giniana's fingers, Johns gave the Ashes a last nod. Then he and Giniana followed the dancing kitten through the doors to outside that opened for them upon approach.

Once outside the kitten stopped, squealing, hopped around. *Me SEE. Me see all kinds of flowers. Me SMELL excellent poop and pee smells of other animals and FAMS … and nice flower smells … and acceptable human smells.*

Giniana started forward, but Johns caught her fingers in his own. "Let her look around and experience the joys of living other than in an alley." He touched Giniana's face so she'd meet his eyes. "The emergency in there, and D'Ash's offer, should help relieve your gilt problems, right?" He hoped they could now spend more time together.

"Perhaps." Her shoulders tensed, then she moved them, her body easing as she deliberately relaxed. "I'm speaking with D'Willow during my afternoon break. There have been … developments."

Her grim tone warned him that she didn't want him asking about such developments. Bad developments, he reckoned.

Squeezing her fingers, he murmured, "Perhaps you will be able to make a more regular schedule. Get more sleep, not have to rely on energy potions or spells or Flair from Residences or FirstFamily Lords."

"Johns—"

"I'm concerned about you, because I care for you. And you are caring more for Thrisca than yourself."

"For this little while."

"And when did this 'little while' start? How long have you been pushing yourself?"

When she scowled, he raised a palm. "Never mind." He scanned the area for the kitten, saw her sniffing around and under the bushes.

Since he didn't want to kiss Giniana in the glider, always awkward, he stepped close. He put his hands on her upper arms, slid his fingers down to hers, enjoying the physical thrill that pulsed with his action. Reverberated between them.

He inched closer, now loosely embraced her, rubbed her tight shoulders and back, along her spine, touching her, letting their nerve endings connect, telling her with touch what he'd said in words. That he cared for her, more than easy sexual lust, that he'd support her. That he wanted to learn her, know her.

Then he angled his head and feathered his lips over hers for the merest taste of her. And suddenly fire ignited throughout his veins and he yearned to feel all of her against himself. He pulled her close, but not as intimately as he'd have liked, and savored the press of body to body, standing in the summer sun with light streaming on them, around them, throbbing through them like their pulse.

His mouth opened, his tongue gliding along the seam of her lips, plunging in as she opened to him. And her tongue tangled with his, sucking as if she relished his taste.

Lord and Lady, so good. Better than anything in his life. "I want you." The words followed the need tearing from him. And because he wanted to take her here and now, his sex hardened for that, his hands tingled with the need to grab and yank closer still, and hold, he surveyed the landscape for a good place to make love.

At the sound of her small choked noise, his attention pinned back on her, enjoyed the flush of color in her face, her dreamy eyes, her lips plush from their kiss. "I think I want that, too," she admitted.

Pure desire flamed through him.

She placed a hand between her breasts. "I feel the intensity of our bond. It's more than lust. More than basic attraction … more."

"When?" he demanded, ready to blow off any other appointment in his life.

"Not—"

But he didn't want to hear "nots." "Tomorrow morning,

instead of breakfast. No. You need the food and the rest, dammit."

"Wait, I mean—"

He didn't want to hear that, either, so before she could continue, he took off after the kitten who'd finished squatting under a bush and now dug determinedly, flinging dirt. He scooped her up, gestured Giniana to take the driver's side of the glider, stuck the kitten in a sling on a side window in the back, sat in the passenger seat and lowered the door.

"You think of the time and place." Emotions poured rough from him. He nailed her gaze with his. "Let me know."

Since her hands didn't grip the driving bar, he took one, put it on his own heart. "We have a bond. Think of that when doubts and lame rationalizations plague you to retreat from this relationship. As for me, I expect to see you for breakfast at the Thespian Club tomorrow morning, at least." And have her in bed—hers or his, he didn't care—soon.

In confused silence, mind warring with emotions, Giniana programmed the glider to leave Noble Country and drop Johns—her would-be lover Johns—off at a round park that served most of the public carrier lines of the city.

Her spirits had lifted unreasonably. She recognized that as a very good thing to battle the smear of depression that seemed to have covered her the last few weeks of unrelenting work and the dreadful teeter-tottering of hope and despair about Thrisca.

And the morning's work … the morning's impulsive generosity at helping a sick and feral FamKitten, had paid off immeasurably, for her as well as Johns.

Perhaps, even with the greater price of the Time Healing Procedure, Giniana could remove her name as a Healer from the emergency roster of all the HealingHalls where she'd registered.

She'd like that. Hadn't been brave enough to tell Johns how many months she'd filled her life with work and Thrisca, narrowed her life to such a thin focus.

CHAPTER 13

DESPITE THE RUCTIONS of the morning, Johns arrived punctually for his volunteer time at the Moores House for Lady-Blessed Children. As he descended from the public carrier, he wondered whether Raz Cherry would really come through on his offer to sell Johns a glider at a wholesale price.

Until then, he'd walk, take the public carrier, and occasionally teleport, as usual. He sauntered down a couple of blocks in the golden sunshine to the medium-sized but distinctly run-down building holding the Center. Just the idea of being with the kids lifted his spirits.

A branch of the Maidens of Saille, celibate nuns of the Divine Couple, the Lady and Lord, ran the facility for those children unable to join any grovestudy groups.

Last Samhain, New Year's, he and others of the Thespian Club and Theatrical Guild had participated in a publicity opportunity of giving gifts and lessons, and interacting with the children.

He'd liked the event. The children had touched him. His childhood hadn't been full of advantages, but he'd had drive and skill and Flair. The children at the Moores House usually lacked one of those qualities, if not all.

But they embraced the simple joy of every moment, every day, and that lifted his own spirits. He couldn't donate gilt, but he could give his time, and he did, once a week.

At the place, he received a warm but distracted welcome from the young nun-counselor. And his brows raised as she smiled and nodded, then left him alone with the children who ranged from about six to early-teen. He'd never been trusted completely alone with the kids before, without even an introduction.

But he smiled and reminded those who'd forgotten him who he was, gravely acknowledged a new girl and boy, both about ten.

They talked a little, then he went into story telling. He always read a simple story first, then acted it out to the children, taking all the parts. Then the children did a performance, too.

The last septhour of the afternoon rang with laughter that rolled into his ears and sank into him.

Near the end of the session, when the children took turns dramatizing their day, an older nun who managed the school gestured to him and asked about the last couple of games he'd be playing. He stated he'd end with "Poison Eyes."

At that her expression lightened. On a sigh, she said, "The children love dying dramatically."

Johns grinned back. "We *all* do." He paused a moment. "Why don't you join us?"

She blinked.

He rolled a shoulder. "It's a good way to release tension, express negative emotions," he reminded her.

"Yes. Hmm."

"When was the last time you had fun?" He sensed her emotional aura clenched tight around her body.

She glanced at the office. "I can't."

"Next week, then."

Her face became even more strained. "No. Yes. Perhaps." With a nervous gesture, she adjusted the yellow head-dress that confined her hair, denoting her as a celibate Maiden of Saille, gave Johns a weak smile, and left.

At the end of the period, after a good game of Poison Eyes, he settled the children on their quiet time sponges. On his way out of the Center he stopped by the minimal office to tell the Maidens he was leaving, and found both nuns there. They sent another volunteer, this time a young woman dressed in the colors of a journeywoman mind-Healer, to watch the children.

Closing the door behind him, he asked, "What's wrong?"

Both nuns sighed. The elder gestured toward the narrow window. "As you saw when you came in, this area of the city is becoming more popular. Our landlady did not renew our lease. She plans on demolishing the building and constructing boutique shops."

Johns grunted. "Do I know this person? Any way I can speak with her, perhaps persuade ...."

But the women shook their heads.

A smile twitched on and off the older Maiden's face. "We are hoping that either the Saille House for Orphans or D'Sea's Mental Rehabilitation Facility will be able to find space for us at their locations."

"Neither of those is ideal," the younger Maiden stated. "They come with significant restrictions."

Johns's perscry pinged. "I'm sorry, I need to go." He bowed to them. "I *will* volunteer here as long as you'll have me."

"Very good to know." She paused. "Can you come Mor Day next week instead of Midweek Day?"

"Yes, but first thing in the morning."

"Many thanks!" the nuns chorused.

He nodded. As always, he walked away with a spring in his step. The affection of the children for him, their enjoyment of the stories and games he played with them, chased away any incipient brood.

He'd be reluctant to give up volunteering for them, but didn't know if he'd be allowed in one of the locations that the Maidens had mentioned. He frowned, wondering what he might be able to do, grimaced. Everyone around him seemed to need gilt. Including him.

But summer surrounded him and he shoved out of his mind all negative thoughts, grasped at the positives continuing to come his way the last few days.

He'd helped a friend, come to the attention of a First-Family GreatLord, T'Spindle, in a good way, gotten an offer for better training from GrandLord T'Marigold, and a glider at cost from Raz ... though that would eat into his long-term savings.

Patting his trous pocket, he felt the silver token T'Ash had given him, a fantastic boon.

On the whole, despite his job ending, he felt his life took an upward slant.

Cheer filled him. Because of the woman, that one fascinating woman, who he hoped to make his lover tomorrow.

Giniana Filix, Healer, wary of actors, so a challenge layered on the humming desire between them. A kind woman with a good heart who smiled at him when she'd heard he volunteered at Moores House for Lady-Blessed Children.

An extremely caring woman who'd take in a kitten, who pushed herself to her limits for her Fam.

The smile fell off his face. Another challenge, a Fam. He knew that if Thrisca didn't like him, Giniana wouldn't associate with him, dazzling attraction or not.

He hadn't met many Fams, and never one who'd treated him well.

Nope, stop any incipient downer immediately.

Switch to dwelling on how he'd make love to Giniana Filix, maybe he could get a meal in her tomorrow evening before they went to their respective jobs. And share passion with her, too.

On the relatively long public carrier glider ride to his home in the southeast corner of the city, Johns occasionally feather-touched the connection between himself and Giniana.

He'd understood the flow of pleasant comfort when she'd returned to T'Spindle estate and her cottage, the love when she'd greeted her Fam. Some ensuing excitement—introduction of Thrisca and the kitten? The general focus of a mind preparing for work, and the busyness when she practiced her craft.

She seemed fine to him, now and for the moment. He'd sure keep an eye on her, though. And, if he was lucky, his hands and another favorite body part.

He walked the half block from the carrier dropoff to his land, teleportation-hopped over the wall and hedgerow near the rusted-shut front greeniron gates, then for the first time in years, he turned in a circle and *looked* at his property.

Behind him, the fancy gates his forebears had paid good gilt for twined with leaves and flowers. Before him a wandering footpath to the front door. Everywhere plants. Some weeds, some medicinal plants that looked like weeds. Like many estates, hedgerows framed the boundary edges within the walls and lined the gliderway.

By no means as huge as one of the great noble's, or any of the the FirstFamilies', his property still included a good chunk of land any noble would be pleased to claim. Johns thought one or the other of his herb-merchant forebears could have *tested* to become a noble, but they'd been proud of their status as upper middle-class Commoners.

The state of his land and home appeared a few years shabbier than it had, but not beyond repair, yet. If he labored at it.

He'd be able to do that if he didn't pick up another acting job right away, and should definitely carve out septhours a day to work on it. And soon if he contemplated bringing Giniana Filix here.

Which, he realized with a strong shiver down and up his spine, he did. No way he could match the beauty of T'Spindle's noble estate that had been tended for four centuries, but he could make his house and the grassyards and gardens around the house...acceptable. Clean them up until they were worthy of showing off again.

As he scanned the area, he imagined the place after some work and gilt had been spent on it. He visualized another summer's day and an afternoon gathering he hosted as an actor of wealth and fame and influence.

A sigh wrenched from him at the gratifying vision.

Then his gaze took in the present circumstances and he grunted at the amount of effort it would take to make property a showplace.

Right now, he didn't have a lot of time or gilt to bring his home back into great shape. Not between matinee and evening shows, the networking after performances, and, most importantly of all, developing his relationship with Giniana.

But as he continued to stroll up the main path to the house, using Flair to banish weeds as he did so, he became aware of a difference in the land under his feet. It *felt* different than any other ground he trod, than any stage, or the Spindle-Flair-infused land where Giniana lived.

Saint Johnswort ground.

A surge of satisfaction accompanied the realization, gave him a little boost of energy so he could groom the path more without worrying about the Flair he'd need for his performance that evening.

As soon as he stepped through the front door, he heard the continuing peal of chimes announcing a package in his mail cache. He glanced at the scrybowl in the mainspace and noted fancy gold stars floating up from the bowl in a wavery atmosphere. Lily Fescue's icon. Lord and Lady spare him from such silly symbolism.

Before he crossed to that scrybowl, he took out his perscry pebble, found she'd left a message there, too, completely ignored in the activity of the day.

Steeling himself, because he knew she'd left a "see message pickup" and if he didn't watch the scry message Lily would hound him for days, he played the home scry instead of the one on his pebble cache.

"Johns!" Lily lilted. Someone had once reported that "Lily lilted" and she liked that particular alliteration. So she lilted far too often in his opinion. Her face beamed. "I'm so glad you decided to pursue finding the Amberose script that will save your career."

He winced. Snot. Narrowing his eyes, he wondered if she'd meant to be offensive or not. Maybe not. Maybe she only wanted to provide incentive.

Any other time, any other playwright, and he'd've consigned the whole idea of looking for the script to the Cave of the Dark Goddess merely to be recalcitrant with Lily.

"I spent *septhours* reconstructing everything I could recall about Amberose's fabulous script." Lily patted her forehead with a softleaf. "I sent myself into a *deep trance* to wring everything from my memory! I've sent you a copy of all the notes I made regarding the plot and characters. I'm *sure* I have large swathes of dialog."

Johns figured not.

"Now I'll let you read the script and see for yourself just how brilliant the roles are! Particularly mi—the main hero's, modeled after you, as I told you before." She smiled indulgently, waved her fingers. "Don't bother to scry and thank me, I'll be preparing for my matinee today! Later!"

He hoped not to scry or see her later. He'd forgotten how tiring and pretentious she could be.

Nearly trudging, he went to his home cache and pulled out the sheaf of papyrus she'd translocated. His brows raised at the sight of so many pages. A good twenty pages of obviously dictated-to-the-page stuff.

Maybe it would be worth his time and attention to look at them.

With a sigh, he sank into the chair in his downstairs sitting room and began reading the sheets.

More than a septhour later, when sun pouring through the window heated his legs, he surfaced from the world Amberose had spun of a mystery in a haunted Residence ... and he'd better take off his good trous so they wouldn't fade.

Lily had a better memory than he'd given her credit for, and she must have read the script more than once. If it had been him and he'd had such an incredible story in his hands and lost it, he'd have conjured all the memory spells he could, settled into a trance, and tried to record every single word he'd remembered. He hadn't believed Lily went to all that effort, but maybe she spoke the sheer truth for once.

Much of her part, maybe thirty-five percent, looked very close to word-by-word. The male lead's, *his!*, about twenty percent, maybe. The language, the rhythms and word choice drew a person into the story, crafted by a master. And he loved the plot. The twists of the mystery, the thrills of the suspense. This role *would* propel him to stardom, he could sense that in his bones. A rich character, tormented guy who hid his true self behind a lightly amused mask. A man who wouldn't give up, who ultimately triumphed. Very layered part, demanding. It would stretch him, his acting and performance techniques, but he could do it.

The notion he could have such a once-in-a-lifetime role burned in his gut, throughout his body, igniting need. A different need than the one he felt for Giniana Filix, but a yearning just the same.

Like imagining his home a showplace earlier, he could visualize himself on stage, *being* this character.

He walked to the kitchen room and got a cup of caff from the no-time, leaned against the counter and sipped. Fabulous dialog, the beat of it. Fascinating plot structure.

And he'd be playing opposite Lily Fescue. A woman he didn't think understood her own character in this instance because there seemed to be glitches in that character from time to time, as if she'd already put her head into how she'd act the part and modified the script at points.

He'd sink into the part.

Lord and Lady, he *did* want this. Lily had hooked him. He could look for the script, hope if he found it, he'd get even more of an edge in landing the lead role.

Though he had no doubt Lily had continued to scry Amberose's agent, the man who'd given the script to Lily, and *might* have another copy, or at least would be a contact point for the playwright, Johns scried him again. No answer.

Wandering from the kitchen to the side sunroom eating nook, he didn't notice the shafting sunbeams, still caught in the glittering houseparty in the haunted Residence, the first scene of Amberose's play.

Until a boy Johns had never seen before jumped over the wall and hedgerow and landed in Johns's side grassyard— side *weedyard.*

Johns choked on his coffee, kept his head enough to barrel

out of the door between the sunroom and the veranda that wrapped around the sides and front of the house. He surprised the boy who stood looking around.

At first the boy flinched, then jutted his chin. "Hey, GentleSir Saint Johnswort!"

Huh, Johns hadn't realized his neighbors to the east had changed. Wait … there'd been a niece who'd joined her g'aunt who lived next door, hadn't there, months ago after Samhain, in the winter? Maybe the boy had come with the niece

The boy grinned, showing a dimple in a childish round cheek, though Johns estimated he'd be hitting his teens soon. And the youngster intended to use that dimple.

Johns said, "I'm an actor, boy, I know a false innocent smile and expression when I see it." His voice came out gruffer than he'd anticipated but made no dent in the boy's manner.

"Ha!" the kid snorted. Even from meters away, Johns could see clever calculation in the boy's eyes, so different than the children Johns interacted with at the Moores House. "I could clean up the sideyard and maybe back grassyard for ya. Maybe some of the rest of your estate, too." He stood tall and his chin took on an additional jut Johns hadn't figured it had, since it'd looked so stubborn before. "For the rest of the summer and autumn, maybe."

CHAPTER 14

JOHNS CONSIDERED the youth's offer. Whatever grassyard there'd been in back would be as weedy as this, with stickers, and who knew what shape his FatherDam's vegetable and flower gardens were in. Not to mention the ancestral medicinal herb gardens.

Nope, didn't know the condition of any of those, though he vaguely recalled the nice scent of flowers wafting from … somewhere, like from the neighbor's place.

"Yeah?" Johns asked. A lot of area even for one very active boy to clean up.

The boy quoted an outrageous price. Johns doubled over in laughter, only part of it show. When he straightened, he shook his head. "You got gall, kid. Impudent boy."

The youngster grinned. Johns figured he knew really well the definition of "gall" and "impudence." Sweeping out a dramatic arm, Johns intoned, "Mine is a multi-generational family who has lived on this land since the colonists landed here on beautiful Celta from the mysteries of deep space on the starship *Nuada's Sword*, centuries ago."

His audience's eyes widened as if his mind whirled with the brief vision Johns had conjured. Johns stamped one foot, and the ground seemed to ripple under him, all the way toward the back and front of the property. Surprising, but he didn't let that show. He could think on his feet when he had to. "This is our land, it knows me, and I know it." True enough, though guilt surged through him at the notion that he sure hadn't been caretaking such ancestral lands—and the much younger house—very well.

Not quite as bad as Giniana's father, Mas Filix, who'd brought a wife and daughter to his land, then mortgaged it and let it go to some other family. Johns had been absent-mindedly neglectful rather than downright dishonest.

Drawing a breath, dredging up knowledge he'd learned hard from his FatherDam, he narrowed his eyes and focused on the weeds, separating them in his mind from the plants his FatherDam had instructed he keep and tend. Which he really hadn't. Too late for that past mistake now.

Another sweep of his arm and huge effort yanked out of him, causing him to sweat through his clothes, sink into his balance before dizzying exhaustion took him down.

"Zow!" screeched the boy, a little too high for Johns's newly sensitive ears. He'd used a lot of Flair and all his senses now seemed too sharp.

Opening his eyes that he didn't recall closing, he squinted at the sideyard. Yeah, he'd ripped out all of the weeds and they lay in untidy bunches against the wall, revealing clean and turned dirt ready for planting good groundcover.

"Zow. You really did a great job on the sideyard," the boy said. He ran a few steps up and down the newly bared flag-stone path, halted just outside arm's length from Johns. The kid stared at Johns. "But looks like that effort took a lot outta you, since you aren't botanically Flaired like me."

Johns straightened from his slump, didn't think he had the energy to go up the few steps to the veranda and lean against one of the supports. What had he done? He'd need all his strength and more than a little Flair for his performance tonight. Hell.

"Huh." The boy turned his stare back to the clean side-yard. "Guess your generational link with the land can let you do something like that."

"I would say so," Johns replied dryly.

"Somethin' to tell my Master of Botanical Studies." The youngster gave Johns another wide grin. "I'm an apprentice and will soon be a journeyman."

Johns grunted.

"But I can surely plant somethin' that'll sprout quick and look good in that newly turned dirt. And I can groom the resta your yard. Landscape it, too."

From the gleam in his eyes, Johns thought he'd like that. "You enjoy your work."

"Well, yeah!" The youngster shrugged. "Why do it if you don't enjoy it? And it's my *Flair*!"

For a few mindful breaths, Johns thought of his own Flair and felt great gratitude from it, murmured a silent prayer to the Lady and Lord for all the abundance his life had brought him.

"Don't let following your Flair and career take over your life," he advised the kid.

"Huh?"

"Never mind. What really brought you onto my land?" Johns asked, though he thought he knew. Color rushed to the boy's cheeks. He grimaced then jerked his chin toward the back grassyard meters away and toward one of Johns's huge trees with limbs hanging over the east wall. At the bottom of the tree stood a small pink playhouse that Johns had designed for a little girl as a sample. He'd built two or three of them in minor nobles' yards after his mother had died and he'd become an adult. In that period of his life, he hadn't been making a living acting and needed gilt.

And in the huge branching tree itself, Johns had built his first treehouse as a child. As he'd aged, he'd added onto it. He'd trained branches so the structure could be a fancy castle Residence like the FirstFamily Nobles, or a sailing ship, or an airship. The tree also held a thrusting deck that he'd used for practicing his lines when he determined to be an actor.

Sure enough, the boy pointed to the treehouse.

"Thought so," Johns said. He didn't ask if the boy had snuck onto his property on the evenings of his theater performances. He eyed the tree tops he could see in the neighbors' yard. "I can make you one," Johns said, then added, "With your mother's permission. And it will need additional spells from someone *not* me to shield it so you can't fall." Thankfully, he'd kept those shields funded in his own treehouse. Now that he thought on it, he usually spent a septhour or two in the treehouse during warm months. Earlier in the month he'd slept there one night after he'd been revved from the theater and had trouble settling down inside the house.

"Can you, please, please *please*!" the boy squeaked.

"Sure, for your continued work in my yard." Slowly the sun and the land beneath him seeped Flair into Johns. "I'll have to get permission from your folks, though."

The boy frowned. "Hmmm."

Johns waved a hand at the pink playhouse, the extensive treehouse, and the other two small buildings further back in the yard that he'd constructed as samples. "You've seen my work. I'll need to take a look at yours."

Clapping his hands, the youngster moved a short step ladder to the east wall, gave his own flamboyant gesture, a poor imitation of Johns's. His had been casually elegant. Nope, the boy wouldn't be an actor.

"By all means," the youngster pronounced in pompous tones.

Johns suppressed a grin. Just talking to the boy gave him

enjoyment, all that optimism. He hadn't been around a lot of optimistic and savvy people lately. He figured the kid would be fun to watch, too. Good entertainment value. Had to keep in touch with younger generations, too, to understand their tastes.

Gingerly, Johns took a step, found his energy returning. He walked over to the two meter-high wall, gauged whether the kid would prank him by toppling him off the steps, decided the boy wanted a treehouse too much—that need radiated from him.

The boy continued to grin at him, so Johns took the steps up and gazed over the wall to the neighbor's back grassyard. Simply breathtaking with green grass and flowers, and an extremely tidy and *pretty* vegetable garden. He kept his expression easy, turned his glance back to the boy who stood, smirking.

Yeah, focus on the kid. Do *not* look back at his own pitifully untended land. He angled his chin. "Your work?"

"Only some. Mom has really good botanical Flair, too." He laughed. "She would *love* to get her hands on your land!"

"I'm sure," Johns said.

"I did the landscaping."

Johns raised his brows.

"Well, I helped. That's what I like best, and will specialize in when I have the chance."

"Uh-huh."

"I could landscape *your* place." A young, winning smile.

Johns saw gilt running out of his savings into his land. Well, it needed some money spent on it, for sure. "I'll consider that."

The boy deflated a little.

Johns stretched, popping his muscles. The boy sighed. Yeah, the kid would be the long and lean sort, not as big or muscular as Johns. He said, "I'll make you the treehouse you want, as elaborate as my own." Another elegant flick of his fingers. "I give you permission to visit *my* treehouse as much as you want, and your folks—"

"My mother and G'Aunt," the kid put in.

Nodding, Johns said, "—as much as your mother and G'Aunt, allow." The boy was being raised by two women, like Johns had been, and of similar ages to him as Johns's mother and FatherDam. Yeah, Johns would have a weak spot for this child becoming a man. "And," he pointed at the boy, "if you get me a design of the type of treehouse you like, I'll build it to your specs."

Big brown eyes widened at him. "Zow."

"That's my offer," Johns said.

They stared at each other for a couple of minutes. "Um…" the youngster began, then his gaze cut away from Johns's. "Can I landscape … please?"

Wanted to practice his Flair more than the boyish tree-house. A surge of pride flashed through Johns. He looked at his land, his weeds, his shaggy hedges, his out of control bushes, his trees again. Needed something for sure. "No mucking with the medicinal herb gardens." Who knew if one of his descendants would have that familial skill? Would probably show up sometime.

"Those gardens, there are plants nowhere else in Druida City, my mother weeps—" The boy sniffed and placed crossed hands over his heart.

"She and I will talk." Johns paused. Lord and Lady knew what he could offer the woman in trade. "Maybe she'd like to harvest some of the herbs—or take cuttings—"

"Yes!" Then the boy sidled aside a pace and Johns figured the neighbors had already done a bit of harvesting or cutting. Huh.

He studied the youngster, recalled his own apprenticeship and journeyman experience. "I can talk to you and your

Master about the landscaping being a training project for educational credit."

That caused more wide eyes and another squeak. "Yeah? Yeah?"

"Yes. I'll drop off the land boundaries and maps to your house and meet your mother later?" He frowned. "What are you doing out of your training program on a summer's afternoon?"

"Master gave me the afternoon off."

"Which Master?"

The boy gave Johns a name he didn't recognize, but could contact. "Right. You have any training work to finish today?"

"No, sir." Another cheeky smile. "Only working here to show you my good will and technique."

"All right." Much as Johns didn't want to, he angled back to see his yard, let his face go impassive instead of wincing. "I have tools—"

"I have my own tools," the boy said. "I can bring them over."

"All right." Johns glanced at his timer. "Start in a quarter-septhour. Go get your tools, then come around to the side-yard gate and I'll let you in and key it to your Flair. Maybe you can plant ... stuff."

"Yes, *sir*!"

It occurred to Johns that he should ask the kid's name, but the boy had already raced away.

§⚓

Less than thirty minutes later, Johns had settled Marti Samphire with his tools in the east sideyard. Yeah, his jaw tightened when he realized that from the huge bundles of weeds Johns had yanked out, it had been in even worse shape near the gate than his back grassyard. Obviously an eyesore to the neighbors as they looked down from their second story windows. The whole place an insult to those with a botanical talent, no doubt. Tough.

Johns *had* puttered around in the house's stillroom, checking the plant no-times that kept cuttings and seeds as fresh as they went in, however many years ago. He could only hope that the seeds he found remained viable. He'd also found a long-gone forefather's design drawing of the estate, designating what should be planted where for sun and shade or whatever. Or what had been planted where. Perhaps.

He copied the map and put it back in the archival no-time, then handed copy and map over to Marti. Saw the widest eyes from the boy who then choked and whooped. Waving the papyrus, he danced around. "This is fan*tas*tic! Real ancient design and notes from *centuries* ago. Can I show my Mom? Can I show my Master?"

Waving a hand, Johns said, "Sure. The map is yours."

"*ZOW!* And the seeds. The antique seeds." He stared at the packets. "I dunno that we should use these to plant this sideyard. Dunno if the botanical gardens have such seeds archived."

"Use them," Johns said. "It's what I have."

"I dunno. Maybe we can trade them up for something equally good here."

Johns scanned the sideyard, couldn't really think what would look good.

With a frown, Marti glanced up at him. "I don't think I'll plant these seeds here just yet. Would rather talk to Mom and Master."

"All right."

"In a coupla days, we'll get plantings in for ya." Marti promised.

"Sure," Johns agreed.

"I'll head into the back and do general cleanup, weeding and chopping and trimming," the boy said with relish.

"All right. I'm hoping it will look good." Johns flicked his fingers. "Proceed. But don't interrupt me for the next, ah, fifty minutes or so."

"Why not?"

Impertinent question, but Johns answered it all the same. "I'll be taking care of the house." Cleansing and tidying spells. Or resting. Or looking at Amberose's script again. None of the kid's business.

"Oh." A pause. "Why are you getting everything nice? You gotta woman? A HeartMate? Getting married?"

Johns choked on his spit, coughed. "I—"

"Mom reads the newssheets about you and it says you're seeing the newssheet guy's sister, Morifa Daisy. She coming here?" Marti scanned the area, shook his head doubtfully. "I dunno that anything we do'll impress her, a minor noble."

But Johns had reeled back into the wall siding, an exclamation of horror emerging without thought, "No!" How could that rumor *ever* have gotten started? He'd ... ah ... he'd exchanged pleasantries with the woman in the greenroom a couple of nights back, barely said "greetyou."

Marti nodded. "Good thing you're not bringing her here. This place'll take years before it impresses anyone from noble class or somethin'." He picked up a tool, and began work, using his Flair. "So why you doin' this?"

"It was time," Johns said simply. Time, again. "Time to take care of my responsibilities."

"For sure," Marti said, "You let this go too long."

"I am aware," Johns said before he left the sideyard and went back inside to handle a good quarterly house cleansing.

No, he couldn't visualize Morifa Daisy here. She'd certainly be disdainful, and trail toxic energy onto his land and into his home.

On the other hand, despite what he'd told the Samphire boy, Johns could, *had been* thinking of bringing Giniana Filix here. Despite the fact she lived on a beautiful FirstFamily estate, she wouldn't be dismissive of his home and land.

He smiled in pleasure and checked their bond again, found her, once more, thinking of her FamCat. His lips curved down. If she stayed any amount of time with him— and his mind and body had already danced in that direction! —Giniana would bring the cat. *Both* cats would arrive with her, and Johns was all too aware what disapproving cats could do to the interior of his home.

He'd have to anticipate that, maybe go to the ritual room to handle a preventative cleansing-shielding-whatever. There must be notes from his FatherDam on deflecting cat piss, since she'd pampered and loved her miserable cat.

But not today. He'd spent too much energy already, and would need more for his actual work.

A last glance out the back windows, to see Marti working hard on the back grassyard close to the house. It already looked a thousand times better and would have taken Johns a couple of weeks to clear-up, if he'd had the desire. Well, he and Marti were glad of the trading services deal.

And as light sifted through the leaves of the large trees, he could imagine the FamCats lounging in the lower branches, maybe taking one of the buildings as their own. Maybe he could palm the pink playhouse off on them as their own place, since he preferred the other buildings.

All in all, the day had turned out well. He hoped the evening performance would, too, but didn't think he'd get the bump of excitement from feeling Giniana in the audience again. She'd be off on her own jobs.

Too bad.

But breakfast tomorrow! And definitely some loving tomorrow, maybe her afternoon break, if he had his way.

CHAPTER 15

GINIANA SET her afternoon break to begin with just enough time for her to walk from T'Spindle Residence, out the gate and across Bountry Boulevard to the public carrier plinth for the vehicle heading further into Noble Country and toward T'Willow's estate.

Unexpected jitters traveled along her nerves. She'd have to ask for something, perhaps plead. She wasn't accustomed to that, preferred to completely rely on herself. Safest.

She hated the idea of not being able to meet the price for Thrisca's treatment. Loathed that she'd circumvented Palli Willow to speak with the FirstFamily GreatLady herself.

As Giniana walked through the gate up to the colorful T'Willow castle Residence, she met D'Willow herself. A tall woman with brown hair and smoky blue eyes, the First-Family GreatLady greeted Giniana with a wonderful smile that gave Giniana hope.

D'Willow gestured to a path from the gliderway toward the neat trail that wound around the Residence.

"Let's walk outside a bit, shall we? I've been inside and embroidering on a special robe, including a bit of time in my stitches, and would like some fresh air."

"Lovely," Giniana croaked, strove to sound casual, hoped they'd move into shade so she wouldn't sweat too much. Sunlight seemed to reflect off the rich gold plastered walls of the Residence. Rather pretty, but she preferred the more subdued pale stone, smaller and more horizontal T'Spindle Residence.

She let the silence grow between them, and thought that if nerves didn't plague her so much, she'd have liked being in the presence of and walking with this woman. This woman with the odd aura that could only indicate her most unusual Flair.

As they stepped onto a narrow path between hedgerows straight and towering green on both sides that provided privacy, Giniana drew in a discreet and steady breath and said, "I am having a problem coming up with the fee, and my FamCat Thrisca is failing."

Giniana had already given Dufleur D'Willow the report that Thrisca could not be Healed from the cough, a requirement before the FirstFamily GreatLady would take a person as a patient for her Time Healing. "I wanted to talk to you about options and, perhaps, solutions."

"You aren't the first person who's contacted me personally about the time procedures and you won't be the last. I *will* find a good option for you, but you must keep this meeting between us strictly confidential."

"Of course."

"I only consider financially helping those who take the extra step of meeting with me and whose outcome of not having the time treatment will be fatal. And I'd like to hear your ideas, first."

Giniana must control her rapid pulse, slow it. "Perhaps it would be possible for you to, ah, shorten the time period between this procedure and the next, within a month, perhaps?"

"I'm very sorry, I can tell you love your FamCat very much. It's a matter of my own Flair," D'Willow stated apologetically. "You must understand, as a FirstLevel Healer, that certain great Flair workings can deplete your energy for ... well, in my case, months, after a proceeding. Though I *do* plan my sessions around Family demands, truly I am able to move several beings through time and back only on a very limited basis."

"Which is why you made your treatments at quarterly intervals," Giniana said.

"Exactly."

Giniana knew she couldn't afford a private session at all. She deliberately moved her shoulders to release tension. "Perhaps we can negotiate payment plan? I have approximately three-quarters of the fee now."

But D'Willow shook her head. "I'm sorry. My contract with my assistant, Palli, is that I make no financial arrangements. That is her provenance. I'll lose her, if I do." A regretful smile. "And she is fiercely organized, and not afraid of working with me, or time experimentation." D'Willow raised a hand and let it drop. "I went through twenty assistants in two and a half years before I found her. And she's a member of the Willow Family. I can't afford to lose her."

Well, not exchange such a gem for a favor for Giniana.

"On the other hand," D'Willow's voice lowered and she stared toward the end of the straight path, grimaced, "I think I was the most impoverished person to marry into the First-Families. I understand what it is to need gilt."

Giniana caught her breath, she hadn't known that.

"We *will* find options for you."

The hedgerows turned from groomed to spiky and thorny, like the conversation. This time D'Willow spoke first. "I know you wouldn't want me to delay this session since others are depending upon it—"

"No."

"I have other, private consultations, but, I think, I might be able to ... flex the next appointment. Can your FamCat hold onto life another month?"

Inhale and exhale. "I think so."

"We could do that, and I could charge your appointment against the annual NobleGilt the councils pay me for practicing my Flair."

Truly a solution for someone without any other remedy. "I ... I'm shocked," Giniana said.

"It would go on next year's Noble Gilt since I've fulfilled my salary for this year. In two and a half months you *would* have to show up the first day of the New Year, Samhain, say, at one minute after midnight, here at T'Willow's so the accounting would be proper."

"Yes, of course," Giniana replied faintly. She should be near swooning with relief, but the magnanimous offer didn't take her like that. She'd be breaking the rules to get something she wanted, something necessary for her FamCat.

She wouldn't be paying her way. More personally important, she'd be dragging this whole thing out by months. Her spirit quailed at that.

Get it done, get it out of the way and finished. That's what she preferred. That's what she had planned on.

And she knew herself, she'd continue to work as hard as possible to come up with as much of the gilt as possible. Pride would force her to do that. For months.

A burden she wouldn't be able to shift seemed to land on her shoulders, bowing them.

At that moment, the narrow path opened into a lovely grassyard and gardens. Two cats zoomed by, playing. Both stopped, nearly tumbled, and stared at Giniana.

She smells like FamCat, said the smaller, rounder, dappled Fam, female.

The dusty brown tabby male sat next to her. *I smell her, too, and more. FamCat is the Oldest of the Old.*

They both did the open-mouth, tongues curled sensing-action in Giniana's direction.

"Interesting," D'Willow said. "How old did you say your FamCat was?"

"I know Thrisca grew up with my FatherSire, Teris Filix."

"Oh! The great actor. We have many of his viz recordings."

"Yes."

"The oldest of the old," D'Willow murmured, looking at Giniana with the mist of time in her eyes. She valued old items and beings who'd moved through time, lived through time for years.

Turning to look at the castle-like structure of her Residence, she said, "The Willows are a largish Family, and none of the Willows have trained or are training in medicine. We could use a Healer ...." she paused, coughed delicately, "at your same rate of pay, of course."

The GreatLady's statement simply took Giniana's breath. "I ... I hadn't anticipated anything like this offer."

D'Willow waved a casual hand. "It's an option. And Thrisca would be welcome to live here, too, of course."

Perhaps more welcome than Giniana. She straightened her spine. She'd *always* given good service for the gilt paid her. "Thank you very much for your consideration. I'll think about it."

"Surely."

The woman's calendar sphere popped into existence, announcing, "Appointment with your HeartMate and T'Willow Residence in five minutes."

"I'm sorry, I need to go," D'Willow swept out an arm. "Please feel free to explore the estate and the ground floor of the Residence." She paused, studying Giniana. "If you'd like to see the suites we could offer you as the staff Healer, please speak with the housekeeper. I've already informed her of the proposal I've made to you. And, of course, my offer of employment is good until Thrisca moves into the Time Procedure Room for this next session." Again, she paused. "I think you liked that solution better than the personal appointment?

So much to think on, Giniana's mind fuzzed ... at the wrong time. "Yes, though I need to consider all you've so generously offered me."

The FirstFamily GreatLady inclined her head. "I'll need to hear within two days whether you'll want the private appointment so I can inform my other client in an acceptable manner."

"Yes." Giniana swept a deep curtsy. "And thank you for discussing this with me. I'm very honored that you would think me, and mine, acceptable to live with your Family."

With a nod and another smile, the GreatLady hurried down a more direct path toward the Residence than through the tall hedges.

Giniana stood until she noticed the deep shade of the trees cooled her too much—she *had* sweated and now that chilled unpleasantly on her skin. She crossed to a bench in the dappled light and let herself *be* instead of thinking, so she'd be able to think clearly.

Until she became aware that the two cats sat before her, ears rotated, whiskers quivering, radiating wariness at her.

I am the TIME FamCat! snapped the female, mentally. *I am Dufleur D'Thyme's FamCat. I am Queen Cat of this household.*

The male growled briefly. *I am the WILLOW FamCat, Saille T'Willow, the GreatLord, is My FamMan.* Then he stood, raised his tail high in pride, flicked it, as if knowing a serval cat, which Thrisca was, couldn't hold her tail straight up. *I am alpha and Tom Cat of the Residence and this land and everyone answers to Me.*

The female sniffed but didn't contradict him. Whatever their relationship to each other, they presented a united front to Giniana.

She answered them mildly, *I live on FirstFamily GrandLord T'Spindle's estate ...*

We don't know him, projected the cats in unison.

So he isn't important, the queen stated.

Thrisca— began Giniana.

That IS the name of the Oldest of the Old, I remember! the female informed the tom, who'd crossed to nose at the hedges now that he'd stated his dominance.

Giniana continued, *Thrisca and I do not live in the Residence where other Familiar Companions would.* So far none of the Spindles had bonded with Fam animals, though Giniana thought they were on D'Ash's waiting list for compatible Fams when intelligent creatures were born or came in from the wild. *Thrisca and I live on a cottage outside of the Residence.*

The male abandoned checking out his territory to stand before Giniana. He waved his tail back and forth. *There is no such place for peoples to live outside the Residence on My land. Outbuildings serve other purposes. All humans live IN the Residence, who cares for Us.*

"Ah," Giniana said. Her own calendar sphere pinged that she should leave now to catch the infrequent public carrier that ran through Noble Country and up into the busier part of Druida City. She stood and curtsied briefly to each FamCat in an excess of courtesy they would expect.

They watched her walk away.

Depression and grief dogged her steps as she left the Willows and boarded the vehicle. She hadn't been able to negotiate a fee and an appointment that fit in with *her* plans. How she'd anticipated that. Hubris and pride. She'd always believed that if she worked hard enough, planned intensely enough, she could solve all her problems, finesse every situation to her advantage.

Not this time. And she knew exactly what her FamCat would say in this instance: "You are young."

Giniana didn't feel young, but as if each septhour of every day weighed her down with *life*.

Deciding to take the private appointment would be sacrificing her pride, her sense of being able to provide for herself without help, provide for her family, Thrisca. Giniana didn't think she could change one of the basics of her character so quickly.

A different kind of grief went through her as she realized she loved her job, and her little house, and the Spindle estate, deeply admired the Spindles.

What she knew of the Willows impressed her too, but they were a younger, more vigorous, more intense household. More demanding, less … mellow and … sweet than the Spindles. Yet, working for the Willows *could* be a good option.

The last resort, if she failed to raise the fee before the day of the Time Healing Procedure.

Right now, Giniana would have to work harder, take every job she could, pray the Daisys would keep her on at night, and give instruction to Danith D'Ash.

She had no doubt her relationship with Johns would suffer. He'd said he'd wait for her, but she didn't *feel* he meant that. Their affair would be nipped in the bud, never to bloom.

Another sorrow. But, whatever the cost to herself, she had to save Thrisca, no matter what.

Giniana walked through T'Spindle's outer wall, and heard tiny mewing. She stopped in her weary tracks. She'd totally forgotten about the kitten.

She huddled, a minuscule rounded shape, under a thorn bush in a hollow that could only house a very small animal, one of the few remaining swatches of her long hair caught.

And her eyes appeared crusted, perhaps a delayed reaction to being healed. Or maybe not.

Giniana's heart squeezed in shame as she sank to her haunches, delicately untangled the kitten, and drew her from her hiding place.

Me waiting for My human, she projected in a cheerful tone that added guilt to Giniana's shame. This being had known so little goodness in her life! And Giniana hadn't done a follow up examination before she'd left for her appointment with D'Willow. Giniana hadn't *fed* the small cat, and she knew from her patients that kittens ate more frequently than other cats. Certainly more frequently than Thrisca.

Frowning, Giniana tried to recall what kind of food she might have for the kitten.

She cradled the kitten in both hands, vanished the eye-grit and cleansed her. The kitten sneezed as dust puffed around her small body. *Welcome back, FamWoman. Me waited long, long, LONG time for you.*

Thrisca added in a chilling tone. *I am watching door to sickroom. Man is moving around lots, opens door and looks out, sees Me and closes door. Does this time and again. No doubt his secrets press on him.*

"Oh," Giniana said aloud.

I could not watch Kitten, too. I could only hope She did not make young mistakes. She decided to explore as soon as You left.

Me DID explore. Me walked along big wall. Me sniffed interesting smells. Then fell asleep a little. Big Day!

"Yes," Giniana said. She hurried to the back of her cottage, feeling the vibration of the kitten's purr in her hands. When she got there, Thrisca rose creakily to her paws.

The kitten squirmed from Giniana's grasp and landed on

her paws. *Here is the other Cat again!* The kitten ran ahead, stopped in a small squiff of dirt when Thrisca padded out onto the path.

The kitten stared up at Thrisca. *You very old.*

You are very young, Giniana's FamCat riposted, then added, *You should hope to live to the great age that I have.*

Very big, too! The kitten's whiskers twitched.

You are small. You will never make a big Cat. And you are a standard domesticated Cat while *I* am a serval.

Then it happened. They actually sniffed in unison and a stream of cat images or language zipped between them. Giniana understood that Thrisca had demonstrated her dominance and authority over the kitten.

The kitten turned and stood side-by-side with Thrisca.

I'm sorry, Giniana projected to both of them.

You did not care for the Kitten, Thrisca accused.

I know, I'm very sorry.

Kitten is hungry. Thrisca thrashed her tail.

ME IS! the kitten caroled mentally.

Giniana crouched down, let the little cat bounce up to her, give her a couple of quick licks on her fingers. She ran her hands over the youngster again. No round tummy like a kitten should have. A too lean silhouette, like Thrisca. Giniana winced.

Greetyou, FamWoman!

She is called Giniana, Thrisca instructed. *I care for Her. She is My responsibility.*

Greetyou, Giniana, the kitten said, hopping around her. *You have a box that keeps food in the building! Me ready for more food!*

"Of course you are," Giniana murmured.

Take care of the man. I will talk more with the Kitten. Thrisca herded the little cat away from Giniana. But her FamCat's continuing disapproval lanced Giniana.

She walked up to the door, sensed the man pacing inside

the small sickroom, yet be-dewed with fever. Giniana banged on the door and ordered, "Take a waterfall, make yourself presentable, sit in the armchair. I'll be back shortly, to check on you, your linens and no-time food storage." She also set a shield on the door that he couldn't leave without alerting her.

Pivoting back to her cats, she saw Thrisca and the kitten touching noses, obviously communicating on a deeper level.

Thrisca joined Giniana, glanced up at her, whiskers twitching. *She is NOT Your Kitten. Not Your FamKitten. Will not be Your FamCat.*

"No?" Giniana asked faintly, mind scrabbling to find someone who'd take the little female. Maybe Danith D'Ash ....

She is MY kitten. Thrisca sniffed, turned and walked through the Fam door into the cottage, then sent back, *Come along, Melis. I will ensure FamWoman feeds You, and sets no-time controls for You.*

As the kitten gamboled by her, Giniana said mentally, *Greetyou, Melis kitten.*

Jumping and nearly bending double, the kitten projected, *That is My new Name!* She sounded thrilled. She hopped over Giniana's foot, sending affection, then headed through the FamDoor.

Giniana entered the cottage through the front door and meekly followed Thrisca's imperious instructions, getting food for both cats and programming the no-time to open for little Melis every two hours, upon paw-tap on the bottom of the appliance.

Melis slurped her food eagerly and Thrisca ate steadily and well.

This could be very good for Thrisca. Or very, very bad for the kitten.

CHAPTER 16

AT THAT MOMENT banging came on the back wall of the cottage, along with a short shout. "I'm here and I'm ready to talk!"

Her male patient sounded bull-headed and arrogant, but Giniana sensed a spike in his fever. She touched the scrystone linked to the sickroom. "I'm coming."

"I'm ready!" he reiterated.

Thrisca grunted. *We will come when We are done with Our food.*

Giniana preferred they didn't, but said nothing.

Muzzle still in bowl, Thrisca advised, *Ask him about his secrets.*

"I don't think—"

Best for ALL of Us, Me and Melis and You and Spindles.

"All right." Giniana left the house and walked around to the sickroom, knocked politely on the door.

"Come in!"

He sat slumped in the cushiony armchair, his weedy body covered only in the standard loose trous Giniana had provided. She checked the temp and the freshness of the atmosphere, left the door open and thinned the window glass to swirl a breeze through the small room.

Yes, she sensed he remained solidly in the third stage of the sickness.

She removed new linens from a corner cupboard and remade the bed with bespelled and herb infused coverings, sent the old sheets to the deep sanitary cleanser.

Translocating a Healing and soothing mixture, she handed it to him. He grimaced, then stood up, swayed. She put her hand out, but he scowled at her, angled away from her to cross to the bed and fall sitting onto it, wiggled against the newly plumped pillows.

We are here, announced Melis, sitting on the step outside the open door with Thrisca.

Giniana's FamCat sniffed. Melis sniffed a few seconds later.

Note the smell, Kitten, Thrisca said, doing the open-mouthed, curled-tongue sense. *The man smells of secrets he hides.*

Thrisca stared at Giniana. *Ask the man his secret.*

"So, what secrets do you have?" Giniana asked casually, as soon as he lowered the potion tube.

Narrowing his eyes, his mouth flattened before he answered. "I had, *had,*" he emphasized bitterly, then rushed his words, "a very important … document. Originally, then it was stolen from a person I lent it to, then the thieves contacted me to see if I wanted the thing back and of course I did and we were supposed to meet during the party here … that night, whenever that was, and I was supposed to get it, but they were stupid enough to fliggering try to rob gliders and teleported away." He paused for breath. "I'd have believed they lied and set me up for a fool, but I found that …" He pointed to the papyrus page she'd set on his bedside table, frowned. "It's still all crumpled up and dirty." Raising his brows, he looked back at her.

"It seemed important to you, and none of my business."

A couple of heavy breaths of silence. "Oh. Thanks"

But a chill shot down Giniana's spine and spread outward. What had he done? What had *she* done in harboring him? "Did *you* let the thieves into the estate to meet you and give them money? Those evil men who wrecked the Spindles' pleasure in their party?"

"What? No! They just said they'd meet me here!" he yelped. Since sweat now beaded his face and he'd gone pale, Giniana believed him.

His chest compressed in a big sigh. His fingers relaxed and the potion tube fell from them onto the bed, then dropped onto the floor and rolled.

Giniana bent down to pick up the tube, cleaned the floor of the last spattering of liquid, and translocated the tube back to the deconstructor.

And by the time she'd straightened, he'd grabbed the papyrus and began smoothing it out, muttering. "Must find any and all of the pages that they lost here before or during that damned party. *Must*, Lord and Lady help me, or I'm doomed!" Then he vanished.

Giniana gasped. The man had teleported away. She sensed he hadn't gone far, but he'd used energy that should have been saved for his body's Healing. She hadn't realized he'd been so close to tipping into delirium. Because she'd tended the cottage and his external needs and responded to her own curiosity and her FamCat's prompting instead of personally examining him. *Stup!*

Hide and seek, Thrisca said sardonically, as aware as Giniana that she'd made a beginner's mistake.

Me find him! Me, Me, Me will FIND him. SEEK! trilled Melis in a loud telepathic tone. She hopped from the threshold down the drop, for her, of the step and zoomed off.

I think She is a good Mouser and I can make her better, Thrisca stated, trotting after *her* kitten.

They found the man quickly. He held three more sheets of papyrus. Obviously he'd had a connection with this important document.

A few minutes later, Giniana had examined him and settled him back in bed, double-checked the infirmary and shielded it.

Back in her own beloved private space, she put kibble out for the cats. Thrisca had actually munched a few bites along with the kitten.

Giniana's calendar sphere pinged and she jumped in surprise.

Time for you to go to Residence and work, Thrisca stated, sitting and licking her paw. *We will watch closed door of sickroom outside, and slink and hunt, and listen to man inside with our Cat senses and I will teach My kitten much, much, much.*

"Uh-huh." Giniana noted the kitten on the arm of a chair Thrisca would have to walk by to the door, ready to pounce. Of course Thrisca knew the kitten's position, too.

Settling into her balance, Giniana did a brief cycle of breathing and meditation. The afternoon break-visit with D'Willow had discombobulated Giniana, set her mind scrambling for some sort of decision as to the options she'd been given. Her subconscious hummed and her emotions rolled from gratitude to irritation at herself, to weariness at the thought of keeping going so long and hard for a couple of months.

She could do it.

She could do anything to save her FamCat, and the kitten who now bonded so closely with Thrisca. But there would be personal costs. Perhaps scrapings of her pride, but also her budding relationship with Johns.

❦

Johns woke from a deep nap featuring himself onstage and standing in front of the curtain after Amberose's play, bowing to wild applause. In real life, his agent rang on his perscry. Disappointing.

He caught the scry before it went to his message cache.

"Yeah," he answered, scrubbing hands over his face before staring into the pebble on his bedside table.

"Checking in," his agent, Chatt, said. "I know you like to be kept apprised on a regular basis."

"Any nibbles?" Johns asked, not sure whether he really wanted a new play or not, since he *did* want to star in Amberose's missing one.

"Not yet. I heard you dropped by the Theatrical Guild."

"Yeah, want people to see me, keep me in mind. Best to do that in person."

"Right. And, ah …" Chatt's face was strained. "Heard you breakfasted with Lily Fescue at the Thespian Club this morning."

Oh, Chatt trying not to laugh. Johns let his own expression go impassive, then forced one side of his mouth up in an amused quirk he didn't mean. "Yeah. Funny fox."

Chatt snorted. "Yes, from what I heard."

"He, not I, got my breakfast," Johns said lightly, though that still stung. Narrowing his eyes at Chatt, he wondered what his agent had heard about Amberose, her new play, what the guy thought. But Chatt didn't only represent Johns. And Johns wasn't the agent's most important male client, who'd also love the plum role.

Still, Johns wanted to star in that play, and to do that, he'd have to find the script...or talk to Amberose, and he sure wasn't at *that* point yet. Quit floundering!

Not a totally honest face to Chatt because he didn't want

Chatt to see how much he desired the part. Casual. He translocated an empty caff mug from the kitchen below for a prop, pretended to drink from it. "I was approached by an agent saying he repped Amberose. Had a script with a part written for me."

Chatt snorted, hurting Johns's feelings, but the guy didn't realize that and said, "I'd heard some second-rate agent was making the rounds. He didn't approach *me* to talk about talent." Chatt flicked his hand. "Speaking with actors himself as a representative of a playwright? That is *not* professional." An exaggerated shrug, spread of hands, "*And* I heard the reason this Blakely Wattle did so was that Amberose insisted on having full artistic control of the production." Chatt snorted again. "As if she was a producer, not just the playwright."

"Might be why she chose a second-rate agent. A first-rate one might not want to try and peddle a script with such strings attached."

Chatt's brows rose. "Perhaps. If this Blakely Wattle really does represent her. If she really *has* written a new script. In *my* professional opinion, that is unlikely. *Ppphhhttt.*" He ended with a rude noise and a wave of his hand.

Johns rolled a shoulder. "Might be true, a new script."

But Chatt shook his head. "You just want that because *Firewalker*'s run is coming to an end. And it would have to be a *brilliant* script for Amberose to get her way with any sort of input on the cast from one of the standard producers here in Druida City." He pursed his lips. "Or even those smaller producers in Gael City."

Johns's gut churned as if he'd really drunk some black stomach-lining-eating caff. His hopes had been high. But he'd also seen the script. The truly brilliant script—in the places he was sure Lily Fescue recalled correctly.

"Later!" Chatt said and signed off.

Yeah, Chatt made a couple of salient points, but that hardened Johns's determination to find the script, figure out if he could put it in good hands. He'd read pieces of the play and wanted to act the role.

Strolling over to the no-time in his sitting room to get a real cup of caff, he wondered how much Amberose wanted to see her work produced—come to life outside the words on papyrus. After ten years, how hungry for that would she be? How interested in compromising her artistic vision? Johns sure didn't want her to compromise on who she liked to play the lead.

He sipped his caff, considered, then scried Amberose's agent and got nothing. After a bit of hesitation, Johns left a message for the man to call him.

Glancing at the timer, he began preparing for his evening work, but put in a quick scry to Lily Fescue. She appeared pleased she'd hooked him on trying to find the script. But she had no information on Blakely Wattle and said she'd leave the whole matter in Johns's capable hands. Since, of course, she was still working in her own long-running play.

The Wattle guy had been at T'Spindle's party, so he'd have button-holed that wealthy lord to produce, and Johns reckoned the lord would have brushed the agent off and moved on to whatever next project interested that First-Family Lord. Easy-going or not, he'd want control of the production he put gilt into. No use trying to contact T'Spindle, or asking Raz Cherry do that, since he knew the lord better.

Mouth turning down sourly, Johns knew there was no chance in talking to the producer of his current play, *Firewalker*. Not only had the man forfeited Johns's good will by closing a profitable play, but Johns wondered about the guy's intelligence. Sad but true.

Who else might have heard of the script? Bought it? *Found*

it? Johns couldn't fathom the answer, but he could keep his ears pricked for any rumors on the topic, and he would.

During a half-shift at AllClass HealingHall that evening, Giniana's perscry rang at a rare non-busy moment when she could spare time to answer it.

Johns looked out at her, garbed in his *Firewalker* costume, with stage makeup and spell enhancements magnifying his features.

Her heart squeezed, thumped hard in her chest. First at the sight of his rugged attractiveness, then in near revulsion at the recollection of seeing her parents with theater enhancements.

He *was* an actor, a pretender, and she should remember that. What was she was doing, mooning over him? Considering a relationship with an actor?

But his eyes lit as she accepted his call, and when he smiled, it went to her heart, pumping up her pulse, and through their link she sensed his sincere pleasure at speaking with her.

And she remembered their kisses.

He'd given her joyful moments in a life currently congested with dreadful decisions and lingering sorrow.

She needed to work to gain gilt to pay for Thrisca's treatment. But should she deny herself all joy to do that? If she'd been consulted as a Healer by a person with her symptoms of exhaustion, what would she advise? What scrip of Healing would she write?

To choose joy.

Naturally, she'd been considering whether to meet him for breakfast the next morning. A bond already linked them since she could feel his emotions. Though she thought she revealed less to him, he might be able to figure hers out, especially now they began to know each other better. Despite his rough and tough appearance, he was sensitive to emotions, and not only hers.

He continued to observe others for his craft. She even thought he might have an internal file on *her* where he kept her reactions to Healing, her professional expressions and gestures and language.

"Giniana?" he caressed her name.

She blinked. "Yes?"

"Just checking on you." He smiled. "I'm about to go on, and after that I have the green room." He pulled a face as if he didn't care for networking after a performance, or the praise people would gush at him that he didn't quite believe.

He continued, "So this is my last chance to speak to you before you leave for your work. I'll see you a little after dawn for breakfast at the Thespian Club." Though he smiled, his gaze had sharpened as if daring her to cancel that appointment.

She smiled weakly.

"You have to eat," he reminded in a brusque tone.

"Yes." She paused, recalled the ancient good luck phrase for actors, all the way back from Earth. "Break a leg."

A quick grin. "If I do, I'll call you." With fingertips he blew her a kiss. "Tomorrow, sweeting."

He logged off as she realized that he'd called her by a pet name and her heart compressed again. She couldn't recall the last time or the last person who'd done that. Or maybe it was her father before he'd abandoned his family and she didn't want to remember the hurt.

Me hungry! You can open the no-time for food! the kitten, Melis, danced into Giniana's small mainspace and hopped over her toes to get her moving.

So Giniana turned her mind and emotions to the companionship of cats.

The next morning, Giniana passed the care of the Daisy baby girl back to her parents and waved goodbye to them as the blue-white sun rose over the horizon, spilling summer light across the city.

Even as she told herself to take the public carrier home to her cottage on T'Spindle estate, she waited to board the vehicle going to the Theater District.

Once at the edge of the grand plaza, she didn't need to think about how to get to the Thespian Club, merely recall a few turnings from the main carrier stop to the place. As the daughter of two full-time actors, one of whom came from a generational acting Family, her father had purchased her a lifetime membership the day she'd been born. She hadn't bothered with the paperwork to repudiate her association here, that would have revealed more bitterness than she wanted to acknowledge.

All too soon she stood under the half-round blue canvas awning in front of the building. Glancing at her wrist timer, she saw that she'd arrived ten minutes before her appointment with Klay St. Johnswort, and wondered again why she'd let him convince her to meet him for breakfast. The door opened as a trio of giggling young women exited. They eyed her up and down, then dismissed her as any kind of competition in their profession.

Giniana wished she'd worn Healer colors. That would have garnered her more respect. And why should she care? Touchy after the long night with a fussy baby?

No, wary at being here. She dragged in a breath to the bottom of her lungs and her nostrils caught the scent of actors, a mix of perfume and aftershave, a hint of makeup, and the underlying sizzle of a thousand enhancement spells. A wave of reluctance and sorrow lodged with the air in her lungs and she let it out in a whoosh. If she left, she'd consider herself a coward.

One old hurt to newly face that she'd never anticipated before she'd met Johns a few days ago.

So another large breath and she walked toward the double smoky-glass doors. The threshold spell swung open the portal before she reached it, and she strode in with a confident air she'd learned in her own profession, then moved into the main lounge.

CHAPTER 17

GLANCING AROUND, she saw that the Thespian Club didn't look any different than it had since the last time she'd been in it with her mother, more than a decade ago. Giniana's stomach pinched at the sight of the shabby elegance, slightly flaking gold tint over cheap wood, excellent but worn furniture handed down from the Residences of arts patrons. All more surface elegance than real. Like actors themselves.

An old man rose from a comfort chair beside, not behind, a long and glossy wooden counter on her left. After blinking a few seconds, a smile broke over his face and he came toward her, offering his hands. "GentleLady Filix, it's been so long since we saw you!"

She took his hands, memories falling through her, and replied, "It's good to see you, Hudson. You were always a cheerful note in my life." She spoke the truth, let a real smile unfurl from her heart.

"Are you finally fulfilling your talent?" he demanded with a falsely fierce scowl.

Laughing, she squeezed his hands and let them go. "You know I never had much acting talent. But, yes, I have a lovely career. As a Healer. I work for the Spindles."

"That's wonderful."

They beamed at each other and the outside doors opened again and a gust of wind swirled. A male couple entered, older character actors that she couldn't name because though she'd seen them on stage, they hadn't been part of her parents' glittering set. They nodded to her and she nodded back, then one continued with his conversation, voice an amused gurgle "—yes, yesterday morning, *on* the table where Johns and that Lily Fescue sat." The men laughed, crossed the lobby and went through the door to the dining room.

Giniana raised her brows at Hudson, ready for a tale. He appeared pained—his outer expression when his eyes showed amusement—as much an actor as the people he served.

But before he could speak, the doors opened again, bringing the scent of Klay St. Johnswort. The fact she knew that fragrance shocked her. She composed herself before she turned.

"Greetyou, Hudson," Johns said.

"Greetyou, Johns," the man replied, his smile widening as Johns took Giniana's hands, raised them to his lips, and kissed the back of each one. After he released them, he set his fingers at the small of her back, causing tingles.

"This is your companion for your reserved table for two, Johns?" Hudson asked.

Johns's spine went straighter. "Yes."

"Very good. I'll lead you to it." Hudson pivoted on his heel and walked toward the dining room.

Giniana followed with Johns, but she could only prevent herself from satisfying her curiosity, along with a twinge of jealousy, until Hudson ushered them into the dining room. "You were here yesterday morning with Lily Fescue?" she asked casually, looking around the dining room, not at Johns.

A surge of irritation pulsed from him and his expression soured. "Business meeting with..." He glanced around, stopped speaking aloud and sent the rest telepathically down their personal channel. *Lily Fescue, one of the most annoying actors in the business. If she isn't trying to manipulate you, she's spreading negativity all over the theater in which you're working with her.*

More people came in and milled around, greeting Johns and looking at her with questioning gazes.

Johns took her elbow, and she liked the size and warmth of his fingers, the steadiness of his grip. He'd keep her from unbalancing in a crowd, and he'd stop her from falling, as he had before. Supporting her physically, at least.

Dared she think he'd be a source of emotional support, too?

"Big drama yesterday," he said aloud.

People laughed. "Everyone heard about the FoxFam and how he ate your meal, Johns," a woman teased.

"After he threw Lily Fescue into a tizzy," an older actor said dryly.

They clumped together and moved to their table, repeating variations of the story.

One man glanced back at her and Johns, sent an edged smile toward Johns. "I've heard the kitchen here has adopted the FoxFam as a mascot."

"Just great," Johns muttered. He glanced at Giniana. "I'll expect you to keep him in line if he shows up."

She tilted her head at him and smiled. "Be glad to."

"Thanks," he replied, but he seated her stiffly.

"You said yesterday you had an incident with a FoxFam?"

He took his own seat, whipped the fancily folded softleaf on his plate onto his lap, sent her a hard look from steel gray-blue eyes even as his smile curved for outward show for others. That shocked her a little, since he seemed to have been completely honest with her before. But that was privately. And not in a room with his colleagues who watched him—them.

Johns said, "A large steak, prime quality, gone before I had more than a bite, not to mention the rest of the meal."

Giniana winced. "Expensive." She could relate.

"Yes."

And she felt him tamp down irritation, pull up a calmness to replace the negative emotion and that impressed her. This time when he smiled, it was sincere … and ironic. "I've never found Fam animals worth the trouble they cause."

Well, the very cute and smart kitten he'd rescued now belonged with Thrisca, and that would have come *after* the fox had munched his costly breakfast. Giniana had the notion that when he'd been alone with Thrisca, the FamCat hadn't been nice to him. His viewpoint appeared rational to him, and skewed to her, a discrepancy that they'd have to work to overcome, if he couldn't accept Thrisca and Melis.

Or Thrisca couldn't accept Johns.

The waiter came by—probably a young out-of-work actor —and Johns ordered a modest meal as she did.

To keep them both occupied with pleasant conversation, she asked about the other people in the room whom she vaguely recognized. Johns flashed her a quick grin and began telling brief stories about each—and none of those stories contained mean elements or self-absorption on his part. Once again the bond between them flowed even and steady with attraction and as she relaxed she spiraled into desire.

They ate, and dealt with the occasional visit of someone who wished to greet Johns or her or them both. Each time she informed them that she followed her mother's family's career as a Healer and worked for T'Spindle, the individuals relaxed, obviously pleased with the news, and that a new competitor hadn't entered the Druida City theatrical scene. That reminded her that her parents, both of them, *had* talent. Her father had abandoned the family for his own career in Chinju, her mother had preferred an easier life of being kept.

Giniana really had to accept that.

Once again alone, and their plates clean, she sat watching Johns, reluctantly aware she should be standing up to leave and walk to the public carrier line for a vehicle home to T'Spindle's estate.

Her perscry rippled the Spindle tune. Johns withdrew his hand from her fingers.

"Greetyou, Healer Filix," the Captain of the Spindle guards, an older but fit man, said.

"Greetyou."

"I am calling to cancel your first two annual examinations of my guards this morning. I'm sorry, but my guards and I are due at the Druida City guardhouse with regard to the continuing investigation of the burglaries and vandalism three nights ago."

"I understand. We can re-schedule those physical exams the first week of next month if that is agreeable with you and your guards?"

"Yeah. Pretty sure our part of the investigation will be done shortly, but I know you've got your own schedule for the staff exams. I'll check my rosters and we'll get everything figured out."

"Of course," Giniana agreed.

"Later, Healer," he said.

"Later, Captain." Giniana ended the scry.

Glancing at Johns, she found his expression set in stone, but emotions roiled through their bond.

"You don't need to be at work for a while," he stated, his look searing.

"No," she whispered, suddenly not nearly as tired as she had been.

His nostrils widened, and this time she believed the pure lust he sent down their link was intentional, and her own body reacted.

Her heart beat fast, she became aware of the extreme sensitivity of her skin, how she wanted his hands on her, sliding along that skin, skimming nerves pleasurably. Her nipples had tightened, along with her core. All from a bond she hadn't formed with any other man ... ever. She swallowed.

His eyes darkened from smoke blue to a deeper shade. "Upstairs," he gritted. "There are a few private rooms for rent."

Air stopped in her lungs. She met his dark and hungry gaze, and desire ignited between them. "Yes."

With deliberate motions, Johns folded his cloth softleaf, set it on the table, rose and strode with that intent and gliding step toward her, stood behind her chair waiting for her to rise. When she did, he removed it with the grace of a trained waiter ... or an actor who'd played waiters ... but the thought didn't bring the usual bitterness.

Instead she sipped shallow breaths due to the heated atmosphere between them. She stepped one pace away from the chair. Johns hard arm came around her waist, his *presence* seemed to curve around her, protective, possessive.

She barely noted amused and knowing glances, the upturn of busy conversation as they walked from the dining room, through a hallway to the club lounge, across the faded red carpet to the counter. Hudson stood there, and behind him she noticed keys hanging on a board.

"Hudson, are there any rooms available?" Johns asked in a strained voice.

Heat washed through her at the grit of his words, his yearning cycling to her and back again.

"The personal parlor suite is open until this evening," Hudson said, eyes glinting with approval.

Lady and Lord. Giniana flushed more, embarrassed at

their obvious desire, but not enough to stop her body from leaning toward Johns.

Not so much that she minded people knowing she'd be taking Johns as a lover.

"Put the rent for it on my account," Johns said. When he held out his hand for the spellkey, delight swirled through Giniana as she noticed his hand shook.

A few minutes later they'd trod upstairs to a lush suite that appeared to be more of a stage setting than a place Giniana actually ever expected to stay in ... or have sex in. Though the furnishings inspired sensuality. The thickest carpets she'd walked on in the club, the richest jewel toned colors. A curved settee of ruby velvet with sapphire silkeen and dull gold pillows. The bed in the next room canopied with layered swags of rose and pale peach and dull gold.

The bedsponge looked thickly sumptuous, ready to cradle lovers' bodies, letting them revel in the erotic arts. And when Johns bent his head to her neck, kissing, nibbling, swells of heat and need swamped her and her mind shut down.

She turned in his arms, pressed against him, felt the strength—and tension—of muscle and sinew. A fabulous physical specimen of a man. And all hers to play with.

Achingly aware of the thick length of his sex against her, and how her body dampened, readying for sex, for him, for *Johns*, she ran her hands up his tunic, murmuring an "undress" spell and nearly swooned as his shirt fell from his body. His scent rose to her then, the faint musk of perspiration, and some earthy herb.

Her hands stroked his chest, feeling the rough softness of his hair, skimming his beads of nipples and he jerked. She kept going, to arouse him more, to hear the fast, unsteady panting of him, feel the uneven rise and fall of his chest, know she excited him with every feathering of her fingertips.

Felt her own body clench with desire, with the need to be

filled and fulfilled.

She leaned in and ran her tongue along his clenched jaw.

He broke.

He lifted her and tossed her on the bed. Should she have expected that? She gasped mid-air.

And she saw sparkles flickering from his hands. "Disrobe!"

Her body flashed heat from inside, shooting out. Her clothes fell away. She landed on the soft bedcover. How did he do that spell? Her turn to pant.

He prowled toward her, face tight, stern. Looking nothing like his character in the play before he kissed the heroine. All Giniana's.

Before he reached the bed, the rest of his clothing split along the seams, he stepped out of shoes and liners and her gaze focused on a fully aroused, virile man.

Blood pounded in her ears. She moved her right leg, opening herself to him.

His gaze slipped to her damp sex, but yanked back up to meet her own eyes, his stare burning. The lust throbbing through their bond didn't only hold physical sexuality, but more, a hunger for intimacy on a level she didn't know she could give.

But which he demanded.

Then he leaned over her, grabbed her shoulders and lifted her from the bed, no Flair involved, pure strength. She twined her arms around his neck, her legs loosely around his waist. Closed her eyes as his lips touched hers, his tongue penetrated her mouth to rub on hers, her breasts flattened against his chest, her nipples sensitive to the slight abrasion of his chest hair.

He changed his grip, sliding her down, then surged up and into her, and she cried out at the sheer pleasure of connection.

Lord and Lady, he felt so good inside her! Sensation ruled. She craved movement. Action, tilted her hips, began a rhythm, pleasuring herself with him.

Feeling the buzz of hot passion sizzling through them, only shocks of delicious sexuality reverberating, physically, emotionally ...

He rumbled something she didn't hear, only felt through their bodies meeting ... mating ... then fell backward onto fresh-smelling and cool linens.

Finally he began to thrust and instead of holding on tightly, she spread herself wide, arms, legs, so he could take as well as give and she lay open to all, saturated with mounting bliss, rising, rising ... shattering.

His shout of climax and release, his body bowing on hers. Too much. She orgasmed again, sounds of her own wrenching delight escaping her lips.

Then they settled, entwined, in the shining golden summer light radiating through the room, and through her and both of them, through their bond. She lay there, peaceful, satisfied.

He filled her, covered her, breadth and length and weight. And for the first time in her memory she felt enveloped by someone who'd care for her. Protect her.

Support her and keep her safe on all levels.

Her breath caught at that. Someone else providing for her. Shades of her mother.

Stupid to feel he'd tend to her. But his scent wisped to her and derailed more thought and tears pushed to the back of her eyes.

Stupid to be so emotional, wanting someone to cherish her.

Stupid to bond so much with this man.

But the sheer relief of the comfort emanating from him, sinking into her skin, muscles, even bones, slipped her into sleep.

Lazily he soaked up the warmth of the summer's day, listened to birdsong and insect chirps, spooned against his new lover. A perfect moment in his life. One he'd remember always.

Though he'd rather, of course, engage in more incredible sex moments ... as soon as he revived. But for this perfect moment, he experienced simple satisfaction.

Until he sensed depression smirching her dozing mind. Not acceptable. So, he pulled her against him, enjoying the softness of her body, her too slender body, under his palms, and nudged her mind awake.

"I need to return to T'Spindle's," she murmured sleepily, released a deep sigh. "Or try to pick up a half-shift at a HealingHall."

He tensed, made himself relax immediately. "Well, I got some food in you. I guess your gilt situation hasn't been resolved?"

"No." She sounded fully awake now.

"I'd help you—"

"No!" She did more than flinch against him, she thrashed away and out of his arms.

"—if I could," he ended, though he would raid his savings for her. Foolish notion. Stup. Giving gilt to a new lover. But she impressed him as honest. More than honesty, her pride wouldn't allow her to take from him. He understood that.

And she'd stopped her rolling motion away from him, or onto her side to face him, he didn't know. Instead, she scooted back to their previous position, but the perfect moment had cracked and fallen away. Now he held a fully awake woman in his arms.

"Your show is ending," she said.

"Like I told you before," he continued lightly, "I have savings." He suffused his voice with enthusiasm, "And I have prospects."

"Prospects? Truly?"

"Yes. I take it your conversation with D'Willow did not go well?"

"Not as planned, no, though *I* have options." Her voice cooled, shutting that topic down.

He didn't press, just stroked her side, the curve of her hip, the top of her thigh with his hand. Not sexually, but soothing.

"New prospects?" she asked.

"Let me tell you." And he did, in an upbeat tone, from the meeting with the agent at T'Spindle's party and the mystery of the theft and loss of the script and the missing agent.

But most of all the pride expanding his bruised ego that *the* major playwright of generations had written a script for *him*. And when his shaft began to stir once more, he withdrew from his superb lover because he knew that her sense of duty wouldn't allow another bout.

He rolled out of bed, rubbed at his chest, glanced down at the delightfully tousled—*wild*—looking Giniana Filix. Until now, he hadn't truly noted that she'd been extremely tidy. But most Healers exemplified that trait.

Sending a longing glance at the luxurious waterfall room, since she wouldn't join him or stay while he actually washed, he gritted his teeth and said a gentlemanly cleansing spell that really scoured parts of him he preferred to have a gentle touch. But it used the least amount of Flair and didn't flagrantly wave those parts around in an embarrassing fashion.

Then he picked up his clothes and began to dress without spells to stretch out the time with her.

CHAPTER 18

GINIANA STARED AT HIM, her face a full frown, looking prepared to reject him again, so Johns spoke, "You still need to eat," he said lightly.

She gave him a straight look. "I don't think either of us can afford breakfast at the Thespian Club every day."

He paused in his dressing. Since her gaze lingered on his body, he'd gone slowly. "No," he replied, carefully keeping the immediate reaction of insult from showing in manner, expression, voice. Reminded himself that he'd already planned to drop the breakfasts as too expensive. "We can meet for caff, or I can bring snacks to share for your morning break. Or lunch to you on my days off."

"You'd come to me?"

He wanted to say, "always," but that sounded too intense and a touch desperate—more desperate than he wanted to acknowledge to himself. He shouldn't want to be with her this much. He peeked at their bond. *That* shouldn't have been as strong and thick and reciprocal in this amount of time. Nothing like the puny links he'd developed with previous lovers. Should scare him silly, but it didn't. He'd fallen too far, too fast, he supposed, and now only needed to hit the unforgiving ground with a thud. Later, much later.

And he stood staring at her too long. "Yes, of course," he said, adding. "Currently my schedule is more flexible than yours."

A slow nod from her. She sat up and his gaze went to the soft sway of her breasts. Very nice.

"How are you for time today, for other meals?" she asked

His heart gave a hard thump. "Morning is free. Matinee and evening performance so my mealtimes will be odd. No rehearsals." He grimaced. "Owner has cut rehearsal time, too. If we want to rehearse, it's on our own time and without pay and not in the theater. Stup."

"I think," she said deliberately. "I've found your missing agent."

That rocked his balance a bit and he had to steady himself. "What?"

"He's a sick man in my infirmary behind my cottage."

"I need to—"

She lifted her hand. "He's *sick*. Perhaps tomorrow he'll be able to talk."

He sucked in and let out a breath, now his mind surged with thought, he could figure out how the whole situation had occurred. "You'll check on him? Perhaps he'll be able to say something about the script later this morning? I could come over."

"Naturally, I'll check on him as soon as I reach home, but if he'd fallen into a deeper fever, Thrisca would have notified me sometime during the night, and she didn't. You may come tomorrow," she said firmly, slid from bed.

His mouth might have fallen open at the sight of her beauty, but he didn't think he drooled. To get more blood in his brain, he picked up her garments. As he straightened, he flicked each out, murmuring a cleanse and smooth spell.

She said a couplet to wash herself with actual water—a trick he didn't know and would have taken too much of his Flair.

He lay her clothes on the bed, was torn between having her check on the health of Blakely Wattle and being with her longer. He crossed to the no-time, scanned the selections, wondering what he could offer that might keep her from leaving. "There's pie."

She paused before pressing the last tab closed on her tunic, hand at her left shoulder. "Pie?"

He waggled his brows, swept a hand toward the no-time appliance, gestured to the small table set for an intimate meal for two next to the window looking down on a pretty side flower garden. "Several flavors."

After finishing dressing, she joined him at the no-time, read the flavors and chose a mixed fruit pie that struck him as being far too healthy. He took out a warm sweet nut pie, himself. Plenty of work to keep him active today.

She sat, relaxed yet vibrant, and he congratulated himself on pleasing her out of bed as much as between the linens.

Pouring fragrant amber tea into delicate cups, she smiled at him and said, "Thank you, Johns."

And it struck him that he wanted his given name on her lips, from her more than anyone else in the world. "Call me Klay."

"Klay?"

"Please." He added quietly, "I may be 'Johns' to everyone else, but I'd like you to call me 'Klay.'"

"Should I be honored?"

He shrugged. "If you want." He matched her gaze and revealed a further truth. "It can be lonely when no one you know, not even your best friends, call you by your given name."

She inhaled harshly, coughed, sipped tea. The motion

almost hid the flattening of her lips. He angled his head. "Don't you have good friends?"

"I have Thrisca and the kitten, of course."

"Of course," he echoed.

"I'm not lonely!" she protested.

He kept his mouth shut.

"Fam bonds are important," she said.

It stabbed him that she'd bonded more with an animal companion than himself. He felt the hurt, let it go. He dredged up a smile. "Most of my friends are actors, and some are also friendly competitors, like Raz Cherry."

She nodded and they ate their pie in comfortable silence. He refrained from pressing her about human friends because he'd been totally honest with her. He liked being honest with everyone, but some people would only use that to manipulate him, so he put on a mask. Being with Giniana where he was completely himself was special. Restful, even.

When only a few crumbs littered their plates, they rose. He took her hand and they both glanced at the bed, the table, the rest of the suite. Yes, absolutely used, but not awful, and not their job to clean up, especially for the cost.

They were in accord in their feelings. Good.

Once on the street, he squeezed her hand as her public carrier glided up to the stop. She met his eyes as he'd wanted. "I *will* continue to speak with you every day." He tried out a lopsided smile and liked how her lips curved in response. "And we'll see if I can manage a meal with you, at least, every day."

To his surprise, she lifted on her toes and kissed him. "Maybe." Then she left.

He was on the carrier and close to home when she pinged him on his perscry pebble and told him Blakely Wattle wanted to speak with him.

Unfortunately, he was met by the Fams.

Johns's gut tightened as he walked up to T'Spindle guard-house, sensed the animals coming along Giniana's path to meet him.

Two Fams. Two Fam*Cats*. Great. But he had face to save before the guards, so he'd use his acting skills.

He'd learned from others that people who dealt often with Fams tolerated the intelligent animals more than Johns did. Others actually *liked* them. Including the T'Spindle guards.

He suspected Giniana wanted him to like them, too, and sent these two to try and charm him, maybe. His previously rare contact with Familiar animal companions seemed to be over. Maybe he could endure such intelligent Fams. In any event, if he continued his relationship with Giniana, he would have to learn to get along with Thrisca and the kitten.

He stopped near the front gate to identify himself and explain his visit. Before the Spindle guards opened the wall door for him, the kitten capered under the greeniron gate and cavorted around his feet. He'd trip if he moved, so he stood still.

I remember You! she squealed loudly enough mind-to-mind that the guards smiled. *You helped Me in the alley and brought Me to My new home and Fam who teaches Me much! You acceptable man.*

He'd freed the trapped kitten, damn well saved that kitten's sight, perhaps her life. Did she mention that? No.

"Greetyou," he acknowledged.

I am now called MELIS. I am part of an Important Family, she said. *Thrisca told Me. We are all very important. We live in the cottage and We help the Healer Giniana and We try out new toys. Thrisca says We are the BEST FamCats in Druida City. But I KNEW that!*

A Spindle guardswoman coughed, obviously covering a laugh, waved him into the estate.

Johns nodded to her and said, "Thank you." Then, two paces in, Thrisca sat regally in the middle of the path.

The kitten hopped onto his shoes—as he walked—leaving scratches through the polish and damaging the leather. She swarmed up his trous before he got her, hooked her claws into his shirt, no doubt leaving tiny holes.

Thrisca rumbled a loud purr. *Melis welcomes You, as I do!* She strode over to strop his legs, depositing a goodly amount of beige hair on his black trous. Squinting, he saw a thick mat or two, and sniffed a hint of cat piss from them.

Definitely should have studied up on Fam spells. He would when he got home. Maybe change all his Giniana-visiting clothes to beige.

Right now, he inclined his head to Thrisca. "Please remove your stinky mats from my trous." She appeared clean and he wondered if she'd saved the mats just for him, to irritate him. He wouldn't put it past her.

She glared.

"All right, I'll let your FamWoman take care of my trous, use her Flair and spells and time and energy …"

Thrisca arched, and extended her claws on one lifted paw. The mats fell away. Left an odor, though. *You are not worthy of MY FamWoman,* she sent mentally.

"Probably not," Johns agreed. "But while you're causing trouble for her, I'm trying to support her. She's doing all this extra work for *you.* What are you doing for her?"

Melis moved across his shoulder to head-butt his cheek. When he turned to look into big eyes, she said, *We must do something for Our FamWoman?*

"Be nice to her. Obey her quickly when she asks you to do something—"

Thrisca snorted.

"*Respect* her."

The kitten's eyes got rounder. *I LOVE her!*

"Then you want to make things easier for her, right?" He hesitated, probably not a good idea to point out that Thrisca might move on to the Wheel of Stars and Giniana might need help with her grief. He got the notion the kitten had already bonded well with Thrisca. For sure the little one's language had already improved.

He didn't know how FamCats thought about death, and, frankly, didn't want to learn.

Thrisca turned and began walking the path to the Healer's cottage. Johns followed.

Managing to balance and sit on his shoulder, Lord and Lady the kitten was small, Melis said, *I am new to Human Rules but I learn FAST! We are supposed to be nice to FamWoman?*

If she had to ask, he had to emphasize. "You are supposed to treat her like the most important person in the world. She feeds you. She houses you. She gives you love and pets." He glanced ahead at Thrisca, who waved her tail in what he believed to be a too casual manner. That cat acted, too. "I know gratitude isn't something a *common* cat feels, but you're supposed to be an evolved animal."

Thrisca turned her head back, upper lip lifted in a sneer. *Like humans evolved?*

"So they say," Johns replied. "I don't know any apes, do you?"

Only you.

He snorted with laughter, waved fingers. "See, I can laugh at myself."

Foolishness. Thrisca sniffed.

Before they moved from the gravel path to the packed dirt, rounded the end of a hedgerow, Johns said, "Stop. Let's make an agreement." And by saying that he knew he'd given the upper hand—paw—to Thrisca. But face it, the FamCat had decades on him and should have learned *something* during all those years, especially when dealing with actors.

Another, slighter, sniff, then she turned and sat squarely in the trail.

Melis kitten sailed with Flair down from his shoulder to the ground, ran toward Thrisca, licked her and took off to explore. Thrisca herself didn't move except for her ears pricking forward, nose lifting. *Yes?* she asked telepathically.

Since she'd planted her butt on the ground, he walked close to her, where he judged he might be in her personal space, within paw reach. Hell, Melis had already damaged his shoes. He thought his trous would protect his skin from a good swipe.

"If you don't harm me, I won't harm you. Physically, emotionally, whatever." He stared at the wandering kitten. "That goes for you, too."

The small animal stopped peering under a bush, skittered back to him and looked up at him with big eyes that didn't engender any affection within him. *How could I harm such a big, strong man like You?*

He grunted, brushed his fingers over his shirt. "You can ruin my clothes, or just make them stink, like Thrisca and her mats earlier. I had enough of that a long time ago. And, emotionally, you can lie to Giniana about me."

Thrisca lifted a paw and gave it a cursory lick. *And what do We get for this consideration?*

"Just what I said. Mutual … respect. I don't lie to Giniana about *you.* I don't manipulate her feelings or make her choose between us."

She would not choose you, Thrisca scoffed.

"Maybe not. I will be completely supportive of her in the weeks ahead. Maybe it would be good for her to have a *human* to rely on?"

Maybe. A long pause while he and Thrisca stared at each other and Melis ate some leaves. When Thrisca rose to her paws and sauntered down the path, Melis accompanied her. *I agree to the terms you proposed. Now, FamWoman and the sick man await us.*

Melis shot ahead. *I hear FamWoman, too! Yes, I DID! Toy. Toy! TOY!*

"Toy?" Johns murmured, his nerves tweaking as he considered his FatherDam's cat's favorite toy, a crumpled piece of paper—perhaps Amberose's script. He prayed not.

It took Johns a few minutes to settle down outside Giniana's cottage infirmary with her and Wattle. And for Johns to study and gauge the value of the man. Guy impressed him as a sleazy agent, but Johns kept his manner casual. Giniana sent him a glance. Yeah, he was acting.

They sat in chairs set outside the sickroom, facing the tangle of woods left wild on the estate, lush and green. The FamCats played with a green-brown camouflage mouseykin toy the agent had bespelled, Thrisca helping the kitten hone advanced hunting skills.

Johns said, "All right, enough chitchat. And, yeah, the cat toy looks and moves great. You got a Flair for that sort of thing. But you must know that Druida City guards are still looking for the thieves. You *did* speak with the guards, right? Since you were contacted by the thieves and were going to buy back the script?" So Wattle had briefly informed Johns.

The agent's eyes slid sideways, more toward the pouncing noises of the cats. He cleared his throat with a squeak. "I, uh, was going to talk to them, the guards, right after my appointment with T'Spindle that morning, was, uh, actually on the way to the station."

Like hell.

"Did you see the thieves?" Johns persisted, roughly. "Or know any of their names?"

Wattle translocated bits and pieces of Flair tech machined pieces and fabric, dropped his gaze to his fiddling hands, creating what looked to be a Celtan rabbit, a mocyn, on a small scale.

Johns grunted to prod the man back into speech. Wattle met Johns's gaze and the agent twitched, making metal parts squeal. He flinched, then finally replied, words tumbling, "No, no, no. Was s'posed to meet the thieves that night, but they *didn't wait for me!* At the time of our appointment they'd already started *breaking into* and *rifling* the gliders, Lord and Lady dammit. Didn't see any script. And I didn't want anything to do with *theft*! And I wasn't feeling so good."

Giniana sighed. "You'd already contracted the sickness but didn't take care of yourself."

"Guess not. And I didn't get the script back, that's for sure. Only found a couple of pages, later." He held up his hand, flat, and with a long huff of breath, he translocated three sheets of papyrus.

CHAPTER 19

BLAKELY NODDED TO JOHNS, who stood and took the pages. Of those three pieces, two were blank.

Johns kept his face expressionless through bleak disappointment. He returned to his seat and smoothed the printed papyrus page on his knee. It only held the title page of the script, the byline, the verification of Wattle as Amberose's agent and his information. Not staring at the man and keeping his tone conversational, Johns said, "From the rumored conditions Amberose demands, I don't think T'Spindle will fund this play."

After hissing out a breath, fingers busy, Wattle said, "Because Amberose wants full creative and *artistic* control. She wants to name the actors to the play, watch the rehearsals—"

Nope, savvy producers wouldn't go with that. And the savvy people Amberose worked for previously wouldn't, either. This particular script would be a very hard sell, especially after a decade of no work.

Johns said, "It's pretty much all over Druida City that thieves took the script." No comment. "Not sure how Amberose will like hearing that, when she does."

Wattle barked a laugh that turned into a cough. "Not well. Sure have dealt with easier people in my career." He sighed dramatically. "And this has killed my business. This mistake. If I hadn't fallen sick, I'da managed to get the full script back ..."

Johns didn't think so, but if the guy wanted to rationalize his failure like that, who was Johns to dismiss it?

"I'll tender my resignation to Amberose," Wattle grumbled. "I made the rounds of all the Druida City and Gael City producers, shopping the script like she wanted—full creative control for her—to no avail." His face folded into an unmanly pout. "I did my best."

Johns shared a look with Giniana. Wattle's agenting career hadn't been stellar in the first place.

"I'm sure you did your best," Giniana soothed. "But maybe that wasn't the right career for you."

Wattle grunted. "I followed my G'Uncle in the business. Don't know what I'm going to do now." The pout deepened. Not a good look for him.

At that moment Melis kitten shot back into sight, zoomed to them and landed on all fours on Wattle's lap. She set her teeth in the outsized ear of the toy he'd been constructing. *Is this mousie for Me? Just for Me? Put Me—Melis on it!* she demanded. With a shaky finger the man did as told, though Johns couldn't read the actual letters.

Mine, mine, mine, mine, mine, mine! She leapt off Wattle's lap, carrying the toy—which, to Johns's dismay, seemed to thrash like a caught animal—into the bushes.

THRISSSSCA! I got MY toy. MINE!

Johns looked at Wattle to find him deeply flushed, except for the mole on his cheek, and Giniana studying him thoughtfully, her fingers clasped around his wrist in the ancient practice of taking a pulse. Jealousy spurted through

Johns. He didn't like her hands on another man, not even one so ill. And he did look sick.

Standing, Johns took a stride to the man, reached down and hauled him up. "I'll help you inside."

"Yes," Giniana said. "You appear feverish, GentleSir Wattle. I'll set the sickroom to circulate fresh, cool air."

"Good," the guy mumbled, leaning on Johns. The scent of sick-sweat rose from his skin. "Guess I overdid it."

"Yes. And you know, GentleSir Wattle, I believe there's a market for your Fam toys, and even better, individualized toys like you made for Melis."

Johns stared at Giniana. Seriously? His mouth dropped open and he shut it. Who on the planet would prefer to mess around with *Fam* stuff instead of the theater? Crazy ideas.

"Really?" Wattle panted as they took the step up into the infirmary. A swift scan showed the simple room to be serene and comfortable. Johns would like having a similar space in his own home. Or change the current dark and heavy furnishings of the meditation room—no, he liked those in winter—he'd make a summer meditation room.

"Need to scry Amberose, first, resign." Wattle swayed, shot a bleary look at Johns. "I'll give ya the woman's scry locale and *you* can speak to her. Very difficult woman."

Johns's pulse spiked. "I'd like that."

A wave of limp, white fingers. "Yeah, yeah." He sent Giniana an appealing glance. "You really think I could make gilt by creating Fam toys?"

"I do," she affirmed.

"Always better to create, if you can," Johns added, lowering the man to the single bed, all clean linens.

"Think I should start with a mechanism that includes a good range of motion to attract kitty notice ..." Wattle rambled. He looked at Johns with glazed eyes. "Then a tough material, finally a soft furry covering ... that's what Thrisca and Melis like best ..."

Johns scowled. Just how long had the guy been here to have gotten such info from the FamCats? Of course he must have paid more attention to them than Johns.

"What about Amberose?" Johns asked, as Giniana swung the soon-to-be-ex-agent's feet onto the bed. She drew up a light cover, then murmured for the man's clothes to fall away from him and slide to the floor.

But the guy only continued to mutter about Fam toys while Giniana finished making the room comfortable. Johns looked for any business cards of Wattle or Amberose, saw the man's scrypebble on the bedside table, but didn't take it, then reluctantly moved away and all the way out the door.

At the stoop, he told Giniana she should check Wattle's scry for any information on the thieves, the call that Wattle said he'd received. She'd raised her brows at Johns, and activated the scry, wrote down a couple of locale links. "No visual," she murmured.

Too bad. And too bad she'd been too honorable to copy Amberose's information for Johns.

Giniana closed the door behind her and stood beside Johns, grimacing. "And I think that the wretched man relapsed. He'll be here for another couple of days instead of able to return to his own home tomorrow morning." She glanced at her wrist timer, stood tip-toe and brushed Johns's jaw with a sweet kiss. "Must go. And so must you. I'll have the cats show you out."

"Great."

The whole event left an anti-climactic feeling within him, with only a slight touch of additional hope he might actually manage to get the leading role in the play that could make his career.

But at least she'd called him, and they'd spent more time together. He'd continue that pursuit.

Over the next six days, Johns kept his ears pricked for rumors about the script, acted his best in *Firewalker*, and continued to clean up his estate and home. Most of all, he romanced Giniana ... or tried to. He learned of Giniana's steely will, but her less-than-iron constitution. He knew she pushed the boundaries of her health, sleeping little and only eating a good meal when she dined with him, otherwise she subsisted on nutrition bars. She worked as much as humanly possible —her day job at T'Spindle Residence with emergency shifts at HealingHalls during the weekend, overnight at the Daisys, and even consulting with Danith D'Ash. All to accumulate gilt for the time procedure that might Heal Thrisca.

But he kept his mouth shut about her schedule so she wouldn't dismiss him. He figured she needed his support, even as he continued to fall for the dedicated and driven woman.

Along with his obsession with Giniana, Johns brooded about the Amberose script. Every night he read the notes Lily had given him, let the phrases Amberose wrote resonate in his mind. Began to obsess over the play, plan on how to portray the character.

He wanted to find the script and read the full play, judge for himself if it would be a good vehicle for him. But he couldn't shove it to the back of his brain. The temptation of a role written especially for *him*, by the great Amberose, whose plays had made actors' careers, sang to him. What a coup it would be to have a part that showcased his talent.

The timing seemed right ... and wrong. Even if someone jumped on the play now, it would take weeks to cast the thing—Amberose's preferences not withstanding—practice and produce the thing, market the play.

So far, he had no nibble from another employer, but it was early days. Chatt had mentioned some inquiries as to Johns's availability, but nothing solid.

Keeping an open mind, if he got a good job offer, would he forsake it for the hope of starring in an Amberose play?

He didn't know. It would depend. He loosed his jaw from gritted teeth. He intensely disliked indecision.

After Healing more from his sickness, Blakely Wattle had informed the city Guards of his dealings with the thieves. The man hadn't gotten any names or a good look at the thugs before they began robbing gliders at T'Spindle's party. The agent *had* left a brief scry message in Johns's cache that he'd heard a woman had purchased the script from the thieves, but that was all. The same gossip drifted to Johns's ears. He'd called Lily Fescue and she'd pouted that *she* hadn't been offered the script. Not that she'd have paid for it.

Rather naturally, Wattle dragged his feet in notifying Amberose that her script had been stolen. Instead, the ex-agent concentrated on his new career of making Fam toys, which he found much more fun and satisfying. Someone had hooked the man up with young Laev Hawthorn, who'd loaned Wattle the money to develop a line of Fam toys. With a sigh, Johns figured the industry would hit big.

Every Fam he knew wanted toys. More than one.

He'd even succumbed to blackmail and purchased a few for Thrisca and *her* Fam, Melis kitten, resenting the gilt spent. The truce with the feline Fams held, mostly because he and Giniana breakfasted at cafes, managed only three bouts of morning sex at the Thespian Club. Not nearly as often as Johns liked.

He slipped Giniana some energy when he could. Since it went down their link, and he timed it during their erotic foreplay and climax, he didn't think she noticed. Thrisca stated that T'Spindle Residence also gave Flair to Giniana during her work sessions. Which the woman might also not recognize.

For a person adamant in not taking gilt, the fact that others supported her with Flair seemed a blind spot. Or an issue tied to her feckless parents that she didn't realize. Which Johns thought. Gilt had been primary for her parents.

Well, it was primary for most people not born to wealth. His mother and FatherDam and he had struggled too, though they had the estate to shelter them and provide some food.

So Giniana could accept energy, Flair, emotional support, but not gilt. He was glad to provide what he could.

One evening, Johns caught a glimpse of the famous cartographer, Del D'Elecampane, whom he'd met at T'Spindle's party. A striking woman with curly blond hair, she moved with a loose athletic stride. A fascinating character to study. Interesting, too, and at the top of *her* career. A minor noble and wealthy beyond anyone's wildest dreams.

But she sparked absolutely no feelings in him other than cool curiosity and a hint of a prospective friendship. He didn't know that she'd stick around Druida City long enough for friendship to develop. She most often lived in the wild and on the road. Nothing like the fevered near-obsession that flourished within him at his every thought of Giniana Filix, at his need to be with her.

Another night he noted a brief encounter Raz Cherry engineered between himself and the mapmaker. The sexual tension sizzled between them, and with narrowed eyes Johns watched their auras flow towards each other, mingle in a wondrous mixture. Breath hitching, Johns realized he witnessed the meeting of HeartMates. People destined to be with each other...though Raz didn't seem to recognize that. Johns thought the woman, older than both he and Raz, did understand it. She played the contact extremely cool, another arresting situation Johns studied. Maybe she'd even come looking for Raz. Fascinating.

Though when the pair parted on a casual wave from Del to Raz, yearning for such a bond flooded Johns. The three dreamquests to free his power, his Flair, had happened early and each had become stronger as the years passed, but he'd never experienced a connection with a woman who'd be a HeartMate.

That moment of observing Raz and Del crystallized Johns's awareness. He couldn't imagine a better woman for himself than Giniana Filix. He'd leave Raz and Del—or Del and Raz—to their journey to a HeartMate bond, and concentrate on keeping the hot and steamy sex rolling with Giniana, interspersed with too few tender moments.

So the hectic weekend of matinees and evening performances had passed, and he'd moved into the penultimate week of the show. At the end of the month, his job was over, his career in hiatus. The knowledge lived under his skin, running along his nerves like an anxious fever.

And finally, finally, on the second business day of the week, a week and a day from T'Spindle's party and the night he'd met Giniana and the last sight of Amberose's script, Giniana scried him during her morning break. She relayed information Wattle had just given her—how to contact Amberose. Wattle hadn't resigned from the job, just moved onto his new enthusiasm.

From the gossip, Johns knew that no one trusted the genius playwright Amberose to make good business decisions with regard to her play.

Maybe it was time to contact the woman herself. The very thought made Johns catch his breath. That would take balls. To tell such an important person that the agent she'd chosen wasn't ethical, that the script itself was missing.

How much did Johns want this part? Enough to risk completely irritating Amberose for it?

He supposed he could rationalize that Amberose should know what was going on in Druida City, since she lived on a country estate nearly a day away by airship.

Walking along his gliderpath from gate to garage, removing weeds, he contemplated options. Amberose had given a single copy of the script to her representative, and the minute she did that, it was out of her control. Wattle had lost it—thieves had stolen it from Lily Fescue—so now Amberose's creative manuscript was definitely beyond her control. She couldn't know who had seen it, papyrus pages or in its entirety. Who'd read the piece, understand the story. Might crib the story.

So her need for privacy had triumphed over her need to show the play to people who'd buy it and produce it, otherwise she'd have accompanied the manuscript to Druida City and kept better track of it.

Or maybe she just understood her lack of business acumen.

In any event, her masterwork was out of her control, and Johns just bet she didn't know that and would hate it.

He put himself in Amberose's position. If he'd created something, given the fruit of his genius to a trusted representative and the item disappeared and his rep didn't keep him updated, would he want to know?

Hell, yes.

So man up and inform the woman. Let whatever consequences—ill or good—happen.

Be factual, unbiased.

He could do this—and, if lucky, find out more about the script itself and any role he might have in it.

After a last scrutiny of the gliderpath that he'd put in good shape in case Raz came through with the at-cost glider

Johns hurried inside, took a waterfall and changed into his best business tunic and trous.

Still enough time to scry Amberose before NoonBell and lunch. He practiced breathing exercises, tongue twisters, and made a brief outline of points he wanted to cover on a papyrus that he could refer to. He'd put it out of scry pebble view.

Now he'd find out just how much charm he could master, and maybe, even how much of an actor he was. For an instant, he wished he'd passed all the info and this particular chore onto Raz Cherry. But that man sure had problems of his own, what with those break-ins and thefts at his house and dressing room and glider—and with the added distraction of HeartMate energy swirling around him.

Johns's lips quirked and his gut unclenched a bit—that last oracle reading he'd done with his breakfast group a week and a half ago had been damn well correct. Raz might be willfully blind as to the identity of his HeartMate, but pretty much anyone with eyes could figure it out. And that particular morning, Raz had drawn the card indicating a HeartMate coming into his life. But Johns had flipped over the card of The Oak King, solid and continuing success in his career. Yeah, he could do this. He could contact Amberose. He sucked in and puffed out a couple of breaths. He *would* do this.

He manually set Amberose's scry locale in his pebble, embedded his St. Johnswort house banner to show his identity, flicked his thumb on the pebble and initiated the call.

His held breath released when an older, regal-looking woman with silver-stranded auburn hair waving to her shoulders answered. Amberose herself.

CHAPTER 20

JOHNS BOWED, keeping his eyes focused on hers. "Greetyou, FirstLevel Writer Amberose. I am Klay Saint Johnswort, MasterLevel Actor in Druida City."

Her blue eyes narrowed, squarish jaw flinched. "I know of you," she stated shortly. "And I presume you've seen my script." Her lips pursed, then thinned, and narrow vertical lines remained.

"No," he replied, then went on, "Blakely Wattle and Lily Fescue were, perhaps, not the best people to receive the only copy of your work."

A deeper frown, then a snappish, "Why not?"

"Wattle couldn't interest producers," Johns stated. "He hasn't the best reputation. And of the, ah, prospective cast, he showed it to Lily Fescue first."

"I authorized that. You don't like her?"

Sip a breath in, keep the concerned expression. "She is a ... challenging ... actor to work with." Lopsided smile. "But we are professionals, after all. In any event, that's not why I contacted you. T'Spindle experienced a couple of thefts on his properties, including the Primross Theater, and thieves stole the script from Lily Fescue's dressing room."

"What! When? Wattle hasn't been in touch!"

"He fell ill. The script went missing a week and two days ago." Johns couldn't stop himself from clearing his throat, but hoped the woman didn't notice his nerves, and spoke smoothly, "However, I believe I am the most concerned of those who know of your play in finding the lost script."

"Are you? Why?"

"*Firewalker* is closing."

"Is it? I hadn't heard. This whole thing sounds rotten. I still have contacts in Druida City theatrical circles, I'll check it out."

"Sure, call the T'Spindle or the Druida City guards—"

She hissed. "That would stir up rumor, would it not? Perhaps catapult all sorts of unknown people into searching for my script. I do not want that. I will call a chatty friend and listen to gossip."

"It's rumored to have been sold," he said, heard her grind her teeth.

"Who knows who has it?"

"No one I know," Johns stated.

"I do *not* want my work circulated widely, the plot revealed ..."

"No one could match your language, your fabulous writing, your technique," Johns soothed.

She shrugged, but her expression eased. "I will discover what I can of this and scry you later, since you are in Druida City and I am not." She paused, then ended grudgingly. "Thank you for the information on this matter. I will keep you in mind." She cut the call.

No time to finesse getting a copy of the script, dammit. And exactly *when* would "soon" be? He hated waiting for calls.

❦

Giniana dragged through the standard three weekend days, the following day and the next morning when she released Blakely Wattle and got paid by him, and finished the Spindle staff physical evaluations. Now she'd only be on call for standard Healing at the Spindles ... but that would include a Cooking-For-No-Times class starting later in the week and facilitated by FirstFamily GrandLady D'Spindle. Giniana would have to be on hand during the lessons to handle any cuts, scrapes or slices.

She ended work at T'Spindle Residence mid-morning, sent Amberose's scry information to Johns, then returned to her cottage. She knew the moment she drew on a thin sleepshirt and fell onto her bed that she'd sleep the whole afternoon and evening until she could grab a quick meal just before she left for her night job at the Daisys. But the image that followed her into sleep showed Klay's caring face.

When the long summer evening light dimmed and she awoke, she stretched every muscle in her body and let the exhaustion and sleep fogginess slough away slowly. Let herself rest in the moment, gently rise to consciousness. She'd overburdened herself, rushed through life instead of savoring it.

And she forgave herself for doing that, murmured her mantra, *only for a little while more*. She'd done evaluations on Thrisca every day, of course, and having Melis as her Fam perked up the older cat. She'd definitely been eating better.

If everything continued as is, and no financial crises came up, Giniana should be able to pay the full fee for Thrisca's Time Healing a day before it occurred at the end of this week, Midweekend Day. She wouldn't have to make the decision to desert the Spindles for the Willows or have the other option of a huge fee hanging over her head for months. True blessings.

She sipped in cautious optimism with the heavy scent of

summer flowers—full summer soon to fade to autumn, and Giniana felt Thrisca *would* live through the following winter, and more winters to come, Healed by D'Willow.

Now, as Giniana ate eggs and porcine strips and the FamCats watched, Thrisca sitting tail curled while Melis bounced around the dining room, her FamCat addressed Giniana in a stronger voice, *Summer nights are very good for hunting. We will be ranging further into the estate tonight, and will patrol humans' favorite gardens for pests.*

We will hunt and eat and sleep WELL, Melis added.

Yes, We will sleep well in the gardens in the morning and when We wake, We will get special catnip pillows as payment from Spindles at T'Spindle Residence. D'Spindle told Me to come tomorrow morning. Thrisca licked one forepaw, then the other, and groomed her claws. *We will also check out the Residence inside and the closer grassyards around it.*

Many peoples will admire Us! Melis enthused.

Knowledge exploded in Giniana's mind that the Fams would be gone all morning. Except for any Spindle emergency, she had the day off. Klay St. Johnswort only had an evening show tomorrow. He had most of the day off, too.

They could make love and sleep late into the morning. Eat a leisurely breakfast, a meal she'd prepare from her no-time here in the cottage.

We ate earlier, but would like another portion of food before You leave, Thrisca stated.

"Absolutely," Giniana said, aware the back of her brain buzzed with plans. She automatically finished her food, gave the cats their late dinner, set the dishes to cleanse, then dressed in loose clothing for the Daisys.

After a few minutes of petting each Fam, and some playtime with Melis, she held the front door open for them to leave and watched them trot away.

Alone. Now, and in the morning, all morning. With free

time she *wouldn't* fill with work at a HealingHall, or even any consultation with Danith D'Ash.

She would cherish the day, and the man.

On the public carrier to the Daisys, she acknowledged that Klay had been an immense support, with Flair as well as emotionally. And she valued that personal connection with him more than anything else.

He'd given her much more than she had him, their relationship tipped in unequal scales that way. But she could offer him a bit more now. More time with him, more sex with him, and, hopefully, more intimacy, learning of each other out of bed.

When she reached the Daisy Residence, she walked into a tense visit of T'Daisy's sister, Morifa, arguing with the Family, and heard Raz Cherry's name mentioned in a demand.

Ructions involving an actor—Raz Cherry—from Morifa who liked to bed actors and who moved in theatrical circles.

And Giniana's lover, Klay, was deeply embedded in that world. He'd acted normally around her—or, rather, hadn't *acted* at all. Been sincere. Even when they'd gone to the Thespian Club for sex, they'd only walked through the usually empty lobby.

She hadn't ever been with him in his professional setting. Her throat tightened at the very thought of it and she stood stiff and still in the hallway outside the sitting room where the Daisys argued instead of taking the staircase to the nursery and her charge, baby Maja.

Morifa Daisy slammed into Giniana as she stomped from the room, snarled, "You flitch of a servant. You get out of *my* way!" and stormed out of the Residence, slamming the door behind her. Giniana's windmilling saved her from falling, and she absently whispered a couplet to remove the pain and any bruising of her body from the contact with the furious woman.

Meanwhile, she heard striding around the sitting room and moved forward to check on her employers. Neither GraceLord T'Daisy nor his wife appeared as if his sister had pushed or slapped them. Good.

"I print what *I* believe to be newsworthy," T'Daisy grumbled. "Even in the society column and the play reviews. And Raz Cherry is brilliant in his role and I won't say differently because he cut off his association with Morifa."

"Of course not, dear," D'Daisy soothed. She took his hand. "And here's Healer Giniana to mind the baby for us tonight, a blessing." D'Daisy stood tiptoe and kissed her HeartMate's jaw. "Let's take a lovely walk down by the stream and talk about widening that slow part into a pond …"

T'Daisy, a large-boned man in his mid-twenties who'd begun to put on weight since he'd inherited the title, made more rumbling sounds but nodded to Giniana and let his wife lead him out of their house.

Hiding a smile and taking baby Maja to rock to sleep in the nursery, Giniana wondered if the couple would make love outdoors. Or in the gazebo at the side of the house. Or hurry back to their bed. In any event, she'd seen the gleam in D'Daisy's eyes, and the softness of affection, and the wish to comfort her husband. Because she loved him.

And they were HeartMates.

Giniana hadn't given HeartMates much thought. Before her time with the Spindles, she hadn't known any Heart-Mated couples. Both the Spindles and Daisys—noble houses who prized HeartMate bonds—were HeartMates. When one of the couple died, the other would pass within a year. She'd seen a little how true love and companionship worked, how they melded their lives together, and respected each other.

The Daisys had left the house hand-in-hand, the strong bond between them minimizing the conflict with his sister, comforting them both. In tune. HeartMates.

But the after-image in Giniana's eyes showed a tall, slinky, sophisticated woman against the open door, leaving in fury that her affair with an actor had ended before she'd decided she was done. Darkness, and more, disgust, swirled in Giniana as she contemplated the limited and nasty society of the theater.

Klay was an actor. If she continued to be with him, develop a relationship with him, she'd have to step into circles and a milieu she'd hated since childhood. She'd have to accept his profession, because his career was as integral to him as hers was to her. Could she ever accept a man who hated her being a Healer? No. And she shouldn't expect Klay wanting to be with her if she despised his profession.

But she liked him as he was. So far he hadn't *acted* with her. Could she live with him if he *acted* around others in social situations? Would he? Of course. They all did. Well, her parents and their ilk all did. The actors she'd met in T'Spindle Residence usually did.

Huge obstacle.

After struggling with her ideas and memories of actors all night, Giniana surrendered to her own instincts and scried Johns, requesting that he meet her at her cottage since she had the morning free. The way his eyes lit as he took her scry, his smile that they'd be together, reassured her as well as filling her with apprehension. They would have to address this issue, and sooner rather than later.

What was worse was that she could mentally discuss the issue, make plans based on such discussions, but, at the core, this problem tangled up all her emotions, and that didn't mean an easy solution.

When she arrived at T'Spindle Residence soon after dawn, Johns stood by the public carrier plinth and after the glider door opened, he reached in and set his large hands at her waist and swung her down. She heard sighs behind her from the other women on the glider, with an excited murmur of, "That's Klay Saint Johnswort!"

Not only warmth from the delight of seeing him splashed through her, but pride at being with him. Of course, at touch their intimate bond thickened and the emotions flowing between them clarified.

And in all her night deliberations, she'd nearly forgotten this, the link that wound between them so quickly and easily. So strongly. The bond that had felt good and right from the first, which she figured must indicate they … matched. An odd thought that she, who spent much of her life only living with a Fam companion, might match with a man.

But Johns stood looking down at her and had taken her hands. He'd said nothing, but now pushed satisfaction at being with her through that bond.

What would happen if the bond went away? Had she already come to depend upon it? Yes, a scary thought.

She squeezed his fingers and let go of one of his hands, and they walked through the wall door. Johns greeted the guards with a wave and a smile but didn't speak. The serenity of early morning silence enveloped them, settled the sparking attraction between them into a smooth rhythm.

Birds singing the day awake, the last nocturnal insect whirs sounding then fading, were acknowledged and cherished by both of them and Giniana became aware of her other senses. She understood that Johns often absorbed the sensual cues around him. Woodchips scattered across the path to her cottage released scent as she and Johns trod upon them, leaves turned lighter in the low-angled sunlight, and a thousand shades of green surrounded them.

At her cottage, she gestured the shieldspell away, opened the door and led him through the empty quietude to her bedroom and her bed, just big enough to hold two adults.

His palms curved around her upper arms, and she looked

up, got caught by his gray-blue eyes and the tenderness in them. He smiled, touched the tab fastenings at the top of her shoulders and her loose tunic fell away. Another sweep of his fingers released her breastband, baring her torso. His gaze dropped from her face and his pupils widened, then his stare rose slowly and she blushed as she sensed him looking at her breasts, her collarbone, her throat.

No, he didn't speak, aloud or telepathically, but she *felt* hot desire rush through him, then flow to her through their bond, bursting her own passion into a huge tide of mind-washing need. Her nipples tightened and her core throbbed, her body readying for sex, for more, fulfillment on the most primal level. She lost control of her breath and began to pant unevenly.

His fingertips stroked her neck and he bent to kiss her under her ear. The intimate scent of him rose to her nostrils, earthy and pungent for a man who worked creatively—but used his whole body as an instrument. In control of every muscle. She swallowed.

His tongue came out to taste and her knees weakened in ancient feminine response. One of his brawny arms circled her waist, supporting her, his other hand moving along the waistband of her trous and pantlettes, loosening them so they fell to her feet.

He lifted her, eyes glinting a narrow silver around large black centers. He liked what he saw. With one long stride, he lay her on the bed and her legs fell open for him. He glanced at her sex then away, and she could feel herself plumping, moistening.

With a short gesture, his own clothes fell away from him, separating at the spell-seams, including his boots and liners. At first she only noticed the outline of his large, well-muscled body. Then she blinked and took in his features, fiercely set, the slight perspiration gleaming on his body and his erect shaft. She gulped at the thrilling sight that went straight to her core, of him as ready for her as she was for him.

Her heart thudded so she only felt her pulse, her yearning throbbed with every beat, waiting.

But he didn't come to her in a rush, as they'd often done at the Thespian Club. He didn't speak, by voice or mentally. Instead he lay on his side next to her, scanned her from her feet still in sturdy shoes upward, his mouth curving.

He put his hand on her heart, met her eyes again and she couldn't look away. His hand cruised over her, touching her breast, plumping it, flicking her nipple with his thumb and she gasped. Pleasure inundated her through their link and her vision blurred and she could only focus on the feathery touches and glides of his fingers over her body, stimulating her. How he toyed with her nipples, brushed his hand along her abdomen to her core and drove her mad with rising ecstasy until she crested.

The sound of her own excited whimpers brought her mind back to think, at least enough for her to move toward him, her fingers reaching for his cock. But he placed his hand behind her neck, leaned over her, and kissed her, his mouth moving on hers, his tongue plunging inside to tangle with hers. He tasted marvelous, of a needy man, a man who wanted sex. She wound her arms around him, and his hands went to her hips and he rolled to cover her.

They joined. He surged inside her, then stopped. Her eyes closed to experience the huge swells of pleasure passing between them. Sensation only. He filled her, and she felt the driving need of his desire held in check as they lay together in the most intimate of embraces, male and female fitting together.

As passion cycled between them and built, built, built, spiraling higher to the point of orgasm, she savored it, all her senses attuned to him. When she believed she couldn't bear one more instant of craving, he moved. Once.

They climaxed together, harder, deeper than she'd ever known, her body clenching around him, part of him, him feeling like a part of her.

Gently, gently she coalesced from the rapture, discovered he'd rolled them to their sides. She whispered a Word, the veriest puff of breath, and the windows of the cottage opened, swirled with morning breezes. His hand cupped her face and he trapped her gaze with his intense one, pressed a slight kiss on her lips, ran his palm over her skin. Then he closed his eyes and his body eased into sleep.

All in silence, no words, no mental thoughts sent to each other, only the opening and following of each others' needs pulsed through their bond. An incredible experience she'd never imagined. All sensation, all emotional and physical connection. With a hoarse and muttered couplet, her shoes and liners fell from her feet and she, too, subsided into sleep, with her last coherent thought that the actor had said no words to her that morning. No practiced phrases. He'd let his body tell his story, let the link between them speak, reverberate.

Unbelievable.

CHAPTER 21

TWO SEPTHOURS LATER, Johns watched Giniana move
gracefully through her kitchen to set a plate of toast with
steaming cheesy scrambled eggs and porcine strips before
him. He salivated at the rich and buttery scent, the snap of
fresh herbs. A simple and different dish than any the Thespian Club offered, and more welcome for that.

She put her identical plate down but remained standing
beside her chair. He glanced up to find her scrutinizing him.
"What's wrong?"

"You're an actor."

He forestalled his reactions, any change of expression.
"That's right," he replied mildly.

"And you're as much an actor as I am a Healer. You define
yourself by your profession."

"Also true."

She frowned and he understood that she'd nearly
forgotten his career since he hadn't *acted* around her and
she'd been crazy busy and they, as a couple, had seemed to
move in a a romantic bubble. But whether she thought so or
not, whether she valued the knowledge or not, she knew
Johns, his hopes and fears, the risks and the demands of his

career. Understood the life of an actor, even if she disdained it. All he had to do was convince her not to disdain *him*. That actors could be honorable, that *he* was honorable.

Now that felt like an uphill battle.

She sat and began eating, though he didn't think she tasted her food.

"Yes, I'm an actor. My run in *Firewalker* ends the last day of this month, in about a week and a half. I'm concerned, but hopeful, and primarily have been trying to find Amberose's script. I called her yesterday."

That distracted Giniana from her thoughts. "What did she say?"

"She didn't know about the thefts, the missing script, or that Wattle stopped representing her."

Giniana winced. "He's abandoned that career, but didn't do his client the courtesy of informing her?"

"That's right."

Giniana's face stiffened. Johns pointed a piece of toast at her. "Don't think that kind of unethical behavior happens only in theatrical circles. There are stups in every profession." He paused. "Including the exalted one of Healers."

"I didn't say Healers are exalted," Giniana muttered, but began eating again.

"You didn't, I did," Johns informed her. He forked eggs on his toast, glanced up and met her startled eyes. "And I believe that. You're wonderful and *most* Healers I've met have been good, compassionate people."

She ate a bite, then said, "Unlike actors."

Johns dipped his head. "We may have many more narcissistic and egotistic and downright rude people in our profession. It can be a strength as well as a flaw, the focus on self and the flexibility of molding self into a new role. I will give you that." Now he raised his eyes and locked gazes with her amber one. "But I don't think of myself as overly self-absorbed. I have a code of honor, like many men in every walk of life. I am passionate about my career, like other men from GreatLords to City Maintenance." He paused. "It's true, I *do* put up with people I dislike so I can advance in my career —also a practice not only of actors." He raised his forefinger. "But I associate with people of like minds and like hearts and like characters. Those are my friends." Though most of his friends *were* actors.

Giniana let her gaze roam over Klay, his bent head as he ate his food with relish, his broad shoulders, and the link between them that revealed no shadow of insincerity. She blinked as she focused on the hominess of her cottage instead of an internal bond running between her and Klay, and questions buzzed in her brain. Didn't her parents have a bond, and didn't they check it? And weren't they sad when it showed deceit? Maybe they were accustomed to shadiness in their bonds, not only in any links between the two of them, but in their connections with other lovers and friends.

She didn't think either parent kept good bonds with any friend. How odd and sad.

Klay wouldn't be like that. He spoke of his friends with affection, and approved of their honor like his own. So he *would* have such bonds. She hadn't met any of his friends, the time they'd spent together lately had been meals and sex, or sex and meals. Though she vaguely recalled him being polite to people he met in the Thespian Club, he certainly hadn't lingered for any conversation.

He'd put her first...well, perhaps. He'd put sex first, at least.

Glancing up, he met her eyes and smiled. "I've also been busy," he said.

And though she'd continued to work as much as she could, she'd been aware that he practiced his craft, too, starred in matinees and evening performances of *Firewalker*.

He'd spoken more of volunteering at Moores House and refurbishing his yard. So he'd kept busy with his own life.

But, as he'd stated at the beginning of their association, he'd made sure she'd eaten a meal a day with him, usually breakfast, and while they'd dined, they'd talked. She realized she enjoyed their discussions. If she hadn't been so preoccupied with surface conclusions about him, if she analyzed their time together more, she would know him more deeply.

"Giniana, you said you only have to work your regular jobs for now? Has anything changed?" And he turned the conversation back to her and her issues, his face showing true concern. Ready to support her as he'd done all along.

"D'Willow asked me to come by and meet her staff," Giniana muttered, knowing reluctance dragged through their emotional bond.

He raised a brow. "You haven't refused her offer to become the Willow Family Healer?"

"I want to keep my options open," she muttered.

"Completely understandable," he said, munched some thick toast, swallowed, looked at her, but now she didn't connect with his gaze. She didn't want to talk about herself anymore.

Klay's scry pebble went off in his trous pocket. As he reached to silence it, Giniana smiled and said, "Go ahead, take it."

His lips quirked. "Speaking of friends, this is the tune I assign to actor friends." His eyelids lowered and he smoldered at her … also sincere, since she felt the heat of sexual tension through their link. "Not at all like the seductive music I assigned to you."

She laughed. "Answer the scry, Klay." Since they'd both finished, she rose with her plate, then moved behind him to pick up his, just as he flicked his thumb on the small glass oval.

"Greetyou, Johns!" an actor warbled. Giniana paused, she knew this woman, or had known her in their childhoods.

Trillia Juniper, always a cheerful person, smiled at Klay. "I heard that *Firewalker's* closing at the end of the month." Her face folded into sad lines. "I hate when that happens! But thought I should tell you that one of the actors in my play here in Gael City is quitting to study for his MasterLevel in Toono Town."

Quick fear spurted through Giniana, trailing pangs of hurt at anticipated loss.

"Yeah, what part?" Klay asked. Though he kept everything —manner, voice, expression—casual, Giniana felt the perk of his increased interest. "The Captain's role?"

"Ah, sorry, no. It's the villain's. But you could do it, for sure," Trillia enthused.

"Don't they usually play him ... spindly?" Klay shifted. Watching his muscular body, Giniana absolutely agreed that 'spindly' could never apply to this man.

"Yes, but think of the challenge!"

"Playing a thin, manic villain a half-decade younger than me would be a challenge, all right," Klay said.

"Oh, Johns." Trillia puffed out a breath. "I just wanted to help."

"I know."

Trillia narrowed her violet eyes from under dark brows— her natural blond hair obviously tinted—and demanded, "Who's that behind you, Johns? Who? She looks familiar—" Then a high-pitched squeal. "*It's GINIANA! Giniana Filix.*" The actress began jumping up and down, waving. "I haven't seen Giniana since grovestudy. *HI, Giniana!* Have you hooked back into the theatrical world after turning your back on us to be a Healer? That's *so* great. I'm *so* glad!" A close-up of Trillia's face as she peered in her scry pebble to study them. "What, what? That body language—you're lovers! Giniana is lovers with Johns!" Trillia pulled back and clapped, angled more toward Johns and winked. "Good job, Johns."

To Giniana's surprise a dull, red flush began showing on Klay's skin, from his cheeks all the way down his jaw to his neck. Interesting, and she wondered how much lower it went ...

She sensed a push of deep discomfort from him, then it struck her that Klay and Trillia must have been lovers at some time, and that she'd been clued into that fact by his manner, something that wouldn't have happened with a good actor. Did the man not act around her at all?

"Greetyou, Gee!" Trillia ... trilled.

"Greetyou, Trillia," Giniana replied, twitching her lips up in a smile. She felt stupid and stiff.

Klay caught on, of course, slid from his chair to stand behind her, and her spine straightened even more and now *she* flushed.

"I'm very happy in my relationship with Giniana," he said, though the words didn't fall as smoothly as she'd have expected.

"Wonderful!" Trillia's dimples flashed, then faded as she scrutinized Giniana. "Oh. You must be *new* lovers. Well, Johns didn't bring any woman to T'Spindle's party ten days ago and didn't mention anyone the last time our group breakfasted together." She wet her lips, lifted her chin. "A good and solid relationship, I hope, Johns?"

"Yes."

Trillia shot Giniana a winning smile. "Not like that week of fun *we* had when we met in our late teens."

"No," Klay spit out the word.

Shooting a finger at Giniana, Trillia said, "Don't be a stup about this, Gee." Then she beamed another smile. "I can see why you don't want to leave Druida City right now, Johns, but I'll keep my ears open about any parts down here in Gael City or even openings in the traveling troupes."

"Thanks," Klay said dryly.

Now Trillia shook her finger at Klay. "You're a snob, Klay, wanting a career only in Druida City."

"As you were, two weeks ago. As most of our friends are. And *you* have a *major* role as Fern Bountry, Captain Lady of the starship *Nuada's Sword*."

"This is true." Trillia preened. "A prime part and I am being very well paid. Later, Johns! Later, Gee!" And Trillia blew them kisses before Klay cut the connection. Then he stepped back, circled Giniana to take their plates from her hands, and put them in the cleanser. "So you know Trillia."

"Yes." Warmth flushed through her. "We went to the same grovestudy group for children of actors. Trillia dropped out of grovestudy to become apprenticed to the Eyebright acting Family." Giniana had thought at the time that Trillia might have fallen in love with the old actor, particularly since there had been a lot of infidelity going on in her own home with her mother and father. Both had had lovers.

Looking back, Giniana thought she might have misjudged the girl.

She didn't like that the thought of Klay having sex with Trillia, even so long ago, still irked. It *did* play to Giniana's prejudice against actors, and that irritated, too. She managed to keep her lips closed over questions regarding his previous love life. Not her business. And she disliked herself for feeling such petty jealousy. Just being around Klay, as an actor, stirred up negative thoughts. And poor character traits in herself that she hadn't dealt with before. Aspects she hadn't realized were a part of her.

Klay moved away from her and Giniana wondered if he sensed those negative thoughts spinning through her mind. He walked across the small dining area through the front mainspace room and opened the door to the natural land-scape beyond her cottage. She watched his chest expand as he drew in the flower-and-woods scented air.

Then he glanced over. "As you stated earlier, I, too, am trying to do keep my options open." He grimaced. "Though my agent hasn't called and I haven't heard of any upcoming *good* roles." With a sharp gesture, he dismissed the offer from Trillia. "But if an acceptable project does appear, I'll have to weigh that with regard to prospects regarding the staging of Amberose's new play. Someone bought it, though I haven't discovered who that might be." He frowned. "I don't think a producer did, because Amberose still wants creative control." He shrugged. "There's an outside possibility a producer might buy it, with or without her conditions."

His blue-gray gaze met Giniana's eyes. "And, yes, I brought the conversation back to me since you didn't want to talk of yourself. I *am* an actor. A good actor and I hope to be a great and famous one."

She noted his body tensed, as if for a blow, saw a large swallow, then he said, "We've spoken mostly of me today, and my life—and Trillia and the fact of my affair with her a decade ago—interrupted our discussion and I believe you reacted poorly to that. If you can't accept me and my career, we should not continue to see each other." He slammed shut their link.

Sudden tears backed behind her eyes, her breath strangled in her throat, horrifying her. *No!* She *depended* on him—and how had that happened? She needed his stalwart friendship.

Perhaps.

His mouth thinned as if he'd surprised himself, too. He angled back to face more outdoors—outside her home and cottage, the world beyond T'Spindle estate. But before he turned his head, she'd noted his gaze, steely and distant.

His words hung between them, the atmosphere

thrummed with the ultimatum, with the demand for an answer from her, the press of a decision needing to be made.

No, she hadn't expected this. The absence of the bond between them was downright painful. Her throat dried with that stuck breath and she couldn't swallow as he had. Couldn't swallow any kind of notion that they'd break up at all. That he would really leave her, but she knew his words to be true.

"You're different than other actors," she murmured, and he looked back, staring.

He opened his mouth, shut it.

And her mind clicked back to his reaction to Trillia's scry. He hadn't been acting at all during that scry or with Giniana. He hadn't shielded his embarrassment from her. And she sensed that he'd never acted when he'd been with her. Not in or out of bed, not during any of their conversations and inter-actions.

She set her hands in her hair, pressed fingertips against her head. "The reason we haven't spoken more about me is that I don't know what to do, I change my mind about what I should do from septhour to septhour."

He stood stiff by the door, her plea not softening him. He'd given more than she, so if she wanted this relationship to continue, she must give more. Tears continued to pool within her, ready to rise and push those already in her eyes down her cheeks.

She couldn't match Trillia in optimism, in her delight for being a part of the theater, but Giniana *could* match and surpass the woman's friendship with Klay that trailed memo-ries of hot sex.

More often than not, Klay had made the first moves of loving, sweeping her into his arms and onto the bed, stroking her. Definitely her turn, now.

So she went to him, reached for his hand and drew him

into her home. He came readily, stood before her, didn't flinch when the door shut behind him, blocking the whole world out. In fact, as usual, he focused on her though he didn't open their link.

She placed her hand over his heart, felt the rapid beat of it, and a trickle of relief at that. This close to him, she smelled the slight perspiration on his skin, believed if she glanced down, she'd see him erect, another positive sign.

On her part, she opened her side of their bond very wide, let her emotional waves lap against his block.

Then she traced his jaw, curved her hands around his face, felt the prickliness of his morning beard against her palms, cherishing even this small intimacy. Trillia might have shared pleasure with the boy, but Giniana knew the man. And she absolutely *refused* to think about Klay's other lovers. Re-fused. Allowed herself this one last moment to be disgusted with her jealousy, she was human after all, but better to concentrate on *her* relationship with Klay. *Their* very real bond.

"I don't want this to end." She drew in a ragged breath of the air of home, tinged with Klay's scent, and that seemed to also mean "home," or, at least, support. Stroking his face, she met his eyes. "I care for you more than I thought. And I value you." She forced the next words out. "And valuing you, I must value your passion for your career, as an actor."

Rising to the balls of her feet, she kissed him, sliding her tongue along his lips, closing her eyes to truly savor his taste, sending her desire for him, the physicality of that—her weakening knees, her melting core—to him.

Their bond blasted open with his passion, his need, swamping her. Only sensuality mattered. She tugged on him, swaying the few steps to the couch, trying to pull him down.

"No," he groaned roughly. "Your bed. *Your* bed."

"Of course." Her lashes sprang open. Whipping around,

she took his damp hand and rushed them into the bedroom, tore back the covers and yanked on his hand.

He laughed, gloriously, tone deep but joyfully light, stirring all sorts of incredible feelings within her, happiness and tenderness and sheer delight that this incredible man was her bedmate.

With a quick gesture of her fingers, she whisked away his clothes, disrobed herself, then pounced on him, fitting herself to him in a delightful slide that sizzled through her.

Joy filled her, *he* filled her, and she let thought go, all doubts melt away. She met his eyes, kept her gaze locked with his as ecstasy drove them to the edge of climax and over.

She lay against him, head below his chin, she said, "Don't give up on me."

His hand cradled her skull, stroked. "I won't."

"And don't leave me." She wanted him to promise forever, but she wasn't willing to do the same, hardly looked ahead beyond the time experiment, the end of the week. Didn't want to spend needful energy visualizing what her life might be after that. Especially if she lost Thrisca.

"I won't leave you, this morning or ever, without talking to you," he replied easily. She sensed a slight wariness through their link from him that hadn't been there before, she also believed his words, this man who dealt in words, so she drifted into sleep.

CHAPTER 22

JOHNS AWOKE LATER to find Giniana sleeping, and he pulled his arm from under her neck, rolled away. He let out a disappointed sigh that she had this day free and he would work that night. Twelve more days to go in the run of the play, ending the last night of the month, the night before the dark twinmoons that signified the beginning of next month, that of Ivy. In thirteen days he'd be out of work and living on his savings.

Just taking a deep breath of end-of-summer air and the scent of Giniana's cottage and *her* banished the depressing thought. He had her, for now, and, he hoped, for the foreseeable future. He didn't know when his yearning for her would fade. Their bond appeared strong and healthy and growing.

The ultimatum that had spurted from him had clutched his gut, but they wouldn't be in a intimate bubble of a new relationship forever. She'd had to accept him as an actor or he couldn't continue to be with her.

And she had. He'd sensed shock and dread, incipient panic from her at breaking up.

They'd gotten through it.

As they would get through the next five days until the

time Healing of Thrisca, hopefully, and *not* her demise, and through the finish of *Firewalker* at the end of the month ... and, hopefully, too, not the end of his career.

He contemplated staying here in bed with Giniana, but sweat coated him—heat sweat and fear sweat and sex sweat, and he needed a waterfall. He rose and went to the other door of the bedroom and opened it, then stared at a tiny, windowless workroom converted from a closet. It held a small desk with delicate metal tools he didn't recognize, and many shelves of ... rocks.

Looking closer, he saw a bowl of different-colored polished stones, some incised with runic glyphs, some with inspirational words such as, "Believe," "Create," "Trust," "Revel." She used copper, silver, gold and glisten metal to script the cut runes. Outlined drawings of animals were also carved in the stones.

Fascinating.

With a fingersnap, he set a lightspell orb to see better, and a gleaming flash of crystal set in rough rock caught his eyes. It showed repeating variegated bands of nearly black deep purple, then blue-green, a soft solid green, and a few horizontal streaks of white. Reaching for it, he took the rock and rough crystal down from the shelf, examined it, feeling the texture of pure Celtan rock and smooth glass angles.

"You like that piece?" Giniana asked behind him.

He smiled. "Yes. Obviously you have a strong creative Flair as well as your Healing."

"Thank you, though it's a hobby only."

"Understood. You're a Healer and this is to relax."

She nodded, her eyelids lowering as she scanned his body. He might feel grubby, but she liked what she saw, and his body reacted to that. He wondered at the space and sturdiness of her waterfall enclosure. "Let's head for the waterfall." His voice dropped low.

Her brows raised, then she tilted her head, smiling. "Just checking on my FamCats to make sure they're busy. This is one of Thrisca's quarterly days up at T'Spindle Residence."

"Free from Fams all day?" His spirits lifted.

"Yes."

Then his calendarsphere pinged and stated, "Your first session in the Johnswort Ritual Room, celebrating the anniversary of the construction of the house, is scheduled to begin in one and a half septhours—"

"Cancel—" Johns began.

"No, don't," Giniana interrupted.

"It's not a hard and fast appointment for me," he pointed out.

"But it's important." Her face wore an arrested expression. "I thought of that when I met you, but not since. You're from an old Family."

"An old family who prized their middle-class merchant status." He twitched a smile, but didn't pretend that his lips curved in pleasure. "The last few generations of the family deteriorated to near poverty." Squaring his shoulders, he stated, "But I *am* refurbishing both house and yard. I have time and Flair to labor on them now."

"Then it's important that you keep your appointment."

He strode to her and lifted her fingers to his lips. "I'd rather spend most of the day with you."

Her smile radiated sincerity. She ducked her head a bit, peered up at him through her lashes. "Perhaps you'd like to show me your house?"

Thank the Lord and Lady his place should be in good shape! "I'd like that." Bracing himself, he said, "I'll even invite Thrisca and Melis."

"Hmmm." But her lips twitched. "They are hunting and showing their skills and being spoilt today by T'Spindle Residence and that Family."

"You might be right. It could be quite a comedown to visit a shabbier estate—not really an estate, but a large house and parcel of land."

"I'm sure the FamCats would think so, and I'm sure they'll try to milk this treat at T'Spindle Residence for as long as possible, perhaps late into the evening."

And her scrypebble shrieked. "Giniana, please, please Giniana, we need you here at AllClass HealingHall, transnow!" begged a woman.

Giniana stiffened. "That's FirstLevel Healer Lark Holly."

"Of the FirstFamily GreatLord Hollys?"

"Yes. I must go! Whirlwind spell, professional Healer attire!" Giniana commanded, and Johns shuddered as he saw her roughly scrubbed by the cleansing spell, her hair yanked back into a professional coronet and Healing clothes whisked on her. As soon as the nasty wind ended, Giniana brushed a light kiss on his mouth. "Please secure the cottage, and I'll see you later, I hope!"

"Yes," he said as she teleported away.

No Whirlwind Spell for him. As he headed toward her bathroom, he contemplated the thought that he must accept the fact that there would be times like this, when Giniana answered a call for an emergency Healer. Such an instance could happen at any time: when he took her to a fancy dinner and they'd begun to sit down, in the middle of the night, maybe even while they made love.

He *had* accepted her as a dedicated Healer, but he'd also been quite aware of the mantra she shared with him, "Just for now. Just for a short time." But that wouldn't necessarily be true if a HealingHall scried with an emergency. He didn't see Giniana ever refusing such a plea.

An aspect of her profession he hadn't totally acknowl-edged until now. It scared him a little that he accepted that she might leave at any moment so easily. As he had moments before, no hesitation on his part, or selfish demand, he so totally supported her.

He lingered as long as he could under the waterfall, enjoying the luxurious herbal and medicinal silky liquid falling from a ledge over his head, but neither Giniana nor the cats returned. Fulfilling his promise, he set spellshields on her cottage, then took the public carrier home.

Some minutes later outside his ritual room, Johns oiled the door hinges and ensured the slab of wood swung smoothly before he entered the chamber. Since he used this space at least quarterly to keep the basic housekeeping spells going, not much dust accumulated and the brass pentacle-within-a-circle inset in the floor gleamed in the sunlight.

He looked at the place with fresh eyes. Bare white walls, no furniture, no rugs. Clean, smelled fine of herbs, tidy altar. At least he'd fulfilled his minimum responsibilities of his family home.

The altar still showed trappings of his Summer Solstice ritual. He winced. He'd done those necessary spells perfunctorily in a short ceremony more than a month ago.

After that, he'd focused on himself and his career. Had definitely not been in the proper state of mind to feel the immense gratitude for all that had been given him in his life. Nor had he expressed such gratitude in this chamber for far too long.

He experienced gratitude now, and predominantly for his new and wonderful lover. A woman who he hoped might visit that very afternoon, for more than just sex. His previous relationships featured casual lovers. None of those ladies had asked to come to his home and he hadn't offered. More casual than he'd thought, since he never spoke to prospective lovers about how he wasn't looking for long term, that was understood up front by both parties.

Not like Raz Cherry emphasized the unimportance of his affairs to his women. But Raz had a wealthy noble Family behind him. Johns, as a guy on his own, and dedicated to his craft of acting, wouldn't be seen as a good marriage prospect. Just as well. Oddly enough he *felt* as if he'd been saving all his emotional attachment for a certain driven Healer.

The moment he'd seen her, desire had sizzled through him. It hadn't faded, not after one session in bed, not after ... and he didn't know how many times he'd had sex with her, and usually the back of his mind kept track, lowering as that was.

A window banged, yanking him from wandering thought.

He crossed to the center of the room. Since today didn't demand directional precision, he moved the mobile altar to the south where it stayed in summer. Then he returned to the middle of the brass pentagram set into the floor.

The windows on two sides of the room poured in light. The quality of that golden sunshine and the notion that this room featured in his earliest memories—even when his mother had been alive—caused deep satisfaction to well through him.

He held that, the satisfaction, the peace, the knowledge that *this room* and the whole house belonged to him. Had belonged to his family for generations. He hadn't thought of that, been grateful for it, for years.

Appropriate thoughts and feelings for the anniversary day of the raising of this House.

Then he let out a large breath, angled until the sun rested on his face. He began the prayer to the Lord and Lady, drew on his own inner Flair and initiated the greater housekeeping spell he hadn't done for too long, using his Flair to power it.

Then energy surged up through him from the floor, nearly burning his feet.

He choked on a ritual word, but only one since he *was* a professional, kept on with the rhythm of the chant when his eyes blurred with power infusing the atmosphere around him, heating it, too.

What was that?

us. The tiny whisper came in his mind, a faint squeak and equally fleeting vague image.

But a huge current of feeling.

Power, energy, Flair *waiting* for him to access it, to use it for the house and property. And the instant he thought of his land, strength rolled through him, tickled the underside of the ground and the thread-roots of millions of blades of grass, supplying *them* with energy.

He thought he heard a boy's surprised yell outside, Marti Samphire working in the yard. But Johns focused on his feet, on the wooden floor below him, then into the basement, and further … down a minuscule shaft he didn't know about. Latching onto the flickering image, the hint of murmur, he sent his mind to the source. *Felt* them better.

Runestones, all touching, in a circular pattern. He couldn't discern the mineral type containing the carved glyphs.

Runestones. *HeartStones.*

Yesss! Not truly a word, just a feeling of affirmation and joy.

Johns rocked back on his heels, sending most of his attention to the stones, sucking in a big breath, too, as the realization pinged through him.

His ancestral house had a—not a HouseHeart because there was no chamber—but definitely House*Stones.* His home was becoming sentient.

Lord and Lady.

Talk about responsibility.

He continued to recite the middle of the spell. Energy pulsed through him so greatly that he seemed to swell with Flair from the inside out, stretching his skin. He pushed that power, along with his own contribution, back through the house—the *H*ouse—and downward, sensing the complete thrill of the stones as they received such energy.

Sounds rustled around him, impinging on his awareness. The floorboard creaked, the window glass in the room thinned of its own accord, setting the small crystal chandelier above his head that he'd forgotten about sparkling and dancing and chiming.

Joy.

Lady and Lord, *why* had he waited so long to do this? But he hadn't known about the HeartStones, and who knew, for sure, when they'd managed to gather that last bit of energy to puff them into intelligence? As he settled back into his balance, he considered that if he hadn't let the HouseStones gather Flair and energy, if he hadn't left them alone, if he'd drained them regularly, they'd not yet be sentient.

A rationalization for sure, but it worked for him. He ended the spellchant with thanks to the Divine Couple and the House, and bowed in all four directions. Then he let the power sweep and hum around him, cleansing the whole house.

His legs wobbled as he sank down to sit in the center of the pentagram. Hell, his whole insides seemed to ripple, radiating from his gut. Amazing.

can we sleep now? murmured the tiny voice, then answered itself, *sleep. until next turn of year.* A slight pause. *would be better if more than one human abiding here.*

Johns opened his mouth, and his mind, to reply, but felt the teeny flickering of the rune HeartStones' essences subside into darkness—sleeping and listening and learning to all that occurred in the House. To him.

Zow.

He wanted to share this wondrous event, and with Gini-ana. No scry bowl in the ritual room, of course, and he'd taken his perscry pebble out of his pocket and placed it on the table outside the door for items not to be brought into ceremonial chamber.

He rose to his feet and exited the room, tapped the latch shut with a stronger verse-spell than previously. Checking their bond, he found her still working, but it seemed she might be finishing up. So he left a message in her perscry that he'd provide lunch here for them both, reminded her of the address. He'd also sensed that the other Healers, or the HealingHall itself, had flooded her with energy.

Then he stopped and sniffed. The hallway smelled good, and breath stopped as the scent wisped around him, bringing back memories, once again before his mother had died when he'd been seven years old.

Without thought he strode upstairs to his suite, looked across the hall. He blinked blurred eyes and saw the rich dark scarlet of the door opposite him. His mother's suite. He couldn't remember, now, how long it had been since he'd actually entered those rooms. A bit after his FatherDam had died, he thought. The women had loved each other as mother and daughter, though his father had died of a sickness soon after Johns had been born.

No, not ready to set foot in his mother's rooms. Some-thing he could need help with, from a strong person, like Giniana.

So he banished sadness with the contrasting thought that he, *his Family,* now had a permanent companion, the House. Incredible and uplifting.

&.

While he strolled through the house—his House, since it had begun to be self-aware—looking at the gleaming rooms and out the pristine windows at bushes that had blossomed with flowers, grass that had grown, his perscry emitted a standard call ping. "Saint Johnswort here," he answered.

A laconic man in a Cherry Shipping and Transport pilot's uniform stared at him. "I'm calling to deliver an Alder Classic glider to you. ASAP, I was told. Can accept a gilt chit from you." He named a large amount.

Johns nodded coolly. "I'm at Saint Johnswort estate now and will stay until you arrive."

"Right. See you soon."

Letting out a pent up breath that he'd sucked in at the price, Johns allowed himself to lean against the kitchen counter, wiped sudden sweat from his forehead. The price on the glider really was a deal. It was a good investment. The vehicle itself could last him a lifetime if he treated it right, which he fully intended to do. It was also a statement that he had enough gilt to own the thing and enough Flair to power it.

Having a glider, now, would signal others in the business he wasn't worried about his career or future.

Johns thought he'd always worry about his future.

But paying for the vehicle would deplete his savings. He'd need to land a job much sooner.

Picking up T'Ash's silver token from the no-time appliance where he'd cached the treasure, he examined it. On the face showed an Ash tree, *the* Ash tree in the center of the Great Labyrinth. The obverse pictured T'Ash's and D'Ash's profiles with the date inscribed. Impressive.

He rolled the coin in his fingers. Like most people, he'd never earned any kind of any Family token before.

Good enough to purchase a glider?

Immediate rejection of that notion. Like the terrible idea

of mortgaging his home and land Giniana had brought up days ago that he'd dismissed instantly. No.

He believed in himself, in his ability to pursue his career, in his own sheer determination. Save the token, the estate, minor as it was, for the future.

He'd stash the coin in the safe in his mother's rooms when he got the guts to go there. Perhaps with Giniana. It *was* the main suite of the House. Wouldn't it be tied to the HeartStones, the vibrations of that space resonate most for them? He'd have to seriously think about moving into those rooms.

It was time.

A thought snippet floated through his mind. He'd like living in the suite so much more with Giniana.

Too soon for that option! Not until they'd all survived the time procedure. If Thrisca *didn't* live through the process, maybe Giniana and Melis would like a change of scene—no, throw those pessimistic thoughts right out.

Analyze his own career. He'd be handing over a large amount of gilt shortly. He should really get down to business and determine how much food all the House no-times contained—indifferent tasting or not. Look at his wardrobe … and if worse came to worst … make those tiny play houses, tree houses, forts, for noble children.

He would have time to examine the MasterSuite and refurbish it. Working through it might be odd and sad, but he could face the echoes of the women who raised him now.

They'd be proud of him, he was sure.

He flipped the silver token, watched it catch the light as it spun through the air before he snatched it back. There might very well be other family treasures or tokens in that suite that he could discover.

CHAPTER 23

WITH HIS NEW sensitivity to the House and grounds, Johns knew when the glider flowed through the gates he'd told Marti Samphire to open before the boy left. Johns felt the vehicle travel up the newly-weeded flagstone gliderway to the front of the House.

He hurried down to open the door, step out onto the deck of the wrap-around porch, greet the driver as the man drew up.

Johns's gaze fixed on the beautiful machine as the guy lifted the driver's door and exited, patted the hood before he rounded the glider to meet Johns.

Staring at the vehicle, Johns handed the man the gilt chit without any tiny bump of anxiety. "Beautiful."

"That she is," the Cherry driver said, grinning. The pilot saluted him and vanished, teleporting away with a small pop.

Jumping down and over the steps, Johns went to the glider and ran his hand over the classic lines and slight curves of the vehicle, excitement pumping through him at his new acquisition. Truly, beautiful, worth anything he paid. A *new* glider! Just for himself! He'd never had anything new until he'd made his own gilt.

And a new scent added to the estate, the heating metal of the glider.

He glanced at the sun. Pretty weather, he could drive with the roof and windows thinned to nothing. He had six septhours before he needed to be at the theater for the show. He wanted to share his good fortune, this lovely moment of pleasure in a stream of sticky negative luck. He wanted to take Giniana for a drive, spend time in her company, and, all right, show off the glider. Didn't matter she knew the circumstances of how he got such a good deal on it.

He wouldn't lie to her. Rarely lied, was dishonest, with anyone. Against his honor. But since she felt so touchy about actors he sure wouldn't lie to her, not even fudge the truth. No pretense at all, and he'd have to watch his innate posturing for best advantage.

Impulsively, he called her again and her live image swirled into the pebble in his palm, and, yeah, his heart did a squeeze-thump at seeing her.

"Here," she said.

"Greetyou, Giniana."

She smiled, one he thought she might aim only at him and everything inside him tightened. He wanted to bow, but gestures like that looked odd on a perscry. "I've received my new glider," he let his voice reverb with extreme satisfaction in his voice, "and I'd like to take you for a ride in it, to celebrate."

Her glance moved from him to a point over his shoulder. Through the small bond that spun between them he felt discouragement and weariness, knew she planned to say 'no.'

"Just a soothing ride," he coaxed. "I invited you for lunch, and we can have that here at my place." One of the fancy meals in the ritual no-time for summer solstice, light and bright. "But if you'd rather just ride through Druida or the countryside, we can do that instead. Go anywhere you like. Unless ... do the Spindles need you?"

"No," she answered absently. "My day is free of work and Fams, but I remain on call for emergency situations."

"And I remain understanding of that fact."

Her gaze arrowed to him and she scanned his face. He wished she didn't continue to doubt him. He stopped his mouth from flattening with insult and irritation. "Have you eaten since breakfast?"

"Nooo."

"You should. With me, as usual. I can pick you up at T'Spindle's in twenty minutes."

She hesitated.

"You'll be better for a ride in a new glider, relaxing before your Fams return to play in and around your cottage." He probably shouldn't have pressed on both lunch and a ride, but dammit, he wanted more of her in his life. Focus on getting her to himself.

Her brows rose. "And I'll be better for being in your company?"

He smiled. "You'll be better for food, for sure. Summer salad greens, fruit, a nice slice of hot bread and butter ... Food and some relaxation."

She raised her brows, "Relaxation?"

"A pretty ride, good food, time on an estate where you're not an employee, with no expectations of you," Johns said. He would *not* mention sex. Oddly enough he wanted to show her his glider, his home, himself in those two situations, more important than sex today.

She sighed. "Come on by, I'll be ready."

"Wear one of those new-fashioned summer dresses." The request spurted from his mouth.

Giniana laughed. "All right. I can do that."

"I'll thin the glider windows and roof. It will be fun."

Raising a hand, he said, "And if you want, I'll keep quiet. You can relax, even doze, on the way from the Spindles' to my place."

Her aura brightened. Good.

"I'll be waiting."

"I'm on my way." He tapped the roof of the glider and the door rose.

"See you soon!"

His scry pebble went dark. Slipping into the glider, feeling the soft leather under his ass, had him grinning. And opening the nav to Giniana's coordinates, saving them as the first location, was perfect.

"*Bye, Thrisca! Bye, Melis!*" Giniana sent telepathically to her FamCat and the kitten, though their minds showed they dozed in GrandLady D'Spindle's parlor. They'd already eaten their snack-after-lunch.

As for her own luncheon, when Klay had told her the menu, she wondered if he might be pulling a meal from a no-time, as she did so often. Did he cook at all? Her own skills were basic, though she could make excellent FamCat food.

Goodbye, FamWoman, Thrisca purred languidly down their link.

Goodbye, FamWoman, Melis's tone zipped along their bond.

Sleep! Giniana sent the suggestion to the kitten, felt her body relax and her yawn.

I will sleep, curled by My FamCat's belly. Melis's thought vanished into animal images and the cadence of sleep.

Giniana twitched the skirt of the new-styled *sundress* that she'd been wearing when Klay had called. A floral pattern, the full longish tunic—and no trous—fell to her calves. She also wore sandals, a treat, since her feet were usually fully covered in case of accidents at HealingHalls.

Her whole body felt buoyant, not just because she'd donned lighter clothes. Or slept well into the day. More like because she had sex and breakfast with her lover, and the recollection diminished the wearing anxiety for Thrisca.

Giniana had received a flash of energy from Klay when he'd called, his demeanor unwontedly cheerful.

So that other actor, Raz Cherry, had come through and sold Klay a glider. And Klay had enough gilt to buy one, even at a discount. It didn't seem as if he should worry about gilt and not having a job as much as he did, as much as she did.

Perhaps he *was* more concerned about the interruption of his career rather than gilt. Her shoulders tensed. Her father *had* been interested enough in his career to leave her and her mother to debunk to the continent of Chinju across the ocean.

Don't think of that other man who'd broken her child's heart. Let optimism return and *feel* Klay. His pleasure emanated through their link as a strong but gentle glow.

Well, he *was* a Master level actor. Maybe he borrowed gilt to pay for—no, she wouldn't believe that. Gilt and the presents it could buy had played too much a part in her mother's life.

Giniana wouldn't think Klay had wheeled and dealed and managed to get the gilt in some shady way like her parents would have. In fact, the man seemed solid. She hadn't asked around about him, nor asked the T'Spindle ResidenceLibrary database about Klay St. Johnswort and his family. She might have done that, perhaps should have done. She'd just spent time with him and listened to his stories and believed them, pretty much trusted him.

Her steps picked up pace as she walked down the path to the gate in the wall. Klay had enriched her life.

She spent the few minutes it took for him to arrive talking about him with the guards. The female guard made jokes about her envy of Giniana in having such a fabulous lover. The male guard spent most of the time pacing outside the gate to see a new gilder a man his age had managed to buy.

The sight of Klay driving up in a pristine, classy vehicle made her catch her breath. The actor Raz Cherry impressed her as the more elegant of the two, but Klay appeared powerful, successful, and confident of his place in the world. Though he'd spoken of his impoverished childhood and revealed his current doubts, he must, at his core, embody assurance and determination.

Or maybe that's what having such a machine did for his sense of self. As Raz Cherry promised, the steel blue matched Klay's eyes.

"Ooooooh," she and the guards let out admiring breaths.

Klay hopped from the open vehicle, landing lightly on his feet beside it as it floated a meter above the ground. He strode around the glider, picked her up and whirled her, set her inside the glider. She managed to angle her legs into the passenger side without looking like a clumsy fool. The fact that it never occurred to him that she might fumble the action generated even more tenderness with the man.

Their connection expanded with sheer exuberance.

The guards cheered, waved, and went back into the gatehouse, the female dragging the man away, since he wanted to spend more time ogling the glider.

"Where to?" Klay asked as he pulled away, the speed of the vehicle whooshing the air around them, but his voice perfectly clear and intimate by an actor's trick.

She turned to look at him, strong and striking features, continued to feel his energizing joy, let herself relax, banished all *her* doubts.

"I'd like to see your home and eat lunch with you."

His white teeth gleamed in a smile. "Excellent."

Seeing the city move by while sitting in a luxurious seat instead of the PublicCarrier, and heading along an unfamiliar route, engaged Giniana. A few minutes later they turned onto a gliderway between simple but elegant greeniron gates, under overarching trees not planted too closely together to obscure the front grassyard and gardens. When she saw that yard and wide flower beds, the large but relatively simple house—not a FirstFamily castle Residence—her spirit seemed to open to it. Almost as if it were perfect for her, or just plain *right*.

A very dangerous feeling.

They circled to the front of the house and Klay parked the glider before the low steps of a deck that wrapped around the front and side that she could see. Nothing like the tiny stoop standing before her cottage, nor the elegant portico of T'Spindle Residence. As with the rest of the property, she liked the look of the deck.

While she still stared, Klay whisked her up and out of the glider, up the stairs, and set her on her feet before the golden brown wooden door carved with herbs and shining with polish. She turned in place to look along the porch, the front grassyard. Everything seemed a work in progress, some portions newly cared for, flower gardens with rich earth showing and not one weed, some edges shabby with long grasses not yet mown waving shaggy tops in the gentle breeze …

Klay touched the gleaming brass latch and the door swung open on a short, wide hallway of tile, dim with refreshing coolness in the summertime, and opening into a sunlit mainspace. Her whole body sagged with the release of tension at the obvious welcome of the house.

He showed her the main floor and public rooms before they ate. She loved the airiness of the kitchen and eating rooms angling off it, one for casual dining, a small glass breakfast room, one for formal dinners. Apparently the previous St. Johnsworts had been interested in food. From the corner of her eye, she scanned Klay's tall, broad body. Extremely nice, but it appeared as if he'd lost a little weight. Perhaps he'd been skipping meals to conserve food.

She enjoyed her lunch, the textures and tastes, and Klay confirmed that a previous St. Johnswort made it for the Summer Solstice ritual. That he would offer her such bounty touched her.

After the meal, she looked out at the back grassyard, staring at a massive tree-fort, and several small and charming playhouses.

"I built those," he said.

"Lovely." She frowned. "Some of them are as large as my cottage."

"Yes." He shifted toward her, smiled. "I could build your cottage," he paused, "or other cottages as outbuildings on other FirstFamily estates."

A depressing thought speared her mind, and she murmured, "You could build me a cottage on T'Willow's estate."

His smile faded, but he nodded. "Yes, if you could negotiate that with D'Willow as part of *your* fee in becoming Family Healer in exchange for her carrying out the time procedure on Thrisca, I could build it." His eyes had darkened to a deeper blue as he picked up on her sadness. "You'll get through this. Thrisca will get through this. Melis will get through this, no matter what. We'll all get through this together."

Giniana swallowed.

He reached and took her hands in his own, met her gaze again, expression somber. "You must not give up hope." He squeezed her fingers. "You must believe that Thrisca will prevail and survive the time process."

She loosened her jaw. She'd clenched her teeth. "I know."

Klay lifted an eyebrow. "Thrisca wants to live. She'll fight."

"Yesss." Giniana's breath hissed out. She pressed her lips together, then said, "And I should have just enough gilt on this Midweekend to pay for the whole thing." Her spine straightened. "Without taking the job with D'Willow." She stretched her mouth in a fake smile, mocking her qualms rather than Klay.

"But you'll have no gilt reserves?" he pressed.

Glancing away at a colorful patch of meadow herbs, she replied, "I'll be fine. I have my employment with the Spindles and the Daisys. I have my cottage at the Spindles. I can pick up extra work, if necessary, as I have been doing, but not as much."

He scowled and that looked good on him. He opened his mouth, but a loud telepathic stream hit them both.

Where ARE You? plainted the kitten. *We want to show You Our ribbons and Our collar charms and how wonderful We look! We want to bask in Your praise and attention.*

You want more petting, and from me, Giniana sent back.

Yessss! both cats hissed mentally.

Sighing, Giniana decided to cut the time with Klay short. He'd need to leave for the theater soon anyway.

"I'll take you home," he said.

"That's out of your way."

"Not so much. We can leave right now." He touched her back as he led her to the front door.

When they stepped onto the porch, Giniana saw a boy rushing away from the glider to a nearby tree, picking up a garden tool he'd left there.

"Hey, Marti," Klay said, raising his hand in greeting to the boy, then said to Giniana, "He's a neighbor kid helping me out with the yard."

Marti shuffled his feet. "Hey, Johns. I didn't do anything. I didn't touch it."

Not quite the truth, Giniana saw a handprint on the metal of the hood, a slight sweat dampness on the leather of the driver's seat.

"No big deal, Marti," Klay said as he lifted Giniana into the glider, though she sensed he'd seen the marks, too. But the scent of him had her resenting her Fams. She'd have enjoyed sex with Klay upstairs in his bed.

As he walked around the vehicle, he smiled at the boy, who straightened as if a personal hero glanced in his direction. Klay said, "I'd take you for a ride, Marti, but I must get Giniana home, then head on into the theater. Tomorrow is matinee and evening performances for me. What about a ride the next day, during your noon grovestudy break?"

"Sure!" Marti sounded thrilled.

"We'll call it an appointment, then." Klay slid into the glider beside her, but continued to talk to the boy. "I need to head into town to the Theatrical Guild anyway, you could come." A lopsided smile from Klay. "Probably not very interesting for you, but you could look around a bit. I won't be long there."

"Sure!" The boy puffed out his chest. "No one in my grovestudy group has been to the Theatrical Guild. It will be educational, so I can miss the rest of the day and start my weekend early. I'll go ask Mom!"

Giniana laughed. "A child usually likes to cut grovestudy short."

Klay waved at the boy who was already in movement toward a cut in the hedge between properties. "Later!"

CHAPTER 24

THEY DROVE BACK out through the gates, and Giniana thought this neighborhood had fallen out of fashion decades ago, maybe as much as a century. Too big pieces of land and too large houses to tend, too far from CityCenter for the more upwardly-mobile middle class and lower nobles, though she liked the almost rural feeling. Not that she'd ever lived anywhere except in Druida City.

A comfortable silence of slow summer spun between them until they reached the busier part of the city they must traverse before entering Noble Country where all the First-Family estates, including the Spindles, were located. The bustling atmosphere affected them both. Klay's fingers drummed on the steering bar, then he translocated a piece of papyrus and offered it to her. "This is my schedule for the rest of the month. If you want me to take you to and from jobs in the glider, please scry." His intense eyes met hers. "Anytime I'm free."

She heard his harsh inhalation. He let his breath out on a demand, "I *will* drive you and Thrisca and Melis to D'Willow's workshop and the Time Healing Procedure on Midweekend. You'll all get there fast and privately."

Her throat closed at his offer and her trapped words whispered around the tightness. "Thank you. I appreciate that, *we* appreciate that."

He grunted and turned his gaze back to the road, though he'd set the glider on auto nav to the Spindles'. She fumbled the papyrus into her pursenal, then said, "I've seen the procedure before, we can watch through an observation window in the wall." She nibbled her lips. "I think D'Willow put that in for nervous relatives who hated seeing their loved ones disappear into a room and the family had to wait in a lobby. Though there isn't much action *to* see."

Klay turned to her, eyes wide with interest. "Hard to observe time."

"Yes. I'm allowed one guest for moral support, since space at the window is limited." Again she knew the curve of her lips wasn't really a smile. She seemed to throb with huge need. "Will you come with me? With us?"

His twitch of lips didn't much count as a smile, either. "Melis doesn't count as your guest?"

"A kitten? I'm sure not. You or I could hold her."

"Good. I'd love to go with you. A most fascinating proposition."

She leaned back into her seat. "Thank you."

"Always welcome," he said, then, "I'm sorry I didn't get to show you the upstairs of my home, the MasterSuite and—"

She found a chuckle. "I'm sorry, too. I'd've liked rolling around on a large bed with you."

To her surprise, his face flushed. "Not all our time is all about sex."

She touched his hand on the steering bar, "I know that, Klay."

He took his hands off the bar, letting the auto nav work, swept his fingers through her hair. "I like our bond, and we're getting ... close." She sensed his irresolution, and when he spoke it was with indirection instead of the straight-talk he usually delivered.

"Your Fams love you," he said.

"Yes."

"In their own way."

She chuckled. "You could say that."

"I did say that. And knowing you love and support her will help Thrisca fight for life."

"I believe so."

"Love can always support you." Another long pause. "You know I'm here for you, in any way."

"Yes." But their bond throbbed with such overwhelming emotion that she closed her eyes, shut herself away. As they proceeded through the city, her problems dropped back into her mind and onto her shoulders like weighty burdens.

Three days until the morning of the time experiment, and her nerves wound drum tight and she hung onto her strength and hope by the merest of threads.

The silence continued as he drove to Noble Country and dropped her off at the Spindles'.

She scrambled out of the glider and through the postern door before he could kiss her. For some reason she thought that if his lips touched hers, she'd shatter into pieces she couldn't put back together.

Playing with the kitten behind her cottage eased the huge and dangerous tsunami of feelings that had threatened to overwhelm Giniana that moment in Klay's glider. She ran around, wiggled a string, hopped here and there to avoid pounces, then finally activated prototypes of several of the toys Blakely Wattle had left and sent them in different directions.

Thrisca lay in a patch of clover, appearing too exhausted to leap to her favorite birdbath, understandable if she'd hidden her condition from the Spindles, done her duties at the Residence and/or directed Melis to fulfill those duties.

So though Giniana's stress at Klay's unspoken declaration diminished, her gut-anxiety over Thrisca's health hitched up more notches until Melis curled near to Thrisca and dropped off to sleep.

When the frenetic activity ended, Giniana slumped in one of the chairs looking out onto the elegant tangle of T'Spindle's woods. Her Fams slept, Melis napped with the quick but profound sleep of kittens, Thrisca with too-extreme weariness. For one awful instant, in Giniana's own fatigue, the terrible wish that Thrisca would pass on to the Wheel of Stars and end all this revisited her. The next moment, she'd shored up her strength with hope. All this would be resolved shortly. By this time on the day of Midweekend, the time procedure would be over.

Closing her eyes and relaxing as the sun sunk in the sky, angling toward evening, the memory of Klay taking her hands and holding them, lending her support through their bond, returned to her in a wash of warm tenderness.

He'd hinted at love, that he might love her, hadn't he? But Giniana wasn't sure what "love" meant. She'd observed the Spindles—HeartMates—the affection, the tenderness, even interrupted the odd passionate kiss now and then—from people older than her own parents. So she saw HeartMate love.

But regular love? No.

Both her parents had said they'd loved her. And they might have, in their own way. But she understood she treated Thrisca with more care than either of her parents had taken with her.

That sounded whiny and bitter, so she relaxed muscle by

muscle until she fell into a doze herself, but kept her perscry close and set for any HealingHall emergency alarm.

Perhaps she could grab a full half-septhour of sleep before jumping up to run at full speed again.

Johns acted well, the play going brilliantly, as usual. The theater continued to be packed with sell-out crowds, since *Firewalker* closed in a week and a half, the last day of the month, Midweekend.

And Thrisca's time Healing was *this* Midweekend, now in three days since the clock rang midnight as Johns drank a winding-down soother in his dark kitchen before going up to bed.

This Midweekend, the day of the time treatment, he had matinee and evening performances. If things went poorly in the morning he'd whisk Giniana and Melis to the theater. The new space and people would keep Melis occupied, and the environment of her childhood might give comfort to Giniana. He didn't know.

If best came to best, he thought the little Family would like to spend time together, and that wrenched at him. He'd rather have them all, even a frisky Thrisca, at his home, running around *his* grounds, not T'Spindle's.

He paced, undoing the work of the soother, considering and abandoning plans in his brain.

Finally, he decided to wrangle his previous understudy to take the performances—even pay the guy extra. That actor might like the credit on his resume, since he'd never actually performed *Firewalker* on stage and before a live and public audience. Johns hadn't missed one performance.

So he left a viz message in the actor's perscry cache, along with a chit on Johns's bank account. When he ended the call, he found his mouth twisted. This relationship cost him, a little in gilt since Giniana would *not* let him help out with the amount needed for Thrisca's Healing. Cost him a lot in time, and a huge amount in sheer emotional vulnerability.

The afternoon with Giniana had consisted of golden moments, summertime and pleasure and his lover, never to be separated into distinct events in his mind, but every nuance to be cherished.

But she hadn't stayed to examine the MasterSuite. Time for him to do so. Without turning on any light, he retrieved T'Ash's token from the kitchen no-time he'd stashed it in, moved to the back staircase ... and tiny white lights appeared under each tread. His heart thumped and he swallowed, said in resonant tones, "Thank you, HeartStones," and trod with deliberate steps, sending energy down into the earth where the runestones lay.

He'd been giving Flair to quite a few beings, lately. He didn't begrudge it to Giniana or his home, but maybe some to the Fams.

When he reached the wide upper hallway, the lights ran along the baseboard of each wall, this time blue, then stopped and pulsed before his mother's door—no, the MasterSuite or MistrysSuite door. Sucking in his breath, Johns placed his fingers on the latch, tapped them in the opening spell, then stepped inside.

A lamp with a fancy stained-glass shade lit, showering the sitting room with colorful light. Another swallow, some blinking as childhood recollections of this place, of his mother and FatherDam, rushed through his mind, hitting his heart. When his vision cleared, he noted the few remaining fine furnishings that his ancestors had purchased.

The silver token seemed to warm in his pocket. He could provide a treasure for future generations, too. He drew in a breath, then stopped, frozen at the lingering scent of his mother. Panting, he was torn, wanting to save the scent forever … and wanting to charge forward in his life.

With stiff steps, he went into the small dressing room and his eyes stung. Perhaps a true Residence might have a spell to save scents—he was pretty sure the new HouseStones couldn't do it, and he could not bring himself to push them to try.

He swept aside lovely dresses dating from the time when his mother met his father, before his father died and they'd lost his potential, the last of the business and most of their gilt. Tapping on a wood panel, he revealed the hidden no-time safe. No gilt inside, of course, no coins of any denomination. Only a bronze jewelry box.

Breathing shallowly through his nose, he took out the jewelry box and moved to the shabby and faded green armchair near the lovely lamp. When he sat, he smelled his mother again, puffed out a sigh, drew up a small wooden side table with chipped veneer, placed the jewelry box on it and opened up the case.

He stared at the ugly piece of diamond and topaz jewelry, the necklace that had been in the family for centuries. Despite all the vaporous wraiths of ancestors lingering in the back of his mind, protesting, he could sell it for enough to recoup what he'd paid for the glider and keep his savings, even add to that account.

He didn't like to draw on his savings when he had no income. Other than his career, he wasn't a gambler. Being an actor made his life risky enough.

Not a gambler. But he would bet on his own career, his own talent.

He tossed T'Ash's silver token atop the necklace without looking further through the jewelry box, snapped the thing shut, put the box back in the safe.

He'd been poor but not destitute, he had the land and the

house. He fully intended to put more gilt into them when he made enough to do so, but who knew what would happen in the future? He was sure his merchant ancestors never imagined the family finances would be so low that a descendant of theirs would live off fruits from the estate gardens, as Johns had done as a boy.

His mother and his FatherDam hadn't sold the necklace to make all of their lives easier, he wouldn't either.

Worse came to worst, he could sell the damn glider in a few weeks.

He'd pass the necklace and token down to whomever came after him—and, yeah, he now understood he wanted a wife and children someday, maybe even with Giniana, and that notion thumped his heart fast.

Keep the necklace just in case one of his descendants needed it more than he.

Still, his mouth dried as he recalled making out the chit for the vehicle from his savings account.

Lost in the past. No. That would send him into a deep brood.

Move into the present now, and onto the future. He rose and stuffed his emotions into an inner closet, examined the room with dispassion.

The oldest, worn furniture needed to be hauled to the large deconstructor and reduced to individual components that might only be worth enough energy to power a few minor House spells.

Better yet, plan how to make these rooms most comfortable for Giniana! Get rid of the sad and change around with more cheerful, patterned pieces. Squinting, he thought of a book with cloth pieces in it that his mother had once shown him, so it lay somewhere in the house. And wasn't there a sample with a pale yellow background?

Dubiously he stared at the walls. What he could see indicated a green gone gray. Definitely not uplifting. Next time he sensed the HouseStones ready to communicate with him, he could talk to them about it. Or he could trudge up to the attic in his oldest clothes and take a look, for the book, any wallpaper, gently used furniture.

Perhaps the attic had been cleaned lately with the house-keeping spells, though he'd concentrated more on the grounds and the public rooms. Perhaps.

Embrace the recent past. When he'd met Giniana, his career, his rise to fame, was the most important thing in his life. And at that time, he'd have said he'd have done anything to pursue it. But not now.

The revelation staggered him. Giniana Filix had risen to become the first priority in his life. With her in mind, he'd worked on his House—and discovered it was becoming intelligent—and labored on his property, that he'd neglected before.

At the beginning of the month he'd been focused entirely on himself.

But from the moment he met Giniana Filix, experienced that connection between them, the one including attraction, hinting at the prospect of love, he'd begun changing.

It was the love. Who knew he'd been so lonely, so needing true intimacy? He hadn't. He'd had his career, his friends, his friendly rivals, acquaintances.

Obviously that had not been enough.

Now he had Giniana.

And FamCats. Urgh.

But HeartStones!

Such blessings he'd received that he murmured a prayer of gratitude to the Lady and Lord.

Then he left the suite, closing the door and the flow of memories behind him, and walked across the hall to his own sitting room, part of the HeirSuite. Yes, the past was past.

The future he might plan for, but would do nothing about until he learned Thrisca's fate in three days.

Live within the now.

And within the now, he could reread the notes on Amberose's script, his own personal obsession. He'd begun to memorize those lines he sensed Amberose had written and Lily Fescue had not made up. He also started practicing gestures, donning the character of the hero.

Amberose hadn't returned his scry. Would he annoy her by pressing her on the matter of her script? Where it was? How she was handling the matter of finding it, selling it, producing the play? He thought she might very well be annoyed if he called.

He'd let that sit as long as he could and hope when his patience snapped he didn't ruin everything.

Johns awoke with the lightening of the sky the next morning, his body becoming accustomed to short sleep and rising early so he could meet Giniana.

Today he could pick her up himself in his glider and bring her here, his home, for breakfast, and perhaps sex in his own bed.

Dressing in casual clothes and jumping stairs to get to the kitchen and his first cup of caff of the day, he moved fast so he wouldn't miss her, surprise her instead.

He reviewed the list of food in the kitchen no-times. His FatherDam had liked cooking breakfast best, and had gone fancy every after-Yule morning, when most of the family—their tiny family of three, then two—remained awake after keeping Yule all night long. That meal would be perfect this morning.

Everything prepared for an intimate breakfast for two in

the sunroom, he left before his calendarsphere rang the note reminding him to depart to pick up Giniana.

Counting today, three days and a few septhours until Thrisca's procedure. He wouldn't let the pressure of that dim his mood, and if it smudged Giniana's emotions, he'd distract her.

CHAPTER 25

GINIANA SAID her usual goodbyes to the Daisys upstairs in the nursery, placing the fed and sleeping baby into her mother's arms. As Giniana walked downstairs, she sent mental probes to her Fams—or her FamCat and her FamCat's kitten —and found them out and hunting, uninterested in any communication with their human.

Scanning Thrisca at a distance, Giniana noted the cat felt as if she'd recovered from her long day yesterday. Giniana had received some energy from Klay and T'Daisy Residence at times during the night, and siphoned some from herself to her FamCat.

Now the cats would hunt until the sun rose solidly over the horizon and banished all twilit shadows, then sleep.

As usual, Giniana's stomach pinched at the thought of the time experiment. She thought of that process more as an experiment than a procedure, because the threat of Thrisca dying was greater than what a Healer would consider during a routine practice. Reaching into her trous pocket, she took out a belly calming pill, swallowed it down.

Only when she opened the door to see Klay leaning against his glider, waiting for her, did all her cares fall away.

They shared companionable silence as he drove to his home, and a beautiful constriction in her chest as she saw the house amidst the gardens touched by the first rays of the sun.

In the glass room they ate a large, savory meal that probably came from the ritual no-time again, and to which Giniana didn't pay as much attention to as she should.

Klay translocated the dishes to the cleanser, took her hand and tugged so she rose. With a wave of his hand, music filled the air and he began to dance her to the sweeping staircase in the front of the house. Naturally his training had included dancing. So had hers.

And his body brushed hers in the waltz and the atmosphere heated with sexual tension around them, and her body began to yearn for fulfillment, her mind to blur.

Leaning down, he whispered, "Your tension is disappearing, sent into the steps of the dance. You follow me, your body responding to mine. Very good."

Then, to her surprise, he swung her up in his arms, and ascended the stairs. He continued to murmur in her ear, the movement of his lips brushing her skin, sensitizing her to his touch, making her core dampen with need. "Sex can be relaxing or energizing, depending on how it's done."

The door opened to a room filled with sunshine, and he set her on her feet next to his bed. Then his large hands slid under the shoulder tabs of her tunic and opened them. His palms touched her and the skin-to-skin contact caused her nerves to sizzle. Everything but the compulsion to make love with this man dissolved.

For Johns, the rest of the day passed in work.

He'd only had a brief conversation with Giniana after sex

and before she teleported home—as he'd been trying to convince her to let him drive her.

So instead of spending that while with her, he laid in three hearty breakfasts, through the morning of the time process, though he believed that neither he nor she would eat well that morning. And Giniana and her tiny *FamCat* family might want to stay at their cottage at the Spindles the night before.

He'd rather have them all here, close, where he could keep an eye on them and be most supportive.

As far as he knew, Giniana had made enough gilt to pay D'Willow for the treatment. Otherwise she'd have been working up to the very last moment. That reminded him he needed to grab a few minutes to speak with T'Spindle. He'd decided that much.

Johns felt sure that Giniana hadn't revealed a hint of her financial straits to her employer—a man with deep inherited and generational wealth, and one who appeared to care for his staff. The guy should know what was going on with his Healer. Johns would want to be informed if someone he employed experienced trouble, if he'd been in the FirstFamily Lord's position.

Several people had made Johns's "must contact" list, though he was considering whether to meet in person or scry.

One call would be to Raz Cherry to thank him for the discount on the glider. And to update that friendly rival about the situation regarding Amberose's script. The secondary male lead seemed to have been written for Raz, and as far as Johns knew, the man hadn't been informed about current developments of the situation. Perhaps Raz could put a little pressure on Amberose, too.

Since he filled his day with morning yard work, afternoon

and evening theater work, and calls with Giniana when he could grab a couple of minutes, Johns managed *not* to irritate Amberose by scrying her. He ended the day by reading his notes on the play.

The famous writer called him Midmorning Bell the next day, didn't bother with a courteous greeting but went straight to the point. "I confirmed that my script is missing. That someone supposedly bought it." Her naturally solemn expression hardened into stern lines. "I also wrung as much as I could out of that Blakely Wattle. My *former* agent. Designing Fam toys now, by the Cave of the Dark Goddess." She snorted, then her piercing gaze seared into his own. "Who is your agent?"

A direct question, and he'd been himself with her, no acting persona, so answer the direct question. Don't blow it now. "Chatt Geyer." Johns drew in what he hoped was an unobtrusive breath. "I don't think he represents writers, only actors."

She inclined her head in a regal manner. "I am not sure of that, either. However, as it happens, I requested one of my distant relatives to check out the rumors in the theatrical community. He did inform me that the general opinion of Blakely Wattle was poor. He also conducted research about current playwright agents." Her smile showed edged and knifelike. "Since this is the first time I've spoken with my family members in Druida City in a decade, and I am the wealthiest person in the family, my relative was glad to proceed further than my initial request."

Johns wanted to clear his throat. He didn't, so his voice came out creakier than he liked. "I'm sure."

Another inclination of her head. "Yes. I received several agents' names and interviewed a few by scry."

"Ah."

"I hired Austro Gentian."

Johns inclined his head. "A very well-respected man in the business."

"Yes," Amberose agreed. "My new agent is dubious that I will be able to keep casting and creative control over my own piece of work."

"I heard that." Johns gave her a sympathetic smile. "Most producers want that control." He waved a negligent hand. "Financial people want to make sure their gilt goes the way they want." Well, that wasn't phrased well. Damn.

"I understand. But we will try selling my play on my terms first," she replied austerely.

Johns figured Wattle already attempted that, and the fact Amberose now had a better agent wouldn't change things. Johns just nodded.

"I would like you to continue looking for the missing copy of my script, and who might have purchased it. My agent believes if he pursues those inquiries, it could lead to extortion, as the purchaser would like to maximize her or his profit."

"It could," Johns stated, but figured Austro Gentian didn't want to do that job, probably thought he had a tough enough task and an overly-demanding client that may or may not be worth a lot of his expensive time.

"I promise that if you provide me with the name of the person who bought my script, other information, or, particularly, the script itself, you will have my greatest appreciation." She ladened her voice with unspoken promises.

He inclined his torso in a short bow. "You are known to be a person of the highest honor. I will do my very best to fulfill that request." And hope that he could come through.

"I will tell my agent to contact your agent if the sale goes through and a production will be mounted."

Again Johns nodded, radiating gratitude. Which he felt, but damn it, the job and the role seemed as far away as ever.

After the call, to soothe himself, he walked around his property, admiring the results of the labor he and Marti had put in, and perhaps Marti's older female relatives when Johns wasn't looking. By the time he'd made a circuit, he felt calm enough, and rehearsed enough, and determined to contact T'Spindle and tell him about Giniana's problems.

Johns hoped she wouldn't think he betrayed her.

Marti Samphire, freshly scrubbed with gleaming wet hair, arrived promptly at noonbell for their excursion to the Theatrical Guild. The boy wore clothes that had Johns's brows rising and his bones feeling old, since the garments obviously reflected the pre-teen's generational fashion sense. Bright blue trous, red shirt with puffed sleeves like nobles wore, screaming yellow vest with cream embroidery of... stems and blossoms, probably reflecting his family name.

Keeping the glider roof and windows thinned, Johns sped through the streets a little over the limit, enjoying Marti's blissful expression.

Since gliders remained few, Johns parked right in front of the wing of the Druida City GuildHall that housed the Theatrical Guild, and ushered Marti into the impressive building, their bootheels sounding on the marble floors of the two-story entrance.

Since the Theatrical Guild shared space with all the other guilds—merchants and mercenaries and weavers and herbal-ists—and appearances mattered to the theatrical community, the set designers had created an imposing atrium.

Just walking into the area made Johns stand straighter. As

with the first time he walked down this hallway, slightly older than Marti, holding a crumpled slightly-damp application, wonder and pride filled Johns. At that moment, he'd proven to himself and others that he was an actor. He would pursue an acting career.

Now, though he felt the quick upsurge of that initial delight, he kept his face in a casual expression, his stride easy. A few clumps of actors stood around, but Johns knew more would be lounging in the elegant but more comfortable sitting room beyond the atrium.

When Marti tugged on his sleeve to be introduced to this or that female actress—usually voluptuous—Johns obliged. He kept his ears pricked for gossip about Amberose's play, dropped a few idle comments to steer conversations without appearing too interested.

The compliments on his work in *Firewalker* gratified him, and he heard buzz about upcoming projects, but nothing solid.

As he strode by the closed door of the Actors' Representative's office, he recalled how Ovata Forsythia had used general funds allocated by the Thespian Club to re-activate Giniana's lifetime membership that her parents had begun, paid the whole thing off.

That got him thinking about her childhood and those who should have supported her, financially as well as emotionally. Had her parents been deleterious in that, too? He knew that her mother had drifted from lover to lover who'd paid Verna Winterbloom Filix's bills, perhaps fed and housed both mother and child if he had the room and the means, but what of Giniana's father, Mas? Legally, he would have been obligated to send gilt to support his child.

And Johns figured the easiest way to transfer such gilt from one continent to another would be through the respective Theatrical Guilds. Mas could pay on Chinju and it would be credited to his account, or his wife's for their daughter, here in Druida City on Cambria Continent.

One simple question might ensure this had been done, have Ovata or the Guild accountant verify the child support.

At that moment, Ellis Gardenia, the-actor-turning-counselor, sauntered from the Actors' rep office, a contemplative smile hovering on his lips.

"Hey, Johns." Ellis lifted a hand in greeting,

"Greetyou, Ellis." Johns looked past him to Ovata Forsythia standing in the open doorway of the office, staring at Ellis.

Projecting his voice to only reach Ellis, Johns asked, "Resigning from the Theatrical Guild?"

"Trying to." Ellis rolled his eyes as he joined Johns and Marti. "Ovata convinced me to only downgrade to a subsidiary membership, so if I wanted to return to an acting career, I could. The lady is persuasive."

"That she is," Johns agreed. But she'd been generous in dealing with Giniana at the Thespian Club. Johns could talk to her about Mas Filix and any support he'd made of Giniana.

"I know you," Marti said, frowning up at Ellis. "You were the grovestudy teacher in the viz, *The Origin of Centaury, the Boy Celtaroon Killer.*"

Ellis laughed. "Yes, I was."

Marti slid his gaze to Johns. "And you were the stup character who died in *Firewalker.*"

"That, too," Ellis said amiably.

Johns met Ovata's gaze and respectfully nodded.

Ellis glanced at Johns, then looked down at Marti with an indulgent grin. "Hey, they're casting a new show, *Centaury, Further Adventures of the Boy Celtaroon Killer.* I know the director, and I think he might like a real boy's opinion on the actors."

Marti gasped. "I *love* those stories about Centaury! I could help, I could!" He wiggled with excitement.

Ellis met Johns's eyes. "Why don't I take Marti along to the auditions for a while ... maybe three-quarters of a septhour?"

Dipping his head in unspoken thanks, Johns said, "Sounds good to me."

"*May I*, MasterLevel Actor Saint Johnswort?" Marti nearly gushed.

"Sure. We'll meet back here in a septhour, why not?"

Ellis angled toward a tiled narrow hallway and Marti, anticipating him, shot down it.

"Thanks," Johns said. "*I* don't know that director, and this will be a real treat for Marti. His Flair is for botanics."

Winking, Ellis said, "I know you don't know that director. I've been around longer than you, and you want to talk with the rep."

"Yes." Johns smiled, sincerely. "You'll be a good counselor, Ellis."

"I know that, too." He ambled after a waiting Marti.

MasterLevel actor Ovata Forsythia stepped back from the threshold of her office as Johns strode toward her. Once inside, she closed the door behind him.

"I've been wondering about the financial support Giniana Filix should have had during her childhood," Johns began bluntly.

"Odd you should say that." Ovata took her seat behind her desk and Johns sat, too. "Gossip is going around the Thespian Club and here that FirstLevel Healer Filix might need gilt."

Johns shrugged.

Ovata continued, "And I thought about the Healer and her family, too." Ovata gave a delicate cough. "But I'm not sure I should talk about confidential information." She met his eyes in a significant stare, then glanced away. "It occurs to me that when Healer Filix's father, Mas, went to Chinju, he would have been expected to send money to this guild for his own membership, and he didn't. I looked at his account and it has been inactive for years."

"Since he abandoned his family."

Another study of his person from Ovata. "You know, pursuant to Celtan law, Mas must provide support for his child since he left her before she reached adulthood."

"When she was ten years old, I believe."

"In Mas's case, I'd expect him to pay such funds to the Theatrical Guild of Chinju and they'd transfer the gilt to the Theatrical Guild here, but Mas Filix's Chinju Theatrical Guild account is also disused."

Johns discovered he ground his teeth. "Interesting. I'd wondered."

"Naturally, Giniana's mother, who was also a lifetime member of the Thespian Club and the Theatrical Guild, should have notified the Guild if such payment from Mas *wasn't* made. She never did. Her account shows absolutely no activity for even longer than Mas's."

"Huh." More boggling of Johns's mind at Giniana's parents actions … inactions. Red began to seep into his vision, surprising him. He'd thought he'd been prepared for this news.

Mas hadn't sent enough funds to see Giniana housed and fed and clothed and raised well? Her mother hadn't bothered to demand such support, the gilt due her daughter from her father? Anger sizzled and he felt it rise to flush his skin.

Ovata fixed her gaze on a point above his left shoulder. "I understand that Verna Winterbloom Filix lived with her lovers." Ovata rolled a shoulder. "I didn't know Verna. She was older than I, and she … made choices I would not have."

Johns belatedly remembered Ovata had three children and

no current husband herself. From what he recollected, all three of her children were doing very well.

"I wonder about Mas's account," Ovata emphasized.

Johns narrowed his eyes at the woman, *heard* the sub-text, studied her manner and her body.

"Of course Mas Filix might have send funds to support his daughter to the main GuildHall instead of our Theatrical Guild, but I can't simply request such files from the main GuildHall clerk. Someone," Ovata gave another tiny cough, "with more clout should do so."

Johns blinked.

"I understand you are ... interested ... in Giniana Filix. Or you wouldn't be here," Ovata added. Her voice took on a persuasive note. "And FirstLevel Healer Filix is the staff Healer for T'Spindle. And you did a favor for T'Spindle a week and a half ago."

He got the idea. Ovata Forsythia wanted him to ask T'Spindle to intervene on behalf of Giniana. He'd already decided to do so, but she gave him some extra information as ammunition. Johns leaned back in his chair. "Tell me, Master-Level Actor Forsythia, would you, as an independent woman, like a ... gallant of yours to interfere in your business? Your financial affairs?"

She pursed her lips. "Perhaps. But I would definitely want my legal due."

"What if you're excessively proud?" Johns had begun to think Giniana held that flaw.

"Ahhh," the actor shook her head. "Youth."

"Perhaps *you* could speak with T'Spindle ..."

But she shrugged and the movement rippled down her body in a sensuality that he manfully ignored.

"It's evident you don't listen to old gossip," she said. "And good for you. But the ancient story regarding ... ah ... conflict between myself and T'Spindle is true. I lied to him and wronged him. That FirstFamily Lord would not listen to me."

A burst of knowledge of past rumors surrounding Ovata and T'Spindle flashed like a light through Johns.

Lied to him and wronged him, she'd said.

The same underlying attitude Giniana had with Johns's profession.

CHAPTER 26

GINIANA WALKED BACK to her cottage after Healing a broken leg for one of the inside Residence staff. She took care to enjoy the day and the blessings her senses brought her and murmured a prayer of gratitude to the Lady and Lord.

Then her scry pebble drummed in staccato and her pleasant mood instantly evaporated. Palli Willow, D'Willow's assistant called.

Blowing out a hard breath, dread looming like a dark cloud heavy with lightning threatening her, Giniana answered. "Greetyou, Palli."

The woman's lips curved up in a rictus smile. *She* certainly could use some acting lessons.

"Anything wrong?" Giniana asked, keeping her voice cool and her fears stuffed away. Then she realized she herself acted during daily life, staying calm when patients exhibited panic at wounds or sickness. Yes, she had a professional mask and manner like the other Healers she worked with.

Palli's smile widened, making her look even worse, her cheer more false. She glanced down at a sheet of papyrus and read words quickly and woodenly. "It's exactly two days from the end of the Time Healing Procedure and I am scrying to confirm your FamCat Thrisca will be participating."

"Yes, of course," Giniana stated, but checked her bond with her FamCat and the kitten, both snoozing in her back garden.

"Good. Good." Palli coughed. "About this time we begin receiving calls from people who might have second thoughts about the treatment."

That had never occurred to Giniana. Not many people ducked out of a standard Healing procedure, no matter how long and involved.

The whole Time Experiment Healing session expense was shared by the participants, so when the number dropped, the amount each person had to pay rose. Don't hyperventilate. She could handle this.

"Have any previously scheduled Time Healing Procedure sessions been canceled at the last moment?" she asked, with her own much better serene smile.

Palli's forehead lined. "Yes, of course. The GreatLady can't work for a minimal amount." Palli frowned. "Some participants have actually failed to show up. Very rude. Thus I scry to confirm, as I am so doing."

"Thus," Giniana said. Her mind had gone wild with sparking fear, zooming through all her options for gilt again. She had enough for the procedure if no one dropped out. Thrisca couldn't survive until another session, not through the chill of late autumn or winter.

Palli looked down at her papyrus again, read: "And I am reminding you that we need a final, pre-procedure report from your Healer about your state of health."

"My FamCat and I are stopping by Danith D'Ash, the Animal Healer, on the way to the Time Experiment. The appointment is set."

Palli looked up, flushed. "It's not an experiment."

"The Healers of Celta deem it so, and that's probably why you have dropouts," Giniana replied. "You may mark me down as attending to observe—"

"You may bring only one guest!" Palli snapped.

"—and my FamCat, Thrisca, attending as a participant."

Palli picked up a writestick and slashed at the papyrus. "We'll see you in two days." She ended the scry.

"Unfortunately," Giniana muttered. She wobbled to the next bench along the path, one set in a beam of sunlight but surrounded by trees. Lifting her face, she closed her eyes, let the heat caress her face. She was so weary, and she'd stopped working whatever job she could get, relaxed and played with Klay.

Her absolute best option would be to accept D'Willow's offer of employment as the Willow Healer, easiest. And Giniana could rest these last two days, not worry about a last-minute session cancellation.

But she loved her cottage, her sense of independence, and working for the easy-going Spindles.

So she prayed and hoped for the best. And pulled out her scry pebble and let all the HealingHalls know she could take shifts.

After Johns strolled to the board with the postings of upcoming shows—few at this moment and none suitable for him—he checked that his name was on the books as wanting a role after the end of the month. Both antique procedures hearkened back to ancient traditions.

He spoke to other actors, those in productions and not, fulfilling his secondary goal of seeing and being seen. He stayed friendly and affable, projecting a manner that he'd be easy to work with. No brooding here, he'd save that privately and for later.

And yes, he acted a bit, and would have felt the need to be truly sincere if Giniana had been by his side, and was glad she wasn't. Eventually she'd see this particular slight mask of his persona, but he'd rather keep it to himself now, and it fit comfortably.

Several minutes later, Johns collected an enthusiastic Marti Samphire. The boy burbled about his experience as a casting consultant all the drive home, as Johns once more turned over options in his mind.

It had taken him a long time to decide to interfere in Giniana's business, in her personal finances, but everything he learned made him think that her draining herself in Flair, energy and gilt when she had other options was wrong.

And the new information regarding her father's lack of any support increased Johns's determination to help her, and do that indirectly since she wouldn't accept gilt from him. Not that he knew what the time Healing would cost, but anything provided by a FirstFamily Lord or Lady tended to be fantastically expensive. And messing with time …

Johns left Marti at the gate of the Samphire property, cranked open his own sticking greeniron gates with Flair, parked in front of the House and marched up the steps to pace through his home.

Should he talk to Giniana about this? Probably, but he had no solid information that her father had been delinquent —Mas Filix might have made arrangements with the Druida City GuildHall or a bank.

An itch told him to contact her, anyway, and he put a scry through and reached her message cache, which made him think she might be working, again, sapping her resources. He didn't want to discuss her father with her in a series of messages. Better in person, but at least face-to-face in a scry.

So Johns left a message for her to call regarding an important matter.

Now, should he scry or pay a personal visit to T'Spindle?

If Johns had wanted to speak with T'Spindle on his own behalf, he'd have made an appointment with the FirstFamily Lord's assistant, at the lord's convenience, shown up a little early, well-groomed and in his best clothes.

This wasn't for himself.

So scry the great man himself, ask to speak to him personally.

But Johns must ensure he made a good impression, because the guy produced plays and *could* shoot Johns's career to the top, if the GrandLord wanted. Definitely groom—waterfall and shave again—and dress in his best and most fashionable clothes. Also … Johns stared around his sitting room.

The FirstFamilies *were* that, First. Their ancestors had funded the starships and the journey from Earth to Celta. Had paid for the ships and the generational crew. The First-Family Lords and Ladies had purchased the right to sleep in cryonics tubes for the long trip. They'd also been the best in Flair on Earth, and had developed it since. They'd been the leaders from the moment they'd stepped onto the new planet's soil, four centuries and seven years ago.

But the St. Johnswort family had developed within the first century, as herbalists providing folk with mixtures, tinctures, potions. They'd become merchants. They'd claimed this land and built this big house at the turn of the second century. His family was old, too.

Even if he was the first actor, even if his family had declined in influence and wealth, he had the pedigree and blood of a long-established family, one respected by the First-Families.

Show that.

After refreshing himself, he went through the house to the paneled ResidenceDen, pulled a little Flair from himself and the House to polish up the chamber.

Johns spent a few minutes choosing the best scrybowl and positioning it right, then he did a couple of mental exercises before circling his finger around the rim to initiate the call. The GrandLord's assistant answered and with a note of insistence, Johns requested to speak with T'Spindle.

The adjunct stared at Johns with cool and calculating eyes, as if the younger man knew who he was and judged exactly how necessary Johns believed talking to the First-Family GrandLord to be.

Johns stared back with his most impressive stone face.

A couple of seconds later, too quickly for Johns to huff out a relieved breath, T'Spindle looked at him, the lord's amiable mask in place. Being the most genial of the FirstFamily lords didn't mean the man wasn't dangerous.

Donning a smooth manner escaped Johns, because this was so important for Giniana. Mattered about his own career, too, but mostly Giniana.

"I'm scrying to speak to you about Giniana Filix," he said bluntly.

T'Spindle's brows went up and down, and he let his surprise show. "I know you've been seeing her."

Of course he did. Anytime Johns stepped foot on the estate T'Spindle would be notified.

Johns jerked a nod. He wanted to clear his throat but didn't, he *did* choose his words carefully. "I spoke with a Theatrical Guild rep today." A self-deprecating smile, as if it was primarily his own career he'd been concerned about. "And was asked about Giniana." Not a lie. "Our guild has no record of any gilt being transferred to it from the Chinju Theatrical Guild from Giniana's father, Mas Filix, after he arrived and took the job in Chinju." A good career move for the man, and Johns knew it had made Filix famous and wealthy, able to choose his roles.

"Are you saying," T'Spindle began carefully, "that Mas Filix never sent gilt to support his young daughter?" The lord's voice chilled and sliced his words.

Johns couldn't take a drink to soothe his dry throat. He didn't even have a tube of water on the desk, an oversight. "That is my understanding though Druida City GuildHall might have an account of such payments." He paused. "I am not in a position to request such records from the GuildHall."

"I understand." T'Spindle's lips thinned. "I will check into this. Thank you."

"Thank—" Johns began, but the lord waved the scry connection cut.

Whoosh. Johns actually heard the air compress from his lungs.

And he wondered if FirstFamily GrandLord T'Spindle knew about Thrisca and D'Willow's Healing process and why Giniana needed gilt, could use all the back gilt her father should have paid her over the years.

Johns yet sat collapsed in the rarely-used desk chair when T'Spindle scried him back and he had to look calm and collected again, drag up those acting skills.

The GrandLord appeared angry, but spoke smoothly and told Johns that no funds had been collected by the GuildHall on behalf of his daughter from Mas Filix after he'd abandoned his small family to pursue his career in Chinju.

And T'Spindle subtly indicated that he expected Johns to take care of the matter of contacting Mas Filix. Which left Johns stunned.

While he wrapped his mind around the notion, T'Spindle disconnected. But the FirstFamily Lord was right. Johns had made the matter his business. And he got the impression

that following through on this matter would be like a test—
an audition—for T'Spindle.

Johns glanced at the antique clock on the wall, figured the
local time for the continent of Chinju, discovered all his
muscles too tight. So he stood and ran through a modified
fighter training kata, simple enough he wouldn't sweat in his
good clothes, then scried the Theatrical Guild of Chinju.

Johns got the Actors' representative in Artisan City,
Chinju, and stated he was calling on behalf of FirstFamily
GrandLord T'Spindle with regard to Giniana Filix, daughter
of Mas Filix. The rep stared at Johns. "Klay Saint Johnswort. I
know of you. Saw your viz."

The one and only viz Johns had done, a cheap adventure
flick.

"I'm sorry," Johns winced, tried an embarrassed smile.

"Huh. Guess it was you and not the writer or director who
made the hero as nuanced as he was."

"I did what I could."

"Good job." And to John's surprise, the guy zipped him
right through to Mas's perscry ... and a recorded viz of the
handsome actor requested the caller to leave a message and
ended with a too-charming-for-Johns smile.

He didn't want to bring up Giniana, didn't want to talk
too much and put the man off. So Johns left a brief message
that he scried on behalf of T'Spindle, figured that would get
Mas to call back. Johns also noted the time difference and
stated he'd be working that night.

When he stood, he found himself sticky again, went to his
suite to disrobe, and set his best clothes in the cleanser.
Returning from another, more refreshing, waterfall, he
dressed in lounge clothes.

Restless, he paced his suite. The notes of Amberose's
story caught his eye. He wished he'd been assertive enough
to ask her for a full manuscript. He picked it up, saw the

description of the second male lead, which reminded him that he needed to scry Raz Cherry to thank him for the glider. Johns should also update Raz about what was going on with the script. He might be a good person to help turn up the missing manuscript.

Johns sat and picked up the story once again and got lost until his calendarsphere pinged that he must leave for *Firewalker*.

Giniana didn't contact him before he went on stage and his irritation sparked as he sensed she worked a regular shift at some HealingHall. Did she need more gilt?

He'd make sure she'd have enough, one way or another.

The next morning at dawn, both he and Giniana slurped down nutrition drinks at his home before she jumped him for sex. Exacerbated nerves shimmered through her, radiating to him, not only along their bond but buzzing in the very atmosphere. Tomorrow Thrisca would be Healed or not.

And Johns figured out Giniana felt she must keep busy every minute of the day to stay sane. He tried to slow the sex down, to no avail, to get some real food into her, also futile.

After mating, he stroked her body in bed. He wanted to comfort and began in a soothing voice, "Let's talk about—"

She hopped out of the bed to land on her feet. "No." Flinging out her arm, finger-pointing at him, she snapped, "Don't you use that actor's voice on me! Don't you dare."

Jackknifing up, he said, "Hey, I've only been honest with you."

Sniffing, she flung out both arms and ordered, "Whirlwind spell."

"Just a minute," Johns protested. "*Calm down.*" This time

he *did* use an actor's voice, projected serenity that he didn't feel.

But her spell zoomed around her, dressing her in standard daytime Healer garb, flinging her previous clothes away, probably to land in her cottage. And the second the scouring wind stopped, she teleported away.

He stalked from the bedroom to find a piece of papyrus of the script notes on the floor. Picking it up, he used it to soothe his own self. His obsession. One he could use to put hers out of his mind for a while.

CHAPTER 27

JUST STEPPING into the Thespian Club to meet Raz Cherry lifted Johns's spirits. As usual he donned a slightly different aspect of his own persona to interact with his tribe. He'd scried Raz and asked his friendly rival to breakfast.

When Johns reached the dining room, he automatically chose the table where he and his friends usually sat, though he'd set his appointment with Raz for a different time.

Raz had been approached by Wattle at the same party Johns had, before the fight, but Johns didn't think his actor-friend had heard anything further about Amberose's script. And Johns could use another interested party to listen for more rumors about who might have purchased the original. Not to mention, Raz had a more sophisticated and *noble* manner than Johns, might interact with Amberose better, if Johns wanted to point him in that direction.

Perhaps Raz could convince the playwright to give up creative control, a remaining stumbling block to seeing the play come to life.

And Johns owed Raz big, too, for selling him the new glider at cost.

Johns rose when the man entered, followed by Raz's

obvious lover, GrandLady Del D'Elecampane, surprising Johns. They appeared happy, though Johns believed the woman knew they were HeartMates and Raz was in denial.

Johns accepted statements that Del could keep a confidence, and her compliments on his work soothed any annoyance away.

He shared information about the script, confirming its existence, that it had been given to Lily Fescue, Raz's current leading lady, and been stolen from her dressing room during the thefts at T'Spindle's theater.

Also Johns fibbed and stated he'd seen the script—he *did* know enough of the plot and the character arcs, had spent septhours with it enough to understand the story—and he wanted to hook Raz. Johns mixed in the truth that the two male roles had been written for him and Raz.

That *did* excite Raz. He knew as well as Johns that such a play could launch them into greatness. Johns noted Del D'Elecampane frowned. A cartographer, she spent her life on the road, away from cities, mapping the huge and unexplored planet. Probably not a city person, and *the* place to make acting career was Druida City.

Could be ructions ahead for those two, but not his problem.

He teased Raz, flirted with Del ... was on a confident and cheerful roll until the damn FoxFam interrupted, and left drool and hair on him. Then Johns discovered the fox belonged to Del.

On the whole, the meeting didn't go as Johns had anticipated but hadn't devolved into complete disaster. He walked away with the knowledge that Raz was beginning to share Johns's obsession with Amberose's script and a respect for GrandLady D'Elecampane, if not her Fam.

As he passed into the lobby, Lily Fescue nearly sprang

from a chair and actually hurried to catch up with Johns as he proceeded toward the street.

She grabbed his arm and pulled him aside to stand in an alcove that also included a statue of a great actor who'd lived two centuries ago. Johns idly wondered if he'd ever have a statue here. That would be fabulous.

"Johns!" Lily hissed.

"Yeah?"

"What's going on with Amberose's script!"

Johns shrugged. "I contacted her. She said she got a new agent. Amberose will probably give the new guy a copy of the script."

Lily gasped. "BW won't be handling her?"

Johns figured Lily was calculating how much effort she'd made to cultivate that man, now wasted. Too bad for her. "No," Johns said.

Huffing a breath and tapping her foot, Lily said, "Have you heard anything about who bought the original?"

"Have you?"

"No." She frowned, then, as if she thought the expression might cause wrinkles, she smoothed out her face but continued to look as if she was thinking. "Wouldn't have been any producer, since she's still demanding artistic control?"

Johns shrugged.

"No producers. Maybe a woman, that was the latest rumor." Lily glanced up at him. "I saw you breakfasting with Raz and that creature he's hooked up with." Lily sniffed. As usual, she hadn't practiced her observational skills. Anyone with good Flair should recognize the couple's HeartMate status. "Did Raz, or even *she*, have any news of the script?"

"No," Johns replied.

Lily lowered her lashes and pouted. "You're not being much help to me, Johns, my boy."

Impassive face and a negligent shrug seemed to be called for, so he did.

One pointy-nailed finger poking too hard into his chest, Lily said softly, "And you're irritating me." A smile as sharp as her fingernail. "And I'm not very nice to those who irritate me."

He'd like to dismiss her with disdain, but never insulted people in the business, no matter how they exasperated him. "Feel free to take over the task," he said.

"Maybe I just will," she huffed and flounced away, but he understood the empty words. Woman said empty words, made empty threats.

As soon as he reached home, he scried Mas Filix in Chinju. The man answered, blinking morning sleep-fogged eyes a shade darker in amber than Giniana's, but set in the same bone structure.

Johns stared at the man revealed in the Flaired image comprised of tiny water beads hanging over the scrybowl. He'd had some face sculpting done, outrageously expensive, and looked strikingly handsome in a way Johns thought appealed more to the Chinju sensibilities than those of Cambria. Johns himself probably would have a harder time landing jobs there. Or perhaps be wildly successful as a contrast. But he could end up playing thugs for the rest of his life if he abandoned his lover, his property, his nascent House, and went to Chinju.

"Greetyou, MasterLevel Actor Filix." Johns dipped his head, apprentice to Master.

Giniana's father preened. "Yes?"

"I'm Klay Saint Johnswort—"

"I have heard of you. Calling to ask my advice about a career here in Chinju?" The man studied him, shook his head, angled his face so the light in his chamber highlighted his features. "I don't think you'd be successful here."

Another, accepting, dip of his head, Johns continued, "I'm scrying on behalf of FirstFamily GrandLord T'Spindle."

Mas's eyes lit. He straightened from casual slouch. "The producer? Wonderful to know he'd like me as a star—but I must regretfully refuse, my life is here—"

"There seems to be an accounting problem," Johns stated.

The ends of Mas's mouth turned down. "I never worked for T'Spindle."

"He's also your daughter's employer." Johns couldn't quite suppress his disapproval.

"I knew that! She's never contacted me since she's been an adult." Mas's bottom lip protruded, as if the guy calculated his daughter's age.

"It's regarding the financial support she should have received from you during her childhood."

"Huh?"

"The gilt you should have been paying to your wife to house and clothe and feed your child."

"I *did* pay it, to Verna."

"I hope you have receipts," Johns said lightly, "because your Theatrical Guild account there in Chinju, and here in Druida City, show no activity, no deposits from you or disbursements to an also unused account to Verna Filix with no notations that the support was for Giniana."

"The Druida City GuildHall accounting department—"

"Has no record of any transactions by you, either. As you might remember, FirstFamily Lords and Ladies have great influence here, and T'Spindle checked."

Johns let his expression fall into naturally stern lines, allowed a whip-thin of anger into his tones. "No records in the Guildhall or the Theatrical Guild of gilt you contributed to Giniana's upbringing. Not one silver sliver all of her life." Johns showed his teeth in a famous edged smile that cued villains that he was about to take a bite out of them.

Mas reared back, paled, recovered quickly. "There must be some confusion."

"I would say so, yes." Johns paused, angled his muscles, his body, his attitude to intimidate, made his voice softer to begin delivering the threats he'd reasoned might goad Mas Filix into the correct action. "We Celtans love our children. None should be in need if they have a capable parent." He dropped his tone to ice. "But you aren't capable, are you?"

"I ... I—" Then Mas shut up before impulsive and unadvised words poured from his mouth.

Johns continued, "And Chinju's population is as sparse, planet wide, as here on Cambria. The Chinju people cherish children, too. I wonder what would happen to your career if your adoring public found out that you never supported your child?"

"I ... no one would believe ..."

"Furthermore, I know the Daisys, the primary newssheet people here in Druida City." Morifa Daisy, the sister to the present GraceLord, had continued to pursue Johns, flirting after the show in the green room, sending the occasional perscry he even less occasionally answered. "I believe the Daisys' newssheet is read by all the movers and shakers there in Artisan City?"

"I—" Then the man scowled. "How do you know so much about my business?" He jutted a square chin. "And *I* have influence, too, Johnswort. Even in the theatrical circles of Druida City."

Johns's gut did a quick clutch that he didn't show. "Feel free to talk to T'Spindle about me. He's the main producer I'm interacting with now." Not quite a lie. "And, of course, you know that T'Spindle's Family Healer *is* your daughter. So you'll be able to explain to *him* how you honored your financial obligations with regard to Giniana."

"I will double-check what happened to all the gilt I spent on support. I know I set up an account at a bank here—"

"What bank?" Johns demanded.

"Reed's Merchants'—" Mas replied as automatically as Johns hoped.

"Ah, an offshoot of FirstFamily GreatLord T'Reed's bank. I'm sure GrandLord T'Spindle will be relieved. If you need any help in locating the receipts, please let me know and I'll have T'Spindle speak with T'Reed and he can request them from his bank there. I'm sure we can get this straightened out, can't we?"

Mas's face froze, not a good look for him, since it empha-sized his age, and Johns wondered that he couldn't do a better job of acting. Though, of course, when a person faced imminent scrutiny by a FirstFamily ... well, no one wanted such powerful people mixing in their business. And Johns had become a little accustomed to T'Spindle, and occasionally saw other FirstFamily Lords and Ladies around town. Mas had been in Chinju for more than a decade.

And the threat was real.

Johns picked up a writestick and made a note on the piece of papyrus in front of him. "Good, I'll report what I've learned from you to T'Spindle and one of us will follow up with you next week." Johns couldn't really demand seven years of gilt overnight, could he? Dammit, he should have moved on this earlier. But he smiled predatorily again. "Now that this matter has been brought to T'Spindle's attention, I'm sure he'll pursue the funds with the fervor most FirstFamily Lords show when protecting someone they care about."

With a commiserating look, Johns added, "I'll be glad when this is resolved and I'm out of his sights except as an actor." He shrugged. "Wish he'd asked his business people to handle this."

"Just why *are* you handling this?" Mas gritted through clenched teeth.

"Because, sir, I love your daughter and T'Spindle knows it." Johns's turn to reply without thinking. He let his caring show, added softly. "And she really needs the gilt for an expensive Healing treatment for Thrisca." He paused, and his jaw flexed with renewed anger. "You remember Thrisca, don't you? Your father's FamCat?"

"She's still alive?" Mas asked blankly, with a disregard that riled Johns, though he didn't much care for the cat, either. But she should have been Mas's responsibility.

"Yes, and undergoing a very interesting, very costly proce-dure this Midweekend, tomorrow, by FirstFamily GreatLady D'Willow." Johns shook his head. "Another FirstFamily noble involved." He stared at Mas Filix. "I'm sure that if you contacted her, GreatLady D'Willow, and offered to pay her directly for Thrisca's Healing, she'd accept." Johns frowned. "Not sure if Fams are entitled to financial support or not. You left her, too."

Mas hunched in, posture turning defensive. Truly, the man wasn't nearly as good an actor as Johns thought. Perhaps he'd reached that level of fame where he really didn't *have* to act, just play himself. Johns couldn't imagine that, wanted to be practicing his craft, and well, when he reached this guy's age. More, he wanted to always learn, always get better.

He knew Giniana felt the same way, held the same belief.

Not her father.

Suddenly Johns's disgust with the man raised his gorge and he couldn't speak, even to flick the scry closed. He did manage to remain expressionless.

Mas used the passing minutes to gather himself, put on a haughty air. "I will definitely track this information down and discover what went awry." He squared his jaw. "However, I don't think I'll be able to rectify the situation in time to pay for Thrisca's—" Mas choked on the name "—procedure."

Johns nodded. "Sounds good. You have my scry and viz locale, Saint Johnswort estate." He paused two beats, "And, of course, you can speak to your daughter by contacting T'Spindle Residence."

Mas made a point of looking at his wrist timer. "I'm sorry, I must go. My current viz project awaits."

"Uh-huh—" But Mas's image vanished in a spill of droplets above the scrybowl falling back to their source.

Johns stood and stretched, scented herbs on his clothes, which must have released when he sweated. He hadn't been aware of perspiration triggering the garment-protection spell. But his fury had certainly heated him. What a dishonorable man that Mas was. And he understood Giniana better. She didn't want to claim the man, who would? But she'd been showing her flaw of pride too much recently.

He took another long pace around his House, upstairs and down, while he considered his next move. Giniana or T'Spindle?

Johns felt on a roll, and if he was going to talk to Giniana about finances and why she kept working so hard, may as well be today and now.

If she continued to be aggravated with him, and they argued, that could definitely relieve some of her tension.

But he didn't like the notion of quarreling with Giniana. The idea speared a lance of tension at the base of his skull, seeping into the back of his mind that he could lose her.

Maybe. Hell. But his conscience demanded he help her, no matter what the cost to him or their relationship. She deserved to have the gilt owed to her by her father, and Johns definitely didn't like that she insisted on standing alone in the face of the winds of financial adversity when he, and others, could help.

If Giniana and he argued, she'd have all afternoon and evening to get over it before Thrisca's Healing appointment.

In any event, he'd promised to pick her and the Fams up and take them to D'Willow's facility tomorrow morning, so he'd do that, no matter what.

He had to make this right for Giniana. Or spur Giniana into speaking with T'Spindle.

Or something.

He'd start with another offer of gilt. He'd indirectly mentioned that in passing now and again and she'd rebuffed him.

So Johns arrived at T'Spindle's and a female guard waved open the large gates that would accommodate his glider. Her expression indicated wariness. "You here to speak with our lord?" Obviously T'Spindle had briefed them to expect him if he wanted to meet with the nobleman.

With an easy smile, Johns said, "No, I'm here for Giniana." He angled his chin at a widening of the gliderway. "I'll park there, so my vehicle is out of the way."

The guard didn't smile back and Johns rolled a shoulder. "Driving a glider takes less time than riding a public carrier here, and less Flair than teleporting. I've got a performance tonight I'll need my Flair for."

"Oh. Sounds right. But Giniana isn't home. Primary Heal-ingHall called her in to finish a short shift for a sick healer." The guard grimaced. "That flill sickness continues to go around." She stared hard at Johns. "Good thing we have a Healer and she and the Residence gave us health boosts when we all had our physicals."

"Good thing," Johns murmured. "Can I wait at Giniana's?"

The guard grinned. "Sure thing, Thrisca and Melis are there."

He gave the guard back a fake smile she seemed to accept as real. "Good."

Much as he disliked the thought, he decided to speak to Thrisca about gilt and see if he could convince the Fam to persuade her person to ask for help.

Just as he took the front steps up to the cottage and sent out a mental call to her, *Thrisca,* along the bond between them that he'd grudgingly accepted, Giniana opened the door with a smile. She seemed to have drawn on her inner Healer serenity, good.

He didn't return her smile. "I thought you weren't here."

She shrugged. "I just got home."

"We really do need to talk."

Her lips straightened into a line. She stepped aside and waved him in.

CHAPTER 28

"WHY ARE you still taking outside jobs other than the Spindles and the Daisys?" Johns asked in as even a tone as he could.

She shuddered. "D'Willow's assistant called to confirm, and she says people occasionally drop out at the last minute—don't show up. And the cost is shared, so—"

Though she looked nearly too twitchy to hold, he went up and put his arms around her. She didn't relax, but he thought her muscles loosened a bit.

"Let me help you," he murmured in her ear.

She slid away and he stopped himself from going after her, but let his emotions get the better of him and paced the small mainspace. Thrisca lay on her twoseat. He sensed her amusement.

"You need help," he said roughly to Giniana. He nerved himself to give it, watched all the gilt he'd accumulated in savings vanish with the offer. He stopped before her. "Together we can do this. I have enough gilt to make up for whatever shortfall you lack."

She scowled, crossed her arms. Not a good sign and irritation bloomed inside him that his difficult offer had been summarily brushed aside.

Glancing away, she replied, "I should be able to provide for myself and my Family."

He shot her an annoyed look. "Things happen that strain the resources of all of us. And let me tell you, Giniana, your emotional resources are strained to the Cave of the Dark Goddess and back."

She blinked rapidly, as if she *felt* she'd been to the Cave of the Dark Goddess, some long, dreadful mythical journey and back. "People will say I slept with you because you helped pay for the Time experiment."

All right, his mouth dropped open in surprise. He straightened, angled, *flexed* the body he kept in prime shape.

She choked, as if with laughter. Good. Jutting his chin, he said in a mock-haughty tone, "I'll have you know, dozens of women would like to have sex with me."

He lifted and dropped his brows, teased a smile from her, then asked softly, "What do we care what people say?"

"Actors always care what people say."

With her standard dismissal of himself, his colleagues, and his craft, exasperation zapped along his nerves. He inhaled through his nose, let out the quiet breath through his mouth. "Yes, actors care what people say about our acting, sure. I care if folks comment about my work. I don't care about anything else." He *wouldn't* say anything about any sort of publicity helping his career right now.

Her arms remained crossed, she stared out the window and didn't do "brood" nearly as well as he.

Yet not looking at him, she said, "I don't think I should take your money."

His chest tightened as she kept flinging up roadblocks. Of course she didn't know how much it would cost him, in gilt, but more in the lack of security. He *hated* being poor.

"I am helping a *friend*," he snapped.

She winced, dropped her arms from her defensive pose. "Of course." She took the step toward him and touched his cheek with fingertips, then drew in a breath, and said, "I can't. I just can't take money from you."

"Not even a loan?" he asked.

"Not even a loan," she shot back.

You should let him help us, Thrisca said mind-to-mind, while purring rustily. *I am fine with any help.*

Moving to prove a point physically, Johns set his hands on her waist and lifted her up. She smiled. He didn't. "You are off your feet. I'm holding you. You are in my power."

She frowned. "No, I'm not."

He didn't respond.

"I'm not," she emphasized, and continued, "I could take a number of actions to disable you."

"But you don't feel like I'll hurt you," he stated.

"No."

"Of course not." He lowered her gently, did not pull her body to body as he wanted. Not the moment for a discussion to alter into sexuality. Releasing her, he asked, "Why do you think I'd control you by any gilt I lent or gave you?"

She opened her mouth, closed it.

"You trust me physically but not with gilt."

"Gilt can make things go very bad," she replied starkly.

"Your mother," he murmured. They hadn't explored personal hurts.

"My mother paid no attention to gilt, and we'd get into financial trouble with banks or people she borrowed money from and never repaid so they cut her from their lives and never forgave her."

"And that hurt you, too. They cut *you* from their lives, too."

"Wouldn't even let *me* repay them when I could," she muttered.

Johns had a vision of a young girl offering gilt to people who loaned her mother money and them realizing how much pride she had and refusing ... and not telling her why they rejected her offer. Which hurt her pride and compiled this particular problem.

"Would you trust *me* in this instance?" she demanded.

"If I couldn't afford to pay for something in a life-and-death circumstance? Yes. In fact, let's turn it around. I admit I'd have problems paying for all of Thrisca's treatment if she was the only one to go through the Time Healing Procedure." It would probably take all his savings. "But I *will* pay for her treatment," he said. "You can provide, say, a quarter of the cost. Yes."

I accept, said Thrisca, sounding amused by human behavior.

"I don't." Giniana stuck out her chin.

"All right," he sighed. "All right. But I'm telling you, you have false pride if you can't let friends help you. You're hurting yourself. You're hurting Thrisca, by not allowing others to help."

"I can do it myself," she insisted.

"At what cost?" he demanded, his vexation igniting into something more. She understood her problems but would not move to rectify them. Hadn't she figured out by now that they only avalanched into more? He had. "You aren't eating right, you've lost weight. You aren't taking care of yourself."

She gasped, "And you think you should take care of me?"

"You're very touchy today. I understand—"

"No. You don't." Her teeth set and jaw firmed, she actually pounded a fist on her chest, a gesture far too theatrical for Johns. "*I* take care of myself. *I* handle my finances."

"All right." He kept his voice and manner steady.

"What of your faults?" she snapped.

"I have them."

"Including handling me instead of letting me take care of myself. Big, macho guy. You aren't your character, you know."

That truly stung. He swallowed hard, some hurt, mostly anger so more furious words wouldn't spurt from his mouth. Yet, he needed a few less-rapid-heartbeats before he answered her. "I understand why this is coming up now." His mouth twisted. "And I should probably put this off until tomorrow, but I'm not going to." He sucked in a breath. "I've put off talking to you about it, already. I've contacted your father—"

And she went up in flames.

"You did *what?*" she shrieked.

He over-rode her volume. "I contacted your father to find out about the gilt he should have paid for your support all your childhood."

"*Behind my back—*"

"No. Yes. I guess—"

Now she trembled in fury, not anxiety. "He *abandoned* me! He *abandoned* Thrisca. *I would not take one silver sliver from him!* How dare you go behind my back and contact him about gilt!"

Johns hunkered into his balance, his face setting into stern lines. "Because he owes it to you, you deserve it, and you need it."

More panting gasps from her. "Who do you think you are?"

He snapped out, "I'm the man who's slipped you energy during sex, while we're together in my glider or on the public carrier. And I've seen others do the same. Haven't the Residences you work at helped you? You *are* taking help, you just don't have the guts to acknowledge it. Or have too much false pride to ask for it."

She flung out her arm, pointed. "Get out."

He jerked a nod. "Going. I'll see you tomorrow morning to take you and Thrisca," who was laughing at them both, with the kitten watching wide-eyed as if in the theater, "and Melis to the health checkup, then the time treatment. Later." He paused at the threshold of the door and glanced back at Giniana. "I love you."

Johns strode, energy sizzling from the argument, hurt hammering through him with every heart beat. He loved this maddening woman and she wouldn't let him help her, in any way. She wouldn't let him be a partner in her life. Cave of the Dark Goddess!

He jerked a nod to the guards in thanks as he drove through the gates they'd opened, but seethed. Better get his temper under control, perhaps store the anger and hurt to use later. He was glad he hadn't asked his understudy to take tonight's performance as well as the matinee and evening tomorrow. He'd thought to support Giniana and Thrisca, the night before the Time Healing.

They could support each other, as always. He wondered if he was really welcome in their circle, the only deeply emotional circle he'd made since he'd lost his FatherDam. The one where he was simply Klay, more than he was 'Johns'— the name most of his associates and the theatrical world called him. The Klay of his deepest, most genuine self.

Even as he thought that, his perscry rang with the regular pings for unknown callers. He set the nav on auto to his home, plucked the pebble from his trous pocket, and rubbed his thumb against it. Del D'Elecampane's narrow face came into holographic view, her blond hair springing in cheerful contrast to her serious expression and a line between her brows.

"Greetyou, Johns. I'd like some information."

Absolutely no flirting on either of their parts. Seeing her and Raz Cherry together confirmed the two's lover and HeartMate status.

But Johns liked her, a solid, honest woman of no pretenses, who'd probably worked out her own problems during her long treks on the trails of Celta. He gifted her with his best smile.

She didn't seem to notice, which made him grin.

"What can I do for you?" he asked.

"You're interested in this play by Amberose."

"That's right," he said cautiously, but his brain made the switch from personal hurt and problems to professional work.

"New, important play that can make careers?" she asked, then murmured. "I like her stories as long as she doesn't do deep drama and angst."

"The script is a suspense with romantic elements," he paused, then added. "With the villains caught and happy endings all around."

Del repeated what Johns had told her that morning, "Two romantic couples. And the leading lady someone like Lily Fescue,"

"Yeah, but as I said, Amberose is demanding artistic control at the moment and no standard producer will do the show with such strings attached."

Spacing her words, Del asked, "Do you know where I might find Amberose's agent?"

A spark of hope firerocketed through Johns. "Formal or informal setting?"

Her head tilted. "I think, informal?" Another question as if she asked his advice on a meeting.

"Sounds good." Johns culled through all the gossip he'd heard lately, considered all the networking opportunities an agent might take. "Pretty sure Amberose's new agent will be at a garden party this afternoon, starts in about a septhour." He pulled up his calendarsphere, he'd been invited, and reeled off the information to Del.

"Many thanks, later," she signed off.

Johns sank back into his seat, not even pretending to drive. He'd heard the gossip about the mapmaker: friends of one of the FirstFamilies, connected to them by Family somehow. And extraordinarily wealthy in her own right. And she was Raz's HeartMate … and Johns had ensured that morning that Raz was fascinated with Amberose's play. with the idea of starring in it.

Del D'Elecampane *could* produce such a play. Unlike other backers, she might also allow the playwright creative license, since Del had no background in the theater.

Hell, she could probably buy a theater, and he sensed through the scry, the tiny flickers in her expression, that she'd been more than contemplating the project, more like planning to buy the script and follow through to give her HeartMate what he wanted.

Johns didn't know much about HeartMates. He didn't have one, though he couldn't imagine loving any woman more than he did Giniana, of bonding with anyone closer.

The future of his personal career had brightened in the last few minutes, something he'd have shouted with joy about a week and four days ago. Now the glow of being a theatrical star had dimmed because he and his beloved stood at odds.

Del D'Elecampane was the only reasonable woman he'd dealt with today. He thought about impossible women. Giniana, whom he loved. Lily Fescue that he'd had to deal with—and *her* snotty threats—that morning. Her words that stuck like thorns in his brain ... and knowledge burst into his mind.

A woman had purchased the script. As Lily had pointed out, probably not a producer. There were few female producers, and a legitimate person would simply contact Amberose herself. Not work with thieves.

A writer interested in cribbing the work—as if anyone could match dialog and technique—probably wouldn't have whatever gilt the thieves demanded.

But Johns considered the malice of dishonorable women, how far such a person might go for a little revenge after having an affair cut off before she was ready to dump her lover, then publicly humiliating herself with that lover at a party the whole theatrical world had attended.

An angry woman who'd keep the script from Raz and Johns, Lily, everyone, out of spite.

And Johns just knew who that might be.

Raz Cherry and Morifa Daisy.

Raz, who'd gone on to be snagged by his HeartMate Del D'Elecampane, and Morifa Daisy who'd moved on, once again casting lures Johns's way.

So he followed his hunch and scried the woman.

"Greetyou, Johns," she purred. Her black hair tumbled around her face in deliberate tousled sexiness. She wore facial enhancements or illusion, smudged eyelids, deep red plump lips.

"You have Amberose's script," he said. "I want it."

"Oh, my dear, I can give it to you." She wet her lips. "For a price."

Careful, careful. Be brusque, up front, at least he had a rep for that and the manner should work for him. He shook his head. "Not going to have sex with you, Morifa. I'm in a committed relationship." All right, that sounded wimpy. "I don't cheat on my women, Morifa."

"Not when they are your women," she countered.

"That's right."

She winked. "But I've been around the theater a lot longer than your little Healer. And I will be here after you're done with her."

He made a non-committal sound, and, yeah, Morifa's malicious smile appeared. "Or until she's done with you."

He shrugged.

Leaden silence stretched until he knew he couldn't break it first because he'd be a loser in the game they played.

She sighed, her expression now one of ennui. "I'll come up with a price ... tonight."

"We'll see if it's reasonable," Johns replied. "Bring the script to the green room after the show. I'll pay for it then."

Her thin brows raised. "In public?"

He puffed out a breath. "All right, forget the whole thing. I'm not one for games." Glancing at his wrist timer, he said, "Gotta go. Lat—"

"Wait!"

"Yeah?"

"I'll see you this evening and we'll ... negotiate."

Another patented shrug. "Not one for endless negotiations, either. Show up at the green room or not, set a price for the script or not. You decide, then I decide."

"I offer, you counter—"

"Nope. You decide. I decide. Later." He cut the scry, and felt the matter could go either way. Morifa might or might not show, might or might not play games, might or might not name a price he would pay for the script. Another unreasonable woman.

But he cheered when he recalled Del D'Elecampane and her motives for obtaining the script, for producing a play. And a woman who didn't want anything from him of a personal nature, touched no vulnerable part of him.

Giniana seethed, flung out of the cottage still steaming with angry energy and tromped down a path toward the far wall of T'Spindle estate. From the corner of her eye, she saw the gray of Melis flitting beside her, zooming through and over exposed bush roots.

Thrisca stalked behind her. Just as well, looking at the FamCat's skinny body tended to spur Giniana into impulsive action. And right now, she was all too aware that anger powered whatever energy she had.

She'd trusted Klay—Johns, as most called him—before, up to that afternoon. He'd seemed like an atypical actor. But maybe her parents had been *too* typical actors. She simply didn't know.

But he'd gone too far and she didn't trust him now.

Sneaking around behind her back to contact her father! In Chinju, even! She coughed, as if trying to force out the terrible notion or spew awful emotions out of her innermost self.

Klay had circumvented her, obviously didn't respect her. Hadn't trusted *her* to be capable of running her own life. He'd been disrespectful of her, of her wishes.

He must have known she wouldn't want anything from a man who abandoned her.

We should take the gilt from the man, Thrisca said. *He is right. YOU do not look as well as a human should be to care for Fams.*

Giniana snorted as amusement mixed with indignation and hurt.

Thrisca sniffed, much better than her cough. *And You should sleep now. We do not need You puny tomorrow for My great adventure into time.* Anticipation radiated from Thrisca.

Giniana only felt dread. She stumbled.

Go back to bed, Thrisca commanded. *You have not slept.*

Following her Fam's advice, and the cat's waving tail, Giniana returned to the cottage.

You will feel better after sleeping. Be happier with the man.

Giniana doubted that. She disrobed and drew on a sleepshirt and lay on cool linens.

And We should take gilt from the man. Take it from anyone, Thrisca said. *Take it from the stup of the parent, especially since it is our due.*

No, Giniana snapped mentally.

CHAPTER 29

No MORIFA DAISY showed up with an incredible script in the green room after *Firewalker*. Almost as disappointing to Johns as seeing no scry from Giniana for the whole of the day. He'd checked before he'd gone on, during the two tiny breaks he had during the show, and after the final curtain call.

A few lines of dialog *had* run through his mind on how to reopen their discussion in a reasonable manner, reset their relationship. He thought he could hook his Giniana in a few words if she gave him the chance.

But just as he left the theater, the assistant stage manager handed him a note. "Morifa Daisy left this for you."

Johns grunted thanks and read it: *I have Amberose's script. Perfect role for you, my dear. I'll give it to you for a minimal price. Meet me as soon as possible at the summer house at my home, T'Daisy's.*

Checking his wrist timer, Johns noted that Giniana would already be on shift at the Daisys. He wondered if he dared to drop in on her after his business with Morifa, how unprofessional Giniana might think that.

Still considering his words to woo her from her anger, he

drove to T'Daisy's. Unlike other Residences, the grounds didn't sport a perimeter fence or wall or greeniron gate, but sat behind a front grassyard a third the size of Johns's own.

He pulled up to a fancy pavilion just short of the house itself, a two-story place with white siding and dark shutters around the windows, Earthlike-looking. And that house was already a Residence, but the Daisys were a numerous, chatty, and outgoing bunch. No doubt those HeartStones got a lot of input from the Family, unlike the St. Johnswort ones.

The glow of a dim yellow lightspell showed bobbing in the pavilion as he stepped out of the glider, lowered the vehicle's door and softly closed it.

Insects chirped in the night. Keeping his alpha persona on, not too hard since Morifa annoyed him, and thank the Lord and Lady that he'd never bedded her, Johns strode to the summerhouse.

She awaited him in a gown suited to a bedroom, scandalous to be wearing the slip of a thing out in public.

His gaze went past her to a stack of bound papyrus sitting on a glass table top.

He let himself grunt, she'd expect rough manners from him, so he could get away with them. "Good, you brought the script."

She winked. "Yes." Stepping up to him, her musky perfume wafted over him.

"What's the price?" he asked.

"No sex?"

"No."

She stroked his face and he stood immobile under her caress. "But I would like a little sample, a taste. A kiss for the script."

"Huh."

Then she flung herself into his arms, nearly unbalancing them both since she cultivated a voluptuous figure, and he hadn't been ready for her. Her mouth hit his cheek, slid across to his lips, fastened on and sucked like a leech.

He kept his mouth firmly shut, muscled the "kiss" under control and dipped her in his showiest theatrical kiss. Then he felt her relax in his arms, laugh against his lips and she emanated complete smug satisfaction.

Appalled shock zinged through him, grief. Not his.

"Klay!" Giniana choked.

He broke the kiss, escaped Morifa's grip, spun, saw a horrified Giniana.

"Giniana!"

"I *never* want to see you again," she stated.

"This is a set-up—" he yelled. "And it was a theatrical kiss!"

But Giniana ran toward the house.

Morifa stopped laughing.

Stup! Johns castigated himself. He'd been hanging lately with too honest people, been too honest himself. Too focused on himself and Giniana and their fight and the situation tomorrow to think of Morifa duping him.

Simmering with hurt and anger, wanting to get out of there and unwilling to leave without the script that had cost him so much, he moved around Morifa and scooped up the papyrus.

Projecting his voice loudly so anyone could hear—including those in the room of the lighted open windows of his house—and spurting the thought down the tiny hairlike link between him and Giniana, he said, "Interesting doing business with you, GraceMistrys Daisy. Extortion is always fun."

Grasping the stack of pages between his hands—he'd trust Morifa to hold out on him, yes, he would—Johns closed his eyes and *summoned* all the like-papyrus from *everywhere*.

Morifa yelped as a good section she must have held back

appeared in his hands. Even some crumpled blank pieces of papyrus snapped to him, speckled with dirt and smelling of woods. Probably had been lost on T'Spindle estate.

Fingers curved claw-like, Morifa snatched at the packet. With an easy movement, Johns held it out of reach. "Playing games, GraceMistrys Daisy?" he asked softly, then smiled showing the dangerous edge of his teeth. "Unlike Raz Cherry, I won't humor you or let you down easy with a smooth and graceful and charming manner. You pulled the wrong man to play your stupid games with."

"I will ruin you!" she shrieked.

He raised his brows. "We made a bargain, you reneged."

She wiped a hand across her mouth. "That was no sort of a kiss."

"It was a kiss that was equal to your portion of keeping our bargain, wasn't it?" he mocked.

"I'll ruin your reputation as a lover, too," she spat out.

She'd already ruined his love, but he wouldn't, couldn't think of that right now, let his heartbreak show to this user of a woman. Instead he laughed, flicked a hand. "You can try, but I'll continue to have lovers who will enjoy me."

He saw more lights in the house come on and angled his chin toward the building, "And I'm pleased to tell your brother, who now runs the newssheet, the *Druida City Times*, of *your* activities, so he can publicize them, if he wants. Though I'm sure he knows, intimately, how manipulative you are." Johns settled into his balance, aimed a considering expression down at her. "I'll be taking fighting lessons with Cratag T'Marigold. He and his wife are great patrons of the arts. Somehow I don't recall you treating either of those people well, either. I'm sure this particular story of mine, how you wanted to blackmail Raz Cherry into being your lover—a pitiful thing—will get around those artistic social circles you love to inhabit." Johns let his voice purr. "Which story do you think will be believed? Whatever lies you spin about me, or the hints I drop about you?"

She literally hissed.

He tilted his head. "I know real FamCats who do that better."

And Morifa tried to rake his face with her pointed nails. Johns blocked her with a lifted arm.

"Morifa," chided her brother, the new GraceLord Daisy, behind her.

She spun, stumbled, hopped to keep her balance.

Johns bowed to the man. "Your sister and I are done here."

"Yes?" the GraceLord asked.

"A simple bargain, well-paid."

"Really?" Daisy glanced at his sister, back to Johns, to the sheets of papyrus in his hands. "Paid?"

"In full," Johns said mildly. "I will not disturb your sister, or you, in the future."

"Fine."

And using all his seething emotions, his anger and the terrible raw wound of lost love, Johns left his glider and tele-ported away home. There he began to walk a circuit of his estate, would do so until exhaustion claimed the strength of his legs and he crumpled to sleep where he lay, be it in a flowerbed or the treehouse.

As he paced through the night, sweating so heavily his bespelled clothes couldn't whisk the moisture away, thoughts trickled into his brain.

He'd have to act as he'd never done before. Now he only had his career, he couldn't let people see his distress. He needed his job, his career, the art of acting itself to get through this time.

He'd move through life in a misery for a long time, but he'd endure. Part of that was realizing he had a family name to live up to. He understood now that, deep in his heart, his bones, it composed a portion of his character. Like other families, even great FirstFamilies, who'd come down to a single member of the bloodline, he felt he had a duty to his ancestors. To make something of himself. To keep the name solid and respectable even if he was the very last.

Of course he'd like to have a wife and children but that didn't look good right now. He felt eviscerated, disemboweled by cat claws. He couldn't think of a wife without wanting Giniana, didn't know when he'd get over her. Maybe never.

So, no children.

But he *could* leave HeartStones. He could do his best by *them*, imprint himself and what he knew of his family and his past on them. And write one of those damn genealogical books that counselors pressed people who were the last of the line to do. He'd ensure they survived and the House passed to another family who'd cherish them.

All that in the distant future. Now he could only walk around the anguish.

He didn't know how he'd survive the night, the next few days, tomorrow morning when he honored his word and drove Giniana and her Fams to the Time Healing Procedure.

Crushing betrayal. Actors *couldn't* be trusted. To see Johns with another woman in his arms gutted Giniana.

Actors spend their days lying, and some of them even believe those lies, take them in until they think they are the truth. Heaven knew, her parents had. That they were a loving Family, when they weren't. That they loved Giniana. Lies.

A person didn't profess they loved you one week and abandon you the next.

Giniana stood in the Daisy's nursery, suffering, forcing herself not to weep. She yearned to pick up the baby, hold the softness and innocence of a new person, but didn't want to wake her, or send negativity into her dreams.

"That was interesting," T'Daisy said.

She looked up to see the man standing in the doorway. "But my sister's manipulations are usually interesting." His voice went flat. "Terrible for those she's targeted, and horrifically fascinating to observers."

He paused. "I'm sure you realized that she set you—and Saint Johnswort—up. Asked you to meet her at the summerhouse because—"

"She wanted help in buying a Family heritage gift for you and D'Daisy and little Maja."

T'Daisy snorted. "And she got your current lover here on a pretext simply to cause trouble. Hmmm. Think I've heard she's been after Johns since Raz Cherry dumped her."

D'Daisy came up and her husband stepped aside so they could both stare at Giniana.

"Actorsss," she hissed. "You can't trust them."

"Rather like journalists? People say that about me, too," T'Daisy pointed out.

"I can't love a man who doesn't respect me," she said. He'd betrayed her more than by kissing another woman.

"Don't be a fool," T'Daisy said roughly.

Giniana saw his HeartMate poke him. The man stepped aside, and D'Daisy glided in. "Thrisca's time Healing is in the morning, isn't it? Go home, Giniana, and care for your Fam and yourself."

And Giniana realized that she *had* had more help than she'd anticipated, from all around her, even without asking.

People had spared her pride by helping her without asking, making it easier on her.

She straightened her shoulders. "I—I—you've given me too much," she said. "You've kept me on when you—"

"Not at all," T'Daisy interjected. "We're glad we had you,

enjoyed every moment of sleep and privacy you let us have at night and knowing you cared well for our baby daughter."

"But it's time we take on the responsibility ourselves," D'Daisy said. "Go home and rest for your big event tomorrow."

T'Daisy raised his hand. "I'm summoning our glider for you."

In a daze, Giniana let them walk her through the house and settle her into the glider. Then she had long minutes of the dark ride to try and not think. She couldn't close her eyes, or she'd see Morifa Daisy in Klay's arms again.

Actors couldn't be trusted. She'd spent years seeing and experiencing and feeling that, had embraced the illusion that Klay was different. But he couldn't be trusted.

Their relationship was over.

She had enough hurt and sorrow and lingering anger mixed with self-pity that she 'ported directly from outside the T'Spindle estate gates to the cottage. The instant she arrived, her scrybowl activated. "Please come to the Residence immediately upon your return, no matter the time." T'Spindle's message boomed throughout the cottage. He sounded irritated. Giniana shrank inside. She didn't recall the easy-going lord ever being annoyed at her.

Uh-oh, Melis said, curling tight between Thrisca's front legs.

Thrisca licked her paw. *Uh-oh, indeed.*

Giniana gritted her teeth, spoke aloud and with deliberation. "GrandLord T'Spindle scried and left a message and you didn't notify me telepathically?"

Thrisca sniffed in punctuation and that triggered a bout of coughing. Melis licked her under her chin, and answered mentally, *We was outside with the door open and I sorta heard him but didn't know his voice so I ignored him and—*

"Thrisca just ignored him because she's a cat," Giniana interrupted.

Yes, Melis confirmed. *It was nice outside and We was playing. And You was at work at the Daisys.*

"And playing takes priority to notifying me of a call by my primary employer," Giniana snarled.

Yes.

By ONE of Your employers, Thrisca added. *Besides, You were raging at Johns and not paying attention to anything less than a huge mind shout.* Thrisca began coughing again and Giniana let more tears dribble down her cheeks as she strode over to pet her Fam.

You too emotional! Melis criticized.

Maybe Johns had had a point. Not taking care of herself led to other problems, like less control over her emotions because she had to put more effort into managing them.

After a few pets along her Fam's bony body, Giniana stepped back, settled into her balance and contacted T'Spindle through their professional mind-link. *I will be there, transnow.*

Please teleport to my ResidenceDen, he replied.

She did so and found the man behind his desk, looking every centimeter the FirstFamily Lord, his standard genial manner gone, reminding her of his massive influence, wealth, power.

He gestured to a chair before him and she took it.

The shift at the HealingHall, dealing with the Daisys had been easy, seeing Klay—Johns—difficult, and sitting here in these circumstances, hideous.

"You told me months ago that you wished more and varied Healing experiences and requested that I allow you to work for HealingHalls and, later, for the Daisys."

She swallowed the dry lump in her throat. "That's true." It came out a whisper.

"But not the whole truth," the GrandLord stated austerely. "You also needed to amass a great deal of gilt for the Time Healing Procedure to save Thrisca."

He waited, gray gaze fixed on her until she dipped her head and muttered, "Yes." Then she wondered if Klay ... Johns ... *the actor*... revealed her problems to T'Spindle also. "Did Saint Johnswort contact you?" Giniana demanded. The FirstFamily Lord's eyes flashed and she wished she'd kept her mouth shut.

"Is that your business?" T'Spindle asked softly. "I've heard you've broken up your relationship with Klay Saint Johnswort."

Already? Lord and Lady, but she'd always known gossip zipped through the FirstFamily circles fast. Did one of the Daisy's scry him? Did Melis or Thrisca burble to his wife—

"*FirstLevel Healer Filix,*" T'Spindle rumbled.

Not a good time to let her thoughts shoot in different directions. "My apologies for not paying close attention, GrandLord T'Spindle."

His forefinger tapped on the pad protecting his centuries-old desk. He lowered his voice and she strained her ears. "I am offended."

Her spine jerked straighter, her breath strangled, but she still made a sound of protest.

"You are a member of my staff." He paused and she nodded rapidly. Maybe he hadn't heard of D'Willow's offer that Giniana pay for the time experiment by becoming the Willow Healer. That would offend him, too, no doubt. Maybe hurt him and she *never* wanted that, she respected the man so.

CHAPTER 30

"YOU ARE A MEMBER OF MY STAFF," T'Spindle repeated. "One of my staff who resides on T'Spindle estate presided over by my HeartMate and me. As such, we are responsible for your welfare and consider you our dependent. Do you understand?"

She nodded, but frowned, felt tears back behind her eyes again at the contradiction of his tone, and the knowledge of how he valued her ... and that she'd riled him.

"It is well that you understand my point of view, and my HeartMate's point of view on this, even if you do not precisely agree." Another pause, but she made no reply.

"And we, my HeartMate and I, also employ the FamCat Thrisca, also consider her a delightful dependent."

His words kept falling into the silence and hitting Giniana like blows. "As our dependent, the FamCat is under our aegis and is our responsibility, including her health. I have trans-ferred the total payment for the Time Healing Procedure from our account to D'Willow's account, authorized any addi-tional charges, if necessary." He made a cutting gesture. "It is done."

Giniana's employer actually glared at her. "You should

have understood our feelings and attitude before now, before we had this discussion."

She wasn't doing any discussing at all.

T'Spindle continued, "You should have realized that the cost to us is minimal." He waved a hand at the negligible-to-him amount. "We are offended."

And she knew she'd also hurt him and his HeartMate.

"I—" But she stopped, not sure what to say, try and defend herself? Insist on her independence? But *she* understood the deal was done. She blurted, "I didn't want to accept gilt from an older man, a man not my Family."

T'Spindle stared with steely eyes, shook his head. "I have a HeartMate with whom I'm deeply bonded."

Giniana knew that, of course. Intellectually. But despite the Spindles *and* the Daisys being HeartMates, she didn't truly believe in the bond.

"We've been HeartBonded for decades." The ends of T'Spindle's lips lifted slightly. "And we are not as affectionate in public as in private, and this is a big Residence. So, perhaps, you don't see our bond that strongly. But it *is* time for you to stop believing that you are like your mother. Or that your mother was wrong in what she did to give you both a good life." He paused. "I knew your mother, and I know GraceLord Citronella well. Your mother cared for him."

Giniana opened her mouth, shut it, but T'Spindle raised his brows. "Don't stifle your words, go ahead." Another lift of his lips. "I'd imagine it will do you well to vent."

"Hadn't planned on doing it to you."

"To me, too?" He shrugged, waved. "Go ahead. I'm listening."

Giniana burst out. "My mother didn't care as much for GraceLord Citronella as much as she cared for his gilt! She wouldn't have taken him as a lover if he hadn't been wealthy."

"Perhaps not. And perhaps she wasted her talents instead

of working with them. But, as I was saying, I know Nardus Citronella. He cared for her, perhaps more than she, perhaps less. But he was happy with their arrangement."

"I'm sure she gave good value," Giniana muttered.

"And I don't think you are sure of anything of the sort," T'Spindle snapped back. "And I don't think you respected or respect your mother."

"No. She took the easy way." And even the easy way hadn't fulfilled her, given her joy or peace or happiness. That was the point, Giniana understood. Her mother had ignored her gifts and hadn't worked at them and hadn't achieved what she needed emotionally in life. Therefore she'd failed. Herself and Giniana *and* Thrisca.

T'Spindle inclined his head. "Perhaps she did take the easy way." His voice softened, as did his manner. "But you are not she." His mouth quirked. "I'd imagine you've never taken the easy way during your entire life. But in this instance, with regard to Thrisca, I did as I should. In a life-and-death situation, I cannot allow a dependent of mine to fail, a person to die, for want of a little gilt."

His chest expanded, then compressed and when he spoke again, he didn't look at her. "I'm disappointed that you did not ask me for help, Giniana."

She gulped, wet her lips, replied in the whisper rather than the strong, steady voice she'd have liked, "To me, as a Healer, the Time Healing Procedure is an experimental treatment that I think might help Thrisca. I didn't want to request gilt from you for such a risky and expensive venture." At least she spoke the truth.

T'Spindle dipped his head, then said, "But you are a First-Level Healer, and I respect your *professional* judgment. If you believe this could cure the FamCat, I defer to you." He spread his hands. "I'm a FirstFamily GrandLord and expense will never be an issue for me, nor, I hope, for any of my descendants. Both a blessing and a curse. In this case, a blessing. You should have told me of your need and your struggles and the problems with one of the dependents on my estate. You didn't, for whatever reasons seemed good to you. However, I am now informing you that I've already sent the necessary gilt for Thrisca's treatment to D'Willow, with the understanding that Thrisca *will* take part in the Time experiment, tomorrow."

A quick, quirky smile lightened his face. "And these procedures are quite rare, so I'm glad to take part in one." Like most of members of a FirstFamily, he had a low threshold of boredom and was endlessly curious. The curse of wealth. "I was informed you were allowed a guest observer."

"Yes." And it wouldn't be Klay ... Giniana blinked rapidly to keep tears from falling.

"Go home, Giniana, and sleep," the FirstFamily lord dismissed her, but with a flick of his fingers, energy poured from him and the Residence into her, so she teleported easily to her cottage.

Thrisca and Melis slept outside in the catmint, ignored Giniana when she called to them by telepathy and voice. She sensed they disapproved of her.

So she curled on the bed and wept and suffered.

Despite her restlessness all night long, Giniana fell into an exhausted sleep and awoke later than usual on the day of the time experiment. She ate a nutrition bar automatically, her mind plodding through the plan again.

Her mind seemed fogged, her body stuffy. Forget Klay, she *must* apply herself to check out Thrisca beforehand, then take the FamCat to Danith D'Ash the famed Animal Healer who would also examine Thrisca, then hire a glider to deliver them both to D'Willow's laboratory. Obviously, Klay would not be coming to ferry them around.

An actor, not to be trusted, she assured herself. He'd leave her and Thrisca and Melis to go through this alone, and that hurt. Being abandoned again.

Knowledge burst into her brain, with a flash of white and painful light. *She'd* abandoned him.

She ached. Clear through, from marrow to skin nerves. And something that had seemed to have bloomed and stretched in her had collapsed back into a hard, painful ball. She'd taken emotional risks, not much, but *had* extended herself.

Now she wanted to hide, from her own self-examination as much as the world. Her knees weakened and she collapsed into a nearby chair, scrubbed at her face that felt raw with weeping.

She'd been so very wrong. Afraid of emotional risk, striving to hold on to the only person she felt loved her, or could love her—Thrisca. Had she influenced Thrisca to agree to the experiment?

But that question she'd asked herself before. As Danith D'Ash told her, a cat's nature would demand she fight for survival. And the idea of the experiment, and the experience *of* the experiment, intrigued Thrisca.

And, lately, the stay of the sick agent and the blossoming of Giniana's romance had amused Thrisca.

The FamCat had gotten her own FamKitten to teach. That had perked her up, too.

No, Giniana's need had not forced Thrisca to hold to life when she wanted to drift away to her next incarnation on the Wheel of Stars.

And Giniana had diverted herself from thinking of her pain again, her huge mistake.

She had ended her affair with Klay because of her fear of abandonment.

Slow her fast breathing, the panting and hyperventilating that made her dizzy.

By the time she'd met him, she'd shoved that hurt of being left behind an inner door. She'd thought it had shriveled into a ball, encased in a hard shell. But she hadn't been able to extend the emotional trust to others. She hadn't believed that people would like her enough not to abandon her. Hadn't thought that affection and passion could be honestly exchanged.

She wasn't being truthful enough with herself. Dig deeper, experience the pain, release it.

The core belief that *she* hadn't been enough for her father to stay with his Family. *She* hadn't been enough for her mother to put her first, to love her as Giniana had loved her mother.

Her mother had always needed someone else, a male someone else, to be happy. Had needed gifts to be shown she was valued.

As Giniana needed professional respect to be validated.

And *love*.

Shuddering with freed emotions, she wrapped her arms around herself. She'd abandoned Johns due to her own fears, not because he'd abandoned her. He'd told her he loved her, and through their tiny link she realized he still did, had spoken the truth, had proved the truth with his sincere actions. *Not* pretense. No *acting*, from him, but honesty. Honesty in admitting he wanted to care for her, his bluntness in trying to help, and the words he'd shouted and she'd closed her ears to last night ... extortion, theatrical kiss.

He'd acted with Morifa.

Could Giniana accept that? Hurt reverberated through

their bond, on both sides. Love still throbbed back and forth, too. She loved him.

Tears washed down her face, cooling it, soothing. She gulped and gulped others.

She would have to apologize, to reveal her own fears and truth of her love and hope her rejection hadn't shriveled his love. Open herself, and send him that love so it smothered his senses. Show him.

Show him.

A thought zinged through her. Yes, *show* him.

She sprang from the chair. Energy, Flair, sizzled through her along with gushing hope, banishing the night's weary ills.

Hurry, follow this impulsive need to give him something solid to prove her love.

Give presents? As her mother preferred to get presents to have herself and her love validated? And Giniana *had* given presents to her mother. Some received with strained smiles that had let her know they'd missed their mark, especially those she'd made herself. The more expensive the gift, the more her mother liked it.

Shake that off. All the things she and Klay had exchanged had been personal help. Those gifts had built and strengthened their bond, but had not been because either one of them had been greedy or demanding. Simply, the give and take of those who felt affection for each other. And desire. And love.

She threw open the door to her tiny workroom. He'd admired the large fluorite crystal, the most banded one she had. She picked it up and with one sharp *snap* of her mind, cracked away the outer rock.

A pillar, no, that wouldn't show off the colors well enough. A long, pointed pyramid … no, make it hexagonal, longer than her hand. Curling her fingers around what she'd form into the top in her left hand, she ran her right down it, using Flair to shape, switched hands and created the point, the angles, to best reveal the colors of the long, seventeen-centimeter crystal.

Pretty. She grinned. As pretty a stone as he kept saying she was as a person. The anticipation of the day's challenges kept her energy high. She needed to have this done by the time he picked her and Thrisca up to take them to Danith D'Ash's for Thrisca's physical. Giniana now had no doubt he'd come. He wouldn't break his word, even if their relationship had shattered.

Shatter. Easy, easy on the cutting of the surface and the polishing. Done. All of it would gleam gorgeous in the sunlight. He could put it in that eastern bedroom window of his to catch the light, have the sunlight filtering through it, making it glow from within.

Done. Smooth the base so it will stand sturdily. Done.

Now, deep breaths to steady her nerves so her hands wouldn't shake. She picked up the slim lettering chisel and wrote in her most beautiful script along the whole length of the least interesting facet, *I love you.*

Her breath whooshed out. Pretty. A very good thing she'd been practicing her creative Flair longer than her Healing gift. The letters and words looked well formed.

Reaching for the silver, the metal that would best complement the crystal, she put on a temperature-spell protective glove, heated the silver until molten. Carefully, ensuring with Flair that the crystal wouldn't crack, she poured the liquid metal into the carving. Infusing the silver with heartfelt emotion, her love for Johns, she also murmured blessings upon him. She let those blessings flow too, along with her undemanding love, wafting aside any desires of reciprocity, that he should or must love her back.

Perfect. The best piece she'd ever done, deserving to be a

gift to her beloved. A deep sigh rose from her at the release of creativity.

Flinging out her hand, she translocated a plush velvet bag from her stock, whisked the pouch and the crystal with a brief cleansing spell to make the resonance neutral. Klay could consecrate the hexagonal point and the bag with the qualities he wished, through the ritual he wished.

FamWoman! Thrisca called. She waited by the greeniron main gate. Giniana got the impression of an amused and flicking tail. *I sense FamMan, your actor lover, coming down the boulevard.*

Not many gliders, added Melis. *We are riding in a private glider to Thrisca's great adventure!*

Maybe, Thrisca added, *or perhaps he will simply drive by because FamWoman hurt his feelings.*

He would not abandon US! Melis's mind voice sounded shocked. *Not US.*

Giniana winced. Her heart skipped a beat at the thought of humiliating rejection. She firmed her lips. She *would* do this. Still, she was glad she'd only eaten a nutrition bar for breakfast.

Coming, she telepathically sent back to Thrisca. Then Giniana twitched her Healing robes with T'Spindle insignia into smoothness, inhaled another deep breath, and teleported to the gate.

A blue and steel gray glider pulled up alongside the far pillar of the gate, near the wall that held the person-sized postern door. Just seeing the color had Giniana's throat tightening. Close to the same color as Klay's eyes. She hurried to the door, opened it, and Thrisca prowled elegantly from the center of the gates to the door and through it. Melis darted through the rods of the greeniron gate and to the glider.

The vehicle's passenger door opened upward, revealing the front seat tilted down and a long, padded bench in the back under the slanting rear window. The cats hopped in and arranged themselves in the back.

Klay's door remained closed. He didn't get out to help the FamCats or Giniana. He didn't look at any of them, not one glance, but stared straight ahead, fingers on the steering bar. A muscle ticced in his cheek. His nostrils widened as if her scent drifted toward him.

A quick breath in, released, then Klay said in a creaky voice, "I deeply respect you. I've always deeply respected you. You are a true and honorable and caring person. I apologize for not speaking with you first regarding your father. I also apologize for allowing myself to be manipulated by Morifa Daisy." A pause. His jaw flexed. "Now can we get on with this?"

"I have a gift for you," Giniana said, bending below the roof of the vehicle. His knuckles tightened white on the bar.

"I don't need a damned gift from you," he growled, still not looking at her.

Horror zipped through her. She'd spoken instinctively, said something that would please her mother, had completely botched the moment.

"Sor-ry." Her voice squeaked high with tension, despair, disgust at herself. All so mixed she couldn't tell what emotion ruled. She panted a couple of breaths while nausea acid slopped in her stomach. Managed one good breath of sweet summer air, steadied and quieted and lowered her voice and tried again. "I have a love gift to give you because I love you, Klay."

His body rippled as she said his name, but otherwise he didn't move.

"I was wrong to throw our relationship away impulsively, and I'm sorry I hurt you." At least now her tones throbbed with sincere emotion. She thought the tiny pulsing emotional thread between them expanded. Hope welled, and she continued with words rushing faster. "I was scared and distrustful and hurt and used my past experiences to judge you. I was wrong. I love you. Please say you don' ... do ... not ... ha-hate ... m .. me." She simply crumpled against the glider.

CHAPTER 31

THE SEAT in front of her snapped up, Klay leaned over and took her right wrist. "Get on in." His voice was thick, too, but his face impassive, hiding whatever he felt. Though she thought their bond throbbed with a leap of joy from him.

"C'mere." He tugged, and she tumbled into the passenger seat gracelessly, her longer, more formal tunic twisting around her.

She forgot all about that when his lips met hers. And not only his lips, his tongue swept inside her mouth as if desperate for her taste. She leaned into him, opening her mouth, and his hands came around her shoulders, keeping her stable.

And she let him, depended completely on his holding her to not fall, which she wouldn't have done even last week.

Thrisca made cat-snickering noises from the backseat, echoed by Melis. The last thing other than Klay that Giniana paid attention to, because *his* taste swirled through her and uncontrolled love upsurged through her and her mind spun and thought left her for pure sensation. The strength of his fingers supporting her, but not tightening around her to hurt, the continuing probe of his tongue in her mouth that she tangled her tongue with his to absorb his taste, even his scent—relief and earthy herbs.

Again she felt tears, these of joy, slip down her flushed cheeks.

And her core throbbed and yearned, but her heart craved his taste and scent and touch more. She dropped the bag and it clunked.

"Ouch." Johns pulled back, said a spell Word and the steering stick sank into the dashboard, his seat moved back. He scooped up the velvet pouch by the thick tie that carried through a thread of gleaming silver.

"What's this?"

Embarrassed heat flooded her, flushed her cheeks. She settled correctly into her seat, cleared her throat, and turned her head to meet his equally gleaming blue-steel eyes. Her lips trembled with admission, "I didn't think that you'd be so easy to convince that I loved you."

His sexiest grin flashed. "Oh, yeah, with you I am the *easiest* guy you'll ever know."

"Lie," she muttered, "you are moody and complex." She straightened her shoulders, determined to do this right. "I love you, and I thought I'd have to prove it, so I made this gift."

Klay's expression fell serious and he murmured, "I never needed solid proof of your love."

She flinched. "No, that's just what my mother needed. Probably my father, too, if he'd remained. Though, as I recall, he liked endless fulsome compliments."

Strained silence as Klay watched her. He weighed the pouch in his hand, dipped his head in acknowledgment, then dropped his gaze and slowly opened the gift. As he drew out the crystal, a beam of sunlight shafted through the window and accented the silver lettering. *I love you.*

His face softened in wonder. "It's beautiful, the best gift

I've ever received." And he looked at her with love, with a tender gaze that warmed her through, even as it crisped away any doubt. He stared at her the way she'd seen HeartMates watch each other, as if their spouse were the most necessary person in the universe. He gazed at her the way she knew no other man would ever look at her, and her heart leapt … and wept.

He loved her.

More than anyone else in the world ever had, or ever would.

How could she not feel the same?

He accepted her with her hesitations and faults and problems.

As she would him.

She closed her eyes briefly, and, yes, tears feathered under her lashes to slip down her face.

Then she felt his large forefinger brush them away.

"I will always love you," she said, her lashes lifting.

He opened his mouth but no words emerged. And she realized—she thought they both realized—that he couldn't say the words now, repeat her vow. Not telepathically, and definitely not aloud. He'd stutter them, she'd hurt him so.

Her heart constricted and more tears, these not so happy, flowed from her eyes and she turned away. "I'm sorry."

"I …" He stopped and she heard the breath he dragged in. "I lo—"

"No!" she snapped, struggled with her own emotions, repeated quietly, "No." She put her hand on his thigh, found tense muscle. "Don't force it, please." She looked at him, watched him swallow, then stare toward the front again.

"Words are my business," he rumbled.

That explained everything. "And acting. I don't want you to *act* this, Klay." She stroked his thigh, blinked at the shining crystal, let the light ease her, spoke *her* truth. "I didn't believe you, didn't trust you, and hurt you. Now you hesitate to trust me." Still focused on the gift that he'd accepted, the feelings that cycled through them both, love and pain, she sipped breaths and continued, "You will say the words when you are able." The words she now yearned to hear with all her heart.

She waited until he met her gaze again, gave him her own smile. "I will wait for you."

"Good," he said gruffly, "Because I am definitely not giving up being with you." He grinned and that sincere emotion reached his eyes. "Definitely not giving up on sex with you. Nightly." He gestured. "Daily."

"Of course."

He stretched out his hand and set his fingers under her chin. "I would never have doubted your words of love."

Truth.

"Last night was nasty though." He shuddered and Giniana knew the action for real, no show for sympathy, no playing on her feelings. She rather recalled her father doing something like that, and watching under his lashes to see if it worked.

Klay set crystal and pouch on the dashboard. His strong hands gently framed her face. He leaned toward her and pressed his mouth softly against her lips.

"Well. This is interesting," said the mellow voice of T'Spindle. Jerking back from another kiss, Giniana noted the man standing next to Klay's open window. The FirstFamily Lord's brows bobbed up and down. "I trust you are seriously interested in a long-term-relationship with my Healer, Saint Johnswort?"

Klay straightened away from her, glanced up at her employer. "More interested in her than any offer you might make me regarding my career, GrandLord."

T'Spindle gave the top of the glider two thumps. "Good. Good." He stared at them both, at Thrisca on the back ledge.

"You all look good together." With a gesture, he indicated the larger, expensive and sophisticated glider parked in front of them. "I'd anticipated handling the transportation needs of Giniana and Thrisca today."

"Giniana's character naturally commands loyalty," Klay said, and had her flushing.

"Yes, like attracts like." T'Spindle leaned down and offered her what she knew as his most winsome smile. "I'd like to—ah—observe the treatment."

Giniana blinked. He'd been right in his scolding of her, sincere in his claiming of her and Thrisca as dependents and wishing to help them, when it cost him little, but her so much. But his words emphasized the fact that he was, as all FirstFamily Lords and Ladies were, nearly insatiably inquisitive. She didn't know how many of those people had witnessed such an experiment, but had no doubt in her mind that there weren't many. T'Spindle would be one of a few who could tell others precisely what went on in this new procedure.

A trickle of relief wound through her. "D'Willow knows you paid for the experiment," Giniana murmured. "You're welcome to watch in the observation room with me."

"My thanks."

"And you don't have to take us through our preliminaries with D'Ash. We can meet you there."

He grinned, something she'd rarely seen. "Thank you!" He glanced at his wrist timer. "I will be at D'Willow's Time workshop a half septhour before the experiment."

He inclined his head, but his blazer-like gray gaze latched onto hers. "You will be all right until then?"

Of course, Thrisca said smoothly, then spoiled it with a long and hacking cough that twisted Giniana's insides.

Melis licked her.

Klay looked back at the FamCat ... *their* FamCat. "You all

right? You need me to initiate emergency mode for the drive to Animal Healer D'Ash?"

I love D'Ash, but she cannot Heal Me, Thrisca stated pragmatically. *She can only examine.*

"But can she relieve your cough?"

"Not today," Giniana answered for her Fam. "No medications or Healing or anything. I don't know why." She glanced up at T'Spindle. "I'll see you later."

He nodded, "Later then, Giniana, Thrisca, Melis and Johns." The lord teleported away.

"All right, then," Klay said, and pulled the steering bar from the dash, carefully took the crystal spear from atop the dashboard. As his fingers moved over the stone, slipped it into the pouch, his emotional bond pulsed with fervent delight and Giniana finally relaxed in her seat, drew the door shut, closeting herself in with her family.

They would face the experiment together.

Danith D'Ash scrutinized Thrisca from eartip to tailtip. The animal Healer confirmed Giniana's own conclusions that Thrisca had steadily deteriorated.

Thrisca ignored the diagnosis, but stayed on the examination sponge as it lowered to the ground instead of leaping off it. Then she left the small room with a low and flicking tail showing her annoyance at the whole proceeding.

D'Ash emitted a tiny cough and gave Giniana big eyes from a small, cute woman, asking that she be allowed to observe the time experiment. Not one of her patients had gone through the procedure and she wished to watch.

Giniana gently suggested that the woman make a request of D'Willow, one FirstFamily Lady to another and was told that D'Willow had already refused such an inquiry.

Since Giniana and Thrisca were only allowed one "guest" to observe, Giniana reluctantly refused the woman, but said she'd keep her in mind if she heard of an opportunity through Healing Circles. She already struggled with the notion that T'Spindle would be accompanying her instead of Klay.

They drove to the estate where D'Willow practiced her *time experiments* craft. Not the newly rebuilt D'Thyme Residence on the edge of Noble Country, and, of course, not T'Willow's FirstFamily estate, but a third workshop and laboratory the Lady had set up for herself. This place sat in a northern central area of Druida City, mostly deserted. In the first decades after landing, the colonists had built Druida City with the great machines they'd brought from Earth, expecting their descendants to fill the walled city, then overflow in large numbers to civilize the planet itself.

What with disease, sterility, and low birth rate, that hadn't happened. Many of those buildings yet stood, some crumbled and had been knocked down, though not much had taken their place.

At the place D'Willow used as her laboratory, workshop and treatment room, they piled out of Klay's glider. The building looked like a regular house, not a space for scientific experiments.

When they entered the small lobby, relief filtered through Giniana. Everyone who'd signed up for the Time Healing Procedure had shown up. Her share of gilt would have been sufficient. Most of the people in the room didn't sit, but lined up in front of double doors that led into the former mainspace now bisected into the narrow-width observation room with a half-wall of glass, and the main treatment chamber.

Klay glanced at his wrist timer, but Giniana knew they'd arrived in good time. Palli, D'Willow's personal assistant, met them with a frown in the front room. She held a tablet.

T'Spindle rose as they came in,

"You have too many observers," Palli snapped. "Three people and one FamCat are too many beings. You are only allowed one person if a Fam is a client—" Palli pointed to Giniana, "and that's you. And you are allowed an additional observer. You have two others." She sniffed.

Thrisca sniffed in turn, more wetly. She nosed Melis kitten. *This is not an observer or a FamCat. This is My kitten. She does not count.*

Giniana stated. "Only I and Melis, *whom I will hold*, and FirstFamily GrandLord T'Spindle will be observing."

"I'll be waiting here," Klay said smoothly. He smiled at Palli. "Giniana has many friends who wish to support her. I'd imagine that she could fill the observation area. As it was, we refused FirstFamily GreatLady Danith D'Ash. We *are* following your rules, and Melis will not take up any space."

Palli stared at Klay. "Oh," she breathed out, completely focused on Klay, her face softening into an expression never aimed at Giniana. The woman remained distracted until the doors opened to the next room, revealing the half-glass wall, and the space beyond where the Healing would take place.

Everyone began to file into the next room, including T'Spindle who cast them a wicked smile. Giniana bent and picked up Melis, held the little being, and stated, "My guest, T'Spindle, has already taken a place at the window." In the center of the window, of course, where he'd obtain the best view. As the highest status person in the building, including D'Willow, no one would dispute his choice position.

Thrisca glided slowly and elegantly through the doors, then the far door to the experimental chamber itself.

Palli jerked from her trance, scowled. and made ticks and comments on her tablet, hurrying into the other room.

Once Giniana reached the threshold, she glanced back at Klay, who remained standing with a few others in the lobby. To her surprise, Palli did not shut the doors as usual, and the additional relatives gathered in the opening to see what they could.

Naturally, a space along the window next to T'Spindle gapped, and Giniana stopped there. She folded her arms so Melis could lie on the shelf of them and the GrandLord shifted toward her, enveloping her in his aura filled with energy, Flair and upbeat attitude. She relaxed every muscle and watched the five people lower themselves to the spongy floor. D'Willow herself helped them. No one else went into the room.

Silence hung, tense and dreadful, with tiny sparks of hope firing through the atmosphere and fading.

Thrisca sat in the middle of the floor, surrounded by a few people sitting, a few lying near her.

Then the door clanged shut.

No one in the observation room moved, all gazes focused on their loved ones participating in the time Healing treatment.

Giniana watched, too, wondering if there *would* be much to see.

A brilliant rainbow-colored fog flowed through the room, and she gasped along with everyone else. Billows of the stuff —time itself? only D'Willow knew—thickened and thinned, gathered and dissipated, revealing portions of the chamber and the people inside.

Lightning flashed, blue-white forks zipping up and down the walls, chained throughout the room, but no thunder sounded.

Everyone in the Time Chamber disappeared.

Giniana blinked. No, no one occupied the room, not one person, not Thrisca, not D'Willow herself.

Someone choked a cry, several people shouted names, pressed themselves, their hands, their bodies, to the glass half-wall.

Others must have held their breaths like Giniana had, because when the fog vanished and the people returned, all horizontal, air whooshed out around her, including from T'Spindle and Melis.

"Zow," someone murmured.

A gong sounded and Palli Willow intoned, "The Time Healing Procedure has been concluded. Blessed be the Lady and Lord. Blessed be us all."

People began to rise smoothly to their feet, beaming smiles, patting various parts of their bodies that hadn't worked well before. Several wept.

The door to the observation room opened and Giniana smelt a whiff of *strangeness beyond strange*, then people rushed out until the room emptied of all but one.

Thrisca lay panting on the floor. Everyone else had left. And, Giniana was glad to see, everyone seemed Healed. No doubt they'd hurry to their personal Healer or HealingHall to confirm the cure.

But *Thrisca.*

CHAPTER 32

GINIANA'S HEART SQUEEZED, her eyes filled with tears. The FamCat had been interested and active lately. That had masked how truly sick she was. Dying.

T'Spindle put his arm around Giniana's shoulders. "I'm sorry," he said.

"I'll get her," Klay stated behind them. Giniana hadn't heard him come in.

Melis mewled, *Me go with You!* She sailed through the air to Klay's shoulder, hunkered down there, fur spiky.

Palli, holding the door open to the time chamber, frowned at them all, glanced at the Fam prone on the floor, back at Giniana and her friends. Yes, friends. T'Spindle, her employer, was a staunch friend. Klay, her love and lover, also a great friend.

Klay stopped beside her, brushed a kiss on her temple. "We'll all take care of Thrisca, now and forever." His voice rang with sincerity. She valued that more than she could say.

He could be himself with her. Surely that was important to him, too? Other memories pressed on her, of her parents always acting, never *real*—not even with each other. She didn't know what their relationship had been based upon, the unspoken rules of it, but they hadn't been honest with each other.

She and Klay wouldn't be like that.

Before she could reach out, Klay nodded to Palli as he strode through the open door, crouched down next to Thrisca. He placed his hand on Thrisca's side and Melis ran down his arm. His fingers barely moved on Thrisca's ribcage as she labored for breath.

No, no, NO! squealed Melis, hopping down to land directly in front of Thrisca's eyes. Small FamKitten tongue came out and licked and licked the old cat's face. *I needs You!*

Johns couldn't believe how horrible he felt at seeing Thrisca so sick. Dying and with the last hope of any Healing gone. When had he come to care for the Fam?

Melis shouted telepathically, surely loud enough that everyone in the building heard, *I loves You, Thrisca. I loves You and You loves Me and We loves each other. We is Best Friends! FAMS! Stay here with Me to teach Me what I needs to know!*

At the huge swirl of sibling love between the cats expanded through Johns, a revelation exploded through him. He let his link with Thrisca spiral wide, yanked at whatever warm emotions he had for the old FamCat, projected them to her, added love … easily added the overflowing love he felt for Giniana into his bond with her Fam. He also held out his other hand toward Giniana who remained in the other room near the observation window.

And *demanded*. Demanded she come to him, to them, to share in the love between them all.

Choking, weeping, she stumbled to him, knelt beside him, touching Thrisca as he did.

Melis cried, *We all loves You and each other and needs to SHOW you. We cans show this! WE CANS!* Her small face turned up toward Johns, her eyes a brilliant green. And he could only remember when one of them had been cloudy.

She stretched atop Thrisca, between Giniana and Johns, connecting them all in a circuit and amplifying all their inter-connected bonds.

Love flowed and Thrisca's breathing, her very heartbeat, steadied to match with the rest of theirs. Under his fingers, he felt the strength of all that love, could almost *feel* the final mending of her body that the time experiment had begun when the treatment had destroyed the sickness.

He knew he provided most of the Flair, the energy, the strength, but an equal portion of the love, and that was perfect.

Melis sniffled. *Life is good.*

A roar of affirmation came from everyone, aloud and tele-pathically. *LIFE IS GOOD!*

Giniana sobbed beside him, then T'Spindle was there, a firm hand under her elbow, raising her to her feet. "Come along. You can see she's Healed, you can *sense* it. Let's leave this place."

Johns met Thrisca's eyes, as vibrantly alive as the kitten's, he stretched his arms under the serval. *Don't you scratch or bite me, or I'll drop you,* he warned as he lifted her. Then he felt Melis on his back, and he had to pause hunched over while she ran up to perch on his shoulder. Cats.

But Thrisca actually shut her eyes, let him take her relaxed weight. *Your Flair is better now that you have been with Us. You are better for Fams,* she said.

He grunted, didn't know about that, and lifted her and carried her to T'Spindle's glider, where they all could fit, and, at the lord's instructions, Johns sent his own glider home.

The FirstFamily GrandLord superseded all Johns's plans for the day that he'd made before the turmoil of last night. His understudy would be the lead in *Firewalker* today, and Johns would be swept up in T'Spindle's arrangements. He rolled his shoulders at the resentment that had settled there, reminded himself that being included in the man's activities would be no bad thing.

But he wished he had Giniana alone. Or even Giniana and the cats.

"I am *so* sorry that a glitch in my payment system didn't get my gilt to you during your childhood," Giniana's father, Mas Filix, lied. The scry had come through to her new suite in St. Johnswort House.

Giniana's heart still palpitated from seeing her father—even through a scrybowl image—for the first time in years. He looked the same, but older, and she hadn't realized how much her features resembled his.

Since he seemed to want a reaction, she nodded. She supposed he might have taken that as absolution, but she merely showed that she'd heard his empty words.

He added a sincere smile.

Not as warm as Klay's sincere actor's smile, that Giniana had seen a few times in the past several eightdays when he interacted with others of his ilk.

Sitting in the refurbished MistrysSuite of St. Johnswort House, Giniana donned her serene Healer's mask. She pretended to her father, as well. "That's all right," she said lightly. "I didn't need the gilt much as a child, mother took care of me." Despite everything, she had to acknowledge that. Giniana would never follow such a path to have her own needs seen to, or any child's, but she'd finally lifted her voice in prayers of forgiveness for her mother—and requested the same for herself for the bitterness she worked on erasing from her life.

After she finished resolving her lingering emotions for her mother, she would have to deal with those involving her father. That would be harder. She didn't think she'd ever banish the hurt of his abandonment. Certainly the large amount of gilt that had been deposited in her bank account from him—because he was legally obligated to do that— didn't mitigate his previous complete absence from her life.

But she had a vibrant family now—Klay and Thrisca and Melis—even if Klay still wasn't able to say the words Giniana longed to hear, needed to hear with every passing moment. She *felt* the love from him, but the words remained stubbornly absent.

"I'm glad Verna fulfilled her duty," Giniana's father said, a trifle woodenly. She didn't know whether he'd bothered to find out *how* her mother and she had lived before Giniana earned her Healer robes, but if he hadn't, she wouldn't satisfy his curiosity.

And if he observed her pretense, which surely he did, he ignored it.

Klay would *never* ignore her. In fact, he'd proved that he'd bull ahead on her behalf and without her consent. A flaw, but not one that hurt her as much as neglect, the lack of simple caring.

Mas tried a rueful look, also false. "I contacted D'Willow and her assistant stated T'Spindle paid for the Time Healing Procedure."

"That's right." Giniana's smile felt strained. "I didn't need gilt before last month. But the time Healing treatment was expensive." She waved an airy gesture. "Incredibly interesting, of course, the whole procedure ... the atmosphere, seeing the very winds of time ..." She shook her head. Oh, yes, *this* he wanted a description of, that he could use in conversation to puff himself up, or use as part of his work.

"You know you'll always be welcome here, with me," he said gruffly. She thought he meant that, in this moment.

Another nod.

Before the silence became awkward, the hall door flew open.

"It's set!" Klay strode in, aura blazing, radiating delight. He picked Giniana up and tossed her in the air, out of Mas's scry sight, caught her with easy strength. "I've got the lead in Amberose's new play! Raz Cherry T'Elecampane and Del D'Elecampane are opening a theater at their new resort. A guesthouse of our own on their estate, top gilt, and a fantastic role!"

Giniana noticed the quick look of envy on her father's face. He wasn't alone, Giniana thought T'Spindle felt a bit of that emotion at the idea of a new resort and theater in the country, too. But Mas would also want a phenomenal part in an Amberose story. A play that wouldn't make it to Chinju for months, if ever, depending on the agreement between Amberose and the newly HeartBonded Elecampanes.

Giniana said, "Then I'll accept the Elecampanes' employment offer as their Family Healer, too." Del D'Elecampane was in the midst of a high-risk pregnancy.

"Hey, Mas," Klay said, as if noticing the open scry with Giniana's father. "Good to see you." Klay glanced at her. "Back gilt come through?"

"Yes."

Klay shook his head. "Too bad the whole thing got so screwed up that it took T'Spindle and T'Reed to straighten out." He beamed, "Hey, Mas, I have great news—"

"Sorry, I must go. May be afternoon there, but I've got a morning rehearsal call. I'll scry you later," Mas began.

"Here's our new viz locale." Klay tapped a pattern on the edge of the scrybowl, impressed an image of a lovely house in the scrybowl water.

"Got it. Later, dear daughter."

Giniana suppressed a shudder. "Later."

The droplets forming his image fell back into the bowl

and Giniana let herself sag against Klay and the vitality of the man enveloped and invigorated her. "Sounds like our future is falling in place."

"Yep." He picked her up and twirled with her.

"Where are the Fams?" she asked. They loved *their* new territory, the St. Johnswort land and house. No sharing.

"They went to T'Spindle's, to do a last sweep of the cottage, some of the grounds, and the Residence, before the new FamCats Danith D'Ash is giving your GrandLord and GrandLady arrive tomorrow."

"To get last pets and treats."

"That's right."

Nevertheless, Giniana checked on her Fams. Thrisca hadn't been outside on her own in Druida City for decades before the Healing. Yes, both felines emanated pleasure.

"What of the rest of our plans?" she asked as Klay let her go to forage in the new no-time for afternoon treats. "What about the Johnswort estate and the new little HeartStones?" she asked, right before he popped a cheese and cracker into her mouth.

"Eat up, you'll need your strength." He grinned wickedly. "The HeartStones are sleeping again. Ellis Gardenia agreed to caretake this place in return for a tiny house and that corner of property we'll give him. The Lady Captain of the Maidens of Saille has approved one wing of this place for the daycare of those Blessed by the Lady. The nuns and the children will keep the HeartStones stimulated between our visits home."

Giniana swallowed the cheese and cracker and sighed. "A big day."

"Not as big as I want." He sobered, sucked in an audible breath. "I love you and want to marry you. Today. I've lined up T'Spindle as Priest and D'Spindle as Priestess to officiate the marriage ritual." He lifted both her hands and kissed them. "Invitations are going out and T'Spindle Residence is arranging matters as we speak. The Daisys and the Ashes have confirmed as witnesses."

"Going behind my back again?" she mocked, even as the huge bubble of joy at hearing his words of love burst through her.

Klay winced, dropped her hands. "Sorry."

"No, don't be." She flung herself against him, and, rock solid, he kept her close. "Not this time. I'd love to marry you today."

"Good." He cleared his throat. "That's good."

"And this is the last time T'Spindle will interfere in my life, too."

"One can hope," Klay said, then shouted along their bond with the Fams. *The wedding is ON! She said 'yes.'*

Hooray! Melis and Thrisca chorused.

And when Johns and Giniana made love on their wedding night, in the newly carved HouseHeart of St. Johnswort House, a huge and overwhelming wave ripped through him at climax ... ripped through Giniana, too, he heard her cry of ecstasy bordering on pain. When that subsided, they stared at each other, panting.

Johns blinked, a golden aura pulsed from her ... and from him, and they both seemed wrapped in a golden rope that tied them together.

The HeartStones hummed with energy and excitement and glee, then shut down.

He thought they'd gone up a notch in intelligence ... as ...

"I think I have more Flair," Giniana said. Eyes wide, she blinked rapidly and he saw crystal tears trail down her cheeks. She moved close and hid her face and expression against his shoulder.

He coughed rasp from his throat. "I think I do, too." He sensed the stones, of course, subsiding in deep sleep, but with a continual circuit of brighter energy cycling between them that hadn't been there before. Awed, he said what he felt, "I think we, uh, Heart—, Heart—,"

"HeartBonded, like true HeartMates! I never knew I had a HeartMate before," Giniana's voice remained hushed. "Perhaps I didn't, until now."

"Yes," Johns agreed. "We came together in love, at the same time as this House's stones sparked better awareness, catapulting all three of us into better Flair. You and I became HeartMates and HeartBonded at the same moment."

Cat yowls sounded, along with scratching at the door. *What was that? What? What?* demanded Melis. *All My furs stood all up!*

FamWoman? questioned Thrisca.

Johns pulled Giniana through the waterfall on one wall and she said a quick cleansing spell, then they went to open the door.

Melis pranced in, headed toward a deep bed of catnip, squealed in delight. *This place is wonderful. Thank you FamWoman, thank you FamMan.*

Thrisca strolled in. *Very nice place for Us all, for Family.*

We IS Family, Melis shouted, pounced on Thrisca as the older cat rolled in the catnip.

Johns curved his arm around his wife, his HeartMate, and they laughed together. "Yes," he said. "We is Family."

ALSO BY ROBIN D. OWENS

Please note that these books and stories are primarily romances. They are not appropriate for children.

HeartMate

Heart Thief

Heart Duel

Heart Choice

Heart Quest

Heart Dance

Heart Fate

Heart Change

Heart Journey

Script of the Heart

Heart Search

Heart Secret

Heart Fortune

Lost Heart, a Celta Novella

Heart Fire

Heart Legacy

Heart Sight

Hearts And Swords, a Celta Story Collection

The Ghost Series (contemporary paranormal/ghost story romances)

Ghost Seer

Ghost Layer

Ghost Killer

Ghost Talker

Ghost Maker

Feral Magic, a contemporary paranormal shifter romance e-novella, CURRENTLY ONLY AVAILABLE AS AN AUDIBLE AUDIO BOOK

The Mystic Circle Series (contemporary fantasy)

Enchanted No More

Enchanted Again

Enchanted Ever After

The Summoning Series

Average American women are Summoned to another dimension to fight hideous evil, and, yes, with flying horses!

Guardian of Honor

Sorceress of Faith

Protector of the Flight

Keepers of the Flame

Echoes in the Dark

ABOUT THE AUTHOR

Robin D. Owens has been writing longer than she cares to recall. Her fantasy/futuristic romances found a home at Berkley with the issuance of HeartMate in December 2001. She credits the "telepathic cat with attitude" in selling that book. Currently, she has two domesticated cats (who have appeared in her stories).

She loves writing fantasy with romance or romance with fantasy, and particularly likes adding quirky characters for comic relief and leaving little threads dangling from book to book to see if readers pick up on them (usually, yes! Reader intelligence is awesome!).

Robin spends too much time on Facebook (see link below), loves hearing from readers, tries her best to respond to any questions and has been known to take reader advice for her work. When she receives good reviews or fan mail, she's been known to dance around bored cats...

Contact me here:
www.robindowens.com
robindowens@gmail.com

Made in the USA
Columbia, SC
11 December 2019

84723935R00200